"Tonight, I wondered what I would feel if I had never met you before," he said.

Carefully, as if she were made of porcelain, Ari turned her around until she faced him directly, her mouth inches from his.

"I have to tell you about the past," she said before he could kiss her.

"Damn the past," Ari said harshly. "For right now, for this moment, let's let the past alone."

He grasped her almost roughly and continued, "I want to know you as you are now, Sara. I don't want explanations. I want to forget the past. For one night."

Sara shivered at the implications of his words. "Ari . . . ?"

"But that's impossible, isn't it? There are too many ghosts between us. Too much history."

"More than you know," she said, determined to tell him about their son.

"Ari—"

"Don't, Sara," he said, raising his hand. "Whatever it is, I don't want to hear it. Tomorrow, perhaps. Or perhaps in another eighteen years. But no more tonight. No more."

Dear Reader,

I have several very exciting things to talk about this month; in fact, it's hard to know where to begin. How about with a piece of news some of you have been waiting years to hear?

In 1986, Kristin James wrote a novel for Silhouette Intimate Moments called *A Very Special Favor.* The hero of that book had two brothers, and over the years, I've received quite a lot of letters asking for their stories. This month, I'm glad to oblige with *Salt of the Earth,* the first step in completing THE MARSHALLS, a family-based trilogy. In August look for *The Letter of the Law,* to complete the series. And here's another piece of terrific news: anyone who missed *A Very Special Favor* the first time around will get a second chance to purchase it this fall, as part of a special in-store promotion. Look for it in your bookstores.

If that's not enough excitement for you, here's more: Kay Hooper is back with *The Haviland Touch,* a sequel to her first—and very popular—Intimate Moments novel, *Enemy Mine.* Of course, this suspenseful and adventure-filled story stands on its own, so whether you've read that first book or not, you have a treat in store this month.

Round out the month with Heather Graham Pozzessere's *Snowfire,* a nice wintry story to balance the summer heat, and Marilyn Tracy's *Echoes of the Garden,* in which long-estranged lovers are brought together by their love for their son. In coming months, look for books by Nora Roberts, Linda Howard, Kathleen Eagle, Naomi Horton, Emilie Richards and all of the other wonderful authors who make Silhouette Intimate Moments one of the most exciting series in romance fiction today.

Leslie Wainger
Senior Editor and
Editorial Coordinator

MARILYN TRACY

Echoes of the Garden

SILHOUETTE·INTIMATE·MOMENTS®

Published by Silhouette Books New York

America's Publisher of Contemporary Romance

SILHOUETTE BOOKS
300 East 42nd St., New York, N.Y. 10017

ECHOES OF THE GARDEN

ISBN: 0-373-07387-9

First Silhouette Books printing June 1991

Printed in the U.S.A.

Books by Marilyn Tracy

Silhouette Intimate Moments

Magic in the Air #311
Blue Ice #362
Echoes of the Garden #387

MARILYN TRACY

lives in Portales, New Mexico, in a ramshackle turn-of-the-century house with her artist sister, her son, her niece, two dogs, three cats and a poltergeist. Between remodeling the house to its original Victorian-cum-Deco state, writing full-time and helping her sister with a forty-foot cement dragon in the backyard, Marilyn composes full soundtracks to go with each of her novels.

After having lived in both Tel Aviv and Moscow in conjunction with the U.S. State Department, Marilyn enjoys writing about the cultures she's explored and the people she's grown to love. She likes to hear from people who enjoy her books and always has a pot of coffee on or a glass of wine ready for anyone dropping by, especially if they don't mind chaos and know how to wield a paintbrush.

For my son, Charles,
who inspired Danny and who daily inspires me

Chapter 1

"I don't care *how* difficult it'll be! I can't go, and that's that. You'll have to get someone else."

"Someone else?" Tom Butterfield sputtered. "Someone else! Have you lost your mind, Sara? *You're* the one who asked for this assignment. *You're* the one who had me push it all the way to New York. *You're* the one who insisted—and proved— you were the only person on God's green earth who could possibly do this story. And *now* you want me to find someone else? What in the Sam Hill's gotten into you?"

She could have told him. But Tom Butterfield wasn't the avuncular little editor in a small-town television series who would have moved mountains rather than submit a reporter to a potential personal crisis. He was the hard-boiled manager of the day-shift desk of the nation's largest newspaper service, McMunn-Knapper. The only things that made his eyes soften was the play of a hot story on Page 1 in newspapers across the country, or a huge bottle of Scotch.

If she had told him her reasons for wanting out of this assignment, he would simply have said: "Fine. Get the story, *then* have a breakdown." And all a breakdown would have meant to Tom Butterfield was that he would have to find someone else to fill her desk. Though that would prove difficult after her ten years with McMunn-Knapper, it wouldn't be impossible; there were plenty of hungry journalists out there.

"Look, Gould," he said, "I don't know what bugaboo you've got against this assignment all of a sudden, but..." He glanced at the cable in her hand, the same one that had prompted her severe attack of cold feet. "All the arrangements are made. Kibbutz Golan is willing to put you up. And this is the kibbutz closest to the Syrian front, right where you claim the next bout of teenage counterterrorism is likely to take place."

Her boss looked up and met her eyes. His hardened. "We'll see you back here in one month. *With* the story."

He picked up another reporter's copy and began marking it, dismissing her as effectively as if she'd never been there.

Sara walked slowly back to her desk, sat down and stared at its littered top without seeing the months of notes, the years of stories, the accolades stuffed in amongst the complaints, the letters, the stacks of newsprint, the photographs ranging in shade from a dull sepia to a startling black and white. She didn't hear the usual newsroom cacophony, the clicking computers, the ringing telephones, the multivoiced barking of a bizarre range of questions. She saw only the crumpled cable in her hand, and heard only the too-rapid beating of her heart.

Tom had seen the words, read them, and had taken them as complete confirmation. Sara had seen the sign-off, the kibbutz director's name, and had taken it as complete disaster.

Ari Gaon.

After all these years, a lifetime of living, loving, working, always working—it had been what she wanted, hadn't it?—his mere name still had the ability to rock her, to send her mind careening down a roller coaster to the past, a past of mistakes, of regrets, of shattered dreams.

Feeling the hair rise on the back of her neck, she had stared at the name, numb as a sense of fate spiraled around her, catapulting her into confrontation with that past. Her hand had convulsed around the cable, and she had gone straight to Butterfield to get out of the assignment.

In all the strange fantasies she'd entertained over the years, fantasies of seeing Ari Gaon again, telling him the truth, explaining the past, she'd never imagined it would be on the same ground, the very same place she'd last seen him, the mountainous Kibbutz Golan. These half dreams, half nightmares had been vague, unformed, yet thoroughly grounded in the conviction that she was never likely to see him again.

Now, staring at the cable, she realized that once again she had been lying to herself, doing something with very different motives in her unconscious mind. As Tom Butterfield had said, she *had* pushed for this story, had *pushed* to get back to Israel. The whole time she'd worked to convince everyone that the story was good, was worth what it would cost and worth losing one of their top reporters for a month, she had *known* Ari lived in Israel, *was* Israel.

Seeing his name on the tag line of the cable had shattered all the illusions she'd had about her motives. No altruism here, just pure curiosity. And, perhaps, a desire to set the future to rights.

Ari Gaon.

Dear God, what had she done?

She didn't have a prayer of avoiding him now. And the sense of doom that accompanied that lack of hope forced into sharp clarity the knowledge that a reckoning was due.

Ari Gaon, young commando, man of her youthful dreams, hero of a newborn nation. Ari Gaon . . . father of her son.

When she had asked—demanded—the Israel assignment, she had plowed straight ahead, as usual forthright and determined, firmly squelching any qualms she had about the wisdom of the request. What if she ran into him? What if their paths crossed? Israel was a small country. She'd dismissed these niggling doubts, telling herself the odds against running into him were a million to one. How comfortably and easily she'd planned the complete downfall of her calm, how simply she'd concocted a trap for herself—a trap that could expose most of her adult life as a lie. And she'd imagined she wouldn't see him.

She almost laughed at that notion now. How could she have ignored his deep-rooted commitment to Israel, to the kibbutz life. It was only natural that he would remain connected with Kibbutz Golan, only natural that someone of his capabilities had risen to the position of director.

Now she sat with shaking hands, knowing the lies she'd been spinning for her conscience's sake were neatly exposed by the tag line of the cable. She'd asked for this assignment for the sake of this confrontation, delayed for some eighteen years.

She, who had spent her life searching for truth for others, was finally about to face up to it herself.

And now, staring at his name, memories swirling in and around her, jamming her thoughts, she shuddered. All the years of rigid indifference, the hard, cynical surface required of a journalist of any stature, the quick wit of a master interviewer was forgotten. At that moment she was only Sara Gould, mother of one, keeper of lost dreams. Mother of Danny.

Shaken out of her reverie by the thought of her son, *his* son, and grabbed by a new fear, she quickly placed a call to Paris. To Danny, away from home, winding up the last of his tour in France as a foreign exchange student, scheduled to meet her in Israel for a long-awaited chance to see the country of his idealistic dreams.

Had she been insane? Had the falsehood she'd let Danny believe all of his young life so thoroughly penetrated her mind that she had begun to believe it, as well? Could this have been why, when the assignment had seemed a sure thing, she had agreed to have him meet her in Israel?

Or had she been tempting fate to take a hand?

Let her reach him, she prayed. There was no way he could meet her in Israel as they had planned. Not now. Not with Ari Gaon at Kibbutz Golan. Not with those possibilities—the father staring into the eyes of the son for the first time—the son meeting a man he didn't even know existed.

Oh God, she thought, life has come full circle. Eighteen years ago she'd left Israel, her heart torn, her emotions raw, in search of the perfect story. And now, a lifetime of growing up later, she was in exactly the same position: her heart still torn, her emotions as fragile and uncertain as they'd ever been, still seeking the perfect story. Then she had run away from Ari, from the intensity that had so frightened her, and from the truth. Now she couldn't run, wouldn't allow herself to do so.

But, oh, how she felt like running. Full circle.

"Hello?" her son's voice asked, the timbre of the voice the father's.

"Danny? I'm afraid I have some bad news...."

Full circle.

* * *

Ari Gaon sighed. The recent Syrian incursion into the Golan Heights outpost had resulted in four deaths. The oldest
casualty had been nineteen. How many more of the young
would have to die, before the children would be allowed to live
in peace?

When have Abraham's children ever lived in peace? Ari
could almost hear his grandmother's voice, dry like the
khamsin winds, and old, like the leaves in late autumn. In her
later years, in the early days of Israel, she had said those words
often. They had comforted her.

Those same words made Ari restless with a helpless anger.
He wasn't religious, at least not consciously. He was simply
Israeli. Born there, raised in the tense, belligerent days of Israel's youth, he had followed the dictates of his parents and
grandmother, and had taken up the sword for a nation fash-
ioned out of guilt, but nurtured to ensure freedom. By the time
he was twenty, he was already a member of the Arumakh, a
small, highly trained group of freedom fighters. With them he
had fought for Israel, and with each battle had given more and
more of his soul to the country he loved. Even then, as a young
man, he had seen Israel for what it was, a precious, wonderful holding. More than for his own life, he wanted this land,
this fertile and angry land, for the children. Other people's
children now, since his own daughter no longer ran on hillsides covered with flowers and gently waving grass.

He sighed again, looking out his broad window. It was the
hottest time of the day, and the afternoon sun was sharp,
blinding. Yet he couldn't bear to draw the shutters. When
closed they reminded him of caves, of moonless nights in fox-
holes, of prison walls. Of coffins.

His office afforded the best view in the entire kibbutz. But
that wasn't why he had accepted the offer to direct Kibbutz
Golan. There were many reasons, not the least of which was
the need to lay the past to rest. It was in Kibbutz Golan that
Ari had found love and lost it. Here he had met Yael Shamir
and married her. Here his daughter, little, bright Galiti, gold-
skinned and warm from the sun's kiss, had been born. On the
road leading away from here, she and her mother had died. So
many sweet and so many hard memories lay in the hallways of
the buildings at Kibbutz Golan that they seemed to echo with

his footsteps and walk with his shadow as he crossed meadows and open fields.

But the sun still turned the summer grass to a burnished gold and the air still smelled as sweet. Bees still flew to hives, hoopoe birds still darted their long, curved bills into the soft soil. Nature continued, indifferent to Ari's memories, and equally indifferent to the deaths of four young soldiers.

Ari turned his back to the view and his mind to more immediate matters. He had tried calling the American journalist to suggest her visit be delayed or that she stay elsewhere. The latest incident had been too close. The story she planned to cover was the one thing he didn't want to happen right now.

Beyond that, it was unthinkable that untutored civilians should stay at Kibbutz Golan at this particular time. Members of the kibbutz, young and old, were all highly trained fighters, many were reservists, and almost all had served in the army at one point or another. Still others, army personnel, were using the kibbutz housing, while the supply of housing was expanded at the border outpost. With the exception of the small children, every breathing person in this communal society was prepared for whatever incident might occur.

But he'd been too late. In a clipped, obviously harried tone, her editor had said she'd left the night before. She would be in Kibbutz Golan by nightfall, Israeli time. If he needed to contact her, the man had said, ignorant of the irony, he could reach her at Kibbutz Golan. And given Ari his own number.

A woman, a journalist, untrained, unskilled in weaponry and survival, unprepared for the potential violence and bent on ferreting out the truth about counterterrorism, was one thing Ari did not need to worry about right now. And her son was scheduled to join her later in a pleasure tour of Israel in early summer. Come to the Golan Heights and Have the Time of Your Life! Those fools in Jerusalem, so concerned to keep good public relations with the American press that they'd open any and all doors. Well this was one door they'd just have to keep closed. He wasn't going to be responsible for an American civilian's death.

Half-ruefully he shook his head. He hoped she would be reasonable when he simply turned her around and sent her on her way. But that hadn't been his experience with journalists. He squared his shoulders. There was nothing else he could do but apologize and send her to another kibbutz. If she stayed she'd have her entire story in an untidy, oppressive package.

He jotted down a note for young Shlomo to watch for her arrival. It would give the grieving, angry boy some task and take some of the weight from Ari's shoulders. Shlomo would look for her that night, bring her to Ari, and in the morning speed her on her way south or west. Anywhere but in the Golan Heights.

He tossed the note into an overflowing Out basket, rose and went to the open window. The wild daisies and mountain daffodils were in bloom in the broad meadow, and the sun teased the leaves on the trees to a glittering brilliance. The mountains, tall and purple, shadowed the valley and made him think of days spent lying on blankets, weaving flowers into chains. There had been too few of those days, too few stolen moments.

It was the American woman's fault, he thought. It was because of her that he'd become nostalgic. Her name, her profession, had made him think of another Sara, another American, another time.

He resented the intrusive memories at first, then shrugging, allowed them to come, for he knew, with the fatalistic knowledge of one who has known great joy and equal pain, that memories cannot be harnessed, only resisted. And resistance usually only honed them finer.

The warm, Mediterranean air hung around her face like a velvet cowl. It carried the heady scents of eucalyptus and gardenia, hinted of mimosa and the acres of orange trees that somehow, miraculously, still emitted fragrance after eighteen years.

Touch me, the air seemed to say. Breathe me, take me inside you and let me love you. It's summer again, and you long for a lover's warm breath against your skin.

Sara did breathe, and the sweet caress of the Israeli air in her city woman's lungs filled her with a strange, bittersweet longing. She had spent too many days, too many nights chasing elusive interviewees, racing deadlines, and inhaling exhaust from a thousand ill-tuned taxicabs in Washington, D.C., not to be moved by this gentle air, by the memories. In all the lost, stardust years, she'd often wondered how it would feel to recognize a familiar touch, to hear a once-beloved voice call her name. Now she knew. Now, oh yes, she knew.

With the knowledge came again the surety that she was making a mistake in coming to this country, coming back. Everything about the trip was wrong. It had already caused problems, and if the tingling in her arms was correct—and the tingling was seldom wrong—there were more difficulties to come.

Not only had she and Butterfield argued, but Danny hadn't taken the altered plans with his usual sanguinity. He had protested repeatedly, and she had ended up snapping at him. Their resulting argument had held a note of acrimony that had never before marred their relationship.

"Come on, Mom," he'd said, and she'd almost been able to picture the flashing eyes in his thin face. "It's not fair. You promised!"

"I promised to take you to Israel *someday*," Sara had said, feeling guilty for not telling him the real reason, feeling shame for using the old, parental excuse. How many *somedays* had her father promised her, never to produce those dreamed-of excursions, those alluded-to delights? She shook off the thought; she wasn't her father, and this wasn't the same type of empty promise. But the truth, withheld for all these years, was impossible to tell, especially over a telephone, and she fell back on the timeworn apology of adults everywhere. "This isn't the right time. I'll meet you in Paris on the way back."

Her son had uttered that rude, disgusted grunt that only seventeen-year-olds—and men who've just lost the biggest fish ever on the line—know how to make.

"I speak Hebrew as well as you do," he'd said. "And if your story's about eighteen-year-old counterterrorists, I stand a better chance—"

"Of getting hurt," she had interposed coolly, having latched on to the most recent incursion in the Golan as her reason for postponing their trip. "It's too dangerous, Danny."

"What about you, then? If it's dangerous for me, it is for you, too."

She had drawn a deep breath. "I'm on assignment. I have no choice," she'd said firmly. It was both the truth and a lie. It was a reason, that was all.

Though he couldn't have seen her, she had held up her hand to forestall the expletive she'd sensed hovering on his lips.

"Now that's enough, Danny." She'd empathized with his helplessness and understood it completely. Hadn't she felt exactly the same way, when she'd seen Ari Gaon's name on the cable?

But her son wasn't like she had been; he was like his father, all fire and action. He was brash and impulsive, occasionally willful, always vitally involved. He'd been lucky enough—and so had Sara—to have had the years with Jason, whose trust and confidence had tempered the disappointments life had to offer young Danny, and who had encouraged the vibrant personality of her son without dimming the adventurous spirit. Yes, he'd been lucky to have had those years. Jason had fallen in love with her tiny, bright-eyed boy, and had lovingly, unselfishly fathered another man's child for the years he had been with them.

"Oh, sure," Danny had continued with heavy sarcasm. "And next year you'll think of another excuse." He'd pitched his voice in a mimicry of hers. "You've got to go to college this year," then resumed his own, naturally deep tone—still a surprise to her after the years of boyhood. "And the year after that you'll take some assignment in Alaska, or maybe in the Philippines. Someday you're going to run out of excuses, Mom."

God, was she that transparent? Did everyone see through her as easily as her son? For the first time since Danny had been accepted as a foreign exchange student, Sara was grateful for the distance that lay between them, glad their conversation was over the telephone. If they'd been together, he might have seen the truth of his words reflected on her face. She had been dreading that very day for most of her adult life. And if he'd been able to see her, he would have read her fears like the book he always claimed she was. He carried every gene of her journalistic instinct in his young body, and he'd have pried and pulled and pushed and prodded until the full story unfolded. And when he found out the truth? Would he then be his father's child, his passions running too high to allow forgiveness? Or would he be his mother's, curious but dispassionate, objective?

Luckily for her peace of mind just then, he was also still a child. No matter how deep his voice was now, no matter how old he'd become, he was still that baby who'd ridden in a backpack while she covered a presidential race, the child who'd sworn he'd be the first man to walk on Mars. And he usually still did as she urged him to do. Though he'd hung up with a forced farewell, he'd agreed to do as she asked.

Caught now by the subtle snare of the Israeli air, the million memories that flooded through her, Sara's thoughts centered on Danny, focused on Ari. Not for the first time, Sara realized how often she saw the father's face on the boy. It was more a certain arrested, vital expression than any specific physical characteristic. Except for the eyes. Those incredible gray eyes, dark-fringed and heavy-lidded. Eyes that smoldered in anger and darkened with love.

She opened her own hazel eyes to the Israeli sunlight. Somehow, thinking of Danny, thinking of his father, being here in the balmy, Mediterranean setting, she felt a curious fold in the time continuum. Wasn't it only yesterday that she was here, an excited young news reporter, fresh from college, in Israel for one glorious year on what her father had called her mini-grand tour, bright and eager to grab hold of the tree of life and shake it for all it was worth? Wasn't it only yesterday that Danny had been a dream and nothing more, and life had held every promise ever known?

And hadn't it been just yesterday that she'd met the young commando who had so dramatically altered her life and completely captured her heart, whose hard, shuttered face had watched her as she stammered her tearful excuses for leaving?

She raised a hand to her short, still-brown hair, brushing it from her damp forehead, as if brushing the memories aside. She lowered her hand, looking at it, noting it was no longer a young girl's hand. With a sense of detachment she felt she could see every day of the nearly forty years that life had etched upon her hand. Long fingers, fingertips blunted by years at old typewriters and compact computer keyboards, these spoke to her age, and she had raised calluses between her first two fingers, the inevitable result of years of pressing pencil to notepad, recording the words of innumerable politicians and important somebodies for posterity. Still caught by a strange distortion of time, her eyes fell upon the empty place where Jason's ring no longer rested. The years of wearing it had created a depression in her finger, if not wholly in her soul.

Jason would have applauded her for removing the ring. Two years had gone since his passing. But would he have approved of the timing of its removal? She thought of the ring now in the top drawer of her battered dresser. She had taken it off after reading the cable from Israel—after calling Danny and packing her bags—after she'd known for certain she would be meeting Ari Gaon again, after all these years.

Suddenly, staring at the space on her hand, Sara felt foolish. Her thoughts—her dreams—of yesterday were as insubstantial as the beams of the sunlight she stood in. It hadn't been only yesterday, but a thousand yesterdays ago. She had married, raised Danny, made a name for herself. How foolish she'd been to keep the memory of Ari as a young, hot-blooded commando fresh in her mind. He'd have grown up and changed, as she had. The depression in her ring finger told her how much he might have changed.

Now she wondered about him, not as the young commando of her past, but as the kibbutz director of the present. Had he married? Had children? Was he in love with his Israeli wife? Had he loved, lost, and perhaps loved again? Had he ever lain awake and thought of the young girl he'd loved so tenderly on a spring night, a thousand nights ago? Had he ever softly called her name, as she had done so many, many times in the early years, as she had done only last night?

She drew a shuddering breath, doubly glad she had not allowed Danny to join her. These first few moments of encounter with the past, of memories jangling in her head like so many alarm bells, these she couldn't share with him. When he was staring down middle age, when he'd known the sorrow of losing loved ones, the pain of lonely nights and lonelier mornings . . . when he knew the truth, then, maybe.

She narrowed her eyes against the strong Israeli sunlight, and held her hand against her loose sundress to keep the teasing breeze from baring her thighs. People lined both sides of the double barricade separating the arriving passengers from the teeming crowd outside the airy, modern structure that was Lod airport. Some were garbed in Arab dress, black-and-white-checked scarves wrapped around their heads, loose at their shoulders, covering either long robes or strangely tailored gray or black suits. Others, sporting yarmulkes, waved or whistled to relatives in the moving group surrounding Sara.

Israeli soldiers, some the same age as Danny but none looking as young, stood in the crowd, eyes alert, Uzis casually slung over their innocent shoulders as if the machine guns were mere children's toys. Sara knew it was only illusion. Those weapons could be swung into action with the speed of light and the accuracy that only young eyes could produce. She'd once held one in her hands, had seen Ari use one with uncanny precision.

She wondered if any of these young people would be in her story and hoped they would not. Counterterrorism was a dirty business, initiated perhaps in a noble cause, but sinking, nonetheless, to the same horrifying depths as the original act of terrorism.

In a moment of sharp clarity she followed that thought with another: neither could anything good come of raking up a past long dead, memories long buried. Only a sense of destiny kept her from turning around; there was a fate that wanted the truth to come to light, wanted the past put into perspective. Or was it really herself who wanted it finally done with?

Along with the rest of the weary travelers she was spilled onto a narrow, rough concrete sidewalk. An ox cart filled with souvenirs stood to one side, the oxen bored, the driver gesticulating and shouting to the crowd to come buy his wares. Across the broad, curved roadway a camel rested on a thin strip of yellowed grass, his neck regally arched, his expression contemptuous.

Sara felt her own lip curl in equal disdain. She was no mere girl afraid of commitment, afraid of the strong passion of one man, of the adventures life had to offer. She was a woman now, strong both in soul and in her chosen career. It was time to lay the past properly to rest, to lay the foundation for the future. If not for herself, then for Danny. It was her own initiative not fate that had brought her here. She would meet her destiny with a head held high.

She joined a group of people in a *sherut,* a many-seated, elongated taxi, headed for the north. Sara saw once again, as if for the first time, the asphalt road stretching from the congested airport to the broad, flat plain—the same valley where Joshua stopped the sun and won a respite for his beleaguered army—to the rising hills. The road climbed swiftly, passing Mount Tabor and the Mount of Beatitudes where, dotted along a grassy slope, carved in tall columns of white alabaster, were the declarations, Blessed Are the Meek, for They Shall Inherit . . . Blessed Are the Peacemakers . . . Blessed Are the Merciful . . .

They wove in and out of kibbutz farmland, slowing down for or passing ox carts, camels and army trucks. They circled the mount where the Witch of Endor had uttered her prophecies. Then, stealing Sara's breath, they rounded the curve that allowed the finest view of the Yam Kinneret, the Hebrew name for the violin shape of the famous Sea of Galilee. It lay still, small and impossibly blue, reflecting the cloudless sky and the thick-leaved trees circling it.

It had been at Yam Kinneret that Ari had asked her to stay in Israel, to abandon her fledgling career. There he'd told her of his love for her, his love for his country. There she had known that she loved him in return.

Sara's heart thudded with unaccustomed speed, and her head felt light, as if she were climbing thousands of feet instead of hundreds. What would she say to him now? And how on earth would she ever find the courage to talk to him about the past, never mind the present? Would she have the courage to tell him about Danny?

As they left the flat plains and broad valleys for the pine-covered mountains, the air changed with the altitude, and her thoughts were transformed along with the scents. How she had loved it here. How often she had longed for assignments here, yet had been afraid to ask for them. Because of Ari.

Because of Danny.

She sat back against the seat drinking in the living history, the past existing in the present. With an aching heart she felt the legacy of beauty, the atavistic need and love of land. And remembered how bitter was that long-ago decision to turn her back upon this fertile crescent that was no larger than New Jersey, this tiny garden that remained a promise, a dream come true for an entire people.

The land had changed in the years she'd been absent. The wonderful Sinai Desert was once again part of Egypt. Kibbutzim dotted the borders of Jordan, and the Negev was fertile. And this northern region, made lush and beautiful with tender care in the country's short life, was different, too. Israel again displayed signs of being the coveted land fought for for so many hundreds of years. It was as if she could actually read each plaque beneath the trees that had been donated long ago, could see the young shoots being gently placed into the rich soil. They'd been seedlings when she'd been here before; now they were tall, sturdy trees.

The land, the changes, the fresh determined attempt to make a garden from a desert was an accomplishment to be proud of, to hand down to children and grandchildren with loving concern. Through each tree, each plant, the donors' whispers remained: "This is yours, we grew it for you. Love it as we do."

Would they? Sara wondered. Did any child ever love what their parents revered? Could they? It seemed to be some rule of nature, perhaps the need to leave the nest, that children viewed, with mere tolerance and tepid interest, the home of the parent.

As she had done. Was Danny doing that now? Already gone from home, determined to be schooled in Paris, determined to make any field but journalism his own. And now angry with her over the change of plans and the delay, telling her not to bother coming through Paris. He'd spend the holidays with his host family.

Tossing off the weight of the past, she focused on the conversation taking place inside the *sherut,* following the rapid, guttural Hebrew with unaccustomed ears. Only one of the passengers was dressed in Arab-style clothing; the remainder appeared to be soldiers, returning somewhere after a weekend leave. Four young men and one woman. They talked as though they were family members, arguing, laughing, expounding on the days' events, world politics and their philosophy of life. Lowering their voices, with half-curious glances at Sara and obvious contempt for the man dressed in Arab style, they exchanged rumors they had heard of an incursion in the Golan Heights. The same raid she had heard about before they had, the one she'd used as an excuse for denying Danny.

Some things never change, Sara thought. Eighteen years had gone by, and still the seemingly placid country, scented with orange blossoms, abounded with rumors of skirmishes. Beneath the green grass, the very soil was steeped in the blood of those who had died fighting for it, Palestinian, Israeli, English, Moorish. That was why she was here, ostensibly, anyway.

One young man—Dov something—leaned forward, the Uzi beside him forgotten, his young, tanned face made oddly old by the intensity of his emotion, and spoke passionately of the need for reprisal. Sara caught her breath. This was the seed of her story. A reprisal was the first step in the counterterrorism game.

Knowing she should be listening closely, filing away the conversation for later use in her story, she found her attention nonetheless drifting. Stamped on the young man's face was a passion, an intensity rarely seen on the faces of American youth. Sara had occasionally seen it on her own son's face, but never on those of his friends. Once she had touched such a face, had felt that passion directed at her.

Once. A lifetime ago. Before Danny. Before Jason. So very long ago.

The *sherut* pulled to a halt at the guarded gates of Kibbutz Golan. The young soldiers piled from the taxi and into the welcoming arms of two of the guards. Amid much pounding of backs and overlapping of questions and answers, Sara emerged from the taxi unnoticed.

She took in the rolls of barbed wire atop the fences, marring the view of the kibbutz, dulling the grandeur of the surrounding mountains. When had the settlement become a fortress? The colony seemed more an army camp than the sprawling mountain farm she remembered.

The swiftly approaching evening chilled the air and raised goose bumps on her flesh. In a nervous habit she'd acquired shortly after Jason's funeral, her thumb rubbed the now-empty space where her wedding ring had been.

She closed her eyes for a moment, conjuring up Jason's broad, lined face. In two years, her memories of him hadn't dimmed, the gentle love she felt hadn't ebbed. "Next year in Jerusalem," he'd toasted at Hanukkah, but there had been no next year for Jason. A heart attack had claimed him, and now she was in Israel alone. About to see the first love of her life.

She opened her eyes and saw not Ari Gaon, not the young soldiers at the gate, but the kibbutz itself. They still farmed it. Spring-green grain that would later turn golden, pushed at the late-afternoon rays of the sun, shimmering in the radiance. She could hear the sounds of birds and the distant rumble of a tractor. It was a peaceful setting, if one ignored the barbed wire atop the fence, the young men dressed in fatigues and heavy boots.

The group of soldiers noticed her then, and one of the guards who had been waiting at the gate approached Sara. In his eyes she could see a wariness that aged the boy beyond his years. And behind the wariness a helpless anger, perhaps one born of pain. "You are the American journalist?" he asked in Hebrew. "Sara Gould?"

She nodded. He looked her up and down in a semiadmiring glance, one that told her effectively that while she wasn't any spring chicken, she wasn't too bad. He brushed past her, reaching inside the *sherut* for her bags, and deposited them at her feet.

Sara smiled, vaguely amused by his casual dismissal. He was typical of the soldiers she'd known in Israel. Informal, blunt, brash, with a rather naive toughness. His shirt was open, un-buttoned halfway down his broad, muscled chest, revealing a thatch of dark, curling hair. He would be an American drill sergeant's nightmare, but Sara knew that when it came to fighting, he would outstrip almost any American foot soldier in discipline and drive. Or perhaps just in sheer fervor.

She hefted her bags and her camera, and he steered her to-ward the closed, barbed gate, saying, "I am Shlomo Havinot. I'll take you to the office of the director. He's waiting for you now." Finally he smiled, dispelling the tough expression, transforming him into a young man of Danny's age, but Sara was scarcely paying attention.

She was to meet Ari now? Just like that? After all these years, was she to have no precious moments to gather her thoughts, still her too rapidly beating heart?

Sara saw the other soldiers eye her with curiosity. They didn't offer to help with the luggage, but fell into step with her. One pointed at the battered camera case. "You were going to take photographs of Kibbutz Golan, no?"

Thinking she had misunderstood him, Sara paused before saying, "I was planning on it."

"It is a pity you will not be able to now," the soldier an-swered.

"I won't?" Sara asked, following the group through the gate and into the grounds.

The young man turned around at her question, a surprised expression on his face. Then he laughed, a little self-consciously. "But you will not be staying here."

"What?" Sara stopped walking, her mind a chaotic whirl of questions. Was there to be a reprieve? Had Ari discovered who she was and forbidden her stay? Was the incursion she'd used as an excuse, the one the soldiers had spoken of in the *sherut*, a serious one? Was she in danger? She felt a moment's sharp irony. Then relief: the coward's reprieve.

Shlomo Havinot's hand waved decisively before the other soldier could answer. "The director will explain," he said, ostensibly to Sara, but she saw that his eyes held a strong message for the others. He was obviously a leader in the making.

"This way, please," he said. "You will wish to put your bags in your room first." As heavy as they felt now, Sara would have been willing to put them almost anyplace. "You are in the main building. Building Alef."

Despite the implication of their recent conversation—her stay would be of short duration—Sara couldn't help but smile. She had stayed in Building Alef those many years ago. And entering, she saw that it looked just the same. The high-ceilinged central room was large, with stairs on either side, and several corridors leading into darkness, both on the first floor and the second. Several sofas and a few chairs were scattered around the space in an unattractive, but conversation-inducing pattern.

She found her eyes drawn to a large, rather too careful landscape against the far right wall. It still hung there, she thought, dimmed by the years and several layers of dust. The realization gave her a strong sense of continuity. The picture showed the same view as one could see from the far side of the building, a scene of rolling hills, distant mountains and tall, yellow grass. Sara had known the artist and wondered now, not for the first time, where he was. Would he remember the young girl who had spent a summer on the kibbutz and had so desperately loved and run away from a certain young commando?

The view from the tall windows forming one entire wall had always been the most impressive feature of the central room. It still was, though, of course, the landscape had changed. Kibbutz Golan had grown. Where once a few, barracklike buildings had huddled together on a grassy, river-rimmed knoll, several modern structures now stood. Some were clearly barns; the purpose of others was less obvious. Dining halls? Sleeping quarters? Nurseries, perhaps?

Images, golden in their clarity, a mental sepia tone of a distant past, flickered and fused with the present. With a strong and rightful sense of déjà vu, Sara saw the modern picnic tables become the older rough planks of raw lumber. As she watched, it seemed as if old machinery shed years and became bright and new again.

A breeze, spurred on by the mountain winds, came through the opened door, cool and clear. The air in the Golan Heights felt dry, yet soft, Mediterranean air certainly, but rarified by the pines and the altitude. It ruffled her hair and for a moment made her feel twenty-two again.

Ari heard them before he saw them. Young Shlomo's voice sounded less moody, less angry. If circumstances had been different, Ari would have decided then and there to ask the journalist to stay; Shlomo needed a new interest right now, anything to pull his mind away from whatever restless, ill-considered adventures he might be plotting.

Ari heard the boy's deep voice, hesitant with an evident self-consciousness, yet enthusiastic in his praise of the kibbutz. He smiled. This journalist must be very attractive to make the normally gruff Shlomo so eloquent.

The woman's voice broke in with a short phrase, a half laugh. Ari felt his loins tighten, his stomach clench. His hand gripped the edge of the desk with so much force that he could feel the metal rim cut at his fingers.

He'd heard the low pitch of her laugh a thousand times—in his dreams, his nightmares.

Sara.

The laugh was gone. With its fading, so vanished Ari's certainty that it was *her* voice, *her* laugh.

He found himself on his feet in front of his desk watching the door, his eyes locked on the painted metal. His heart pounded in a strange, almost frightened anticipation.

Chapter 2

It seemed to Ari that as the door opened and Sara stepped across the threshold, the world bucked its normal axis. The sensation lasted for the span of time that it would have taken a bird to wing a single stroke, and yet in a deep recess within himself, Ari felt the dizzying spiraling going on and on, shaking him to his very core.

It was *Sara*. He couldn't speak. As if his body belonged to someone else, he felt his legs take jerky steps across the office; it seemed to be a stranger's hand that stretched toward her.

A myriad of conflicting emotions and sensations assaulted him as she placed her hand in his. There had been only two other times in his life when he had felt this curious displacement: one when Sara had told him she was leaving Israel all those years before, the other when he'd heard about Yael and Galiti's death. Both times his heart had lurched and his mind warred, screaming denial and anger.

Stunned, he felt as if his breath was permanently caught in his lungs and his heart had forgotten how to beat. He was mesmerized by her parted lips, snared by the multilayered messages in her clear, hazel eyes.

He stared at her, half in disbelief, half in an odd despair. *Why now? Why, after all these years?* As he stared, he tried marshaling his chaotic thoughts. He wanted to pull her into his arms and hold her. He wanted to shout for joy and, at the same time, shout at her for the pain she'd inflicted eighteen years ago. He wanted to kiss her . . . wanted to drive her to her knees, make her beg his forgiveness.

His entire body reacted to the slight pressure of her cool hand. His heart began to beat again, erratically, his breath shuddering through his chest.

Sara. He wanted to cry her name aloud, wanted to push her away from him, out of the door, out of his life.

He felt confused by her presence, bemused by the pain and joy of seeing her again. And he was angered by his own confusion. Didn't time heal all wounds? Apparently not. As if it had been only yesterday, he thought of her laugh, her touch. He remembered that sudden, rapt expression on her face when she heard some story, and painfully recalled her voice, husky with suppressed passion.

The trembling in her long fingers kept Ari silent and called his errant mind to heel. In her liquid eyes he read sheer shock. He knew it matched his own. He felt he had conjured her out of the blue study he'd been in all afternoon. He almost laughed. It had been her name that had reminded him. And the real Sara stood before him now. But the reservation read Sara Gould, not Sara Rosen.

He stepped back a pace, feeling the need for distance. He released her hand and moved behind his desk, still feeling the impression of her touch on his palm. Though apart from her now, he could still smell her summery scent, one of wildflowers lazily wafting in mountain breezes. He recognized it. In the dark, in a room full of people, he'd have known that unusual, warm scent. He'd have known it anywhere. Anytime.

Sara. A thousand memories crashed in, wave upon wave, thundering impact upon receding thought. Sara running, half sliding down a hillside, wild daffodils up to her knees, her toffee-brown hair dancing on the early-summer breeze, her skin golden from the sun, blushing at the memory of a recent kiss.

Seeing her now, knowing that it really was Sara, no ghost, no midnight fantasy, Ari was at one and the same time wholly alive and wholly shell-shocked. *Why was she here? Why had she come back?* And why did seeing her cause such a riot within him?

His first impression was that she hadn't changed at all. *Not at all.* In the sunlight, the beams glinting in her hair, he had thought her a figment of his imagination, the same young girl he'd known so many years before. Looking at her now, watching the initial impact of their meeting die from her eyes, he could see the marks of time on her face.

If possible, she was more beautiful than she had been all those years ago. Her body had a maturity and fullness it had lacked then, and her face showed an awareness of the negative sides of life, the downswings. Eighteen years ago, only dreams and moonlight had lighted her face. Now she carried an aura of knowledge, of inner confidence, of acceptance of time and what time could mean. Her features wore the unmistakable surety that dreams can die and moonlight is no sinecure. It was a stamp she had left with him all those years before. The scar deep inside him twisted painfully. Almost angrily he waved his hand, as if to brush the past aside.

Her eyes broke away from his; he could see it was a conscious effort. She flexed her hand and kneaded her left ring finger. *No wedding ring.* Yet she rubbed the empty space as if she'd done it many times, as if it were second nature. Her name was different. Where was the husband who'd claimed her name, but produced no wedding ring?

Despite the desk separating them, she pulled back a step, as if the proximity were too great. The series of emotions that had filled her eyes when she first saw him slowly ebbed. She masked her expression, but he could see it was an effort. Still she said nothing as her eyes studied him, appearing to miss not a detail.

He wondered what she saw. Was she having the same difficulty he was in realigning time and space to link the long-ago past with the stark present? He was no longer the young commando. His hair was almost solid gray now, and his eyes needed the half glasses that enabled him to read. For the first time he found himself wishing he had not crossed the barrier of forty-five. He had scarcely noticed the years passing, but now, seeing Sara again, he was acutely conscious of their departure. Eighteen years, he thought. Almost two decades.

He had to clear his throat in order to speak. "Shalom, Sara," he said. Even to himself, the simple word sounded like a caress and possibly a plea of some kind. Its literal meaning, peace, was all too appropriate.

"Ari," she said softly, her contralto voice falling upon him like the memory of a dream. Yet like her face, like her body, her voice was different. Deeper. Richer. And in her tone he heard a note of something strangely like fear. "It's...it's good to see you again."

Was it good? he wondered. It was strange, even terrifying, but was it *good?* He had the odd impression that a wall he'd erected around a private part of his heart had been suddenly blown to bits. That wasn't *good,* that was *dangerous.*

"It's been a long time," he said, hating the inadequacy of the words and himself for the banality of the phrase, resenting the distance that separated them, the passing of the years and the long-ago pain that had created such a barrier. *Sara.* The only woman he had ever truly loved. The realization made him feel a stab of guilt for Yael, and the guilt made him tighten his lips. He forced them to curve into a smile he didn't feel.

"Yes." She agreed to the length of time simply, adding nothing. For some reason, this both steadied and vaguely pleased Ari. She had not clarified his statement, merely acknowledged it. Was she also acknowledging the importance of their time together? Had he held a more important position in her mind than that of a summer's lover? Often what one doesn't talk about has greater significance than the memories one does recount. He knew this well; he'd never been able to really talk about Yael and Galiti's deaths. He'd never even spoken of Sara.

At the same time as her words acknowledged the past, they also underlined the passage of time, the miles and eons they had traveled separately.

With an effort, Ari assumed the mantle of directorship, again waving his hand—was it trembling slightly?—at one of the cheap folding chairs. Ignoring the rapid beat of his heart and the constrictions it underwent, he watched Sara take a seat and slowly cross her legs, Ari sat down in his own desk chair, willing his features to a calm he was far from feeling.

Seeing the pulse jump in her slender throat, noting the quickened rise and fall of her blouse, Ari felt a shaft of sure power shoot through him. She had come to *him.* Now. After all this time. He'd intended sending this journalist away, simply, directly, like swatting a pesky fly. But this was *Sara.* She was so tense that there was little doubt she felt as out of kilter as he. A long-buried, hitherto unexplored desire for revenge uncoiled in him as surely as his loins tightened at the vision of her beauty, the sense of her presence.

"So, Sara, how long will you be staying with us?" he asked, ignoring Shlomo's surprise and the suddenly intent look on Sara's face.

She frowned, and Ari could see it was more from nervousness than from seeking a possible answer to his question.

"Somehow," she said slowly, "I'd gathered the impression that I wouldn't be allowed to stay here."

Shlomo started to speak, but Ari interrupted him. He was countermanding his own orders, possibly placing her life in danger. But what of his heart? Wasn't that what was really in jeopardy? All the same, he could no more have sent her away now, knowing who she was, seeing her again, than he could have torn his heart from his chest with his own hand. *Your turn,* his soul whispered, but Ari didn't stop to question the possible implications of the phrase.

His eyes flicked to Shlomo's, and he gave a quick shake of his head. "No. When I gave the order that you weren't to stay, I didn't realize it was you."

"It apparently makes a difference," she said, her words ironically begging the question.

For a moment Ari felt nonplussed. Of course it made all the difference in the world. Couldn't she feel that? How could he tell her the magnitude of what this meeting meant? A man of action, not of words, he could only fall back upon weak excuses. But in his heart he knew it didn't matter what he said: anything would be an excuse. She must stay. He didn't want to explore the reasons why. He shrugged. "You've been here before. You know the dangers. You know how to protect yourself."

He saw a spasm cross her face. Was she remembering the hours they'd spent together on a lonely hillside, his arms around her, teaching her to use a gun she'd hated almost as much as she loved her camera? Or was it something else?

She drew a deep breath, as if she'd been sitting there not breathing for some time. It made him slightly more comfortable to see that she was having difficulty, too.

"Thank you," she said. "I—"

She stopped, then apparently decided to forge ahead, but not with what she'd been about to say. "I'm glad I'm here again."

But Ari knew she was lying. He could see it in her wide eyes, in the trembling of her lips, hear it in her throaty voice. He could feel the muscles across his shoulders bunching, stretching with unaccustomed tension.

Again he wondered why she had come back after all this time. What did she want? Stories lay under every rock in Israel. Why had she chosen Kibbutz Golan? Had she chosen it because he was here? Or, judging by the wariness in her eyes, had it been the sheerest coincidence? No, hidden in the depths, behind the shock was the clear message that she'd *known* he was here.

But most of all he wondered why he had a sinking fear that she still had that incredible power to move him as no woman had ever done before her or since. A power that he'd not been able to use in return. She had left him. Now she'd come back. Did she still have that power? Or had the tables been turned, so that now he was the one with the force?

Your turn, the small voice said again.

The silence stretched awkwardly between them as his eyes locked with hers; the room was charged with too many unspoken questions, too many answers withheld.

"Come," he said abruptly, rising and holding out his hand. "I'll show you around. The kibbutz has changed a great deal since you were here." As he waited for her hand to touch his, he found himself wondering what it would be like to do more than take her hand. Would her lips still feel as soft? Would her touch still be as sweet?

He felt her hesitation before she placed her hand lightly in his. He drew her to her feet.

"Everything's changed," she said quietly, her eyes meeting his. Shadows he couldn't fathom hid her from him, yet he sensed her words were charged with meaning.

"Yes," he said, equally quietly, thinking not of the Sara and Ari of the distant past, but of his daughter's name, chiseled in the honor plaque in the center of the garden, of the part of his heart that had been carved there also.

"Yes," he said, "everything's changed," aware as he spoke that nothing could have crystallized the distance they'd traveled quite as much as this sorrowful acknowledgement.

* * *

As they walked, Sara tried keeping her eyes on the dusk-drenched pathways, on the new buildings, on the golden-skinned passersby. She tried looking at anything and everything but Ari Gaon. But she failed. It was the set of his shoulders, the curve of his cheek, the broad jawline, the full lips that drew her attention.

He walked as he had always done, with a relaxed precision, characteristic of Israeli soldiers. He had no rigid movements, but a fluid grace, a raw, unself-conscious sensuality, a casual air of absolute command, total control—a confidence he exuded at all times. It was there today, had been back then. Except for that one horrible day when she'd said goodbye, when she'd told him she couldn't stay in Israel, couldn't stay with him, she'd never seen him without it.

The silver in his hair, the lines on his tanned face only added to his attractiveness. He'd always been a handsome man, not in the manner of actors and statesmen, but in the style of compact, rugged outdoorsmen. He was the embodiment of the Israeli male, she thought. A small voice deep within challenged her: he was the embodiment of masculinity.

Age had done him proud, she thought, and if anything, he looked even more the soldier. Yet unlike the Ari of the past, he seemed controlled and distant. Though the difference in his appearance didn't cause her any concern, the difference in his attitude somehow made her nervous. Surely no one could change that much.

He'd spoken little since leaving his office, and for this Sara was grateful. His deep, heavily accented voice played along her spine, sending shivers up and down her back, making her body liquid. It was almost dark now, but she searched his face looking for evidence of that first encounter's shock. Imprinted on her mind was the swift joy, the sudden anger that had flashed in his eyes.

But nothing showed there now, and the realization served only to underscore the difficulties between them. She'd known it would be strange to see him again, but had never guessed, never dared dream, that he would still feel vestiges of emotion for her. That *she* did, was, under the circumstances, inevitable. But for him to have done so, as well, seemed nothing shy of incredible.

Just being in Israel was difficult, seeing Ari again after all this time was confusing, but hardest to bear was the awareness that she had responded to the casual touch of his hand as though he had kissed her. Had he kissed her she would not have pulled away.

Once again she found herself kneading her ring finger. Quickly she shoved her hand into her sundress pocket and shivered. Was she seeking comfort from Jason? He had comforted Danny and her as easily as some people breathe. Was she asking permission? And if so, permission to do what? Never had she wanted Jason beside her as badly as she did at that moment. A strange wish, she had to acknowledge, to want the husband beside her to give her the strength to combat the effects of a first love. Yet Jason would have understood. He always did—had. She shivered a second time.

"Are you cold?" Ari asked, stopping. He glanced down at the folds of her dress that hid her hand. Slowly his gaze traveled upward. Her body betrayed her reaction to it.

Sara shivered again, feeling her nipples harden involuntarily. She'd been wrong to come back. She should have quit McMunn-Knapper rather than come here to this place. She'd been wrong to assume she could tell him about Danny.

Now she realized all too vividly that she'd been wrong to believe a separation of eighteen years would make the telling easier to this aloof, distant Ari. Wrong to even believe that telling him was possible. She'd known all that back in Washington. There was too much between them to tell him about Danny, to tell him he had a nearly grown son.

Sara drew a shaky breath. She would do the story as quickly as possible and leave. It was better to let the past remain just that: the past. Yet standing before him, her eyes level with his, she wondered. Perhaps it was only the dim light, perhaps it was wishful thinking, but she told herself she could see compassion in his gaze. Compassion, where none had ever shone before. And behind that a wary desire.

Her breath snagged in her throat, as her heart stepped up its rhythm. The Ari she had known had been the consummate figure of passion, not merely physically, but in every way. He was all fire, all intensity, a man of commitment, of drive, of cause. "That's for the weak," he'd once said of compassion, and then he'd meant it.

What did he believe today?

Now his lips were parted, as if he were about to speak. His hands were clenched at his sides, as though preparing for a fight. But he said nothing.

It was up to her, then.

"Thanks for letting me stay." She wondered why she, who made her living with words, should resort to such trite phrases.

"You make it sound like a question," he said. His face was shadowed by the darkening sky, and she couldn't read the expression in his eyes. His back was too straight for him to be relaxed, and she felt the distance between them like a tangible presence.

"No," she lied. But it had been a question of sorts. It was only after seeing her again that Ari had changed his mind. The whys were too numerous to count. Potential explanations were too filled with conflict to verbalize. She wished for one of her battered notepads; it would offer the security blanket she so desperately craved at that moment and serve to place even more distance between them than did the square set of his shoulders.

They resumed walking, neither speaking, not touching. Even when she stumbled against a stone, he did not touch her arm, though he half raised his hand as if to do so. Mentally she clung to that withheld gesture. There were so many things to tell him, so many old debts to pay. Why couldn't she speak?

It took every element of self-possession she had at her command to maintain a calm exterior when Ari asked her if she was married. They were walking along a flower-lined path, cool, evening shadows creeping across the concrete pathways, blessedly hiding her face from his.

God, has it come to this? she asked herself. *The man she had loved most in the world, knowing nothing about her?*

As if her voice had come from someone else, she heard herself say that yes, she had been married to Jason Gould, and that he'd died only two years before.

"He—you loved him?" His tone was short, even cold, but the words were charged with a thousand unasked questions.

She had never been so aware of the years that had flown by. Lifetimes had come and gone, since they had loved so intensely in that long-ago summer.

"Yes," Sara answered quietly, knowing that while it was the truth, it was also a lie. She had truly loved Jason, but never with the depth and the scope she had experienced with Ari

Gaon. Nor had she ever been afraid of Jason, as she had of Ari. Jason had offered the calm mantle of fatherhood to her child, a blanket of security to her own young career. He had loved her without reservation, without asking her to give more than she had to give. And he had known about Ari, had known she would always treasure the memory of the young commando she'd refused in panic one too sunny day on a hillside in Israel. He'd understood her confusion over that and had not pried for reasons.

"I'm sorry," Ari told her, but Sara didn't know if he was sorry she had loved Jason, or was giving her the conventional response to the news of Jason's death. She met his eyes and read understanding there, and more. *Everything's changed*, she heard again, and could see it in his eyes.

Everything *had* changed. The young commando would have had difficulty in masking a possible sense of superiority, the kind that would have said she would always have loved him best. But this new Ari, eighteen years older, looked momentarily saddened. It was as if he took it personally.

"Children?" he asked, his voice so low that it could have come from the shadows themselves.

Her throat tightened, her mind rejecting this bizarre conversation, her heart perversely angry that he couldn't see the truth without her having to speak it. "One. A boy. Danny," she managed.

"Daniel?"

"Just Dan." Her heart thudded painfully in her chest.

"We have a river named the Dan," Ari said reflectively. He turned and met her eyes, a soft smile on his lips. Was he remembering the lazy afternoon beside that river?

"It's a good name," he said.

She nodded, transfixed by his gaze, held still for fear of his next question. Would he understand the connection? Would he leap to the—to her—transparent conclusion? But he didn't ask her if she remembered the quiet nights on Tel Dan, the hill beside the river. And he didn't ask Danny's age. Nor did he comment further.

In the heartbeat of silence, she again felt oddly dispirited that he didn't instinctively, intuitively see the truth. Her reaction was immediately followed by a sharp stab of chagrin, as she realized that there was no way on earth he would make such an assumption. He'd had no knowledge of her pregnancy. She hadn't even known then.

"And you?" she asked him finally.

He sighed, and the depth of the sigh told her he had been married, but was no longer. He stopped walking, pointing across the small, enclosed garden to the tall stone monolith in the center. "I married." He shot her a glance. Was that reproach in his eyes? Challenge? "Three years after you left. Yael Shamir. Maybe you remember her."

Sara didn't.

"Sorry," she said. "Eighteen years is a long time."

"Yes," he answered, but the single word seemed to carry more than acknowledgment.

Staring at the monolith, trying to cull its significance from her recalcitrant memory, Sara said nothing. She had always known it was likely he would marry. But knowing it rationally and feeling it emotionally were two different things. The stab of jealousy she felt was wholly unjustified and completely irrational. He'd asked her, and she'd said no. How could she begrudge him the years with someone else?

She stepped toward the large stone. He uttered a sound, almost a vocal extension of the sigh, but she didn't look back; the significance of the monolith had become clear.

The stone was a memorial plaque. Each name it bore, carved by hand, indicated someone within the kibbutz community, someone who had died in the preservation of their way of life, who had died for Israel.

A small light at the base of the memorial illuminated the names clearly, and after studying the Hebrew letters for several moments she found two names: Yael Shamir Gaon and Galit Gaon. His wife and daughter were among those who had lost their lives at Kibbutz Golan.

"Oh, Ari, I'm sorry. I didn't know," she told him. He said nothing in response.

As though avoiding a direct confrontation with the implications of the plaque, Sara considered his daughter's name instead. He'd known the meaning of her son's name, though he didn't realize its special significance. She quickly assimilated the significance of his daughter's: Galit meant Ice Cream. It sounded silly in its English translation, though it was no sillier than naming a child Candy; it seemed to Sara that children named for a confection always displayed traits of sweetness and delight. Dear God, what he must have gone through to lose a child. No wonder distance had replaced passion.

The thought of Ari having had and lost a daughter racked her and made her realize anew how wrong she'd been to push for an Israel assignment. *If you're going to tell him, tell him now, and get it over with!* Her thoughts beat so loudly in her head that she could hear nothing else.

"It happened five years ago," he said as he approached, and though he didn't elaborate, Sara understood, hearing the weight of pain in his voice. "I didn't remarry."

Sara couldn't have looked at him for all the money in the world. Her heart pounded in a harsh, painful rhythm. She wanted to touch him now, to lay her hand along his muscled arm and murmur magic words, a single, miraculous phrase that would ease the pain from his voice, the shadows from his eyes.

She knew the words, too: *You have a son.*

But she had no right to just blurt it out like that. She'd given up that right when she'd left him eighteen years ago.

"Galiti would have been fourteen next month," he told her.

Though his voice was steady, the words sliced straight and deep across her heart. "I'm so sorry," Sara managed finally, at last able to look at him.

He stared into her eyes for a long moment, then said, "Yes. So am I." He turned away, his shoulders square, head erect, his pride held as fiercely intact as if he used it as a shield. Which, Sara thought, he probably did.

"Tell me about your son," he said after a long silence. He took her arm.

Involuntarily she looked at him. Caught off guard, pinned by his incredible eyes, she blurted out the first thing she thought of. "His eyes are gray," she said, and when she heard her words die away, she saw he was watching her with an odd, arrested expression on his dark features.

"What an unusual thing to say, Sara," he observed, a hint of the old Ari coming through, the Ari who could see through all of her fantasies and cut through all her shams. "You said it almost as if you only just now realized it."

Shocked at the indiscretion, stunned by the accuracy with which he'd interpreted her words, she laughed shakily, looking away, struggling for some explanation. "Maybe I did. I haven't been away from him too often. You find yourself remembering funny things when you're apart."

"I know," he said softly, and her heart constricted, for she could sense he knew it only too well. Then he turned away, and she wondered if she hadn't misunderstood his meaning.

"He's young, then? Danny?"

Sara wanted to spill the truth, to stop this torturous questioning. No, she wanted to scream at him, Danny's not young, Danny's seventeen, Danny's in France, and Danny's yours. *Yours. Ours.* But the silence of eighteen years stood between them. The deaths of his wife and daughter deepened the gulf.

In that realization, Sara comprehended the full scope of the gap. They were not the same people they had been. Years, loves, lifetimes had passed. The thought saddened her inexpressibly.

"Sara?" Ari prompted.

She flushed, realizing she had been standing stock-still, staring at Ari, not really seeing him. She groped for the answer to his question. "Danny? He's just finishing high school," she said, and waited for the—to her—inevitable calculation of age, but it wasn't forthcoming. Then she understood that even if he did make such a calculation, he would arrive at another conclusion. In Israel high school is the level usually reserved for seventh and eighth graders in the United States.

"The first cable said he'd be joining you...."

"No!" she exclaimed, and backed up her too-emphatic denial with a rueful smile. "You said yourself it was too dangerous for a civilian." Not that Danny could in any way be considered untrained. Jason, knowing the boy's background, seeing the future with ever-prescient eyes, had made certain his adopted son was well versed in every form of self-defense.

He didn't argue. "I wouldn't have allowed him to come, but it is a pity. I would have liked to have met him."

He couldn't possibly have known how the innocuous phrase hurt her, made her hands tremble.

"Ari...?"

His eyes met hers, making her heart lurch painfully. The brave words her mind had summoned dissipated, shriveled on the end of her tongue. What had she been going to say, anyway? Ari, Danny is yours...?

"What is it, Sara?" When she only shook her head in help-less speechlessness, he smiled somewhat wryly.

"It's tough, isn't it? Seeing each other again after all this time," he said.

She nodded, but said no more, resuming her pace. The si-lence lengthened and stretched like the night's shadows.

Ari's voice, when he finally spoke again, was low and full. "You know, I've thought of you over the years. Wondered what you were doing, where you were." He looked away, as though searching for her in the distant, night-blackened mountains.

He continued. "I wondered if you were happy."

He turned back to her. While his voice had been dreamy, even sad when he'd spoken before, now his eyes flashed. "And here you are."

"Yes," she said, slightly frightened of the intense gaze that was clearly visible even through the darkness around them. Frightened because this was the Ari Gaon she remembered.

He sighed. His mouth worked for a moment, as if tasting something rotten. Then he said heavily, "In all that time, Sara, I somehow never thought we'd be strangers."

"Strangers..." Sara repeated, cut by the truth of his words, aching with the reality of them. *Strangers*.

She looked away from him again. Those eyes had always frightened her with their intensity, the speculation hidden in their depths, the combination of wariness and desire, the mixture of knowledge of the past and uncertainty about the future.

Yes, they were strangers. Yet in her mind they had been bound together for years, every day, every month, because of her love for him, but most of all because of Danny.

She jumped when he took her elbow and guided her around a turn and in front of Building Alef. Her arm, though his fin-gers held her only lightly, seemed to burn; as if in refutation a chill worked at her neck. In the dim light issuing from the glass doors and windows, she knew he could see her face as clearly as she could see his. His expression was masked. But was hers? What could he read in her eyes? Fear? A wistful hope that the truth would simply deliver itself?

He took a pace closer, and she realized he could read some-thing else: desire. It was there, she couldn't hide that, even from herself. It had been eighteen years since she had seen him, yet her heart beat a rapid rhythm, the blood in her veins seemed effervescent. Her palms felt damp, her lips were dry.

She lightly ran her tongue across their parched surface. Had he read in her eyes a need to lay their past to rest? Ari and she had never really finished. They had never sat across from each other at a rough table, hands clenched, white-knuckled, around coffee mugs, and put paid to their dreams and hopes.

She'd run from him, run from the intensity that lay so close to the surface, that burning passion she'd seen again in his eyes only moments before. Why? Because of that twenty-two-year-old's certainty that she would not be able to match that intensity. But she'd stayed away because of Danny.

Stepping back from him, Sara told herself she was no twenty-two-year-old girl now. She would be forty in two short months, a woman who had raised a son and lived side by side with a good man. She had shot a thousand pictures and written the accompanying stories that had blazed, banner-headlined across the nation's newspapers. The photographs had burned themselves onto people's minds, the stories had moved them.

Strangers. His word settled into her heart and burrowed a home for itself. No, she couldn't tell him. Not now. Perhaps never. Or perhaps just not yet. Not until she knew him better. If she ever did. She hadn't understood him all those years ago and understood him even less now.

"Sara . . ." Her name was a caress on his lips, and her reaction to it—to him—confused her. She wanted him, yet feared that want. He'd always had the power to move her, make her lose sight of her goals, her dreams. She'd used his intensity as an excuse once. What excuse could she use now?

"Yes?" she asked, hearing her voice sound as breathless as her lungs felt. Her smile felt pasted on.

He met her widened gaze with a steady stare and took another step closer. He was close enough for her to smell the scent of his soap, the clean smell of the night on his skin. She could hear his breath coming and going, see the flaring of his nostrils.

"No," she murmured, backing into the plate-glass window behind her. She felt the color rise in her cheeks, then ebb. Her hands curled into the folds of her skirt, her thumb clawing again at the empty ring finger.

Twenty-two again. That was how he made her feel. Or rather, she thought with some exasperation, that was how she let him make her feel. She had never been one of those women who dreamed of being young again, and now knew why. She had been a fledgling then, an untried hint of the woman she had become. She'd been insecure, unknowing of what real life and real love meant.

She wondered if everyone meeting a former lover had that curious reaction. With no years linking them, no continuity of daily routine, no loving, silly rituals—pass the butter, do you want the sports section?—could they only relate as they once had? Or was it merely the fact that a first love never dies? Was that really all they had had? A first love, a love affair that would have died and faded from memory long ago, had not the unusual circumstances, the lack of a last, tearful revocation of love, the stamp of the father's face upon her son's kept it alive for her?

Yet Ari seemed to remember also. His walk, the distancing, wary look in his eyes, the flashes of anger, and now the increasing intensity of passion there, all told her he remembered all too vividly.

He leaned closer and, after a long, searching look, closed his eyes; his lips breached the distance to hers.

Whatever he may have intended by the kiss, an affirmation, an acknowledgment of the past, it was so much more. Lightly at first, his warm lips merely brushed her cold mouth. Then her body was cold no longer as the kiss deepened; he grasped her hand so tightly that it hurt.

Sara's knees threatened to buckle at the enormity of her emotional and physical response. Her very lips recognized his. Even his taste was familiar. Without thought of the intervening years, his lips driving every other rational idea from her mind, she leaned into him, tasting him fully, remembering him, yet more stirred now than she had ever been. She moaned his name, invoking an answering groan from him. He drew her tightly against him, releasing her hand, gripping her shoulders.

The kiss grew more intense. No longer a mere tasting, a gentle quest, it became a fiery demand. Her body thrummed to a rhythm it hadn't known for years and had only vaguely understood then. This was why she'd come back, she thought. This and nothing else.

Her limbs grew weak and her legs gave slightly, causing her to arch against him. She knew the fit, her body sought the stunning familiarity. This was the dream, the fantasy, and now it was reality.

As if doused by icy water, Ari jerked backward, tearing his hands from her shoulders, his breathing harsh in the cool air.

Sara slumped back against the glass, grateful for the cold solidity, aching with desire, aching at the abrupt rejection. This was the moment she'd envisioned, the moment she'd feared.

"Why, Sara?" he asked harshly from the shadows where he'd apparently chosen to hide his face from her. Stunned by the unwanted freedom, still languorous with want, Sara could only shake her head in puzzlement.

"Why did you come back here? Why now? Why, after all these years?"

Helpless, she could only shake her head again. "I didn't know you'd be here," she said.

He expelled his breath in a quick release. He raised his hand and swept it through his curly hair. "That puts me in my place, doesn't it?" There was no hint of humor on his face, no glint of sarcasm.

"I didn't mean . . ."

"You're lying, Sara. You had my cable." His voice was edged with scarcely controlled fury.

"Yes," she said, remembering the fight with Butterfield, the fight with Danny. But it would be useless to explain only one part of the story to Ari. He had been the type of man who saw the world in black and white, no extenuating shades of gray. All cause and glory, all passion and action. Explanations were for people who vacillated in the middle, he'd often said.

"So why did you come?" he repeated.

His hands reached out and took her shoulders, thumbs caressing her cool, bare skin, his fingers tightening into the soft flesh. But this time the grip was not a lover's touch. This time she felt the anger emanating from him, and though there was no physical pain, her heart constricted.

"Why, Sara?"

He shook her slightly, the depth of emotion in his voice as poignant as the unembellished question.

"I had to," she said and realized how ambiguous an answer it was as he sighed. She wanted to say something, anything, to cover the suddenly dangerous ground they'd strayed onto. "Ari, I . . ."

"It's all right, Sara. I understand."

He released her, though his hands ran lingeringly down her arms before he did so, as if he could not help himself. He sighed again and met her eyes.

"I had it right, didn't I? We *are* strangers."

Chapter 3

Ari crumpled the terse message from the border commandant and tossed it onto his desk. It skipped across the stacks of paper and the day's clutter, moving with an irregular rhythm, like a truck with two flat tires. It rocked to a stop, an odd-sized ball containing ominous words.

They had fired cables back and forth all morning. He could have walked the distance and talked to the bullheaded man in half the time. But walking across the mountains was no longer safe. *When was it ever?*

He'd made a mistake in allowing Sara to stay. Not just because of the constriction in his chest whenever he thought of her, or because he'd had no sleep the night before, tortured by the thought of her actually sleeping at Kibbutz Golan. He had wanted to do so much more than just kiss her. All of those reasons were valid, but now moot; now there was danger.

"We've no right to keep her here," he'd told the border commandant with the unlikely name of Harry.

"No one in, no one out," Harry had fired back. "Too few patrols on the border. Reprisals expected."

"Get more!" Ari had cabled.

"Trying, trying."

"Too dangerous for her," Ari had told the commandant.

"Too late, you'll have to keep her," Harry had returned with unknowing irony.

Everywhere he turned he met with irony, Ari thought without humor.

He ran a hand through his hair, as if he could sweep away with a physical gesture all the thoughts in his roiling mind. He hadn't felt this confounded in years. Eighteen years, to be exact. He was not a man who wallowed in self-examination, wondering what made him do this, why he did that; he simply did it, whatever it was, whatever had to be done... unless he was with Sara.

Sara.

She was like a Siren. She was a witch who had cast a spell on him eighteen years earlier, and now had come back to see if it still held. In his arms the night before, lips pressed against his, she must have found the answer: he was still captivated by her.

Yet in his arms, her body arching to meet his, answering his demand with a plea of her own, she had turned back the clock for a moment, making him feel whole again, making him feel strong and young. Maybe that had been why he'd pulled away from her. She was like an intoxicating drug. He'd been addicted once; he wouldn't allow himself to fall for that addiction a second time.

But now, no matter how much he wanted her to go, he knew she had to stay.

The realization filled him with dismay. More trouble was expected on the border. And as Kibbutz Golan was a mere strip of trees and a short range of mountains from the border, trouble could be expected here, as well. The commandant's message said they should expect a reprisal attack. Ari snorted. Reprisal for what? The kibbutz had lost four youths during the last incursion; the border contingent had lost even more. Wasn't that reprisal enough? Or was a Syrian stepping over the boundary the crime? *An eye for an eye.* The same grandmother who had cried for peace would have said yes.

And Heaven only knew when the reprisals and skirmishes would end. Could the final tally ever be considered even? A brother for a brother, a grandfather for a mother, Galiti for someone's cousin.

He turned to the window, as if the golden view would offer him solace. It only reminded him of how far Kibbutz Golan had come in its struggle for survival, how far Israel had come.

And of how many mistakes he'd made with Sara, past and present.

He'd seen the desire in her eyes the night before. It had infused him with fierce pride, with a raw need of his own. But he'd also seen the wariness, the pain—a pain he couldn't understand. And he'd seen the certainty that the past still lived.

Tasting her lips, feeling her body softly arch into his, he had forgotten the years, forgotten where he'd been and what he was now. He had wanted her with the same hot intensity he'd had before, though beneath that want lay the wound she'd dealt him so many years earlier.

He'd called them strangers, had tried to hurt her by saying the words. Yet her body had melted to his, as if they'd separated only the day before. The curves of her slender frame had felt achingly, damnably familiar.

He'd wanted to lash out at her, because he'd resented the fact that she still moved him. Angrily he'd used phrases, snatches of phrases, to hurt her. His pride, like some avenging weapon, had whipped at her, every bit as much as his heart wanted to have her kneel at his feet, as he had once knelt at hers. But he was a man not a child, and she was a woman not a figment of his young-old mind. He had changed; life had changed him. She must have changed as well. This resentment for the lost years was what had made him angry.

With her in his arms, smelling of the same summer scent, her lush body pressed to his, he had lost sight of the changes, lost sight of the present. But in the heat of that moment he wanted to hurt her as badly as she had hurt him. He wanted to crush her, curse her, enact a reprisal of his own: demand a heart for a heart.

He frowned, confused by the implications of their kiss, distrusting his reaction to her, hers to him, while wanting to trust them both.

He turned from the window, picking up the phone. He barked orders into the receiver, listening to the assenting voice of his friend's son, Dov, the newly apprenticed kibbutz security officer, thinking of Sara, of the frightening present.

For now, through his own desire to see the past recreated in the present, he had put her in danger. The border commandant had urged a curfew and a total restriction of outside movement—a basic cordon around Kibbutz Golan.

And what of the restless young people, those angry over the deaths of their friends, their lovers? Ready to disobey orders, they were ripe for dangerous mischief. Ari had seen it too often in his own eyes not to recognize it in theirs.

He hung up the phone. A meeting of the kibbutz managers was slated for that evening after the dinner hour. In the next two weeks soldiers would be pouring in, filling the dormitories, crowding the dining hall, turning Kibbutz Golan once again into a military headquarters. All directors would be very busy, trying to maintain schedules, discipline and calm.

Ari went back to the window and forced his mind to remain in the present. But the present seemed only to contain Sara. Soon he would have to gaze into her soft hazel eyes again and face the price of his youth, the price of his heart. Damn her for coming back; damn her for dredging up the memories he'd wanted as dead as was their long-ago romance.

Sara lifted the camera to her eyes, filling frame after frame with the peaceful setting. A hillside covered with yellow bobbing sunflowers, a distant blue mountain, an old man and woman sitting on a narrow concrete bench, not talking, but relaxed together, their eyes on a tractor humming in a small field far away. Slowly Sara lowered the camera and walked toward them.

"Moshe?" she asked hesitantly. "Hannah?"

The man's seamy, pockmarked face turned in her direction. The old artist's pale blue eyes, rimmed by pockets of flesh and encircled by a thousand tiny wrinkles, stared at her blankly for a long moment, then the shock of recognition focused them.

"Sara," he said. In his voice was all the welcome she could ever have desired. A smile creased his features still more, and he pushed himself up from the bench, both muscled arms outstretched.

She moved into the embrace easily and gladly. Here was a welcome with no constraints, no awkward, terrible memories to blot the present.

"Oh, Moshe," she said as he took her face between both hands and pressed kisses upon her cheeks. "I wondered if you'd still be here, wondered what became of you."

"Sara Rosen!" the woman called. She was some ten years younger than the man, in her late fifties or early sixties. She rose with the same fluid grace Sara recalled from her young days at Kibbutz Golan. "So you have finally come back."

Moshe turned to her. "Of course she came back. What else could she do? We fed her pomegranates, remember?"

"And by that are you implying that this kibbutz is like Hades?" Hannah asked with a haughty arch of an eyebrow. But her eyes twinkled at Sara.

"Only that Sara is like Persephone, my dear. Only like spring." Moshe gave her another hug, then released her to Hannah's cool embrace.

"I hoped you'd both still be here," Sara told them.

"Oh, we are like the rocks we stand upon," Moshe said, waving his broad hand at the ground. He was as grandiloquent as ever, Sara thought, amused. "We remain forever."

He pointed an accusing finger at her. "You are the little swallow that flew away and never wrote letters. We pined each day, waiting for word."

"Oh, Moshe! Give the child some space," Hannah chided. She drew Sara onto the bench. "Tell us everything, my dear. From the day you ran away from us to what you are doing back here, sitting on this bench."

"Yes, tell all, and we will hang upon your very words," Moshe added. "We would tell you all that has happened to us, you see, but aside from the facts that Hannah is now the doctor here and we both have more wrinkles, there is nothing to tell. We are still here."

Sara raised her hands to tuck them into his. He was still as solid as ever, all muscles and brawn, but now age had stolen the straightness from his shoulders and bleached his hair.

"I saw your painting in Building Alef," she said. "It's still where it was, when you hung it up that first day."

He laughed, that same loud bray. "It wasn't dry, and you were afraid it would get damaged. You made me hang it up to save it. And it was such a bad painting! But you wouldn't let me give it to you."

"It belonged to the whole kibbutz," Sara said fondly. "Like your portraits."

"You and Hannah here are the only two who have ever truly appreciated me."

"Don't encourage him, Sara. He's unendurable after someone compliments him."

"I've still got that one of you." He winked broadly.

Sara smiled, remembering. She'd come back from an abortive target practice with Ari, and Moshe had insisted upon doing a sketch of her, right then and there. It wasn't until he was finished that she knew she'd had crushed daffodils sticking out of her hair.

An affection for these two people welled in her, healing the doubts of the past week, reducing the insecurities of the night before—decreasing the tension that had wound within her, ever since she'd seen Ari's name on that cable.

"So our little swallow has come back to the nest," Moshe said, his broad, blunt hands still retaining hers.

"To do a story," she responded.

"Ah!" Moshe exclaimed, sitting down at her other side. "Now that is a wonderful excuse." He gave her a knowing wink.

"Moshe, now stop it," Hannah admonished. "Sara doesn't need an excuse to come back here."

"Doesn't she?" he asked delightedly. "Did you know that Ari Gaon was the director here now?"

"Yes," Sara acknowledged, hearing some of the tension in her terse reply.

"Stop it, Moshe," Hannah repeated with a fierce glance. She took Sara's hand, drawing her attention away from Moshe. "Tell us about your story, dear."

Sara, grateful for the turn in conversation, complied. "It's a story on counterterrorism. Teenage counterterrorism."

Moshe said irrepressibly, "This is the first time I've been grateful to those rascals. If they've managed to bring you home to us, I may have to give them my support."

"Hardly rascals," Hannah protested his statement. "But Sara, Sternit isn't here at Golan. They are more active in the mountains above Haifa. They have been going across into Lebanon."

"From what I could piece together in my research," Sara said, "it seems likely that something will happen here. Especially after that latest incursion at the border."

"Ach," Moshe muttered, shaking his shaggy head. "That was a bad business. Four of our young people died in that one."

"I'm sure nothing like that would happen here," Hannah reiterated. "Ari wouldn't allow it." Sara saw her color up; she must have realized she had introduced the very subject she'd been trying to avoid. Her eyes met Sara's with sympathetic understanding. Sara smiled back crookedly.

Moshe, however, with his typically focused attention, was oblivious to Ari's name now. "They are children, nothing more."

Sara turned to him. "It's a pretty dangerous game they are playing."

"Oh, it's not a game. But they are children, nonetheless."

"I thought that perhaps so close to the border, there might be some of these 'children' here."

He met her question with an amused look. Was he remembering his earlier teasing? "Is that what brought you to Kibbutz Golan? Believing that the wave of child terrorism will infect us here?"

Sara could feel the color rising in her cheeks. "I picked Golan for two reasons," she said.

"You don't have to tell us what they are, Sara," Hannah said kindly from behind her.

Sara turned back to her. "That's okay, Hannah. I picked Golan, because I thought it likely that the young people might try something here, and because I knew this kibbutz."

"Ah," Moshe said. "Those are good reasons." His heavy disbelief was nothing short of patronizing, but it didn't anger Sara as it might have, coming from someone else.

Hannah stepped into the silence created by his patent sarcasm. "I worry about a group of children who have made heroes out of terrorists, who have heard stories of the Stern Gang and decided they would emulate the great deeds of Israel's beginning."

"That's why they call themselves Sternit?" Sara asked.

"Yes, silly, isn't it? Children, putting a child's diminutive on Stern, to form a new word. But all it makes me feel is sad."

"What makes me sad," Moshe interjected, "is that Sara isn't telling us how she feels about coming back here and meeting a not-so-young-anymore commando, who was a great fool and let her get away."

Sara blushed again, as easily as if she had still been that young girl in love.

"Moshe!" Hannah exclaimed. "Never mind him, Sara. He was always a busybody."

"Ha! Calling me a busybody, when you are forever snooping around asking personal questions! Right before you came up, Sara, she had the audacity to ask me if I'd had any indigestion after eating my breakfast!"

Hannah chuckled. "You know it makes you feel loved, Moshe."

"It doesn't make me feel loved," he protested, but the light in his eyes gave him away. "It makes me feel like I'm a source of curiosity. Why don't you just get on the PA system and announce your findings to the whole kibbutz?"

"I'm not the one broadcasting my findings on your health, Moshe Ben Eban. *You* are," Hannah said calmly.

Moshe sniffed, turning back to Sara. "How long have you been here? How long are you staying?" Then, without giving her time to answer, "Have you seen him yet?"

Sara found herself squeezing Hannah's warm fingers. She felt the other woman's hand curl protectively around hers and realized what she had done. She had given herself away.

"I've seen him," she said and could hear the constraint in her voice.

So could Moshe, apparently, for though he ignored it, as he had when she was young, he still pursed his lips. "He's changed."

"So have I," Sara replied.

"Good," Moshe said, patting her shoulder. "That's good."

"I was so bad?" she asked, amused and piqued at the same time.

"You said it, dear girl, not I. I'm a believer in the saying that youth is wasted on the young. You were both great fools. You were so intent on chasing rainbows, but so afraid of catching them. He was so stiff with pride and visions that he wouldn't go after the one thing that mattered to him above all others."

This was stirring up the past with a vengeance.

"Is it so difficult, Sara?" Hannah asked softly. "Yes, I can see that it is. Never mind. We won't pester you anymore on the subject." She turned a hard, quelling look in Moshe's direction. "Will we?"

Moshe ignored Hannah, much as he'd always ignored anything he didn't want to hear, Sara reflected. He took her hand from Hannah's grasp and held it up for all three of them to study.

"You are not married?" The question was rife with conjecture. "Yet there is the mark of a ring."

"I'm widowed."

"So-o-o," he said with shameless speculation. "Ari, too, is alone."

"Moshe!" Hannah snapped.

Sara smiled a little wistfully. She wished life could be as simple as Moshe was implying it could be. She shook her head. "Life isn't that easy."

"No?" Moshe asked. "It is difficult only if you make it complicated."

"There's too much between us," she said.

"Such as?"

"Life. The past. The eighteen years of not seeing each other."

Moshe waved his free hand, as if waving away the missing years. "That's like a minute. Nothing more. You still love him, he still loves you."

"No," Sara said sadly. "I *did* love him. I know that he *did* love me. But that was years ago. Another lifetime, it seems. I've married. I've raised a son. Ari's been married, too."

"And widowed."

"I'm a different woman now. I don't even know him."

"You know him," Moshe told her firmly. "He has gray in his hair now and sometimes wear glasses. But he's still Ari Gaon. He is not a man to change what is deep inside him."

Again Sara said nothing. Were Moshe's words true? Were they true for her, as well? And if they were true, what did it mean to her? She'd run from what was deep in Ari Gaon, run from the intensity in him, the dedication to causes, the highs and lows he experienced with equal passion. She, who had prided herself on objectivity, couldn't remain objective around him, nor could she enter into his passions...except in one area.

"Tell us about your son," Hannah said.

Sara heard the element of pain in the older woman's voice. Hannah had lost her only son in a battle on the Gaza Strip more than twenty-five years earlier. As a mother herself now, Sara knew there were some agonies one could never forget. It made her think of Ari, of the death of his wife and daughter.

"Tell me," Hannah prompted.

Sara smiled, but even to herself it felt wistful. When Ari had asked her, the question had seemed laden with meaning, filled with dangerous nuances. Hannah's request was simply that of one friend, catching up on the life of another.

"He's seventeen," she said. "He's much taller than I am, about six foot one. And he's smart."

"Of course," Moshe commented. "How could he be otherwise, with you for a mother? What is his name?"

For the second time in as many days, Sara found herself giving Danny's name, talking about him. But this time she felt at ease, comfortable, certain of herself.

"And your husband? Who was he?"

Sara told them.

"Ah, Jason Gould. The great helpmate to Israel. I don't think anyone even knows how much money he sent to this country every year. But most people know his name. He never came here?"

"No, he wasn't well. His heart couldn't have withstood the trip."

"I see," he said, and Sara suspected that Moshe did indeed see, and knew from Hannah's thoughtful expression that she did.

"So you are a wealthy young woman, now, Sara," Moshe observed.

Sara saw his tactlessness draw a frown from Hannah and smiled. "Wrong," she said. "Jason's money is in trust for Danny . . . and for Israel. . . . And I'm no longer young."

Again he waved his hand, rather like swatting at a lazy fly. "Looking from my years, my dear, you are a mere baby."

They sat for several minutes in comparative silence, comfortable with each other, the years of absence not marring the friendship the medical assistant, middle-aged man and young girl had formed so long ago. Now they were doctor, old man and middle-aged woman.

A fighter jet shot by overhead, a loud, sleek reminder of how close the border was, of why she was in Israel. The three of them looked up, watching the swift aerial maneuver. As if it were a signal of some sort, Hannah rose, so did Moshe, and finally Sara.

"I must get back to the infirmary," Hannah said. She pressed her lips to either side of Sara's face in the traditional kiss of greeting or farewell. "Come and visit me, Sara. There isn't much to do right now, with everyone here healthy as proverbial horses—except for grouchy old men, who won't do as they are told. I'd be glad of the company."

She walked away briskly, her back straight, the sun's rays catching her frosty hair and creating a halo around her.

"She's a damned fine woman," Moshe said, squinting his eyes, watching her departure.

"Did you ever marry her?" Sara asked.

He turned to her in mock surprise. "Now what makes you think I would ever marry that old busybody? She would nag me to death in a week."

Sara laughed gently, undeceived. He might not have loved Hannah all those years ago, but he loved her now.

The plane that had swept toward the border was already shooting across the sky on the return leg. Both Sara and Moshe watched it disappear beyond the mountains, heading south.

When the roar died away, and the morning once again seemed almost bucolic in its peacefulness, Moshe steered her in the direction of the principal kibbutz buildings.

"We'd better go and find out what is going on," he said. "Fighter planes at the border usually mean big trouble. And we don't want these child fighters of yours getting any ideas."

As they walked back, Moshe stopped several of the other kibbutzniks, asking questions here, commenting there. He was received with the same warm affection Sara felt for him, and although many of the people they talked to seemed to be half listening to something just out of range, they were pleasant when he performed introductions. Only after the two had talked with several of them did Sara overhear the whispered dismay, feel the just-below-the-surface preparation for battle. By way of reply to any of her questions, everyone merely recommended she talk to the director.

Could he answer them? she wondered. Or would five minutes in his company merely raise a host more?

"Go talk to him, Sara," Moshe said, adding his voice to the general suggestion. He smiled that cagey, quit-fooling-yourself look he'd given her so many times in the past. "He may be able to tell you more than you are even asking."

"I'm not asking anything other than what relates to my story."

"Aren't you, little swallow? What is the saying in your country...? Life, Liberty, and the Pursuit of Happiness? I think maybe that is what you really want to ask Ari about. Go now. We'll talk later. I'm still in the same rooms. Come by, we'll have a nice long talk. About you. About Ari." He leaned forward and kissed both her cheeks again. "And maybe we'll even talk about the future of little swallows who have flown back."

By the time Sara finally summoned the courage to knock on Ari's office door, the afternoon sun was slanting long shadows into the hills, and the day's cutting of grass infused the air with a ripe, fresh fragrance.

Ari's expression was guarded as he watched her enter his office. Only his eyes gave away the tension, the anger he barely held in check. She knew a moment's hopelessness. She would never be able to tell him about Danny. If he still harbored a grudge after all this time, how much more intense would that anger be if he knew that he'd had a son he had never seen, never held?

Briefly, without betraying any other emotion than cool annoyance, he spelled out the directive from the border commandant. She thought he waited for her response with caution, almost as if he expected her to argue.

"Kibbutz Golan has been cordoned off?" she asked incredulously, repeating his statement. One part of her was relieved at the news he'd given her. It meant she could focus upon the situation and not the man.

"You'll have to stay here now." He held out his hands as if he wanted to shake her again. The gesture made her legs curiously weak. "I should have kept to my original plan of sending you away."

"It's too late to be worrying about that," she said, trying to look on the news as a convenient way to conclude her story quickly. She was startled by the sudden flash of anger in his eyes.

"Yes, it's too late," he said tersely.

Though she tried to betray no emotion, his words made her quake inwardly. Was it too late? Was it ever too late? His face said it was. He didn't know how like a death knell his words rung inside her. *Too late…too late…* Yet in his arms, his lips pressed against hers, it had seemed that the past had no weight, that lateness had no meaning at all.

"Can you still shoot, Sara?" he asked abruptly.

She stared at him uncomprehendingly for a moment, feeling the color rise in her cheeks, revealing her inner thoughts. "No," she replied evenly. "If you remember, I never could."

His eyes met hers sharply, then cut away. "I remember," he said. His tone was cold, and a small smile curved one side of his full mouth upward in a bitter acknowledgment of his attempted training.

She flushed even more at seeing the memory in his bitter smile. Twice that day this memory had been dragged from the secret places of her mind. With Moshe she had blushed; with Ari, she felt curiously close to tears. Had that been the day? Had that one loving moment set the future in motion?

"I'm sorry..." she began, but the blazing look he sent her caused the rest of her sentence to die on her lips.

"Are you, Sara?" He rose from behind his desk. Involuntarily she stepped back a pace, though her heart quickened its beat. He moved with the lithe grace of a caged panther. He stopped mere inches from her. His mouth worked; he was plainly struggling with those emotions that had always been so volatile, so explosive... so frighteningly captivating.

"I cursed you for coming back," he said at last. His tone held no more feeling than if he had told her that the sky was blue. But a muscle in his cheek jumped, and the tendons in his throat were taut.

She couldn't tell him that she'd been cursing herself, as well. Or that she'd tossed and turned throughout the night, sometimes drifting into a sleep that was filled with his images, filled with the two of them locked in a fervent, desperate embrace, filled with the look of disgust he would show should she tell him about Danny.

Uttering a racked sound, he turned away from her, striding to the window. The hand that grasped the opened frame showed knuckles white from strain.

Sara couldn't stand any more. "I'll stay in the background," she said quietly. "I'll keep out of your way." In her words she could hear the echo of her father's voice, her father's advice on the way to live: *Stay in the background. Stay out of the way. It is the only way to survive. The only way.* That ability to stay in the background was how she had lived her life, was what made her a successful photojournalist.

Ari laughed shortly, a derisive snort totally devoid of humor. Slowly he turned back toward her. Staring at her, his face rigid, his gray eyes blazing, he shook his head. He crossed the distance between them. She was riveted to the spot by his hot gaze. He raised a hand to her face to cup it gently. "But can I keep away from you? That's the question, Sara."

As if his words had released the panther within him, he crushed her in his embrace, fiercely capturing her lips. One hand slid to the back of her neck to draw her closer, while the other gripped her lower back and pressed her tightly to him, conforming her body to his, forcing her to remember. And she did. She relearned how much he moved her and, pressed against him, sensed how much she moved him.

Demandingly, half angrily, he let her see, let her *feel* the torture she'd raised in him.

As she had always done, would undoubtedly always do, she stiffened against the raw emotion in him, then gave in to that burning, searing kiss like an ember craving the spark that revives the flame. Each flick of his tongue, each branding sweep of his hands, each graze of his teeth against her skin put paid to the barriers between them. In his arms, her body alive to his every touch, she felt as though she could forget the past, the years that lay between them, could even forget Danny.

Like a dreamer roused from a nightmare, she shook herself free. He let her go, his face inscrutable, only his rapid breathing and dark eyes giving any hint of the depth of his desire.

She *couldn't* forget Danny. She simply could not give in to that quivering want, that liquid need that Ari inspired in her. Not with the truth about Danny still untold, with the certainty that telling him would make him hate her. Not with the past still between them like an unwanted intruder, an almost physical presence.

"You want me as badly as I do you," he said finally, misunderstanding her reasons for withdrawal.

"Yes," she breathed. Then, "No."

"Yes you do, Sara. But you are still that frightened little girl, who didn't have the strength to stay here. You wanted it all, yet you got out of the kitchen when the kitchen got hot. Run before you get burned—that's still your motto, isn't it, Sara? Isn't that what you told me? That I would burn you up."

He turned from her, his back a solid square against the sunlight pouring into his office. "This time there's nowhere to run. You can't leave." He gave a short bark of laughter, half triumph, half disdain. "So. If you try to run away...this time you won't be able to run far."

Shocked at his perception, tears rising to her eyes, she was horrified to discover she wanted to prove him wrong, but did just as he had sarcastically suggested. She ran from the intensity of Ari Gaon.

She got no more than four steps beyond his door, before he grabbed her elbow, swinging her around. For a long moment he merely stared at her, his eyes hard, his mouth set. Then as he took in the moisture in her eyes, the trembling lower lip, he muttered some imprecation and for a second time raised a hand to cup her face. Slowly, gently, his thumb brushed her closed eyes. His heart seemed to be beating too hard to stay where it was. On his thumb, glistening, lay poised a single tear, a testament to his harsh words and worse temper.

He let go of her face, obliterating the tear in the palm of his hand. She opened her eyes, but wouldn't meet his.

"Sara—" he began, but a quick shake of her head stopped him. He was glad she had; he wouldn't have known what to say or do.

She was shaking. He'd wanted to lash out at her, wanted her to experience some of the pain he'd known all those years before, but hadn't counted on it hurting him, too. And the slight droop of her shoulders, the liquid eyes, the trembling fingers all told him too clearly of the hurt his words had caused. He ached for it, even while a primitive part of him exulted in knowing that he could still affect her.

Yes, he'd wanted her in pain. But now, now that he'd hurt her, he wanted to be able to grab the words back from the air, stop them before they pierced her heart.

"I..." he started again, and once again stopped. Incredibly, she smiled. Just so would Galit smile when recovering from some fall, some childhood hurt. He frowned a question.

She shook her head, but the smile on her face remained. But where his daughter's smile would have been bright, sunny, reassuring, Sara's was wise and sorrowful.

"Not such strangers, after all," she said softly, then turned and left him. Again.

* * *

Sara avoided any possible chance of another encounter with Ari by simply staying in her room. She typed her notes quickly, wrote a long, apologetic letter to Danny, and finally, with nothing left to do, nowhere she could go without running the risk of seeing Ari, and feeling a curious reluctance to respond to Moshe's invitation of a chat, she lay down on the bed, wishing for the sleep that had so eluded her the night before. It eluded her still, hovering tantalizingly on the borders of her mind. While she couldn't persuade sleep to overtake her, she couldn't dispel thoughts of Ari Gaon.

She lay on one side, fighting the urge to just grab him and tell him the truth, then on the other, fighting the urge to grab him, as he had done, then shake and kiss him with all the passion he'd released in her with his kiss, his touch. How long she might have continued this vain attempt at mental reconciliation, she was never to know, for a dull explosion shook her bed, made her room tremble. It seemed, for an instant, that the building rocked on its foundation.

Swinging her unsteady legs from the bed, she flew across her room, and with the instinct of the journalist, swept her camera bag over her shoulder and ran into the hallway. Below her, down the hall, she could hear voices raised in anger, fear and excitement. A siren's piercing cry sounded the alert, a barn door being loudly closed long after the horse had disappeared.

She ran for the stairs, acutely conscious of being the only unarmed person among the swiftly moving crowd. She stopped, momentarily stunned, on the broad stairway. Across from her, across the lobby, where there had been glass only that afternoon, where there had been glass eighteen years earlier, now there was only the dark blue of late afternoon, a blue marred by clouds of dust and swirling debris. She was pushed forward and down the stairs, jostled on all sides, her ears ringing with the sounds of gunfire, of people yelling, the ominous, deadly sound of glass crunched beneath running feet. The smells of fear, burning grass, of dust, dirt, and oddly, gardenia, assaulted her, making the bizarre chaos around her real.

Someone, a man holding his Uzi before her face, but neither pointed at her nor threatening, merely an extension of his arm, grabbed her and pushed her against the painted cinder

block wall. Someone else yelled at her to get down and rein-
forced the command with a rough shove to her shoulder.

Habit, sheer force of habit, ripped the camera from the case,
had her checking the f-stop and the light setting. With the ease
of practice, she looped the cord over her head; its light weight
against the nape of her neck steadied her. Fear and shock
gripped her as tightly as she held the camera. She raised her
protective shield to her eye and began recording the scene.

In a split second, with the detached eye of the camera she
saw shards of glass that glittered and splintered on the lobby
floor, reflecting the blue sky, reflecting the panic of the room's
occupants. The painting of the kibbutz fields, Moshe's painting, lay dizzily against an overturned sofa. People were everywhere, yelling commands, tossing weapons back and forth, as
if playing some game that had no rules. They were upright,
holding sobbing mothers or sisters in their arms, or they were
lying down, teeth gritted against pain, while hands—their own
and the hands of friends—clenched legs, arms, chests.

And there was blood. It stained the furniture, the strips of
cloth held against foreheads, cheeks and mouths, covered the
glass, opaquing the reflections with a nightmarish red. It
overrode the smells of dust, the scent of gardenia, with the
sharp, coppery tang of destruction.

Her camera relentlessly captured it all, the human mouths
crying out in suffering, the cringing, flinching shoulders, as yet
another blast rocked the building. She recorded the horror,
sealed the story, and as she depressed the automatic shutter
release, taking in the chaos and translating it into clear, im-
personal black and white, the camera defused her own fear.

"Sara!" she heard Ari call over the cacophony. Instinctively she turned toward him, her finger depressing the shutter release. Through the lens she perceived the tension, the
worry, the hard lines etched on his face.

"Over here!" she called back, waving her hand high above
her head.

Another explosion resounded, sending Sara sprawling
against the legs of the man who'd pushed her to the ground.
He kicked himself free and ran for the door in a low crouch.
He yelled something to a man and woman who were just behind him. They burst out the doors and disappeared into a
writhing wall of smoke.

"Are you okay?" Ari asked, kneeling beside Sara. She met his eyes gratefully and nodded. With the camera no longer before her, she could see a harsh concern, and something else. So intent was she on that gaze that she gasped when his outstretched hand reached toward her, brushing the hair from her eyes. The gesture was absurdly tender, all the apology for his earlier harsh words that she could have wanted, all the gentleness she'd never suspected he could show. The realization that he'd been concerned for her *now,* in the midst of all this, threatened to overwhelm her. She found herself parting her lips.

"The children!" a woman screamed. "They're all in the nursery!"

Ari turned swiftly and called out three names. "Stay here!" he barked at Sara. Raising the gun in his hand—a gun that Sara had not realized he'd held until that moment—he jerked his head toward the still-open doors, and the four men ran at them.

A short, angry burst of machine-gun fire volleyed somewhere in the distance. A man screamed.

Just as Ari's small band of rescuers was leaving the shattered building, the group who had left earlier appeared out of the swirling clouds of smoke and dust. They had brought the children. Or two of them had. The third person who had gone out through the opened wall was not with them.

Sara raised her camera again, capturing the essence of the rescue. One young man carried a small girl against his chest, her thin arms convulsively locked around his thick neck. Another child rode piggyback behind him, legs dangling, blood snaking down one leg in a narrow rivulet. A child of no more than ten carried an infant at his breast, his long fingers pressing the baby's face into his shoulder, his eyes wide and dull with shock. The woman who had so readily gone with the team held the hands of boys and girls on either side of her, her elbows upraised, as if spreading wings of protection over them. Both of the rescuers' faces were streaked with soot, and Sara could see blood slowly seeping from the young man's arm. All of the children's mouths were compressed, clearly holding in the cries and screams of terror.

Mothers cried out, as did fathers, and arms stretched for the children. Sara's camera caught every gesture of anguish and hope.

"Get them against the far wall!" Ari called, jerking his head in Sara's direction.

"Here," Sara announced, standing, and waving them toward her. Within seconds she was surrounded by some twenty-five children, all strangers, all clinging to her, as if through her touch some semblance of normality could be achieved.

"Get her some pillows, blankets, something!" Ari barked. Several sofa cushions were cast her way, and a blanket came hurtling out of the smoke-filled air around them. Sara, with the help of some of the children, quickly arranged a small island of safety. Dragging around a cushionless sofa, they soon had a low barrier against the commotion.

The woman who had gone to rescue the children eyed Sara with chilly appraisal. "You will watch out for them?" she asked finally, apparently having reached a guardedly positive conclusion.

"Of course," Sara said. After another long stare the woman nodded, then left Sara and the children for an impromptu war conference on the far side of the room. On her back was an Uzi, in her hand a small automatic.

Sara, feeling every bit as stunned as the children, slumped against the wall and slid to the cold, concrete floor. Around her, hands groping for hers, heads pressing desperately against her arms, the children sat, some blank with the shock of the last few minutes of chaotic danger, some watching with intent, fear-filled eyes. Together they watched and listened, as young men and women ran in and out of the shattered windows, each armed with an Uzi, shoulder straps over their bodies, hands over the triggers at the ready.

People yelled. Some talked on a makeshift radio, while others busied themselves in a corner, obviously preparing a quick hospital. Rapid gunfire in the distance drowned even the heavy footfalls on the crunching glass, the whimpers of the children and the moans of the injured.

It was a world gone mad, but in the madness was industry. No one looked in their direction; the children were safe enough.

The youngest of the children, the infant that looked no more than eighteen months old, began to wail in thin protest. Sara, not dislodging any of the others, pulled the crying child onto her lap and gathered the remaining ones as close to her as possible.

"I'm old enough to fight," a small boy said solemnly. He was the young savior of the infant in her arms. Her chest tightened as she took in the old-before-his-time expression on his face; he couldn't have been more than ten. His young face was white with fear, but etched with determination. He turned and gazed balefully at the group of people around a radio that had materialized from some recess. "They think I'm too young."

Sara willed herself to shake her head slowly, solemnly. She wanted to cry, "You *are* too young. You're a baby, you're scarcely older than this infant in my lap." But she couldn't wound his pride, nor could she utter the words of comfort that hovered on her lips. He reminded her of Danny. The thought made her shiver with a new fear. What would happen to Danny if anything should happen to her? Jason was dead. Her parents had long since gone to a peaceful rest. There was only *Ari*. And Ari didn't know about Danny, Danny didn't know about Ari.

Let me have the chance to tell Ari, she prayed.

Meeting the young boy's resolute gaze, Sara forced herself to ignore her heart's silent pleading, the distant gunfire, the shouts of the adults in the room. She reached a hand to the boy's cheek, noting with some detachment that somehow she had scraped her knuckles raw.

"What is your name?"

"David," he said. His eyes met hers with a defiance she recognized from Danny's younger years.

"David, I need your help," she said quietly.

He looked as skeptical as Danny ever had when being requested to render assistance.

"You know all the children. They trust you. They might not trust me." The falsehood of this was patently obvious, as even the baby in her arms had quieted.

But the boy weighed her statement for a moment, then nodded. "What do you want me to do?" he asked.

Sara couldn't think. "Tell them a story."

"What? Tell children's stories while the guns fire?" he asked incredulously.

Sara sighed. The child in her lap was no longer crying, but his breathing had the ragged, hiccup-laced tenor of the nearly hysterical. Automatically Sara kissed the child's damp temple and hummed a snatch of a song. She looked up at David. "Do...do you think it will bother them—" Sara jutted her chin at the busy soldiers "—if we sing? Very softly?"

"No-o," David said consideringly, obviously looking at the question with the weight of new responsibility, adult consequences. "Soldiers often sing while going into battle."

"What do you suggest we sing?"

He thought a moment. "Yerushalayim Shel Zahav."

It was a good choice. It was one of the most beautiful songs ever written. Drafted during the Six Day War, the song had been an instant hit, going on the radio live the first time, then taped a thousand times over. The soldiers sang it as they drove into Gaza, tears on their young faces.

Sara nodded and slowly began to sing. "Jerusalem of gold, and of copper and of light/ for all your songs, let me be your violin." Timid at first, the children mouthed the words only, whispering the chorus, voices breaking in fear and shock. But soon they joined her, their soft voices rising above the clamor.

Ari felt his heart stop. Incredibly, soul-wrenchingly, the muted, yet sure voices of the children painted a picture of innocence defying brutality, of purity overcoming adversity. He slowly turned to look.

As did almost everyone else in the room. For a moment the danger was forgotten, the children's sweet, clear voices driving the oppressive fear from all minds. Then across the room, a large, heavyset man joined in the chorus, his deep baritone contrasting with the children's sopranos and Sara's soft contralto. Another man added his voice, a woman, then another.

Ari sang also, a smile coming to his lips as he saw the smiles on other faces, watched the tension drain, the purpose become focused. It was for the children that they were fighting; thanks to Sara it was the children who were giving them the strength to defend their home, to calmly and prudently survive this afternoon's disaster.

Across the room, children all about her, she sang in her clear, lilting Hebrew. Her eyes lifted and met his. He felt the meeting of that gaze to his very soul.

"For all your songs," he sang with her, to her, "let me be your violin."

Chapter 4

Sara looked at her watch. Incredible! It was scarcely nine o'clock. The mountains were gone, stolen by a velvet darkness, the fields seemed to stretch into the star-studded sky. In and around the kibbutz lights twinkled as if merrily dismissing the afternoon and evening terror.

The fighting had ended almost as abruptly as it had begun, and already makeshift covers had been fitted into place over the shattered glass. The children were safe, most still up, leaning tiredly against relieved, loving parents, who would take the children home with them, rather than letting them sleep in the nursery on such a night. Reports had been sent to authorities at the border, to Jerusalem and Tel Aviv.

A silent and reserved Moshe had helped Sara to process her film, and had then faxed several photographs to a news relay station in Tel Aviv, where they would be placed on the international wire for use by television stations and newspapers around the world.

When they'd finished he had turned to her, gently grasping her hands. "This is the real story, Sara. The deaths of children who want nothing more than a place to live. When you go to tell the story of the misguided youths who are involved in counterterrorism, remember this day. Remember that it is very difficult to tell the difference between heroism and terrorism when the bullets are flying and the grenades are destroying your home.''

He'd walked away from her, his broad, bearlike shoulders bent, his white hair clearly visible in the darkness. He was going, he'd said, to help Hannah in the infirmary.

The kibbutz telephones hadn't stopped ringing yet, and the two public phones still had long lines of people waiting for their chance to let family and friends know they were okay, that the children were fine, that Dov Shamir and Abrahim Ben David were no longer among them. Young Dov, Sara mourned; she hadn't known him well, but only two days before he'd been a vital, barely controlled force who had shared a *sherut* with her.

Sara had given up on trying to phone Danny. She would try later that night, in answer to his terse, worried cable: "Saw photos. Stop. Are you well? Stop. See you soon. Stop."

When she had stood in Ari's office, reading the brief message, she'd been struck by such a strong wave of longing for her son, now grown-up, but infinitely caring, that it had been all she could do not to attempt to break through the cordon and wing her way to France.

Ari's words, after reading the cable she'd silently held out to him, had been like a burr against an open wound. "He's a good kid. I wish I knew him."

Again she felt that irrational stab of irritation that he couldn't *feel* it, didn't guess at the truth.

She would have told him then. Almost had, but someone came into his office, lists of damage reports dangling from both hands. Instantly his attention had been on the work at hand. A man of blacks and whites, he was wholly devoted to duty at that moment, the consummate director of a war-torn kibbutz. Missing years and grown-up sons would only serve as tormenting distractions.

And now, with an odd sensation of having been let down, Sara stood in the small garden where the plaque on the monolith bore the names of those who had died for Kibbutz Golan. Tomorrow two more names would be added to the ever-growing list, both security kibbutzniks. Young Dov had looked a lot like Danny, older, tougher, but for all that, still a boy. Now he would never age.

Ari's words of the night before echoed on the air. *Galiti would have been fourteen.*

Sara had come to the small garden to escape the noisy, triumphant, impromptu celebration taking place in the dining hall, seeking the cool night air, her mind a jumble of thoughts. She hadn't been conscious of where she'd been walking until the monolith stopped her. Its cold lines struck a chill into her heart, burned themselves into her mind. Had she come here, not just to remember the two young people who had died that day, but because of the things in her past that had died as well?

She paced, trying to bring order into her confusion. Most of that sense of chaos was centered around the look on Ari's face as she and the children had sung; he'd looked tender, thunderstruck, and finally proud. What had he expected of her? Nothing good, it seemed. And if he'd been able to read her thoughts then? If he'd been able to see into her heart and into that moment's terrifying realization that Ari *had* to learn about Danny, that her son had to know he had someone else in the world besides herself? If he'd seen that certainty, what would he have looked like then?

He wasn't a man who could dissimulate; his emotions stood bare and dramatically exposed for all the world to see. Now, with the realization that she *had* to tell him, no matter what it cost her, no matter how angry he would be, she knew a moment's fear so real, so deep that it was a palpable presence in the night, standing beside her, urging her to greater cowardice. But she turned, prepared to go back and call Ari aside, to simply and flatly tell him that the good kid he wished he knew was his own son, blood of his blood, flesh of his flesh.

Her heart was full, her legs were shaking, and she drew in the cool night air as if breathing for the first time. It smelled of pita bread, humus, falafel made for dinner and of new-mown grass. And it smelled of shattered concrete and broken dreams. It tasted as bitter as the past.

She wondered later if she had guessed Ari would follow her, as she slid her dinner tray onto an empty rack and quietly left the dining hall. At any rate, she felt no surprise at seeing him materialize in the moonlit garden, coming from the shadows to her side.

They didn't speak at first, letting the night sounds speak for them. The million conversations of a billion stars, the sonorous creak of the crickets and the hum of the other night insects, the dull roar of the exultant diners, all combined to tell a tale of hard-won, temporary peace, of a delicately balanced harmony. And though all the sounds, smells and tastes worked on Sara's senses, her heart and mind were wrestling with the need to tell Ari, struggling to find the words with which to begin.

She could feel the warmth of his body reaching out to caress her skin, could hear his shallow, steady breathing. She shifted uneasily. Out of cowardice? Stepping away from him, she let the night breeze play along her skin, touch her cheeks with scent and mountain moisture.

When her mind was cool, too, when she felt that calm assurance that the timing was right, that *now* and *only* now would serve, she turned to him and said, "I have something to tell you."

"I, too," he responded. His face was in shadow, but nothing on earth could dim the blaze of his eyes.

The words she'd struggled to find suddenly curdled in her throat.

His hand slowly reached to touch her shoulder, and then lightly, ever so lightly, he ran a fingertip down her bare arm. Sara shivered.

"Are you cold?" Ari asked, though she was certain he knew the cause of her sudden trembling. He'd asked her the same thing the day before. But the day before he'd just been mildly curious. Now his tone was seductive.

"Not cold, no." Without anything to blunt the three short syllables, invitation seemed to hang in the air. Ari's hand froze for a moment, then slowly fell to the crook of her arm and stayed there, warm, then hot against her. For a moment it seemed that was enough; they had no need to say anything else.

But Sara did have something to say, something that would change this man's life, her son's and her own. But she couldn't do it if he were touching her, looking at her like that. Sara stepped back abruptly. Slowly, painfully, too conscious of his proximity, too aware of him as the man she'd first loved, still too aware of him now, she tried thinking of him only as the father of her child, and with hesitant words began to build the bridge that would link the past with the present.

"Today, when all of the violence took place..." Sara paused, desperately uncertain of how to continue. She couldn't just blurt it out; the truth was too charged for that. It would explode like the grenade that had taken out the lobby glass in Building Alef.

She began again. "Today, for the first time—" She broke off with a gasp. He'd moved until he was directly behind her, his broad hands covering her shoulders making her shiver anew, making her jump. But he was behind her; she didn't have to watch his face while she continued.

"Today, for the first time, I realized that if anything happened to me, Danny would have no one."

"Ah, Sara," Ari said, his voice as deep as the ocean, his tone as tender as the velvet darkness. His fingers kneaded the tense muscles in her neck and shoulders. At each pressure, her mind lost a little of its precious grip on the need for telling him the truth, the need for telling him *now*. She stepped forward, acutely conscious of the loss of his touch.

"Jason would have taken him, of course—"

"Of course," he interjected. "How not?"

That was the crux of the matter, wasn't it? she thought, to tell him the "how not." She continued as if he hadn't spoken. "But Jason is dead."

Ari's warm hands again folded around her shoulders. He drew her back against his solid body. Her breath caught in her throat and where they touched she felt burned, branded.

"I know," he said softly, his breath playing against the sensitive flesh beneath her ear, his hands slowly, inexorably leaving her shoulders to stroke her full breasts. Lightly, knowingly, but questing, he molded them to his large, callused hands. Cupping them, taking their weight into his palms, his thumb and his forefinger met, trapping each nipple in soft torment.

"No..." she whispered, the word denying him access, even as her body pressed more tightly to him.

"Yes," he murmured, misunderstanding her, lowering his hands to her waist, to caress, to learn her curves, then lower, gripping the planes of her hipbones, drawing her closer, pressing against her bottom in a slow, sensual, rocking motion.

As if speaking in a dream, he said, "This feels so right. So very right."

"Yes..." she breathed. Lost in his embrace, in the liquid demand of her body as his hands roamed, touched, stroked and roamed again, the words of one truth died on her lips, while another demanded to be told.

Her head lolled back onto his shoulder. "Oh, yes," she murmured. "So right..."

Ari groaned her name as his lips descended to her bared throat.

Sara's knees buckled as a shudder of reaction coursed through her.

A low ghost of a laugh escaped Ari's lips, expelled against her neck in a brief puff of warm air and, though she knew he couldn't see it, Sara smiled in response. She couldn't have said exactly why the moment had made them smile, but she knew that for both of them, it was an affirmation of sorts, an acknowledgment that beneath the passion that still seemed to flow between them, there was a thread of tenderness, an acceptance of frailty that had been lacking before.

But would that acceptance continue, once he knew the truth about Danny? Sara's smile faded.

"Today," he said, finally, his hands stilling beneath her breasts, "tonight, watching you, I wondered what I would feel if I had never met you before."

Slowly, carefully, as if she were made of porcelain, he turned her until she faced him directly, her mouth inches from his, her eyes upon him.

"I have to tell you about the past," she said, before he could kiss her again or say anything else.

"Damn the past!" Ari exclaimed harshly. "For right now, for this moment, after the day, after the deaths... Let's let the past alone."

He grasped her almost roughly and continued. "I want to know you as you are now, Sara, not as I remember. I don't want explanations. I don't want might-have-beens. I don't want—" He broke off, looking away for the first time.

His gaze raked the monolith to their right. "I don't want to remember. I want to forget the past. For one night, for one moment."

Sara shivered at the implication of his words, instinctively responding to the pain she could hear in his voice, could read in his face. And to the want she could feel in his body.

"Ari...?"

In answer his hands cupped her face and drew her to him for a hard, silencing kiss. His tongue fused with hers, then broke away to taste, to demand. Weak with wanting him, aching with a reawakened need, she raised her hands to his arms, following the line of the muscles, relearning the set of his jaw, discovering new lines fanning from his eyes.

The world around them faded into oblivion. The only things that mattered were the touch of their bodies, the heat of the desire that had always consumed them. For Sara, Ari was the only reality. She clung to him as if to life, and in his arms she lived.

Suddenly he lifted his lips, crushing her to his chest, pressing her face against the curve of his collarbone. He dragged air into his lungs in a rasped whisper. His hands held her tightly, fiercely. And just as suddenly as he had moved, Sara understood what was going through his mind, his heart.

He was the director of this kibbutz; two more people had died that day. One young man on the threshold of life, another who was leaving behind a wife and young baby, the baby she'd held on her lap that afternoon. Ari, as director, as a man, must feel their loss sharply, and it must conjure up memories of his own, more personal loss.

"I'm sorry," she murmured, wishing, as she had done the night before, that she could think of better, more expressive words.

"I keep thinking there must have been something I could have done, that I should have suspected something."

"There was nothing you could have done any differently," she told him. "How were you to guess that those people would perform a suicide attack on the kibbutz?"

"It is my business to know those things," he said. A shudder worked through him.

"I'm sure your job description doesn't call for you being psychic, Ari," she answered rather tartly.

She felt the tension in his body give way for a split second.

"No?" he asked. "You've seen the contract then?"

"Yes," she said firmly, and used her hands, her body to reinforce the strength of her convictions.

Though his body seemed to relax, Sara could still sense that his mind was far away, lost in memory. His next words confirmed it.

"Dov was the son of a friend. Yigal. Yigal Shamir. Yigal and I served together—oh, a long time ago." He fell silent for some time, but his hold on Sara relaxed. Unconsciously, it seemed, his lips brushed her temples. "When Yigal died, I brought his family to live here. His wife—her name was Ester—died in the same explosion that took Galit and Yael."

Lowering his brow until it rested upon her shoulder, his lips met the bare flesh of her upper arm.

"And Dov was the last," she said, knowing it. *Feeling* it.

"Dov was the last," he agreed.

Sara could only offer whatever comfort her arms, her lips against his throbbing throat could give.

"He was like a son to me," he murmured, unknowingly piercing the fragile defences she had erected around her heart.

Even as she raised her trembling fingers to his face, looking at him sadly, directly, words trying to escape her lips, words that would tell him he *did* have a son, one who would need him, who might rely upon him, he released her and stepped to the large, cold slab. He ran his fingers over the Hebrew letters, pausing over the names of his wife, his daughter, his friend's wife and three or four others.

"There's no one else, now, Sara," he said, his hand lying flat on the unmarked portion of the monolith. "I can't lose anyone else now."

Instinctively she stepped forward, hand outstretched, her lips framing the words to deny this. He did have someone, had a son. Had *herself*.... But he looked up as she approached, his eyes, dark with emotion, shadowed with pain, appearing black in the moonlight.

"And I'm glad, Sara. I'm really glad."

His words stopped her as if he'd slapped her. Stupidly feeling as if the ground had suddenly lost its substance, she remained where she was.

"I'm glad there's no one now. No ties, no commitments. No pain." He paused. Had he seen something on her face, some trace of the shock, the turmoil within her? Sara saw his lips crook into a half-bitter smile. "That's why I didn't want to talk about the past. I wanted to pretend that we had just met. Just now. No pain, no years of wondering if I'd ever hold you in my arms again. I just wanted tonight." His hand raked through his hair, and the moonlight caught the silver.

"But that's impossible, isn't it?" he asked. "There are too many ghosts between us. Too much history."

"More than you know," she said, determined to tell him, determined not to let the moment slip away again.

He held up his hand. "Don't. Don't say anything more. I'm tired. I've had enough of the past. All I wanted tonight was a moment's peace. Love, perhaps, with a stranger. Tonight, though, we are not nearly strangers enough."

"Ari..."

"Don't, Sara," he said wearily. "Whatever it is, I don't want to hear it. Tomorrow, perhaps. Or perhaps next week. Or perhaps another eighteen years from now. But no more tonight. No more."

With that he turned, a man clearly too burdened by the events of the present to hear tales from the past. Her hands clenched tightly to her sides, her mouth clamped shut with the effort not to scream the past at him, to make him listen, for her good, for his. Sara listened as he strode down the dark pathways, disappearing into the gloom. His footsteps echoed on the rubbled sidewalks and in her heart.

It was almost two in the morning before Sara gave up the struggle. At the rate she was going, she would have to sleep for a week to catch up. But Ari's words had chased sleep far away.

And she still hadn't talked with Danny. He was worried, his cable attested to that. She had to reassure him. She missed him, too. But it was more than that. It was a sense that in not having told him the truth about himself, in not having offered him the opportunity of knowing his real father, she had stolen something vital from him.

Her own father had always tried to shield her from what he'd called the "bad" things in life. When she'd chosen journalism as a career, he'd railed at her, calling her ungrateful. He'd tried all of his life to make the world a beautiful place for her, teaching her survival as he knew it—not to make waves, not to be visible, not to put herself in danger as his mother had done by speaking out against the Nazis and being dragged, screaming, from her home to die in Auschwitz—teaching her his brand of common sense. After all this protection, all this teaching, she'd rewarded him by going after all the seaminess life had to offer, compounding it by insisting on that year on a kibbutz in Israel, only to fall in love with and get pregnant by an Israeli soldier.

Though she had continued to see her father before he died, he had never quite forgiven her, and she had never been able to tell him that his very shielding had been part of what had catapulted her into making her so-called mistakes. She had also never been able to reveal that his shielding had worked when it came to Ari Gaon. She had never met such burning intensity and had run from it like the terrified child she'd been. This she only admitted to herself long after her father was dead.

She'd tried not to make that mistake with Danny. There were some things he had to do for himself, learn for himself.

She went quietly downstairs, picking her way along the makeshift railings and out through the newly constructed plywood doorway. The night air was cool and soft against her face, and she was glad she'd put on a light jacket. Soon, she thought, the wind would be dry and hot, as the late-spring khamsin winds approached, sweeping across the fertile crescent, spreading the secrets of the Sahara as they passed.

The two telephone booths were empty and seemed eerie in the early-morning darkness. A single light, high above the dining hall, lighted the area around them, forming a small pool of brightness, like a spotlight directed at center stage. She stepped into the light, dropped in her tokens and waited for the international operator. Within seconds her call was placed, and she heard the sleepy voice of Danny's host mother loudly asking who was there, who was there at this time of night.

Sara apologized for the time, explained—with what she felt was a lamentable lack of French—who she was, and why she had felt it necessary to call.

"But Danny, he is not here," the other woman said, a note of sincere sympathy in her voice. "He has gone with friends to the Dordogne in the south. He will not return for oh, three, maybe four nights and days. He gives me a number where he can be reached. I give it to you, yes?"

Sara took it, aware of a too-sharp disappointment. She rang off with more apologies for having disturbed Madame. After a moment's hesitation, she decided not to wake the people in the Dordogne. The region was largely farming country, and a family who had to rise with the chickens, and was hosting a young American boy for a few days, would be unlikely to appreciate a call from his nervous mother at twelve-thirty in the morning, local time.

"He wasn't there?" A voice spoke from outside her circle of light, making her jump. But she recognized it, knew it as she knew her own name. *Ari.*

"I didn't hear you," she said, taking her hand from the receiver, summoning a smile.

"Come, I'll walk with you back to Alef." He held out his hand and, after only the slightest hesitation, she took it. His fingers curled around hers, threaded themselves between each finger, holding tightly. He looked down at their linked hands as if puzzled. He turned them this way and that, into the light and back into the darkness.

Finally, without comment, he lowered their joined hands to his side and turned, pulling her with him. Sara went, content for the moment to follow dazedly, to let the silence of the night still the tension between them, unable in her tiredness to resist the things he made her feel, the worry over telling him about the past.

Their footsteps matched as they walked, crunching in unison on the now-silent pathways. Sara sighed; it had always been thus. Their minds, their perceptions of life were as different as the wind from the rain, but their steps had always matched, their bodies had melded as if one. As if reading her mind, his fingers tightened around her hand, warm, reassuring, confirming the moment of total harmony.

Wistfully, Sara wished it might continue. They had already grazed the past, opening old wounds. This was the time for them to get to know the people the years had made them. But to speak now, to say anything, might shatter the fragile peace. She said nothing.

Still without speaking, he guided her through the plywood barriers and on up the steps that led to her room. At her door, her heart pounding with sudden anticipation and a touch of fear, she stopped. He turned the knob and pushed the door ajar. He still had not released her hand. He was near enough for her to feel the heat from his body, smell the day on him. The moonlight caught the sheen of his eyes and reflected it at her.

"What I said down in the garden . . ."

"Yes?" she asked softly, breathless as the single word left her lips.

"I lied," he said. His lips twisted.

"About?"

He smiled briefly. "When I said there was no one left."

Tell him, now! a voice in her screamed. Now, before it's too late. Before he makes you forget, before you listen to another word. Then his lips covered hers in a searing, tormenting kiss.

"There is someone...I care about. *You,* Sara." He whispered the words against her lips, against her temples.

Feeling as if she were drowning, afraid she was dreaming, she shook her head, murmuring denial.

"Oh, yes. I've loved you. I've hated you. And tonight, tonight I need you."

Unnerved by his words, the soft pressure of his lips against hers served to cause tears to spring to her eyes, tears of guilt, anguish. Of relief?

He pressed her back against the door, leaning into her, not demandingly as he had done that evening, that afternoon, but gently, tenderly, a question in his hands, a promise on his lips.

When Sara's hands grew limp against his shoulders, her palms curving outward, wrists touching his cheeks, her heart beating in an irregular rhythm, Ari felt as though life had truly contrived to give him a second chance. His mind was filled with a thousand different images of Sara, Sara as she had been, Sara as she was against him now. And in this moment, her lovely body arching to him, her mouth a hot, open invitation, he'd never wanted her more.

In the garden, where he'd gone instinctively to confront his feelings about Dov's death, he'd found Sara. She had served to remind him of life, of pain and of longing. As always in her presence, he'd felt confused by a riot of conflicting emotional responses, and as usual, he'd said things he hadn't quite meant, hadn't really wanted to say to her. They'd been things that could mask the hurt in him whenever he looked into her hazel eyes, whenever he touched her tawny hair.

But he said none of this now, save with his kisses against her soft, pale skin. Without seeming to move, she had curved to meet his body, her warm mouth pressed against his, her arm now stretching around his back, her free hand against his waist, pulling him closer, drawing the need from him, as her own want flowed from her.

He reveled in her slow abandonment. It had not always been so. Once, in those days long ago, she'd been confused by passion, fearful afterward that she'd done something wrong, something negative. But even then she had stirred him, as no one else ever could. Though she'd been afraid of it, she had understood the want in him. And now, it seemed, the same passion stirred in her. The thought sent a shaft of pure adrenaline coursing through him. He pulled her to him, feeling the heightened demand.

"Sara . . ." he muttered against the narrow hollow between her breasts. He raised his head and captured her lips.

Close to fainting, the world seemed to spin as his tongue again met hers. He tasted of mountain air and some sweet, soft drink he'd touched to his lips. His tongue was hot and his need ardent. With a shock, she knew it matched her own. No longer familiar, Ari's skillful lips and knowing hands sought things she wouldn't have known how to give as a young woman, would not have dared given. She'd run from that intensity then, fearful of losing herself in it. But now? Now she could no more have run than spoken.

With a sense of inevitability she knew from his touch, from his hot breath on her cheek, the strong hands kneading her back, that a union between them now would be complete, no holds barred, an utter and total surrender by both parties.

"Sara," he murmured again, his hands roaming the planes of her face, her hair, the curves of her body. And arching against him in answer, she groaned as his mouth nuzzled the soft bodice of her dress, his lips accurately finding the peaks of her breasts, lightly nipping at her through the material. She whispered his name as his hand swept the length of her leg, his fingers flicking against her thighs, teasing, exhorting them to part for him. And when they did, he lifted one of her trembling limbs to his waist, where it automatically curved around him, her skirt trailing unheeded over his hand.

He pulled his head up sharply and, with a racked groan, swore softly.

Meeting her eyes, he said slowly, deliberately, "I want you, Sara. Now. Tonight."

His hands curved around her hips, pulling her to him, letting her know the extent of his desire. What he discovered was the extent of the desire she felt for him.

He muttered something and kicked the door open. He lifted her other leg and with both of them wrapped around his waist, one of his hands upon her bottom, one against her back, his face buried between her breasts, he carried her into her room. Gently he kicked the door closed and didn't release her until they reached her narrow bed.

Moonlight spilled into the room through the opened window, once again catching the light in his eyes. She had the odd sensation that it was not a man who held himself poised above her but some ancient, powerful god, a phantom of her lonely dreams, a miracle of masculinity.

"You're so very beautiful...." he murmured, half straddling the small bed, one of his legs curled beneath him, the other propping him upright, planted on the concrete floor. His eyes raked the curves of her body, taking in the heaving breasts, the legs still resting languorously upon his hips. With a sweep of his hands her skirt was raised, baring her thighs, revealing her to his hungry gaze. He drew in his breath sharply, in an effort to control the pain, the exultation within him. He rested his eyes on the thin layer of cotton that blocked his full view for several heart-stopping seconds, before raising them to meet hers. Had he ever wanted a woman as much as he wanted Sara?

She met his gaze, lashes lowered, half covering her eyes. A small smile curved her parted lips. Her breasts strained against the thin material of her blouse. Ari felt his already tightened loins protest against the barriers between his body and Sara's. He reached for the buttons on her blouse and was bitterly amused to see that his hand trembled. His whole body seemed to be trembling. A thousand times he'd dreamed of this, a thousand lonely, aching dreams, waking to find nothing but air in his hands, the taste of defeat in his mouth.

But now she was here, this was no dream. She aided his fingers with the buttons, and as he pushed the sides of the blouse aside, she ran her hands up his arms. But Ari scarcely felt the soft raking of her nails. His body thrummed with need, his eyes feasted on her lush, full breasts, dusky at the tips, appearing darker in the dim light of the room. Slowly, almost reverently, he bent his head to her dewy skin.

Sara gasped as his moist tongue encircled a taut nipple, and lifted her back from the bed to give him greater purchase. Her legs, sprawled across his, rose to his shoulders, sliding against his muscled arms. She felt as wanton as a total innocent and as innocent as an immortal. In a moment of startling clarity, she understood that while Ari had seemed some phantom god come to her in a dream, so was she to him. They were a matched pair, opposite sides of the same coin. Together, locked in loving, there were no differences, no pasts, no futures, only the intensely glorious, immense realm of the present.

As if she'd spoken aloud, he said, "No guilt."

"No," she said in return, not exactly sure what he meant, neither knowing nor caring why he'd said the words. Stroking his thick silver hair, Sara had never felt as right with the world as she did at that moment. Though never understanding him, she had always loved him. And now, as his hands roved her body, sliding their clothing from them, his mouth driving her to gasping pleasure, she knew that here, at least, she understood him, she could give in completely to the passion that he demanded of her.

They did not meet in gentle exploration. They met in a torrent of pent-up, too-long-denied emotions, an explosion of want and desire, a wild, primitive acknowledgment of need.

Any hesitancy Sara might once have felt, any wavering in her acceptance of the passion that lay beneath the surface of her being, disappeared, leaving her wholly a woman, a woman in bed with the father of her child, the first and only true love of her life. As the narrow bed rocked under them and she with him, she knew a moment of total certainty that nothing in the world could be better—or worse—than this moment.

As he watched the play of emotions on her face, one moment intent, the next chasing that all-too-elusive guardian of completion, he was strengthened by her striking beauty, by the fever that consumed her, and by the fact that the fever bore his name.

Then, as her legs circled his waist and she cried his name, he thought he would die if he didn't give in to the plea in her voice, the urgency in her body, the demand in his own. Holding nothing back from her, her lips beneath his, her breasts flattened against his chest, he thrust even deeper into her, their tongues locking, fighting, imitating their joining. Faster, harder, swifter they arched together, he whispering her name, she begging him for something she couldn't even begin to express.

"You . . . it's always . . . been . . . *you!*" Ari cried, matching his words to the furious rhythm of his body.

That rhythm, his words, the fire consuming her, all met at that instant and fused. It was the culmination of everything she had ever been and would be. The convulsive spasms that overtook her seemed to reach out, draw in and spiral in ever tightening revolutions, until she was lost in the very core of the universe.

As he felt her body grow rigid, her ragged breathing catch, then hold, and she whimpered his name, Ari felt as if Sara had plunged into the deepest part of him.

Come to me!

He could not have resisted for anything on earth. Trapped in her, wanting to be further ensnared, he thrust one more time, deeper yet, gripping her shoulders, shaking, and called her name. The world exploded into shards of glassy light, and the universe absorbed them.

He shuddered, and as she folded her arms around him, a harsh, racked sound of exquisite agony escaped him. Another, almost violent shudder, and he collapsed upon her, his lips pressed against her shoulder.

Ari's body against hers, pressing her deep into the slight bed, was curiously weightless; she pulled him tightly to her, holding him, lulling him, and as the waves of her own climax subsided, lulling herself.

Her body replete, her senses sent spinning by their union, Sara kept him tightly pressed against her, terribly, fiercely conscious of this special night, this one moment of total joining. She was all too sorrowfully conscious that when the daylight filtered in through the now-moonlit window, she would have to tell him the truth about Danny, have to explain the past.

His hand crept to her cheek and gently stroked the curve of her face, stopping at her lips. She kissed the callused fingers.

"We...need...to talk," he murmured, hearing his words slurred by repletion and the late hour.

"Yes," she agreed, stroking the hard, muscled planes of his back.

"In the morn..."

The fingers against her cheek fell still, and his breathing deepened, but even as he drifted into sleep, his other hand curled around hers and held it tightly, trustingly—almost as a child grasps a mother's loving hand for protection from bad dreams, Sara thought. And just before sleep finally reached a caressing hand to her much-tried mind and languorous body, she glimpsed an Ari she'd never known before: the Ari who, in that world of grand causes and total commitment, knew vulnerability and understood uncertainty.

"Yes," she whispered. "We'll bare all secrets in the morning."

Chapter 5

In the morning Ari was gone.

Sara pressed her face deeply into the pillow that bore his scent and smiled. They still had differences, were essentially different people, but last night they had gone a long way to bridging the gulf. This day's telling of secrets would be easier because of that. For the first time since the day she'd felt Danny quickening in her womb, she actually looked forward to telling Ari, thought perhaps she had enough of that courage he'd assumed she was still lacking.

She wondered what her colleagues back at McMunn-Knapper would think of Ari's assumption. The smile she'd woken up with broadened. She was sure they would first stare blankly, then proceed to die laughing.

But she had behaved in a cowardly fashion toward Ari.

Luckily, joyfully, that time was over. For last night, in the joining, if not necessarily in his words, he'd told her in every way possible just how much she had meant to him, how much she still meant. And she'd caught a momentary glimpse of the vulnerable boy in the cause-driven man. Would that she had seen it years ago. Would that she had looked for it then.

Rolling over, taking in the rays of the sun that spilled through her open window, she realized it was much later than

she'd thought. It was close to midday. Sounds from the outside world filtered in through the shutters, a tractor somewhere putted along with a singsong, chuffing rhythm, children
were playing some game that produced high shrieks of excited
fear and a great deal of laughter, and below her window, she
could hear the sounds of saws and hammers.

She rose from her bed swiftly, smiling at the small aches and
pains of her body, a body unaccustomed to passion. She would
quickly shower and dress, then, like the kibbutzniks so busy
reconstructing Building Alef, she would seek out Ari and repair the devastation of the past.

- She had just completed dressing, choosing a light, almost
frivolous sundress, because it exactly suited her mood, when
a knock sounded on the door. Opening it with a wide smile,
she was slightly disappointed to see it was Moshe Ben Eban
who stood before her, a solemn expression on his craggy face.

"Moshe!" she exclaimed, trying to sound enthusiastic. "I
was just on my way to look for Ari. Will you give me an es-
cort?"

Without a smile, Moshe nodded.

"What's wrong?" she asked, a queer, sharp fear piercing
her heart. Something had happened to Ari this morning as she
slept. Her hand grasped his forearm. "What is it?"

"Does he know, Sara?"

"Know what? Who?"

"Ari. Does he know about his son?"

The world jerked sideways, tilting dangerously. "What are
you saying?" she whispered.

"Your son. He's here."

"What!"

"He came this morning."

"Wh—How? How could he be here?" Sara grew hot and
cold at the same time. She felt a dull confusion, a sharp fear
for her son's safety. And sick. Sick with the realization that her
beautiful bubble had burst, exploded into nonexistence. How
did Moshe *know?*

"He doesn't know, does he?"

Slowly, not knowing whether he meant Ari or Danny, she
shook her head. Wearily she said, "No, no one knows."

"I do," the old man said. "You do."

She looked away from him almost wildly, staring out the
window, as if the clear blue sky beyond might give her some

answer. What was she going to say to Danny? What would she say to Ari?

"Why didn't you tell him, Sara?"

"I don't know. I thought I had a reason."

"I don't mean the boy," Moshe said.

She turned then, meeting his eyes. "I didn't know then."

"And you thought he wouldn't find out."

"No, I planned to tell him." She laughed a little hysterically. "This morning."

"I don't think it will be too long before he figures it out."

"Is it that obvious?" Sara asked.

Moshe nodded slowly. "Like my old grandfather back in mother Russia used to say, 'The father's face is on the boy's.' It's pretty obvious."

Sara had the detached, almost humorous notion that if her other hard-bitten colleagues had been in her position at this moment, they would all have been shaking in their proverbial shoes. Every bit as much as she was.

"Damn," she said. There didn't seem to be anything else to say.

For the first time she saw Moshe's solemnity lighten. "You weren't wrong when you said he was smart. Mossad could use him."

"Where is he?" she asked sharply, grasping Moshe's arm. He covered her hand lightly with his own.

"Ari's office."

"Ari's office," she repeated faintly, a new horror dawning, a realization of the full implications beginning to override her other thoughts. "With Ari."

"Yes."

"How did he get here? Through the cordon, I mean? How did he even get to Israel?"

"Why don't you come ask him?" Moshe suggested, patting her hand. "They're waiting for you."

She shook his arm a little. "But Ari doesn't know...." she said wildly.

"Not about the boy, no. But he's fairly concerned that he turned up here, getting past every checkpoint, then just hopping off the truck with the other soldiers, as coolly as you please."

"Oh, my..."

"Come along, Sara. Time enough to faint later."

Moshe's pale eyes met hers gravely.

She allowed him to lead her from her room and pull the door closed behind them. "Is it really that obvious?" she asked.

"I'm an artist, Sara," he reminded her. "A *portrait* artist. I saw it the second I laid eyes on the boy."

"Dear God," Sara murmured. She walked beside Moshe down the corridor, but her legs felt as if they belonged to someone else.

"Who would have suspected that little Sara Rosen would go away and raise the son of Ari Gaon? You say the boy doesn't know, either?"

She shook her head slowly. Her body felt curiously heavy, her stomach leaden.

"Poor little swallow. Life wasn't so easy for you, was it?"

This time she didn't shake her head, but met his eyes, as a strange calm settled upon her.

"Are you going to tell him? The boy, I mean."

"Yes. I was always going to tell him . . . someday."

"Funny how 'somedays' have a way of sneaking up on you," Moshe said, taking her arm and leading her down the broad staircase, as if without his support she wouldn't have been able to manage.

He continued. "And Ari? Are you going to tell him?"

"If it's as obvious as you say it is, I don't think I'll have much choice."

"You never saw it?"

"Well, yes," Sara admitted, reluctantly. "Yes, I saw it often. Both in his looks and his personality. But I always told myself I was making too much of it. That I—"

"Wanted to see it, perhaps?"

She smiled wanly. "Perhaps."

"I think that if he doesn't guess, doesn't see it, I would tell him just as soon as possible."

"I don't think I have a whole lot of choice now, do you?"

"He won't like you for it, Sara."

"I know."

He stepped back for her to pass, then followed her out the main door. "Poor little swallow," he said again.

With Moshe's hand at her back, his solid presence a wall of comfort, Sara scarcely hesitated at Ari's office door. Since last night she had believed the world could explode, but as long as Danny and Ari were safe, she wouldn't even notice the chaotic aftermath.

That she'd been wrong, too horribly wrong, wouldn't make the situation go away. She pushed the door inward.

The dark, somber expression on Ari's face, the hard set of his lips and the reproof in his eyes caused her to pause. The tight, hard-summoned smile faded from her lips, and her limbs, compared to how she'd felt before, were now strangely light, as though she were having a nightmare. His gaze turned from her to the far corner of the office, and Sara followed that angry look.

Her heart seemed to jump once, a hard, painful leap, before resuming its newfound, irregular beating.

"Danny," she whispered. Her eyes drank in his stiff, slightly belligerent expression, the thin body clad in the fatigues of an Israeli soldier, the Uzi draped across his shoulder. Shadows of sleeplessness formed circles beneath his eyes, and his skin was drawn tight. In tension? In high excitement? More probably, she thought giddily, he was just hungry.

She was certain, absolutely certain she was having a nightmare. But she couldn't seem to awaken. Her legs trembled, threatening to give way. Danny stood not four feet from her, young shoulders hunched, arms tightly folded across his chest. His gray eyes met hers pleadingly.

He nodded, his head jerking. A nervous smile crossed his lips. His eyes darted to Ari and back to her. She licked her dry lips. Seeing him there in the same room with Ari, she wondered that the entire world didn't know. They were almost exactly alike. The one a younger version of the other. No wonder that Moshe had guessed so quickly.

She turned to look at Ari, steeled herself to meet his gaze. Did he know? Had he guessed what was so glaringly, painfully obvious?

"Sara?" Ari asked.

His voice seemed to come from miles away. She blinked with strangely heavy lids, as if they were weighted. Perhaps they were, she thought, weighted by the past, by guilt, by the knowledge that the day of reckoning had arrived.

Please let this be a nightmare, she begged. Please let me wake up soon. Let this be only a guilt dream, Ari's arms still around me, his voice whispering my name.

The Ari of this nightmare asked again, "Sara? Are you okay?"

No, she was definitely *not* okay. Slowly, achingly slowly, she shook her head, feeling the blood drain from her face. The room seemed to lurch and spin. She stepped backward, bumping into Moshe, knocking a book from a low shelf. It clattered to the floor with a dull thunk and a brief flutter of bent pages. She stared at it as if it could tell her what to do, what to say.

"Mom?" Danny asked. His voice cracked and shifted to a higher pitch.

"Oh, Danny," she murmured, her right hand going to her mouth, her left thumb frantically rubbing her bare ring finger. For one horrible second she wished she could simply give in to the tumultuous pounding of her heart and lie down upon the floor, never to rise again. The room seemed to swell and shrink, making her feel she was on a dark dance floor, held erect only by the heavy bass rhythm of a too-loud band. She wished she could go ahead and do as Moshe had suggested: faint. Maybe if she pitched to the ground, she would wake up in her narrow bed, Ari's breath upon her cheek.

But she had never fainted in her life, and this was no nightmare; it was simply and horribly the worst moment of her adult life. It was the day of reckoning. A Yom Kippur, a Day of Atonement out of season, out of rhyme.

"Mom?" Danny asked again.

She turned back to him, grateful to escape the bewilderment in Ari's eyes, the puzzled wonder at her reaction.

"What are you doing here? How did you get here?" she demanded. "How did you come to leave France? I talked with your host mother. She said you were in the Dordogne."

He shrugged, hunching further over. The Uzi on his shoulder slid forward, and he pushed it back negligently.

"Why don't you let me have that?" Ari suggested. His voice was not unkind, yet it held a note of steely authority.

Danny removed it with obvious reluctance and handed it to Ari, who set it carefully across his littered desk top.

"Danny?" she inquired, waiting for some explanation. This might be her day of reckoning, but her son also had much to answer for.

Moshe made some sound behind her, and Ari cleared his throat. The two sounds sliced through the spell cast by motherhood and her eyes flew to Ari. Did Ari *know?* Could he see what was so clear to her, so clear to Moshe? Was that why he'd looked at her with reproach?

"I take it this *is* your son, then?" Ari snapped, turning the hard gray gaze in her direction. Fearfully, but almost grateful to look anywhere but at the incomprehensible puzzle her son represented, she met his eyes.

He doesn't know, she thought. If anything, his lack of knowledge made her fear escalate, made the sick horror inside her roil and convulse. She could only nod, moving her lips but uttering no sound. Her stomach clenched and the fingers against her mouth trembled violently.

"Did you know about his coming here?" Ari barked.

She dragged her gaze to Danny, trying to make sense of Ari's question, trying to understand what Danny was doing there, dressed as an Israeli soldier, gray eyes locked with hers in some uncomprehended, unspoken plea. *Oh, Danny, why now? Of all times to strike for independence, of all times to disobey... Why now?*

Apparently Ari's anger was not so intense that he couldn't read her confusion, for he stepped around his desk and said in a softer tone, "He told me he let you know he was coming here."

Looking from the father to the son, feeling the world crumbling around her, not understanding how Ari could stand so close and not *feel*, not *know* he was Danny's father, Sara only half heard what Ari was saying. Danny was standing there, here, thousands of miles from the Dordogne, having lied to his host family, having lied to Ari, depending upon her to back him up.

"See you soon" his cable had said. Sara felt a weak, almost black humor stir in her. Strictly speaking, he hadn't lied... to her, at any rate.

"See you soon," she said aloud, looking at Danny. He blinked, giving her the only acknowledgment that she had guessed correctly. There were other messages there, as well, but in her shock, she couldn't begin to fathom them.

"What?—oh!" Ari said. He paced for a moment, then turned to her son. His son. And like a father who has been frightened, he railed at the boy. "Do you have any idea how dangerous that was? This is a dangerous time. You could have been killed!"

"I saw the fuss on TV. I was worried about Mom," Danny said, speaking the first full sentence since Sara had entered the office. "I had to come."

For a long moment Ari just looked at him. Sara couldn't read his expression, but seeing the two of them, a mere foot apart, so startlingly alike, stubbornness etched on both faces, she wanted to scream herself awake. She wanted to scream the truth at them, the painfully obvious truth.

Moshe pushed past her, stepping between Ari and the boy. "He can't go back," he said.

None of them could, Sara thought bleakly, although she knew that was not what Moshe meant.

"No," Ari agreed, looking from Danny to Sara. "No, it's too dangerous." He stared at Danny for a long, hard moment, then a rueful grin crossed his face.

He continued to Sara. "Somehow, in ways I can't even begin to contemplate, he got through every roadblock, every checkpoint. He got another soldier to lend him a uniform *and* that weapon—" he pointed to the Uzi on the desk "—and he rode with the soldiers coming to the Golan border. He almost made it through the gates here, but after yesterday's incident, Shlomo was checking everyone with more than his usual vigilance."

Couldn't Ari see? Couldn't he feel it? Sara wondered again. She stepped toward Danny. Her legs felt as if they were made of water, her mind seemed fogged. Moshe took her arm and drew her into the comfort of his arm.

"It will be all right," he murmured. She could only look at him wildly. How could it be all right? How could anything be all right again?

"Danny?" she asked once more, unable to form any other of the thousand questions that trembled on her lips.

The belligerence had gone from the set of his mouth, and his eyes no longer pleaded with her. He had seen the grin on Ari's face, Sara thought, and knew he was largely out of trouble. They—Ari—could hardly set him back on the road for France, now that he was inside the cordon. But a lingering air of doubt as to his reception clung to him. He raised a hand to rake it through his black hair. Out of the corner of her eye, she saw Ari doing the same thing. With a sense that fate had stepped in, Sara turned and met Ari's eyes.

He met hers uncomprehendingly, even tenderly, the glow of the night before once again lighting his eyes. Nothing other than a rather exasperated forbearance showed on his face—an acceptance of her son's—*their* son's—daring venture. Again Sara wondered if this nightmare would ever end.

Ari looked from Sara's anguished eyes to Moshe's steady gaze. For a split second he felt he could read a message there, a single flash of warning, then his old friend looked away, and he wondered if he'd been mistaken.

When Shlomo had first brought the boy to him, he'd been shocked to realize that Sara's son was older than he'd imagined, almost old enough to be a part of the army he looked as though he belonged to. Moshe had apparently been similarly shocked. He'd looked as though he'd been struck by a heavy object.

Ari had chastised the boy, of course, but deep within him, he couldn't help but admire the courage and ingenuity it must have taken for a boy so young to have traveled across Europe on a mission to rescue his mother. And he'd admired the boy's immediate acceptance of responsibility for his actions.

Looking at Danny now, he found himself wishing he'd known him when he was younger, wishing he could have shown him the things he'd shown Galit, that he—and his mother—had been around in the peaceful periods, the days and days of nothing but golden sunshine and even more golden grain.

The boy looked up and met his eyes. The slight hunch of his shoulders was gone now, and the gray eyes met his guilelessly. A swift, apologetic smile crossed Danny's face.

Ari's heart lurched in a painful fillip. He felt as if he'd been kicked in the stomach. Just so had his own father smiled. Just so had Galit.

The smile faded from the boy's face, as uncertainty clouded his features.

Ari couldn't seem to look closely enough. The high, broad cheekbones, the slightly arched eyebrows, thick and long eyelashes, so long that they actually cast shadows upon the boy's cheeks, the dark, softly curling hair. Hair like Galit's. Dear God, he thought, hair like *his own*.

Was he so in love with Sara that he was creating fantasies about the missing years? Was he so besotted with the mother that he wanted the boy to be his own? He shook his head, and inadvertently caught Moshe's eyes.

A warning was there, as well as sympathy. Sympathy for Ari, sympathy for Sara. Was the warning for the boy? Ari turned to Sara, his hand going to his hair, to rake it as the boy had done only minutes before . . . as he had done only minutes before.

It was at that moment, perhaps from the fear and the knowledge he could read in her eyes, the recognition of his own unconscious gesture, or perhaps because he could see his own features on the young face, that the truth, the startling *terrible* truth, slammed into Ari's mind with the full force of a runaway cargo train.

He looked deep into Sara's wide, pleading eyes and read the answer to his single, damning question. He saw it in her white face, her trembling hands, her pale, dry lips.

As if his hands had minds of their own, his fingers curled into his palms and pulsated in his clenched fists. He could hear the thunderous pounding of his own heart, smell the tension in the air. He knew how an animal caught in a trap must feel, as he fought the urge to flee the room, to flee this knowledge.

In all his dreams of Sara, in all the thoughts he'd had about her over those long years and in her arms last night, he had never once dreamed that she might have had his son. His mind and heart engaged in a violent war, the rational portion of him making excuses, hearing once again her words of the night before, half recognizing them as an attempt to tell him, the irrational exploding with anger, with an outrage so intense, so bone deep that it shook him to the very core.

How *dare* she keep this from him? How *dare* she leave him and raise his son, his *son,* without ever telling him of the boy's existence? How could she have allowed another man to *raise* him, to *hold* him, to *teach* him, when she had never even told Ari about the boy? Had she hated him that much? That much?

And how come she'd returned, knowing this, *knowing* she'd kept his son from him?

What had last night been? Revenge? Revenge for what? What had he ever done to Sara to make her hide his son from him for eighteen—no, it must only be seventeen—years and then bed the father again, without *telling* him he had a *son?*

And this after knowing how he felt about the loss of his daughter, about the loss of Dov. *Knowing* him.

The scream of rage that fought for release in him was contained only when he took in the look of confusion on the boy's face. On his *son's* face. Danny didn't know the truth. Danny didn't know that the first words he'd ever shared with his father were angry ones. Fearful ones. A rash young boy explaining a misdemeanor to a foreign authority.

Foreign, Ari thought. I'm a foreigner to the boy. To my own son. He looked across at Danny, the gulf of five feet feeling like the whole of the Negev, the length of the Sinai. He had never felt so helpless before and hated Sara for making him feel like this. He opened his mouth to tell her so, but stopped.

It wasn't the boy's fault. If he said something now, he would possibly hurt the boy. He didn't know that his father was dying inside, wishing he could take back the angry words, turn back the clock and wipe the look of fear from his son's young face. Wishing, just wishing, anything and everything.

"How...?" Ari started, unable to take his eyes from his son's face. To his horror he felt his voice break. "How...?" He dragged his gaze to Sara's tear-filled eyes. Her tears stirred him, as they always had, as they probably always would, but he wasn't about to let her know it. Not now. Not knowing *this*.

He couldn't seem to voice a single one of the many questions he had. *The boy doesn't know,* his mind cautioned. *Go carefully.* But his heart needed one answer, at least, so he ignored her tears, asking the one thing his rage demanded that he know.

"How *could* you?" he asked her. "How *could* you have done this, Sara?"

"Ari!" she said, her voice, like his, broken, his name on her lips like an imprecation. "Please..."

Moshe's voice cut through what seemed like fog in Ari's brain. "Ari. Stop. Wait."

His eyes locked with Moshe's for a long moment, then he transferred his gaze to the boy. *Danny,* his mind insisted. *Call him by his name—the name you had no hand in choosing, the boy you had no hand in rearing....* A cry of outrage welled in him, a visceral, eviscerating sword blade of pain.

His eyes on Danny now, as if to memorize every feature of the boy's face, his thin body, Ari couldn't withhold the question that seemed to come unbidden from the very depths of his soul.

He asked it slowly, with awful calm. "Did you... *know* ... about ... *this* ... when you left?"

"She didn't," Danny said, stepping into the tension between his parents, clearly misunderstanding the question. His words came out in a torrent of protection of his mother.

"She thought I was safely in Paris. But when I saw the news, saw her photographs on the air, heard about the attack, and I couldn't get through to the kibbutz by telephone, I just had to see for myself that she was okay. I caught the first plane." A little smile, a smile of triumph, of self-approbation for his cleverness, flitted across his face. Ari saw it fade quickly when the boy saw his mother's look of anguish. Danny put a hand upon her arm and met Ari's gaze squarely, only the rapid throbbing of his pulse at his throat showing his fear, his emotion. "She's ... she's all I've got, see?"

Nothing the boy could have said would have devastated Ari as completely, nor silenced him as thoroughly. You've got *me!* he wanted to yell. You've got *me!* his heart cried.

The boy's words seemed to have a bracing effect on his mother, however. Though Ari could see her blink rapidly, no tears fell from her eyes, and her shoulders, which had slumped so dejectedly only moments before, now squared. If he hadn't been caught in the grip of such powerful, raging emotions, he might have admired the gesture. She resembled someone standing before a firing squad.

"It's true, then," he said. And he could see that it was. He could *feel* it.

"Oh, Sara..." he said, unable to say more.

Sara drew a shallow breath and met his eyes directly. The world still felt off balance, tilting at a dangerous angle, yet deep within a long-held-back sense of awaiting her nemesis ceased its keening cry. This was the moment, the day of reckoning. She had avoided it for eighteen years, had dreaded it for so long, that now that it had finally arrived, she felt strangely relieved.

This was not how she would have chosen it, was not the way she would have had it happen. But fate and pure, blind chance had combined to make this the time, the hour, the minute, in which her past decisions were displayed for all to see.

Moshe had said it all too clearly. "Somedays have a way of sneaking up on you."

"Yes," she answered. "It's true." Even to herself, her voice sounded dull, emotionless, though she felt anything but.

"Hey, Mom!" Danny exclaimed, stepping closer, as if to place himself as a shield. His eyes flicked to hers for a moment, apparently confused by her white-faced calm, then locked on Ari with unspoken, but unmistakable challenge.

Ignoring the look on their son's face, Ari asked her, "Why didn't you tell me?"

Sara saw the anger in his face, felt the waves of fury reaching out to her, but beneath the rage she could also see the hurt. She had known it would be difficult to tell him, but this was worse than difficult, it was torture. Made all the more painful because of last night.

She'd been wrong to assume that their loving would serve to bridge the gap between them, wrong to believe it would make the news any easier. Now she deliberately avoided Moshe's eyes, believing that what she had to say, she must say without the benefit of support.

"I did what I thought I had to do," she said finally.

"But *why?* Why didn't you at least *tell* me?"

She met his eyes squarely, willing herself not to flinch at the fire in his gaze, the burning fury behind it. "I tried," she answered.

"When?"

Sara bit her lips hard to keep them from trembling. Last night they had trembled beneath his kiss. This morning they trembled with memories, of last night, of eighteen years ago, of her son growing up.

"God, Sara, did you hate me that much?"

"Hate you?" she asked blankly. Of all the questions she might have anticipated from him, this wasn't one of them.

"That you couldn't tell me?"

"I didn't know then."

"You didn't know...?" He looked as though everything he'd believed to be true had suddenly proven false.

"Afterward, then," he said finally. "Were you still so afraid that you couldn't tell me?"

Had it been cowardice? "No, Ari. It wasn't fear or hate that stopped me. Not in all those years."

"Then what?" He was so frankly puzzled, so stunned, that she found herself wanting to comfort him. But she shook her head, glancing at Danny.

Like the Wailing Wall that separates the Jewish quarter from the Moslem in the Old City of Jerusalem, Danny stood between Ari and Sara, his seventeen years of life an insurmountable barrier. She could see that to Ari, his son's very being was a breach of confidence, a black and terrible betrayal of his young love for her.

"In God's name, Sara, *why* did you lie to me?"

"I didn't lie to you, Ari. I didn't tell you. There's a vast difference."

"That's splitting hairs, Sara, and you know it."

"It was my decision."

"It was a lousy one!"

"That could be," she acknowledged.

Only her years of interviewing irate and often furious people gave her the ability to remain calm, to stand before him without giving in to the panic within her. Her mother had used tears, her father had employed guilt. She would do neither.

With icy calm she said, "What I did then is done. It may have been a bad decision, but I made it, nonetheless. I can't go back and change it."

He looked as though she'd slapped him. Her words, or perhaps the coolness with which she'd spoken, robbed him of speech.

It was Danny who took a step forward, his jaw set, his narrow body tensed, as though prepared for physical blows. He glared at Ari. Sara saw the glare hit Ari like a blow; a spasm crossed his broad features. He raised a hand, seemingly half in protest, half in some kind of supplication.

"Oh, Sara," he said in a ragged voice. "Do you have any idea what you have done?"

Danny moved as though to strike Ari. Sara swiftly took hold of his rising arm. "Wait, Danny. You don't understand."

Danny's face colored, but his eyes never left Ari's face, nor did the prepared-for-battle stance loosen.

Sara felt flayed by conflicting emotions. On the one hand she knew an instinctive pride that her son was so willing to take up the cudgels in her defense; on the other, she was crying inside for the hurt on Ari's face. She had said what was done was done, but oh, if she could only do it over…if she'd only known then what she knew now.

"What's going on, Mom?" Danny asked without looking at her.

"Yes, tell him," Ari said. His mouth worked for a second, as if he were tasting too many terrible things. "Tell the boy. He has a right to know."

"We'll go," Moshe proposed. One of his broad, blunted hands encircled Ari's upper arm.

"Tell him," Ari commanded.

"Let's go, Ari," Moshe entreated. His hand upon Ari's arm was white with the strain of holding Ari in place.

Without taking his eyes from Sara's, Ari allowed himself to be pulled toward the door. Once there he stopped, shaking his arm free of Moshe's restraint. For a long moment Ari merely stood there, staring from her to Danny, his eyes not blinking, but his hands relaxed at his sides. Then with a curious sound, half pain, half anger, he pushed by Moshe and reached for the door.

"Sir?" Danny said, before Ari could pull the door open.

Ari stilled as if shot. "Yes?" he asked, slowly turning around.

Danny produced a half grin and shrugged with one shoulder. His eyes met Ari's in apology. "I'm sorry I caused so much trouble."

Ari's hand rose to his hair, checked, then dropped limply to his side. Sara could see a hundred different answers rise to Ari's lips, only to be discarded. His mouth worked; the bitter pill he'd been made to take that morning was clearly hard to swallow. Finally, with a meaningful glance at her, Ari yanked the door open.

"*You* didn't," he said, stepping through and slamming the door behind him.

As though the slam was the signal for the puppeteer to drop the strings, Sara's legs gave way and she slumped into one of Ari's battered chairs. She felt as if all her strength were gone; she'd used it all in facing Ari's awareness, his anger.

Now her son moved to her side, uncertainty on his young face and a frowning curiosity in his eyes. This day was not ended. Only half the reckoning had been paid; the other half, perhaps the more difficult half, certainly the worse, was yet to come. How was she to tell her son, the person she'd always loved more dearly, more deeply than any other on earth, that she'd lied to him for seventeen years?

Though she cringed at the idea of telling Danny, she was greatly relieved that Moshe and Ari had left them alone. It was a sensitive gesture, a kindness she didn't believe she deserved. They'd offered her the chance to tell Danny in her own way, provide her own explanations.

The moment she had dreaded all of her life was upon her, much worse than she had ever imagined. Jason had urged her to tell him, had pushed her to explain, but she had never had the courage. Had never, she thought with irony, felt the need. She'd made her decisions and stood by them. Then Jason had died, and she'd told herself she couldn't break the news to a grief-stricken Danny that the man in the tomb was not his real father.

Ari was right in saying that she'd run from him. She had. But she'd stopped running when she found out about Danny. She'd stopped running that very day. This was her son. And for Danny she would do anything. She had done anything. And now, *anything* included telling him the truth about his parentage, even it it meant facing his anger and confusion.

Sara drew a deep breath and gripped her son's cold hand. She pulled him around in front of her and eased him into the folding chair facing hers, then met his questioning look steadily.

"What did he mean, Mom?" he asked. His eyes were curious, nothing more, and terribly trusting. So like his father's had been last night, had been only moments before.

Her knees almost touching his, she examined his hands. They were slender, long-fingered, not like Ari's, but like her father's. The detached, running-from-grief part of her noticed that his nails were dirty. The thought brought back a memory of him at age five, crying because she "cleaned too hard." She wondered when he'd last eaten, and if it had been enough.

When he returned the pressure of her fingers, she looked up and met his artless, puzzled gaze.

"I've got something to tell you," she said finally, having to struggle to get the words free of her constricted throat.

He wore a guarded expression now, as if fearful of her words, anticipating bad news, but willing to take it like a man. Ironically it was neither Ari's expression nor her own, but

Jason's. The imprint of the man who had been so kind to both of them sat well upon his face and lent her strength.

"Danny . . . ?" Her voice broke, and she shivered with the effort to pull it into control.

"What is it, Mom?" he asked, his voice young, anxious.

"You remember when we talked on the phone and I canceled our plans to meet and to come on to Israel?"

"Sure," he said. His tone suggested he would agree to anything, if she would only stop being sad.

"I had just received a cable from this kibbutz, from Ari Gaon." She forced her eyes to remain linked with his, no matter how strongly the urge was to look away, to look anywhere but at the boy whose entire life she was about to alter, whose whole background would suddenly have a different meaning than it had had a few seconds ago.

"I knew him once . . . oh, a long time ago. Before you were born."

Her son was nothing if not lightning quick. "Before Dad?"

Dumbly she nodded. Perhaps it was the sorrow she knew was in her eyes, or perhaps her fingers clenched his too tightly, but she saw a dawning awareness grow in his gaze. Not all the truth, no, but a sense that there was more to this story.

"You and this guy—?"

"Loved each other," Sara interposed quickly. Oh, how very much, she thought sadly, wisely, knowing it was the truth.

Danny shook his head, his brow furrowed. "But if you loved him...and he loved you..." His voice trailed away, and he colored.

She couldn't bear him to be embarrassed in the midst of this telling of a truth too long withheld. It would be unforgivable if she made him feel bad about himself, about his understanding, when the entire decision, the full responsibility was hers and no one else's.

"I was too young, Danny. I was twenty-two, but I was too young. It seems, looking back, that I was about half your age. I would never have been brave enough, or clever enough—though that is probably to the good!—to have done what you did today. I wasn't strong. In fact I was very, very weak."

He didn't say anything, though he seemed to be sifting through her words, looking for alternate meanings.

"I couldn't handle what I thought we had together. It scared me."

"So you split."

She nodded slowly. "So I ran back to the States, telling myself I was dedicated to my career, dedicated to a life on the sidelines, reporting incidents, reporting things, not living them every single second of every day."

"Has he been giving you a hard time?" Danny asked, his jaw squaring.

"No," she said quickly, sadly, remembering the night before.

"Then what's all this about?"

"When I left Ari—" She broke off, then tried again. "When I left *Israel,* I knew I couldn't ever bear to see Ari again."

"And then he turns up here?" Danny asked.

"Well, yes, but that wasn't what I was going to tell you about." Sara drew a shallow, painful breath before boring to the hub of the truth. "You see, when I left, I didn't know."

"Didn't know?"

A spasm of fear rocked her. *Please understand....* She raised Danny's hands to her lips, kissed them gently, then laid them back upon their knees. She forced the tears to recede, then met his gaze evenly. Her voice, when she spoke, was calm, if very low.

"I didn't know about *you.*"

Sara gripped his hands so tightly that she could feel the resistance in his fingers.

A look of stunned awareness spread across his face. His eyes probed her face, clearly looking for denial. She could read in the quickened breathing, the white lines around his mouth, the wide eyes, a morbid hope that he was wrong, and yet behind the hope lay certainty, revulsion. He looked from her to the closed door and back again.

"Him?" Danny asked, his head jerking toward Ari's desk, his voice a young boy's warble. "Are you telling me he's my father? Like, my *real* father?"

Every fiber of her body responded to the pain in him, the wonder, the myriad questions. "Yes," she said quietly, so calmly that he apparently misunderstood her fragile hold on her emotions.

"Yes, she says," he murmured. "Just like that. Wham."

"Danny—"

He jerked his hands, as if to pull away from her, but she held on. She had the feeling that if she let go now, she might never have another chance. "Listen to me," she said.

He looked pointedly away from her. She knew now what the phrase "looks that could kill" meant. It wasn't a question of meeting an angry pair of eyes; it was a son looking away from his mother.

"I'm sorry you had to find out like this. . . ."

He shot her a pained, pleading glance. "Yeah? How would you have had me 'find out'?"

She clung to his hands as if to a lifeline. "Danny. . ."

He turned to her then, face on, the boy having within seconds become a man. She could see in his stillness a touch of herself, something of Ari and of Jason, and oddly, something of her father. A tinge of curiosity crept into his expression.

"What's his name? Ari Garon?"

"Gaon," she corrected. This, of all things, drove home the terrible injustice she'd perpetrated. Ari's son didn't even know his *name*. "His name is Ari Gaon."

"Gaon," he said slowly, emphasizing the second syllable. "Gaon." His lips twisted. "You know, it's really weird, but when I first saw him, I thought I recognized him."

Sara closed her eyes tight, and while his words pierced her heart, even more did the doubts and the pain within her son. She opened her eyes and met her son's gaze again.

"Danny, I love you," she said finally. "I always have. I'm so very sorry I hurt you now."

He said nothing for several minutes. He didn't pull his hands from hers, nor did he look at her any differently than he always had—that curious combination of "explain it to me, and oh, why didn't I think of that before?" Then he looked down at the hands locked over their knees. He seemed to be studying them with great interest, much as Ari had studied hers the night before.

"I don't know that I feel hurt exactly. Just kind of funky. Kind of mad. You know?"

He looked away, a muscle in his thin face working. "Did Dad—did *Jason* know?"

Whatever she had expected him to ask, it hadn't been this. "Yes," she said, not elaborating. "He knew."

Still without looking at her, he asked, "He knew that I wasn't his son?"

"Yes."

"I see," he said. A slight shudder worked through his slender frame.

"Oh, God, Danny, of course he knew! Did you really think—?"

The frozen look of sorrow on his face stopped her outburst abruptly. She could see him taking in the knowledge, assimilating it, trying to set it into the context of the kind, gentle man who had carried him around, who had taken him fishing, taken pictures at his graduations from various levels of schooling.

She saw him rearranging his entire life to accommodate the realization that the man who'd called him Son, the man he'd called Dad had not been his real father.

"He never said anything," he said finally. Slowly. Very, very sadly.

"He wouldn't have," she told him softly, her heard bleeding for her son, bleeding for Ari, aching for Jason.

"No," he answered quickly. But he wouldn't look up. "He wouldn't have. I guess…" At last he looked up at her. "I guess I wish I'd known, somehow. I mean, known that he wasn't my father."

"Why?"

"I don't know," Danny answered, half angrily, then he continued, pained. "Because if I'd known, well, maybe I would have treated him more specially. You know. Like, telling him how great he was and stuff. I mean, I just thought he did all those things because he was my father, and that's what fathers do. If I'd known he did all that and he wasn't really my father…"

"He knew," Sara said, hearing her words catch on a sob. "Danny, he knew how much you loved him."

"Yeah, but I mean, he was really terrific." His voice was deep with unshed tears, unassuagable longing.

"Oh, yes, he was," Sara said honestly.

"Did he know who my real father was … is?"

"He knew. Long before you were born." She looked away then, remembering, thinking about Jason, about Ari. "Yes, he knew."

"Did he mind?"

"Did he mind what?"

At that Danny all but threw her hands back at her.

"Did Da—*Jason*—mind knowing? Did he mind me not being his son? Did he mind raising some *other* guy's son?"

He stood up, his body all action and gaucherie, his eyes cold and filled with manly outrage. With a sweep of his arm, he knocked the shabby chair backward. He towered over her, her son Danny, a young David armed with the slingshot of righteousness.

"No!" she said sharply. "Of course not. He *loved* you!"

A spasm marred Danny's features, then a shudder worked its way through his body. Upon seeing the intensity of his relief, the magnitude of his pain, she felt the keening, responsive cry of her own soul.

"And this guy, this *Ari* Gaon—"

"Didn't know about you," she said swiftly.

"He didn't know," Danny said quietly. Almost as if by reflex, he righted the chair and sat back down. One of his knees touched hers, melting some of the chill around her heart. He flicked her a quick, self-conscious glance.

He said, "Seems weird, doesn't it? I meet this guy for the first time, and he about has my head for his lunch!"

Sara smiled weakly in response. She was filled with a fierce pride in her son, this boy she'd raised, encouraged to think for himself, this boy who had courage she'd never dreamed of having at his age.

"Danny, I'm so sorry," she said.

He looked at her with a puzzled frown. "Why are you sorry?"

"For not telling you."

"Yeah. Well, I don't tell you everything, either." He chuckled rather hysterically. "This is too weird."

Sara agreed one hundred percent.

"I'm kind of curious, you know. I feel like I should *feel* something. Like I should have *known* or something." He looked away. "And at the same time, I feel like marching out that door and asking him why he wasn't ever around when I was a kid! Maybe I should ask him why he didn't ever call, or send birthday cards. Maybe . . ."

"He didn't know," Sara said quietly, honestly, knowing that whatever wrongs she had committed in her life, whatever she had done to Jason, to Ari and now to her son, she could not allow Danny to believe that Ari had neglected him, wouldn't have *cared*.

Danny's leg started jumping in a nervous bounce, much as if he were hearing a rock band playing in his mind. "Yeah, right. Why didn't he?"

"Why didn't he what?" she asked blankly.

"Know. Why didn't he *know?*"

"I never told him. I didn't know about you when I left him."

"He's a creep."

Only the white-edged shock around his mouth, the pinched look around his eyes, and the utter certainty that she stood on the brink of losing him forever, kept her from lashing out at him.

"He's a fine man," she said quietly. She held out a hand toward her son.

He looked first at the hand, then pointedly away, staring out Ari's large, opened window. He said nothing.

Sara felt rooted to the floor.

"Danny...I...I never meant to hurt you."

His eyes shot to hers, the hurt, the uncertainty, the realignment of his life evident in the gray depths.

"Danny, I want to tell you about it...."

"What's to tell, Mom? I've seen it in a hundred movies. I just never really thought it would happen to me, you know? I never even thought about it. Kind of stupid, huh?"

"Don't you *dare* feel stupid about this!" Sara snapped, angry for him, angry at herself. "Don't you dare!"

"Hey, Mom, no sweat. It's no biggie. I mean, I can hang." His eyes met hers in a quick, agonized glance.

"I would like to tell you about it," she told him, rephrasing her words.

"Save it." Danny rose, paced close to the window and back. He stopped some two feet from her. Close enough for her to smell him; it was the same scent he'd had from the first day, when the nurses placed him in her waiting arms. But he was so far away that she couldn't wrap her arms around him. "I guess there's really only one other thing I want to know now."

Sara steeled herself. The look on her young son's face said his next words were hardly likely to be conciliatory.

"Anything," she said, her hands balled into numb fists.

"How many other lies are there?"

When Sara didn't—couldn't—answer, he nodded once, then marched to the door, his back rigid in reproof, the set of his shoulders declaring his confusion.

"Danny—!" she called, and almost to her surprise, he stopped. He half turned, meeting her anguished gaze with his own tear-filled eyes.

"I'm not blaming you, Mom."

"Danny, I love you. I know you don't believe that right now, but I do. I always have. You can always believe that."

His face twisted, and a wild look flashed into his eyes.

"Yeah," he said dully. "I know. I know you love me. I—I love you, too." He shut the door quietly behind him, the soft thud a cannon's roar in her heart.

Chapter 6

Ari half expected Danny to burst through the outside double doors like a stone from a catapult; that was what he would have done at the boy's age. He anticipated a young volcano, spewing molten condemnation of a lie perpetrated for seventeen years.

When the doors opened, he found himself gripping Moshe's shoulder tightly, as if grounding himself, anchoring himself to something solid.

But Danny wasn't any cataclysmic volcano. He was neither running, nor did he appear angry.

Though Ari didn't loosen his grip, he was aware of a curious disappointment, as if Danny couldn't really be *his* child, because the boy was not acting as he would have acted, was not exhibiting the same emotions he would have shown.

Yet he was.

Had he been anyone else's child, Ari would not have been able to read that impassive face, would have misunderstood the careful lack of emotion. Had he been anyone else's son, he would have been any young man, stepping from a darkened room into bright sunlight. He was squinting, his mouth set in a slight grimace because of this.

But Ari knew. Ari understood. This was the same expression that must now be on his own face. It was the conscious, deliberate veil of pride, of pure will driving the scream of doubt churning to a deeper, more hidden region.

He knew. Oh yes, he *knew*.

His *son* walked about three feet, down the narrow strip of concrete that led to the offices, and stopped at the sidewalk, turning to look in both directions, as if crossing a busy street instead of a kibbutz pathway deserted at midday.

This, too, this blindness, this difficulty in perceiving commonplace things in a world suddenly turned upside down, Ari knew and understood.

With the knowledge and understanding came pride in his newfound son. Even from thirty yards away, Ari could see the strength in Danny, the self-respect that forbade him to display the uncertainty that surely lay beneath the surface.

Hadn't he felt just like that only moments before? And not contained it half so well.

He understood the boy's desire to be alone, to be anywhere, everywhere but in that room, hearing things he would not—could not—have wanted to hear. He wondered just what Sara had told his son, wondered again how he hadn't known, hadn't guessed.

Danny, not looking in his direction, began to walk slowly, aimlessly, away from the building, clearly putting distance between himself and the morning, getting away from full disclosure, for Ari instinctively knew Danny hadn't allowed Sara to tell him everything, hadn't let her explain it all. Some things were too painful to have explained, others were better left in the dark and lonely places of the soul until the time was ripe to bring them into the light. This was one of them.

Danny, as if hearing his father's thoughts, looked to his left, looked directly at Ari and Moshe then. Ignoring Moshe, he met Ari's stare, seeing, Ari hoped, understanding. The boy stood there for several seconds, seeking, Ari thought, the courage to approach the man he now knew was his father.

For a single fraction of time he felt younger than the boy before him, less prepared, less able to handle the situation. What could he possibly say to this child of his loins?

Danny's mouth hardened, his lips compressed tightly, his jaw squared with sharp tension. His pale eyes flashed briefly in some strong emotion, then he jerked his eyes straight ahead and, at a fast, stiff-legged walk, moved away from the office building, away from Sara . . . away from Ari.

"Let him go," Moshe said. Ari had forgotten he was there, forgotten whose shoulder he'd been gripping so tightly.

"He needs some time to think," Moshe told him. "He can't go anywhere with the cordon. Those were the last of the soldiers he came with."

"I have to talk to him." Had to look at him, touch his face. Had to understand what he had missed . . . what he had found.

"Give him time."

"I've missed seventeen years. There isn't any time."

"One more hour will not matter." Moshe's voice was steady, but there were, nonetheless, tears in his eyes.

"Every minute is essential," Ari fired back. He broke the contact with Moshe and started forward, unable to take his eyes from the hard, straight back of his newfound son. A bitter ache in his already pained heart, he called his son's name.

Once he'd decided not to run after the boy's mother, deciding it was better to live without her than without his pride. Now he couldn't live without his son. Sara's boy.

"Danny!"

His voice echoed off the buildings around them, hung, heavy with command, in the quiet afternoon air.

Danny stopped, his back still turned to Ari.

His son was made of strong stuff, he thought. The boy straightened his shoulders even more, and hands lightly rubbing against his thighs, he waited quietly, poised. Every muscle on the boy's back expressed reluctance, yet he remained there. Waiting.

Ari walked forward, slowly at first, then faster, fearing the boy would bolt any second. He's nearly a man, Ari thought, with a man's pride, and a man's fear of accepting those things too painful to be borne.

As he moved swiftly toward his son, his body felt both young and old at the same time, and his heart swelled with pride in this newfound son, though mingled with that pride was a pang of sorrow.

He'd missed all those years, missed that strengthening. In that instant Ari both hated Sara for stealing the years from him, and admired her for having done such a fine job. He didn't try to analyze his ambivalence; right now he had thoughts only for this boy who had Galiti's smile, and his mother's gray eyes.

When he was directly behind him, Danny turned around, his face set, his eyes wary and distant. Ari stopped, a curious sense of dismay striking him at the sight of his son's unsmiling face. The boy's back was to the sun, his head blocking the rays from Ari's face.

He's taller than me, Ari thought. The next generation, the completion of his father's hopes, his grandfather's desires. Tall and straight like an arrow, like a dream. He had no idea what to say to this tall, grown young man.

It seemed to him now that he should have recognized the boy at first glance. Not by his looks, though now that he studied his son, he could see the similarities. No, he should have recognized the pure psychic force, the calling of the blood. The fact that he hadn't had those feelings, hadn't reacted as a father to his son, tore at him, made him feel awkward, uncertain.

He was even slightly horrified to feel as if they were two dogs, squaring off, distrust in every taut muscle. Sara's fault, he thought, then: *my* fault.

If he felt this way, how much more would his son be feeling?

For a few seconds neither of them spoke, each appraising, assessing the figure before him. Danny's body was rigid, tense, and his face was almost furiously controlled. Ari was stirred by a strange combination of nostalgia and fear of the future, and wondered if it showed on his face.

Danny didn't speak; it was clearly up to him.

"I didn't know," he said finally, looking deep into his son's eyes. "She—your mother—never told me."

Something flickered in the boy's eyes, Ari wasn't quite sure what.

Like his mother's had during the agonizing time in Ari's office, the boy now turned his eyes some two inches beyond Ari's shoulder. His throat seemed to jump, the blood pulsing too rapidly through his veins, swallowed words struggling to be spoken. Still he was silent.

"I'm *sorry* I didn't know," Ari said, meaning a vast universe of things, but even he felt the words were lame.

Danny's eyes flicked to his, a starkly furious look. The anger was so intense, so much like his own, that Ari involuntarily stepped back a pace, not out of fear, but in total surprise.

"Why didn't you?" Danny asked. His voice was as cold as the Arctic in winter.

"Why didn't I what?" Ari inquired, bemused by the anger turned toward him.

"Why didn't you *know*? How could you *not* know!" Danny almost spat the questions at him. His voice was deep, low like a growl.

Ari felt as if he'd been physically struck. He no longer felt young, no longer felt that time had been lifted from his shoulders. The anger in his son's voice, on his son's face, made him old beyond his years, beyond time. "She never told me," he said, straining to remain calm.

"Oh?" Danny made the single syllable sound derisive. "And that was all right? You never thought to check on her? Never thought to ask? I don't know how it was in your day, *Pops,* but in my time we ask a girl about things like that. We don't love 'em and leave 'em, you know?"

"She left me," Ari said through clenched teeth. He was now almost as angry as the boy. Angry at Sara, angry at the injustice. And angry at this man-boy who dared judge him.

"Big deal," Danny said. "You still didn't bother to check up on her, did you?" Emotion had darkened his eyes and his hands opened and closed against his sides.

For the sake of this boy who knew nothing about the past, who could never understand all that he—Ari—wanted to say to him, he swallowed his instinctive, angry response.

Slowly, measuring the words, he said, "This is no way for us to meet."

But his son was apparently having none of it. "No? Well, I don't see that there was much other way, really. You didn't want to know—*obviously*—because you never asked."

He glared at Ari.

"And I'm pretty glad you didn't, as things turn out, because I had Da—Jason—and I had Mom." He broke away, as if needing a physical outlet. *This* Ari understood. But Danny whirled back equally quickly.

He continued, his youngish voice high with charged emotion. "I didn't get all that crap you were throwing out at Mom in there, not when you were saying it, I mean. But I get it now.

And I'll tell you something. It was *your* mistake, pal. It takes two to tango, and you stopped dancing before it was time to pay the band!''

Danny waved his hand at the low office building containing Ari's office, containing Sara.

"Yeah, I think she was wrong for not telling me. And maybe she was wrong for not telling you—I don't know you, man, so I can't say. But she was always around for me. You weren't. She was there in the hospital when I broke my arm, she was there when I had my tonsils out.''

"I—"

"*She* was the one who taught me that I should never *assume* everything is okay with a girl, that loving and living aren't the same thing, that responsibility is something you own, that I should—''

To Ari's increased horror, he saw that tears had sprung to his son's eyes. His passionate outburst was checked by a choked sob. Overriding his own anger, his instinctive denial of the boy's words, was an even more insistent and perhaps more basic need to comfort Danny. His hand clasped the boy's shoulder. Danny shook it off with a violent shudder.

His next words were blurred and almost inaudible, but Ari heard them as clearly as if the boy had carved them upon his heart.

"She's a class act, and you don't have the *right* to condemn her.''

"Don't condemn me, either,'' Ari said quietly. He had the odd sensation that he'd woken that morning to a world gone crazy. He'd left Sara's bed reluctantly, had walked the golden hillside with new hope in his heart, had heard the bizarre disclosures of the morning with—for him—fairly remarkable composure. But this was too much. The unknown son of his loins, blood of his blood, telling him that *he* was as much to blame as Sara, was entirely too much.

And yet . . . could the boy be right? Hadn't he told Sara to leave, if she wanted to, to run, to cower like a child, but if she ever came to her senses . . . not to even think about coming back? He hadn't meant the words, but he had said them. He'd said them out of an anguish too intense to be swallowed, too deep to bury. And he had never tried to contact her after that. Not once. He'd never even dreamed . . .

Something of Ari's thoughts must have shown on his face, he realized, for he saw Danny shift. His ire was still visible, but some of the tension in his shoulders had eased. Tears still clung to his incredibly long lashes, but now he had the tears under control.

"No matter what has happened in the past, no matter how many years we've wasted," Ari said slowly, his tone measured, "I'd like to try to be a father to you."

"My *father*, the man who raised me, was Jason Gould," Danny said. The clenched hands at his sides told Ari he would launch an attack if the statement were contradicted.

Ari closed his eyes for a second, then said, "I know. I know that. He was a good man."

"The best."

"I never really knew my father," Ari told his son softly.

The boy's eyes took on the look of a hunted animal who hears the predator approaching from some distance away: wary, alert, shaken.

Finally, after obviously wrestling with this seeming non sequitur for several seconds, he asked, "Why not?"

The cold hand that so painfully gripped Ari's heart relaxed its hold a little. "He was killed when I was very young."

"In battle?" Danny asked. No sympathy showed in his expression, but to Ari the question, the curiosity behind it, indicated a hope of sorts.

"Yes, during the original fight for Palestine."

An odd expression flitted across Danny's face. Without looking at Ari, he said, "He would have been my grandfather."

"He *was* your grandfather," Ari corrected.

Danny was silent for several heartbeats, then nodded, a rather bitter twist to his young lips. He shifted, and his lips parted, as if he were about to say something, then his expression hardened, and his eyes focused on something behind Ari.

Looking back over his shoulder, following his son's gaze, Ari saw Sara, standing in the shadowed doorway of the office building. Her hands were hidden in the folds of her sundress, her expression concealed by the blue dark of the shadows. She made no move to join them.

Danny uttered a sound, something that seemed to come from within the deepest part of him, then he turned and walked toward the kibbutz's front gates. This time Ari let him go.

About halfway across the sweeping lawn, Danny turned and looked back, first to his left at Sara, then slowly to his right at Ari.

Moshe, watching the tableau, couldn't have moved at that moment, if his life had depended upon it. Once he had read somewhere that the triangle was one of the strongest and most powerful forces in nature. Looking from the father to the son, then to the mother, feeling the love and confusion emanating from all three, Moshe knew how true this force was.

The three of them were bound together, linked, each at a corner of the triangle. He shook his head sadly, feeling the weight of his years, wishing there were something he could do for these people he loved so dearly, even for this child he'd never met before today. While he knew with an old man's instinct that the three were truly and irrevocably linked, he had the disheartening sensation that they were also destined to be forever separate.

The next two days were a time of unequaled despair for Sara. On the surface they passed as long, interminable days of quiet, of peace, of tractor noises and young laughter, sawing and good-natured railing between industrious kibbutzniks.

Trapped in Kibbutz Golan by the cordon, seeing Ari's cold ire each time she saw him, witnessing the boy she'd raised behave awkwardly, with reserve in her presence, Sara felt as if the entire world had become a never-ending nightmare.

She tried burying herself in her work, interviewing everyone she could, shooting roll upon roll of film, but as she used the kibbutz darkroom facilities, she discovered that she hadn't been taking pictures of potential counterterrorists, young, would-be heroes.

Instead she'd captured the central subjects of her own life: Ari and Danny. Clothespinned to drooping wires were strips of negatives, almost all filled with her own pain: Danny laughing at something Shlomo Havinot was saying; Danny bending over a pretty girl at a picnic table. Was her name Tova? Or was it Chava? Danny staring, solemn-faced, at the monolith bearing the names of the dead; Danny, talking easily with Moshe; and Ari, caught with an unguarded look of longing on his face, as he watched his son stride past him, head averted.

She had tried to talk with Ari, wanting to explain the past, needing to say something, anything that might atone for that bitter morning, that moment of blazing awareness and anger. But he was either in conference in his office or with others in the dining hall. When she had finally, in dull desperation, left a note for him, asking him to see her, he hadn't responded, not by so much as a glance.

He'd assigned Danny a room not three doors down from hers, and through Hannah, Sara learned that he had encouraged some of the younger kibbutzniks to take him around, introduce him to others.

"He's trying, Sara," Hannah said. "But Danny isn't having anything to do with him."

"I know," she'd answered sadly. "I've tried to talk with Danny about it, but he won't listen."

"Ari's confused, my dear. That's all."

"I think it goes much deeper than just confusion," Sara had answered. "It has its roots in betrayal."

"Exactly so."

"Meaning you think he has a right to feel betrayed?" Sara had asked sadly.

"No," Hannah had answered. "No, I just meant that I believe he still feels betrayed from eighteen years ago."

"I know," Sara had replied. "I don't know what to do to smooth it over. There aren't any words to just erase eighteen years."

"Is that what you want, Sara?"

"Of course," she'd responded, but at Hannah's skeptical look she'd had to stop and consider. She wanted things smoother naturally, easier, more comfortable, but didn't want them to be like they'd been eighteen years ago. She hadn't known how to deal with life then, hadn't known that with every pain came joy, with every joy pain.

"No," she'd corrected herself. "I don't want to erase eighteen years. Maybe I just want to set them straight."

"You still love him, don't you, Sara?"

"Ari?"

"No, young Shlomo Havinot."

"I don't know," Sara said, with the merest hint of a smile at Hannah's joke. "I'm not even sure I loved him way back when."

"Then you'd better stop and take a good look into your heart, Sara. Because then you loved him more than life itself, and if you don't remember that, don't *know* that, then you're lying to yourself. And if you're lying to yourself in one place, you could be in several others."

They'd talked longer, she and Hannah, but Sara couldn't have said now what they'd talked about. Her mind kept revolving around what Hannah had said, her heart asking questions she couldn't answer.

She wanted Ari, and now, because of the past, because of eighteen years of unspoken words, she couldn't have him. But was that love?

She wanted her son to once again be relaxed with her, to joke with her, to lose this look of caution that stole over his face whenever he spoke with her. And she wanted him to know Ari, for Ari to know him. Why? Because she loved Ari? Or was it only that she loved Danny?

Ari needed a son, Danny needed a father. She'd been down that road before. Yes, it led to love, it led to respect. But was that what she could feel for Ari Gaon?

No, what she felt about Ari was much more complicated, much more complex. It was all tangled up with hopes, dreams and wishes, clouded by nuances of right, wrong and many shades of gray.

Did she love Ari Gaon?

Had she loved him?

Oh, yes. She had loved him. She had loved him with a girl's unbridled assumption that everything would end up perfectly, with a girl's unchecked faith in a happy future. And when they'd differed, when they couldn't agree upon the slightest of things—everything from what breakfast should be to his commitments to causes—she'd discovered that for her, loving was not enough.

Then she'd met Jason. She had never loved him like she'd loved Ari. She had grown to love him in a different way, in a giving, tender fashion, building slowly, trust upon trust, until that point when he'd died and she had realized with a terrible sorrow that she'd never once really told him how much she had grown to love him. Because it hadn't been like it was with Ari, springing full-blown, fully grown, a ripe apple to be plucked and savored, she'd never noticed how many obstacles he'd quietly removed from her path, in how many silly, small ways she'd contrived to make him comfortable.

She realized these things now, in time to appreciate how much he'd helped her to grow, how much he had put into this "courage" of hers. As if he were with her now, she could almost hear him telling her to listen, to slow down, to stop, and most of all, to allow her heart room to breathe.

"Think, Sara. But think only with others in mind."

She was no coward now. A little heartsore, maybe, a little bruised, but no coward. As if she were outlining a photo layout, or struggling to find the best angle for a story, she considered the situation. The trouble was, she could come up with the hows, whats and wheres, but when she did a story, she didn't have to worry about the "how-to-solve-its." Here she had to take Jason's advice and think with her heart.

On that dreadful morning, two days ago, all three of them had crossed a barrier of sorts—she from the hitherto unrevealed past, Ari into a possible future, and Danny had opened the gate to adulthood.

In that crossing they'd all lost something; Sara a love she'd always wanted, but now could never have; Ari—to judge by the looks he now gave her—his faith in her; and Danny had lost his childhood identity.

Even as she cursed the cordon for herself, she found herself grateful for it when it came to Danny, and perhaps, even as it affected Ari. If the cordon hadn't been in place, if the danger of leaving hadn't kept them there, Danny would have bolted that first morning, would have used that ingenuity of his to flee somewhere, and she suspected it wouldn't have been France or the States. It could have been anywhere as long as it was away from her, away from Ari and the disturbing truth.

The cordon kept Ari there, as well. She knew, as surely as she knew the sun would rise and the wind would blow, that Ari would have conjured up a pressing meeting in Jerusalem or a summons from Tel Aviv, leaving her, running from her and the anger he now felt for her as desperately as she had run from him all those years ago.

With the cordon in place there was a slim hope, a faint possibility that she would be able to smooth over the rough beginning her son and her love had faced. Perhaps if she could do that, one or the other might someday forgive her the past, the years of separation. And if they didn't, perhaps by trying, she might be able to forgive herself.

But where to start? How? Ari would just plow on, somehow, unerringly finding a path. Jason would have slowly plotted, carefully finding an answer that would please all. But where should a bystander, a spectator at life's game, begin to discover how to mend an eighteen-year rent in life's fabric?

For two days this question had held her in its thrall.

Now, once again in the shadows, in her element beneath the red light of the kibbutz darkroom, she held negatives loosely in her fingers, eyes not upon them, but upon the few enlargements she'd been unable to resist bringing to life.

Here, in the quiet, reclusive, yet so expansive closet that photographers live in, she felt the full weight of her years of standing on the sidelines, never the participant, never the communicator, only the quiet recorder of fact, fantasy, and dreams of others, never her own, never hers.

In these sorrow-filled photographs lay exposed every dream she'd ever had—the man she loved, had always loved—and the boy she loved more than life itself. Unlike her usual story-photos, which told others' lives, these pictures told the story of her own shattered dreams, her own lost hopes.

Nothing on heaven or earth could piece her heart together again, but she owed it to Danny . . . owed it to Ari . . . to try something, anything, for their sakes.

But where to start to repair the damage already done? Where to start thinking with that recalcitrant brain of hers?

She felt adrift in a world where no one spoke her language, where love had suddenly turned to hate, interest had flipped to disdain. And in this crazy, topsy-turvy world of opposites, her son turned a cool shoulder, and the man she had dreamed of loving for so long, had loved for so long, deemed her a stranger.

In the photographs Danny and Ari were framed together, Ari's hair seeming more silvery when near their son's dark, tight curls. The lines on his face were more pronounced when contrasted with his son's unmarked, untested features. Yes, she had to do something, for she had deprived them of so many years. So very many years.

And it had been deprivation; she could read it in every nuance of Ari's gestures, every expression on the face in the photographs. She had seen it too horribly clearly when, in that triangle tableau, Ari had met her eyes across the distance. His eyes had reflected the sky, the surroundings, even herself, but she had not been able to read what lay behind them, had not seen even a glimmer of forgiveness. When he had turned away, she'd felt as if the shattering of her world was complete.

Standing there, watching the two of them that morning, she had realized that their moment together, their few hours of joy, wasn't the beautiful beginning of a new relationship, but the tumultuous farewell to something rare and unique that had really died years before. She carried the memory of those hours like a precious gift, hugging it to herself, reviewing it whenever alone, or lying in the dark, staring at the cloudless, starlit sky with tired, sleepless eyes.

In the dark of her lonely bedroom, the memory would wrap gentle arms around her and press goodbye kisses to her trembling lips, and filled with an anguish that surpassed tears, she would drift, dry-eyed, into a troubled sleep in which the sun no longer shone and the clouds were all imprinted with Ari's features. In the dreams she knew the sun would never shine again.

As she couldn't do in her dreams, she fled from the small darkroom, where a false red glow lighted her hands and the pictures she worked with, infusing her world with a gentle complacency. She fled from the room that the sun never touched, and with the small grouping of photographs still clutched in her fingers, ran into the waning sunlight, the tears flowing unchecked down her cheeks.

Feeling stifled by the camaraderie in the dining hall, restless, Ari went out into the cooling, quiet evening. Night was still a few hours away, but the mountains already cast their long shadows across the valleys of Kibbutz Golan. It was in these shadows that he sought some semblance of peace, peace from his weary thoughts, peace from his aching heart. He avoided the garden with the granite slab bearing the names of his wife and daughter, as if avoiding acknowledging the loss of the son he'd never known and the woman he'd loved too intensely.

Instead he sought out the small-garden enclosure of the children's nursery. Even there he recognized the irony: he'd

missed raising his son, missed his growing up. He'd never seen
him on a swing or playing in a sandbox. He'd never kissed a
hurt away nor swung him high upon his shoulder. He'd taught
him nothing and was nothing in his life. He'd come to this
lonely, evening-empty enclosure looking for seventeen missing years.

In the most shadowed corner, unseeing and unseen, he sat
upon one of the empty swings and, not for the first time since
that dreadful morning, tried to answer the harsh questions his
son had asked him. *Why didn't he know? How could he not
have known?* There was only one answer, the one his son had
handed him on a double-edged sword: he hadn't known because he hadn't tried to find out. He hadn't known because
he'd been so wrapped up in wounded pride that he'd never
tried to find her. This was the conclusion his son had come to,
correctly perhaps, but so damningly. It was a youth's conclusion, all black and white, no shades of gray. It was the type of
conclusion he himself would have drawn. Did draw. Had
drawn.

Sara had run from him all those years ago because of the
passions that ran so high in him, had run because he couldn't
understand her holding back from Israel, had run because he'd
tried forcing her to embrace his causes with the same fervor he
himself did. His commitment to Israel was no less intense now,
but for the first time in his life, the passion was gone. He felt
too old, too tired, too emotionally drained to *feel* much of
anything.

The son who should have been raised a sabra, a prickly-pear
native like himself, was a stranger to this land, a stranger to
himself. How could this be his, Ari's, fault, when of all things
on this earth it would have been what he most wanted?

Ari wasn't surprised when Sara entered the small nursery
garden. It seemed somehow fitting, as if their mutuality had
drawn them both here, here to this place of children, to this
living testimony to youth.

Even in the darkening garden, Ari could see the tears that
stood upon her cheeks, could see that she was unaware of his
presence. A sheaf of paper was pressed against her chest, and
her shoulders were bent with the weight of her grief. Whatever anger he felt toward her, whatever confused, chaotic
emotions she conjured up in him, he nonetheless felt a piercing shock of pure sympathy.

He knew these tears were only the scalding release of surface pain, for she must have a well of tears that filled her soul, as he did. With that instinct he'd always had around her—except, perhaps, when it had mattered the most—he knew she cried for Danny, for his pain and confusion. He also knew she cried for him, shed tears for his anger, his sense of betrayal. And he suspected she cried for herself, for the lost, hungry years, for Jason and the many mistakes all of them had made.

She didn't jump when he spoke, but merely stilled, a sob catching at the back of her throat. Like a traitor, his heart quickened its pace, and the blood in his veins seemed to flow with dizzying speed. Even now, even knowing the extent of her betrayal of him, he wanted her. With a sinking feeling he knew he would always want her. Always.

"I didn't know anyone was here," she said slowly, her voice low and roughened by tears.

He didn't say anything, and for a long time neither did she. The evening shadows shifted and stretched around them like ghostly playmates, dancing in and around the playground, jumping from bar to bar, from swing to swing, from Sara to Ari and back again.

Sara moved among the shadows as if accepted by them, as if she were used to their playful ways. Closer and closer she drew to him, until, if he'd propelled the swing any farther forward, he would have grazed her thigh. His heart was beating so rapidly that it was painful. He had so much to say to her, to ask her, and all he could think of was that she was there. Beside him, near him. Close enough to touch. Near enough to kiss, to drive her to her knees to beg his forgiveness. Near enough to press her to the ground and love her, as he'd only dreamed of loving her before.

In the end he did none of those things. He merely jerked his hand toward the next swing.

Grateful for the shadows, relieved to see no traces of bitterness on his face, Sara took a swing, sat down and waited. It wasn't long before he spoke.

"He is a good kid, Sara," he said. He wasn't looking at her. His eyes were on a young tree in the center of the nursery garden. Sara understood the pathways of his thoughts instantly; they were in tune here, if nowhere else.

"Yes, he is," she answered. Her heart thudded in her chest, filled with a cautious gratitude that this would be the first thing he would say to her about their son, filled with a tense, painful optimism. She was too aware of their proximity, too aware of the narrow strip of air that separated them. And she was too conscious of the wide gulf that would separate them forever.

Again silence fell between them, but this time it wasn't a silence that blanketed accusation or bitterness. It was the strange, and oftentimes sweet silence that falls between two estranged parents when thinking of their single, shining conjunction: their love for their child.

She thought of the photographs pressed to her breast, photographs that showed how much Ari wanted his son, how much his son needed a father. She shifted, dropping them to her lap, taking them up in a shaking hand to show to him. To *give* to him.

"You've done a good job with him," he said softly, and Sara could hear the sincerity in his voice. It pierced her heart.

"Thank you," she said, hearing her voice break slightly. Now the silence seemed neither easy nor sweet; it was charged with unspoken questions and unvoiced explanation.

"As—as you said, he's a good kid."

"And you had Jason," he said. He said it without rancor, but Sara felt the sting of the words, nonetheless. His mention of Jason, the reference to the gulf of the past, made her raise the pictures to her chest once again.

"Yes," she said simply.

"Danny loved him." It was a statement that required no answer.

"Yes," she said anyway, pressing the photographs tightly against her, as if trying to press them into her.

"He must have been a good man," Ari said reflectively, yet his words held a question.

"He was," Sara answered. Sadly her thumb traced the empty spot on her finger. "He was."

"Tell me about him."

"Danny?"

"Jason."

Sara was surprised at the question, yet, as she thought about it, she felt it made sense. Danny was fiercely loyal to his—to Jason. Know the father...the *adoptive* father...and know the son.

Beside her, so close that she could smell that mountain scent of his, could touch him if she dared, Ari sighed heavily.

Then he said, as if she had misunderstood him, as if unperturbed by their proximity, "Tell me about that time. Tell me about Jason. Tell me about Danny's birth, his growing up."

When she didn't answer immediately, he sighed again, and pushed the swing backward, as if seeking physical expression for the questions that swarmed in his brain.

"I really want to know," he said.

The Ari she had known when she was younger would not have asked, would not have waited to ask. If he had wanted to know, he would either have found out for himself, or demanded. Thinking this, Sara realized that the girl she had once been would have evaded the questions or would have run by now. But, like Ari, she had changed. And the past two days of agony had crystallized that change.

"I met Jason when I was eight months pregnant," she said. Beside her, she felt Ari give a sudden jerk, heard the snap of the chain against the swing seat, but he said nothing. "I was applying for a loan in the bank."

For a moment, caught by the memory of her own sense of inadequacy, the recollection of the loan officer's contemptuous glance at her swollen belly, Sara faltered in her account of those long-ago days. She had been very frightened.

"Jason was there, talking to a friend of his at the bank. He heard the man deny me the loan." Again she heard the swing chain snap.

"He came up to me then and asked me if there was some trouble. I explained that I had no collateral." For the first time in the past two days, Sara smiled.

"He didn't say anything, he just pulled out his checkbook and wrote a check. He handed it to the loan officer. 'Here's her collateral,' he said. I never even knew how much the check was for." Her smile faded somewhat.

"Go on," Ari said.

"He wouldn't listen to my protests. He didn't even really look at me, just at that loan officer. I'll never know what made him walk by that desk at that moment or what made him stop to listen. He told me later he would have given *me* the check, but he wanted to wipe the fatuous expression off the loan officer's face. That was exactly the word he used. Fatuous." She stopped, remembering again.

"What was Jason? I mean, what did he do?" Ari asked. "I know he was a great friend of Israel. But I don't think I ever heard what he did." His voice was tight, his speech clipped.

Sara smiled faintly. "He was a stockbroker. He was a philanthropist. I think in Jason's mind, one was indivisible from the other."

"He was wealthy, wasn't he?" It was a rhetorical question; he knew the answer before he opened his mouth. Sara wondered if he put the question thinking the response would tell him the reason she had married Jason.

"Yes," she said, but didn't elaborate. She owed no one any explanations as to *why* she had married Jason, least of all Ari Gaon.

"I can't see you having married for money," he said.

"No, I didn't," she answered, grateful for his perspicacity, grateful he saw beyond the dollar bills that usually accompanied the mention of Jason Gould's name.

"But I don't think you were in love with him, either," he said.

Though his interpretation angered her, she said quite calmly, "I wasn't." She heard him sigh, and something in the sound made her add, " . . . then."

The swing chain snapped again.

"Go on. Tell me the rest."

Sara took a deep breath, the anger he'd sparked in her crowding out the pain of the past two days. "After that he came by often. Sometimes he would take me out to dinner, more often he would bring food by my apartment and then fix it for us. I was only working half time in those days, and the closer it came for the baby, the more he was there. I didn't think of him as anything but a kindly man."

"How old was he?"

Sara wondered if Danny had told him. If Danny hadn't, how had he guessed so easily?

"Then?" she asked. She could feel Ari's nod, though he said nothing. "He was forty-eight."

"Twenty-five years older." Ari's tone carried censure.

"Yes," Sara said, without explaining how she'd felt about the age difference, what she'd initially thought of Jason, what their marriage had been like. Now the anger in her shifted and slid into despair. Ari already thought the worst of her; these false assumptions only added fuel to his disgust. No amount of arguing on her part, on her own behalf, would make him understand, make him see her reasons for marrying Jason.

"Go on."

"He took me to the hospital when I went into labor. He stayed beside me throughout it all."

Ari shot past her with a swift kick forward, his swing rising from the ground, as if his temper were too uncertain to remain grounded. He steadied the swing almost immediately. "Was it an easy birth?"

"As childbirth goes, yes," Sara answered with a flicker of humor. "I don't know many women who would call it easy." She sighed and continued. "Danny was a beautiful child."

"And Jason was there? Jason held him?"

Why the interest in Jason? Not just for Danny's sake, obviously. Jealousy? A spurt of hope shot through her and just as quickly dissipated when he said: "That is one of the best moments in a man's life. Holding a newborn child."

"A woman's too," Sara said quietly, feeling as if she'd been chastised, wanting to take him down in return.

"I remember when Galit was born, I just couldn't take my eyes off of her. She was so tiny and so perfect."

Sara said nothing, remembering those first few minutes of Danny's life, remembering feeling as if hers had just begun, as well.

"It was a whole new love, a depth of emotion I never had understood before," Ari said, obviously also caught in his past.

"Yes, it's like that," Sara agreed, aching for him, for his loss, for his sense of having missed that with Danny.

"Jason loved him then?"

"From that moment on," Sara answered honestly. "I think he probably loved him from the very first minute."

Ari was silent for several heartbeats. "When did you marry him?"

"When Danny was six months old," Sara said. "He asked me that first night in the hospital. I hadn't thought of him as loving me."

"But eventually you said yes," Ari added slowly. "Did you love him?"

Sara hesitated. He had asked her that question before, but it meant different things, then and now. In the wake of the past two days, in telling Ari of his son's past, she could offer no less than the unvarnished truth. It was too late for Ari and herself, perhaps, but she did owe him this, as she owed it to Danny and possibly even to Jason.

"Not the way I loved you, but yes, I did love Jason. I loved his gentleness with Danny, I loved his consideration of me and of my feelings. He never pressed me to do anything, never asked questions I couldn't answer."

"Like I did. Like I do," Ari said.

Were the comparisons and contrasts so obvious then? Had that been what she was trying to say? She didn't think so, but it was obvious that he did.

"No," Sara answered his question—his statement—with ambiguity, without elaborating. How could she begin to describe the vast differences between the two men? How could she begin to tell him how many nights she'd been certain she'd made the wrong decision? First back in Israel, then in not telling Ari, and finally in marrying a man she respected, a man who needed her desperately, but a man she could never want in the same ways she wanted Ari? How could she have told Ari that the fire in him that had so terrified her was wholly and absolutely lacking in Jason, and yet Jason had been no less a man because of it?

As they spoke, as the silences lengthened between them, the shadows withdrew like tired children, leaving in their wake a velvet blanket of darkness.

"Tell me about Danny. When he was young. When did he first talk, what were his first words? Why did you call him Danny?"

"I named him after the river here," she said quietly.

"I see," Ari said, and Sara suspected that he did. "I should have suspected then, when you first told me his name."

Sara said nothing.

"But I didn't. I didn't suspect a thing."

"No," Sara agreed.

"You think I should have, don't you?" The chain snapped again. "Sometime, either after you first left, or somehow in the last few days, you think I should have guessed about Danny."

"No," she lied.

"Danny thinks so, too."

"He said so?"

"More or less. He chewed me out."

"I'm sorry," she said honestly, not apologizing for her son, merely extending true sympathy toward Ari.

Ari dropped the subject, resuming his earlier line of questioning. "And the other things? His first words? When he first walked? Does he play baseball . . . ? All those things."

With a deep ache in her heart, Sara told him. Between the answers and the questions, the night settled in fully, wrapping around them, drawing them closer, smoothing away some of the differences and obstacles too visible in the light of day. Twice he laughed, and once, so did she. But finally the well of questions ran dry and her pool of answers seemed empty. And again a silence fell between them. It was the silence of having talked all around a subject, of having broached a thousand different topics other than the one that really mattered.

Then Ari rose, stretching. He walked a few paces from where she still sat, his broad back to her, his hair once again black in the moon- and starlight. "Why didn't you tell me, Sara?" he asked. "When you found out you were pregnant, why didn't you tell me?"

The ax fell. It had hung, silent and deadly for eighteen, long years. It had almost fallen two mornings earlier, but confusion had stayed it. But no longer. It sliced between them, redefining the gulf that stretched across miles and cultures from Sara to Ari. It was the crucial question, and what she would answer was the pivotal reply.

"I had already left you," she said, her voice heavy with memory. She tried reading his expression in the darkness, then was glad when she couldn't see it. She sighed.

"I was young, Ari. So very young. I didn't believe that having told you no, that when you told me to never come back, I didn't believe I should seek you out, only because I was pregnant."

"You loved me so little, then?"

The pain in her heart that seemed as if it were too great to be withstood grew even more unbearable.

"I loved you more than heaven and earth," she answered simply, as simply as only unvarnished truth can be.

He turned at that, stepping closer, though the darkness still masked his expression.

"Then why did you leave?"

Sara half shrugged in sheer helplessness. "As I said, I was young. We were young, Ari. Scarcely older than Danny. I was *young.* I looked at you and saw this immutable passion, this burning, sweeping demand to change the world, and . . . I was afraid. I was afraid I wouldn't—''

She broke off as the whole truth finally settled in on her. She hadn't left him because she'd been afraid of *him,* of his passions, of his drive for a cause. She'd left him, had *run* from him because she'd been afraid *she* wouldn't be able to give him that same passion, either physically or emotionally, that she would shirk from becoming involved in grand causes, that she didn't have what it would take to keep such a driven, passionate man.

She'd run because she'd feared he'd one day discover the real Sara Rosen; then she'd see condemnation in his eyes, find only apathy in his arms.

"It's ironic, isn't it?" she mused.

"What is?"

"I ran from seeing the condemnation, and now, after all these years, because of that decision, I'm seeing it anyway."

"I don't follow you, Sara. You were afraid of condemnation? By whom? Me?" His voice was blank with shock.

She leaned against the swing's chain, as if her head were too weary to hold itself erect.

He persisted. "You said you were afraid you wouldn't . . . what, Sara? You wouldn't *what?*"

"I was afraid I wouldn't . . . I wouldn't measure up."

"What?"

With more heat and more understanding of her younger self she answered, "I was afraid that one day you'd wake up and see the real me—a coward, afraid of living, afraid of giving my all for a cause, for a belief . . . for a man. Afraid that because I couldn't be like you were, you wouldn't want me anymore."

She knew a curious sense of peace. Now, she thought, now the whole truth is out. The truth about Danny, the truth about herself. It's all been said and done. She felt as if she were staring at a blank page and rolls and rolls of new film, a clean, startlingly clean slate.

He murmured something, an oath, an imprecation perhaps. He crossed the distance between them in a single second, and with a rough gesture, pulled her up and out of the swing and into his arms.

"God, Sara," he said against her temple, his arms wrapped around her, pressing her so tightly to him that it seemed he would draw her inside him.

He said now, "I never wanted you to be like me. I never did. I wanted what you were, so vibrant, so loving, so naive. You had no concept of war, of battles, of the things that drive men to them. You were like a ray of pure sunshine. And I loved you. More, I think, than life itself."

With an inarticulate whisper, Sara buried her face against his shoulder, inhaling his heady, male scent, feeling her cheeks flush at his words, his warmth. But though she was touched by his words, though her heart seemed to be fusing some of the shattered fragments, she couldn't help but notice that he had used only the past tense.

He wanted her now, but he'd loved her then. Here, locked in his arms in the dark corner of the nursery garden, it seemed that wanting was enough, that it was in the end, perhaps, all that really mattered. At least it seemed so as his lips pressed a fierce, angry kiss to hers.

As always, when she was with Ari, the world lost its sharp focus, and there were only the two of them, hands to hands, lips to lips, warm, heating bodies pressed one against the other. And, as always, she found that undeniable longing to be one, rather than two.

Only three nights before she had lain in his arms, over him, beneath him, loving him and begging him to love her, inside and out. Only three nights before she had been certain that the morrow would bring good news and heal old wounds. In the aftermath of their joining, she'd been certain the past would be forgiven by the telling of it.

But three days ago she still hadn't been much different from the girl she had once been. She had still been that coward, and while she hadn't lied to herself as she had done then, she'd been every bit as naive, every bit as lacking in understanding of the things that drove men like Ari Gaon. Now she was immeasurably wiser, undeniably sadder.

The past would never be forgiven, couldn't be forgotten. It would always be with them, always be between them.

But one thing could be grasped at, and that was this one moment in his arms. Here she was no longer naive, here she was no longer *young*. Here, in this one place, she didn't have to fear that she had no answering passion within her. She had it and to spare. For all Ari had to do was whisper her name, touch her face, brush her lips with his own, and a fiery liquid injected into her veins, swept her heart and cleansed her mind. She gave herself to his embrace, to his kisses, to his pressure against her, as if in a torrent of expiation for the past, as if making up for every minute of the lost time.

It was Ari who pulled back, holding her from him, drawing harsh, shallow breaths in the cool night air. He held her at arm's length, his elbows locked, the muscles on his arms hard and rigid, showing the depth of control he was using to keep them apart. His face was contorted, and his mouth was drawn into a grimace of pain. When he spoke, it was with words Sara didn't understand.

"No! I must be insane!"

He turned away from her, slamming a fist against the stuccoed wall of the nursery. Still without looking at her, he reached his hand around the corner and flicked on a switch. Instantly their dark alcove was awash with golden light. It pooled around them like water, but Sara shivered in the glow as she saw Ari's hard profile.

She felt wholly exposed, her breasts still quivering with want, her legs shaking. Around her feet, dropped when he'd kissed her, forgotten in the shuddering arousal he inspired in her, were the photographs of Ari and Danny.

"I've had enough of the dark," Ari said harshly. He turned. The stark anguish on his face slapped at her, hurt her. "I feel as if I've lived in the dark for eighteen years. No more, Sara. No more."

Sara couldn't speak. She felt as if all the blood in her were draining into the ground she stood upon, pouring out and onto the photographs at her feet. Life's blood. Love's.

As if reading her thoughts, he slowly lowered his eyes to the ground, took in the pictures. Slowly he stooped to pick them up, and then carefully dusting them off against his thigh, he studied them one by one, then went through them again. He smiled bitterly at the one of a laughing Danny, and wiped his face clear of all expression when he studied the one of himself looking at his son passing by.

Finally he glanced up and met Sara's eyes. His own were bleak, and all traces of desire had vanished. Obviously misunderstanding her completely, he stared at her.

"What have you done, Sara? What in God's name have you done?"

Chapter 7

Moshe Ben Eban heard the boy enter his rooms, but didn't look up. He knew who it was, just as he had always known when Sara had stolen out to sit beside him on the sunny hillsides he'd tried to paint so long ago. He couldn't have said how he knew, he just did; it was like knowing whether or not the sun was shining, whether or not there was goodness in the world.

At Hannah's suggestion, he'd started this portrait last night, long after the kibbutz was down for the night, the low drone of patrol planes accompanying his light strokes. He wondered what the boy would make of it.

He added a touch of burnt umber to Danny's hair, then another dab of black. Slowly, carefully, he blended them with deft, light jabs of his narrow brush. Beneath his brush, Danny's hair came alive, curling tightly, capturing a bright ray of sunlight.

"How can you do that, when I wasn't even here?" the boy's voice intruded.

Moshe didn't answer, cocking his head the better to see the portrait of the boy. It was a good one, one of his more promising efforts. He glanced at another one on an easel nearby, another good portrait, of Ari Gaon, done almost twenty years ago. It looked like the boy behind him. The chin was different, he decided, and possibly the flare of the nostrils, but the similarities were startling.

He heard the boy come closer, felt him standing just beyond his shoulder, understood his wariness.

"It's good," Danny said finally. He didn't comment on the subject matter. After a few minutes, he said, "But I still don't get how you can do it without a model . . . or even a picture."

Moshe continued highlighting Danny's hair. Fifty years ago, when he was a young apprentice to a master artist, Alexei Kagarlitsky, he had asked the same question. "Memory," the master had said, "is the best artist. Only from memory can the real feeling be drawn."

Moshe didn't feel it necessary to mention the sheaf of photographs Sara had left with him.

With a deliberate, tantalizingly slow gesture, he cleaned his brush, set it aside, and wiped his hands on his faded flannel apron. Pressing a hand to his back, he arched, groaned and stepped away from the easel.

This was part of the game they played, he and this boy of Sara's, this boy of Ari's: the boy asking questions, the old friend cum grandfather not answering until finished with whatever project had served as an opening for them. Hannah had accused him of playing Pied Piper to the boy.

Now Moshe turned to him. "Always you are coming in here, interrupting my work, and acting like a little bird in spring, chattering, questioning, chattering more."

Danny grinned, as Moshe had known he would, as his mother before him had smiled. Undaunted by Moshe's gruffness, the boy sought him out. In the past three days they had become friends. They hadn't talked of Sara and Ari, except indirectly. No, for the past three days, they had talked of everything else, Jason Gould often, tales of Israel, the friends Danny had met at Kibbutz Golan, and the boy's dreams.

Moshe suspected that to the boy he was a link to his past, a hold to the present. He also knew that in the boy's mind he, Moshe, was an outsider, was a knowledgeable but distant participant in the events that were so strongly and harshly governing the child now.

But the time had come to confront the past. Moshe felt he owed it to the years of knowing Ari, the years of wondering about Sara. He pushed their little game to a new level.

"You are like your mother was," Moshe said. "I used to call her 'little swallow.'"

"Because she chattered and interrupted?" Danny asked, smiling.

"Partially."

"Why then?"

"I called your mother a little swallow because, like the bird I named her after, she wanted to fly free and unfettered, never landing, except out of necessity."

Like his mother—and his father—before him, the boy took in the meaning of Moshe's words swiftly. "You're saying that's why my mother didn't stick around." A touch of stiffness crept into the boy's voice.

Moshe didn't respond directly. "There is a song about a calf and a swallow that we sing here in Israel. Perhaps you know it? No? No matter. In the song the calf is slaughtered, the swallow is free. I believed then that your mother was so afraid of becoming a calf that she forced herself to be a swallow."

As quick as ever, the boy jumped to a conclusion. "You believed *then*, but now you don't?"

Moshe smiled, proud of the boy, sad for the father and mother. "It turns out that I was wrong. I think she was really so afraid of being an *eagle* that she turned swallow in self-defense."

"An eagle?" Danny mused. "Yeah, that fits her. Dad, Jason, told me once she could be a real spitfire when she got worked up. She never really showed that side to me, though."

"A spitfire," Moshe said thoughtfully. "It's too bad she doesn't show some of that right now."

"Why?" Danny asked.

"Oh, it might clear the air," Moshe said, looking at the boy as if he'd just realized whom he was talking to. As he'd intended, Danny didn't want to brush the subject aside.

"Clear the air of what, for what?"

"Between your father and Sara," Moshe answered. "Maybe between you all."

Danny looked away, his mouth tightening, his shoulders tensing. "It doesn't seem like there's a whole lot of air left to clear. I mean, it's all out in the open now, isn't it?"

"Not all," Moshe said quietly.

"I know who he is, he knows who I am. What else is there to know?" Danny asked shortly.

"You see that portrait of your father over there—"

"I wish you'd stop calling him that," Danny burst out, interrupting Moshe. "He's no more my *father* than that chair is. *My* father is *dead*."

"Jason Gould is dead. Ari Gaon is very much alive."

"I'm sorry, but that doesn't mean a whole lot to me."

"Perhaps not," Moshe said. "But it means a whole lot to your mother."

"What? Why?"

"Because I believe, and so does Hannah, that she still loves your father, that he still loves her."

"What! You've gotta be crazy. How could she love him after what he did to her?"

"And what did he do to her, Danny?"

Danny stared at him with open disgust. "How can you even ask that? He knocked her up and then didn't even bother to find out about it! And you think she could still love somebody like that? Forget it!"

"A rather crude way of putting it, Danny. And not the whole story."

"It is the only part of the story that means anything to me."

"Why?" When the boy didn't answer, Moshe pressed his point. "Why should that be the only part of the story you want to know about? Because you think that way you won't have to get to know him? That you won't discover your father is human, after all? Or your mother?"

"Oh, she's human enough. She used to ground me for lying. Pretty ironic when you think about it, isn't it? She pitches a lie for seventeen years, I don't see her staying in her room."

Moshe couldn't help but laugh, and his laughter brought a reluctant grin to the boy's face.

Danny said sheepishly, "You know what I mean."

"Yes, I do," Moshe said, still smiling. "But don't you think she is being punished?"

"No."

"You barely talk to her, you won't give the time of day to Ari Gaon. Ari won't see her. You don't think that's punishment?"

"Are you saying it's my fault she's sad right now? I told her I didn't blame her. I told her I still . . . you know, loved her."

"Hearing it and *feeling* it are two different things," Moshe said quietly.

"What does she want me to do? Jump around, a stupid grin on my face, telling everybody how *happy* I am that I've discovered a *daddy? Oh, Mommy, thank you for lying to me all those years, thank you for pulling a father out of your magic hat. I really, truly wanted one.* Is that what she wants? Is that what *you* want?"

Moshe looked at Danny for several minutes without speaking. He wasn't sure he could trust himself to. Finally, wiping his hands on his apron again, as if erasing the nastiness in the boy's speech, he sat down heavily.

"You should consider a career in acting, Danny," he said with some sincerity. "You obviously have a flair for the dramatic."

Danny flushed. Moshe suspected the color came as much from anger as from embarrassment.

"You know, Danny, eighteen years ago your mother came to me, blubbering, as full of silly nonsense as you are right now. But when she did, I sat with her quietly, encouraging her to pour out her troubled soul, and instead of challenging her, I soothed her, told her she was right to be worried, right to run, right to do whatever it was she thought she should do."

Moshe stopped his recital of the past, his mind reviewing his advice, reviewing what he knew now.

Finally he continued. "Unless someone really knows what he is talking about, it's usually a lot better to keep his big nose out of things."

"You're butting in now," Danny said, but with less rancor than had been in his voice before.

"Ah! But the situation is different now. I'm a crusty old man who can say anything he likes now. And this time I *know* what I am talking about."

"Just what are you saying?" Danny asked.

"I'm saying that for you to let your anger out on me is just fine, the way it should be, perhaps, but once you let it out, you need to go—"

"To him," Danny said with a jerk of his head at Ari's portrait.

Moshe shrugged. "Is that so difficult?"

"Yeah," Danny answered.

"Why? Haven't you the least curiosity?"

"Sure, I'm curious. Who wouldn't be?"

"Well, then?"

"You make it sound like curiosity and accepting all this go hand in hand."

"It's the first step, possibly," Moshe replied swiftly.

Danny took a turn around the small room, standing first before the half-finished portrait of himself, then the portrait of Ari.

He said reflectively, "In some ways, it kind of makes me mad to look so much like him."

Moshe smiled sadly. "Because that makes it harder to hate him?"

Danny nodded absently. "But also because it...I don't know, gives more emphasis...or something...to genetics. Do you know what I mean?"

He turned and looked directly into Moshe's eyes.

"I think so," Moshe said cautiously. "Because you look at it as an accident, a mistake, it doesn't seem fair that you should look so much like him, that his genes are obviously very strong in you."

Danny's face lightened somewhat. "Yeah. That's it. It doesn't seem fair."

"Would you like to see a portrait of your mother?" Without waiting for an answer, Moshe rose and moved to a large portfolio case leaning against his far wall. He made a pretense of searching for the watercolor of Danny's mother; he knew right where it was. Had always known.

"Ah, here it is," he said, pulling it out, blowing nonexistent dust from it. He propped it on the easel next to the one of Danny.

Danny said nothing, merely staring at the portrait of his young mother. Moshe studied it as well, though he knew it by heart.

She was smiling slightly, and still sported those ridiculous crushed daffodils in her hair. Her cheeks were flushed, and her eyes were bright with dreams. And she looked as though she were about to burst with the love inside her.

"She looks so happy," Danny said quietly, almost fearfully.

"She was happy," Moshe answered.

"She was really in love with him, wasn't she?"

Moshe, not looking at Danny, answered sadly, "Yes. I'd never seen anyone as much in love as your mother was."

"Did he love her that much, too?"

"Yes."

"Then why?" Danny burst out. "I mean, *how* could he have just let her go? How could she have gone?"

Moshe shook his head. "You'll have to ask your mother that. You'll have to ask Ari. And if neither of them can answer you, come back."

"You know, don't you?" Danny said.

Moshe shrugged this time. "Not everything, no. But enough. Too much, maybe."

"Tell me," Danny said.

Moshe looked at him, seeing him as if from a great distance.

He said slowly, "I think she came back here for your sake, Danny. And I think you owe it to her to ask her why."

"*My* sake?" Danny cried. "*My* sake!"

"Consider this, Danny. You are ready for life, now. You have known the love of a good man, the rearing of a good woman. But that man is dead now, and you need someone in your life."

"I've got my mother. That's enough."

"You are so sure of that?"

"I sure don't need *him*."

"How do you know that?" Moshe turned from the boy to the portrait. "Have you talked to him? Have you tried?"

"He didn't even *care* if she was pregnant! He didn't ever even *ask!*"

"When your mother left, I believe the sky was never so blue for Ari again." When the boy didn't say anything, Moshe pressed the point. "Ari loved your mother, Danny. More, I think, than he loved this country—and believe me, that is considerable."

"Then why—?"

"Why didn't he follow her? Why didn't he chase her down, leave Israel and fly to the States, to insist that she marry him? She'd told him she didn't want him. She'd turned him down, son."

"But . . ."

"There are no buts in pride. A man feels he has nothing if he doesn't have his pride. And that was all that Ari had left."

"You're trying to make me feel sorry for him."

"No, I'm trying to make you understand the situation as it was."

"I'll never feel sorry for him," Danny said definitively, pointing at the portrait of Ari. "And I'll never understand him. He loved her, but he let her go."

Moshe shook his head. "You are so like him."

Danny froze, his finger still directed at the portrait.

"You are. You both feel so *intensely.* You both see things as right or wrong, no in-betweens. No middle, fuzzy areas, where things are neither good or bad, right or wrong."

Slowly Danny lowered his arm to his side.

"Your mother, on the other hand, is just the opposite. For her, for Sara, there are only shades of gray. There are only nuances, feelings, questions. For her, at least as she was, there were no absolutes. Or if there were, she never allowed them to consume her, the way they did him."

"I'm not like him," Danny said truculently.

"You are only hurting your mother by refusing to talk with him."

"It's *for* my mother that I haven't. I can't look at him and not see what my mother must have gone through because of him."

"Have you asked her about how she feels? Have you let her talk to you? You don't have to answer. I know. She has talked with me, too."

Danny looked at the floor. "I don't know what to say to her about it." He looked up. "Not that I hold it against her, or anything . . ."

"Don't you, Danny?" Moshe smiled slightly, remembering the boy's earlier words.

Apparently Danny remembered them, too. "Well, not much. I mean, it's not like I can't forgive her or anything." But the look in his eyes was that of a wild thing, trapped and fearful.

"Could it be that you won't talk to Ari, won't listen to your mother, because if you do not, you are gaining some measure of revenge for the years of having been lied to?"

"No!" Danny paced the room a moment, his body electric in its demand for physical expression. "That's not true. That's not true at all." But his eyes acknowledged the possibility of some measure of accuracy in Moshe's words. "Sure, I felt really weird when she told me about *him,* but . . ."

"But what, Danny? You weren't angry with her? You weren't angry at finding out that the man you loved as your father wasn't your father, after all? But what? You weren't upset over the fact that you'd been lied to all of your life?''

The trapped look in Danny's eyes evaporated as a quick anger surfaced. ''What is all this? What do you want from me?''

Moshe, afraid he'd pushed things too far, fearful that he might be doing Ari and Sara the greatest disservice with his interference, persevered, nonetheless. ''What do I want from you? I want you to see beyond the hurt, boy, see beyond the shock. I want you to *understand* that love doesn't always work the way we want it to, that people make *mistakes*.''

''Mistakes? You call this a mistake?'' Danny jabbed a finger at his own chest.

''No, I call you a miracle. I call what your father and mother did to each other a mistake.''

This struck Danny dumb. He gaped at Moshe, a slow, red flush sweeping up his cheeks, staining them. The embarrassed face before him made Moshe sad, made him hurt in so many, many ways. Years before Sara had stood before him, tears on her golden cheeks, her heart in tatters. Then he had done nothing, had said the wrong things.

''Give them a chance, Danny.''

''A chance to what?''

''Give them a chance to correct those mistakes. You know the truth now. You know how much your mother loves you. You know how much your father wants to get to know you.''

''Why?''

''Why what?''

''Why does he want to get to know me? He doesn't know anything about me. I'm just some kid. Just somebody he . . . somebody he doesn't even know.''

''Exactly. But you're *his* somebody. You're *his* kid. You're the son he always wanted, but never had.''

''Well, he could have had more.''

''He had a daughter.''

''So, see?''

''She died.''

''She died,'' Danny said slowly, then, as if struck, he added, ''She would have been my sister. Half sister.''

''Her name was Galit. She was a delightful minx.''

''How did she die?''

"A bomb was in the vehicle they were traveling in. Ari's wife, daughter and thirteen others were killed."

Slowly Danny added, "And his father was killed a long time ago."

"Yes," Moshe said. He felt inexpressibly aged at that moment. "They are all dead. Ari's family. Except for you."

Danny walked up to the portrait and stared down at it for a long time without speaking. Finally he raised his head and met Moshe's eyes.

Speaking deliberately, he asked, "Did you do this—this portrait, this making me mad, all this stuff—on purpose?"

Moshe smiled somewhat sheepishly. "Yes," he answered.

"Why? I mean, what's it to you?"

"A debt, Danny. A debt."

Danny met his eyes levelly. His brow furrowed in a frown. "To Ari Gaon?"

"And to Sara," Moshe answered. And to Sara, his heart echoed.

"And getting me to talk about this with Mom, getting me to talk with Ar—my father—puts paid to this debt?"

Moshe felt his lips curl into a bitter smile. "Partially, Danny. Only very partially."

"Will you tell me about that debt someday?"

"Probably not," Moshe said, sitting down upon his stool. "Very probably not."

Whatever Danny said next was lost as the kibbutz alarm sounded, its high-pitched Klaxon screaming the warning to arm, the warning to take cover.

Moshe pushed Danny out the door of his first-floor rooms and held him back against the outside wall.

The siren was even louder outside, and all around them people responded to the call, donning weapons, herding children, abandoning tractors and fences. Some were wearing shorts, others loose cotton dresses, some army fatigues, but all were fully alert, eyes on the gates or on the clear, empty skies, looking, waiting, ready.

"*Maze?*" Moshe called to a young man running past. "What's going on?" The young man didn't pause, but gave an elaborate shrug of his shoulders, and called out that someone had been spotted in the trees beyond the fence.

The siren ended as abruptly as it had begun, but none of the people seemed to notice. They continued to probe the skies and hillsides, seeking the danger the siren portended.

"Do you have an Uzi?" Danny asked Moshe.

Moshe turned to look at the boy. "What do you want with an Uzi?"

"I know how to use it," Danny said shortly.

Moshe studied him for scarcely more than three seconds, then nodded, jerking his head back toward his rooms. Danny bolted through the still-open doorway. "Bring me one, too," Moshe called.

Danny reappeared in seconds, handing Moshe one of the deadly submachine guns, while expertly swinging the other over his shoulder. Under Moshe's approving eye, Danny quickly checked the weapon out, released the safety, then held it against him, relaxed and easy, as if he carried such weapons every day.

"Danny!" called a male voice.

"Over here!" Danny called back.

Shlomo Havinot stepped from the doorway of a barnlike building, pointing to the other side.

Almost to Moshe's amusement—in any other situation Danny's answering pantomime would have been funny—Danny pointed to himself and then, as Shlomo had done, to the far side of the building. The boy broke away from Moshe and ran in a crouched zigzag, darting across the lawn, until he reached the far side. Nodding to each other, one boy at either end of the barn, both whipped out and around the corners, disappearing from Moshe's sight.

Moshe followed more slowly, and possibly with more caution. If, he thought sourly, caution was synonymous with irritated corns on both of his feet. A burst of rapid gunfire from up ahead drove all thought of pain from his mind and he ran.

By the time he'd caught up with them, the quick battle was over and Danny and Shlomo were both unharmed, though pale. On the other side of the tall, chain-link fence lay a figure, face hidden in the grass, dark splotches on his clothing, his gun now some three feet from his body. He was yelling obscenities.

"What was it? What happened?" Moshe asked, joining the throng around the two young men.

Answers rained upon his ears from all sides.

"He was running at the fence—"

"Shooting at the kibbutz—"

"Screaming he will kill us all—"

"Did he have explosives?"

"Who is he?"

"Syrian, look at his face, look at his—"

"He's wearing a Syrian army uniform."

"Is he dead? Who stopped him?"

Guards from the gate far to their left loped along the fence line until they reached the rocking figure. One confiscated the abandoned weapon, while another knelt over the frankly abusive intruder.

For a brief period, both inside and outside the fence, everyone seemed to be talking at once, arguing, explaining, questioning, answering.

"He's alive," one guard called, signaling for the others to search the nearby area.

"Explosives!" another explained, stooping to pick up a canvas bag that bulged ominously.

"A bomb!" yelled someone from Moshe and Danny's side of the fence.

A quick, derisive denial followed. The guards on the outside quickly checked for identification, and finding none—as Moshe knew was common with single sniper or explosive attacks—swiftly cleared the area of the still-screaming man, and the would-be killer's effects.

Looking around at the gathered group of people, then back to the strip of grass where the man had fallen, Moshe thought that with the exception of the weapons in people's hands, and ignoring the strained look of high excitement on Danny's face, it would be impossible to guess that the entire kibbutz had been mobilized, that a potential murderer was now in custody. Hardest to believe was the fact that Danny had been involved in halting the danger, in stopping the would-be killer.

He studied the boy with new respect and no little approbation.

"They spotted him in the trees," Shlomo was saying, pointing across the way to a thicket of young, full trees. "But we were ready."

"I couldn't believe it when he ran for the fence like that," Danny said. His voice was high and tight. His eyes shot to the now-empty fence line. "Right out in the open." A pause. "Why did he?"

"He was probably expecting us to panic and run." Shlomo laughed. "He didn't know what he was up against.... What did you call us, the dynamic duo?"

Danny flushed again. "Yeah, that's it."

Shlomo laughed again, clapping a hand onto Danny's shoulder. He had to reach up to do it, Moshe noticed.

In contrast to Danny, who had two small dots of color on his otherwise white cheeks, Shlomo looked as though he ran after weapon-carrying intruders every day. Yet, when Moshe looked closely, he could see a curious expression on the boy's face, almost a look of vindication. It was gone as soon as Shlomo's eyes met Moshe's, and the old man nonetheless felt a small chill work its way over his arms and down his back.

It was one thing to defend one's home, he thought sadly, but entirely a different matter when one felt ennobled by killing for it. Nobility and killing should not travel in the same vehicle. Moshe shook his head. It wasn't that he thought the boy had enjoyed it, but rather as if the injuries the man had sustained were to be listed on some cosmic tally card, with Shlomo able to decide which side was right and which was wrong.

More people had joined them by now, asking questions, congratulating Shlomo and Danny for a clever, defensive attack.

Out of the corner of his eye, Moshe watched as from two different directions Ari and Sara reached the circle around Danny. As one the group stood back to accommodate the director.

Ari stepped forward, standing within inches of Danny, and Moshe saw several puzzled glances from Ari to Danny and back again.

Though taller and slimmer, and his hair still jet black, Danny looked enough like Ari for it to be undeniably obvious they were related. A few eyes traveled to where Sara stood, one hand at her mouth, as if holding in some cry, the other clenching and unclenching at her side. Moshe could see that her breasts were rising and falling rapidly; she'd obviously run here.

* * *

Sara listened, her heart pounding in her ears, thudding painfully in her chest. *Danny,* she cried inside. When she'd heard the gunfire, she'd immediately run to her window. The view framed the tense scene below. She had screamed, uselessly, when she recognized her son as one of the two young people, armed, crouching, and making for the fence. She'd also seen the lone running figure open fire.

Powerless to stop it and terrified, certain her son was about to be killed, she'd abandoned her post at the window and had all but flown down the steps and out the back door of Alef. When the gunfire stopped, for an agonizing moment so did her heart. She ran as if propelled by rocket fuel rather than shaking legs and bare feet.

"And that's all there was to it," Shlomo was finishing. She had listened, but hadn't heard, hadn't understood any of what he'd said.

She noticed that Ari, too, seemed to be having some difficulty in comprehending what had transpired. Like hers, his chest was rising and falling rapidly. His hands, too, were clenched into tight fists.

Shlomo threw his arm around Danny's shoulder. "He understood exactly what I had in mind," Shlomo said. The first touch of excitement crept into his voice. "It was almost like he could read my thoughts."

Sara shuddered as Shlomo grinned, rubbing his knuckles across Danny's head. "Someday you'll have to show me how you rolled over those barrels there and ended on your feet, your gun already up and ready to fire!"

"Anytime," Danny said, Shlomo's enthusiasm driving some color into his face and hands. A shy grin flashed. "It's dead easy."

"Where did you get the gun?" Ari asked quietly.

Something in Danny's face died. Despite her fear for him, despite the fact she'd been asking herself the same question, Sara wanted to rail at Ari for putting an end to the moment of unguarded excitement.

"I borrowed it," Danny said, not meeting Ari's eyes, looking at the ground.

"I gave it to him," Moshe admitted.

Sara looked at him in horror.

"You *gave* him an *Uzi?*" she croaked. "How could you? He might have been killed!"

Moshe didn't say a word, and Sara wanted to scream at him for the sympathy that was so evident on his old face.

"He wasn't killed, Sara," Ari observed coldly.

Sara flicked him a dismissive glance, then turned her eyes back to Moshe. "But he might have been. How could you have given him a gun?"

"Drop it, Sara," Ari told her firmly.

She started to ignore his command, her mouth open to remonstrate, when his hand circled her upper arm and he pulled her to the side.

"Danny did what he thought was right," Ari said softly. "You are embarrassing him. Whatever he needs to be told about this will be said *later.* Not in front of everyone."

"But Ari—"

"That's enough, Sara." Ari's tone carried the command of the kibbutz. "Moshe did what he had to do. So did Danny." He dropped her arm and turned back to Shlomo and Danny.

"You've both saved countless lives by your actions. I'm not saying I wholeheartedly approve of nonkibbutz members—Americans, at that—having such access to kibbutz weapons, but I can't fault what you did."

Sara's instinctive terror for her son, checked by Ari's reproof, ebbed thoroughly as she watched her son's eyes rise to meet his father's with probing intensity.

Something passed between then. An intangible, yet palpable message. She knew she wasn't the only one to feel it. The crowd around them was strangely and uncharacteristically silent.

Finally Ari spoke again. Sara noticed that his voice was slightly unsteady.

"We can all be proud this day. No deaths, no explosions."

The crowd cheered.

Beneath the cheering, Sara heard Ari speak again, this time to Danny alone, but she couldn't make out the words. She saw Danny flush, not with embarrassment now, but with an exultant pride. His gaze met his father's, shyly now.

Ari said something else, and Danny looked down at his feet, a small smile curving his lips. Sara could see that her son wanted to say something else, but in this scary and tentative truce with the man he'd sworn he'd never respond to, in the heat of victory, he couldn't. Perhaps if there hadn't been so many people around them, perhaps if his mother hadn't been present, he might have said more.

As the crowd's raucous recounting of the events and praise of such quick action died down, Sara could hear Ari speaking once more.

"Where did you learn such things?" he asked.

Danny mumbled a few names that Sara knew would mean little to the assembled group, but had meant years of concentrated training to her son.

"Would you show us some of them?"

Danny met his father's eyes again. Sara suspected that despite the earlier locking of gazes, this was the first time Danny really *saw* his father as a person. Not as the kibbutz director, not as his mother's lover from the past, nor as a cardboard villain out to wrest his previous misconceptions from him.

"I'd like that," he said quietly.

Sara held her breath, tears coming to her eyes, a strange pang in her heart.

"So would I," Ari said, equally quietly, his words infused with other meaning. "So would I."

Sara sat on the edge of the small pond, her feet just skimming the surface, creating ripples that slowly stretched across the water. The ripples glimmered in the late-afternoon light, reflecting the orange sky, fluid, like her mind. Though her thoughts were chaotic, jumbled and insistent, she felt she couldn't really have been said to be thinking. She was merely trying to create some semblance of order out of the chaos.

One minute so peaceful, so quiet that one might be on an Iowa farm. The next, gunfire, her son responsible for another man's injuries. If he'd been hit any higher, it would have been his death. And if the man had hit Danny? She felt ill at the thought.

Hating the path that line of thought was taking, she jumped as another flashed into her head: when had Danny become a man? Perhaps, she mused, there were moments when every parent encountered the adult in his or her child.

Another flash, another thought. She couldn't condone the violence, the use of weaponry, but how many more might have died had her son not acted so quickly, so instinctively, impulsively? How many more might have been hurt? Intermingled with her concern was the inevitable pride. And he had managed to do this without killing the Syrian.

And finally, the spiraling, coalescing linking of the thoughts: the look on Danny's face... the excitement, the satisfaction, the flush of victory. It was a man's look, not a boy's. When had he grown up? The other morning? Last year? Today?

That led, as always, finally and utterly back to Ari. Ari, who had taken her son's part, had backed him up and finally breached the high wall separating father and son, if only by adding another layer of brick to the wall between her and himself. Despite the horrible pain in her heart when he'd looked at her so coldly, had spoken so callously, she couldn't begrudge him that moment.

He'd asked her the night before what she had done. "What in God's name have you done?" He hadn't waited for her answer, and Sara had believed then that she didn't know. Now she knew. She had offered Ari his son. She had traveled thousands of miles and eighteen years, and in a brief, split second of awareness beneath a blazing sun, in fear and concern she had passed the boy to the man. Where would it lead, where would it end?

"Are you still speaking to me?"

She looked up at Moshe's lined face. "After this morning I thought it might be the other way around."

Slowly, with obvious discomfort, Moshe lowered himself to the ground to sit beside her. His feet, clad in thick, broad sandals, did not go into the water, though the look on his face said he would rather that they did.

"Are you still angry with me?" he asked finally.

"No," Sara said, honestly.

"He's very like Ari."

Sara felt a bitter smile on her lips. "Yes," she agreed.

"I don't mean in looks, though he is that, too."

"I know," she said.

"You *are* angry."

She turned at that. "No, Moshe. I'm not angry. I wasn't even all that angry then. I was scared. Mother scared. There's a difference."

"They interrogated the intruder," he went on, changing the subject. "He's from the village of Na'asum. Apparently his brother was killed last month."

"He looked like a boy," Sara said.

"He's almost twenty," Moshe answered. "It seems the P.L.O. is setting up a headquarters in Na'asum."

"Is that far from here?" she asked.

"As the crow flies, only thirty kilometers. Even I could walk it."

"So close," she said.

"You forget, Israel is not very large."

"No," she said, agreeing.

"Ari is very proud of his son today," Moshe added, turning the conversation once more.

"Yes," Sara said dully.

"This worries you?" Moshe asked.

Sara smiled wanly. "As Danny would say, it makes me feel funky."

"Why?"

"When did you pick up a degree in psychiatry, Moshe?"

He chuckled. "All painters hold degrees in psychology, at least. We're too crazy to go into anything else. And old painters have the best shoulders of all. So why do you feel funky, Sara?"

Sara didn't answer directly. "When he was first born, Jason was right there. From that moment on. I suppose in some fashion, in some recess of my brain, I'll always associate Danny with Jason."

"But you associate him with Ari also. No?"

She met his eyes for a brief moment, then looked away. "It's funny, but back in the States, sometimes I'd look at him, hear him say something just like his father—just like Ari—and it would sweep over me, make me want to..."

"Want to...what?"

Sara sighed. "I don't know. Cry. Scream. Anything. Every day it seemed more and more obvious that he was Ari's son. And even though Jason knew, I'd feel so terribly, terribly guilty. Not over Jason, but over Danny, over not telling him. Over Ari. Wondering if I ever could tell him. But now that we're here, now that Ari and Danny both know, their similarities, oddly enough, didn't seem as glaring. Until this morning."

"I don't think I'm following you, Sara," he said.

"Perhaps because the truth was out, I didn't feel the need to constantly watch for Ari on Danny's face. Maybe I just haven't looked very closely the past few days."

"And perhaps you feel so strangely because you are not certain you want Danny to be close to Ari?"

Sara thought about his words for some time before answering. When she did, she could see by the look on his face that he thought she lied.

"No, I don't believe that, though I've worried about it often enough. I think, now that Jason's gone, now that Danny is growing up—almost grown, he needs to get to know Ari."

"And Ari?"

"Needs to know Danny."

"No, I meant what about Ari . . . and you?" He was looking out across the water, his expression cautious.

Sara shook her head. "There isn't any more Ari and me. That was over years ago."

"For whom?"

"For Ari, for me. Not telling him about Danny served as the final blow, but the relationship was dead already."

"Says you."

"Ari would agree, I believe."

Moshe pushed himself to his feet and held out his hand to her. He drew her to her feet, waited while she donned her shoes, then linked her hand through his arm and led her in the direction of the dormitories. "You know, little swallow, for an intelligent woman, you certainly manage to overlook a lot of facts."

"Such as?"

"Such as Ari Gaon is so torn up with love for you that he can hardly think, let alone act."

Sara smiled wistfully. "I wish that were true, Moshe."

"It's true, Sara."

"No. No, it's not true, Moshe. I should know."

"Why don't you ask him?"

Sara stopped and put her hands onto Moshe's broad shoulders. "Moshe, you are a dear friend. You always have been. You always will be."

She paused, as a funny spasm crossed Moshe's features. It was gone in the amount of time it took to happen. Sara looked a question, but he shook his head slightly, raising his hands to cover hers.

"Go on. You were about to add a but to that declaration of undying friendship."

Sara smiled, relieved. "I was only going to say, *but* you're as wrong as you can be about this. What good would it possibly do to ask Ari if he still loved me?"

"You might hear the truth," Moshe said promptly.

Their stroll had taken them to the makeshift doors and walls of Building Alef. Sara surveyed the plywood nailed into place before answering. "Oh, the truth. I think there's probably been enough truths exposed in the past few days to last a lifetime."

"There's never enough truth," Moshe declared firmly. "Ask him, Sara." He pulled open the plywood sheet that served as a door and guided her inside, drawing her to a sofa grouping against the far wall.

His painting was back in place, she noted irrelevantly. And yet was the observation so irrelevant? The picture was a silent testimony to the fact that some things never changed. Plywood might stand where just a few days earlier there had been glass, Ari and Danny knew about each other now, had exchanged the first, tentative words of truce between them. And she had been made to confront the past, confront the two people who meant the world to her. If only it were the intangibles, like love, like dreams, that remained and not the concrete, tangible results of past events.

"...don't you think you owe it to him, to yourself?" Moshe was asking.

"What? I'm sorry," she apologized. "My mind slipped off somewhere."

"Don't you think you owe it Ari to talk with him about this? About how you feel, about how he feels?"

Sara considered his words, then shook her head.

"Owe it? No. I don't owe Ari Gaon anything. Not anymore. Possibly not ever. Whatever guilt I felt, whatever guilt I might still feel over Danny, is not something I *owe* Ari. I made my decision years ago. I didn't make it lightly, Moshe. I may have made a mistake, probably did. But that doesn't mean I *owe* Ari anything because of it. Danny, possibly, Danny, yes. But not Ari."

"What about yourself?" At her puzzled frown, he continued. "You still love him, don't you? Don't you?"

"Maybe. Yes. I don't know anymore. All those years I'd have said yes, I'd always love him. The other night—" She broke off with a quick blush, glancing at Moshe's dispassionate expression and then continued bravely. "I was certain that I did, that everything could be worked out."

"And why can't it now?"

"You saw his expression that morning. You heard what he said. He'll never forgive me those eighteen years."

"Are you so sure of that?" Moshe asked quietly.

"Oh, Moshe, of course I'm sure. He doesn't want explanations, he doesn't want to know the background, the reasons for the decisions. He only wants absolutes."

"Yes," Moshe said slowly. "Danny and I were talking about that, just this morning. How much the two of them are alike. They both are people of polarities."

"Polarities? Yes, that's right. Well, that says it all, doesn't it?"

"How so, my dear?"

"Love...hate. To forgive...or to revile. There have never been in-betweens for Ari. That's one reason I didn't stay all those years ago. I thought we were so different. Now I wonder if we're not too much alike. That's one reason why we can't work it out now."

Moshe shook his head slowly. Sadly, Sara thought.

"Yes," she said wearily. "You see, Moshe, even if he did love me, as you claim, it wouldn't change anything. The whole past still stands between us. The very thing that should have brought us together, Danny, a son that we created, will always serve to keep us apart. I couldn't live with him, couldn't see him daily and know that he had never understood, never forgiven me for Danny. Or for leaving him."

Moshe pushed to his feet and stood over her.

"Is it Ari that you want forgiveness from...or yourself?"

Sara felt as though she'd been physically shaken. Her thoughts focused on his words with awful suspicion.

"Perhaps, as you said, you are more like him than you know, little swallow. Perhaps you, too, have your polarities, only in your case you internalize them, you judge yourself." He bent down to kiss her cheek. "Think about it, Sara. Think *hard*. Your whole life...and Ari's...depends upon what you decide to do *now*."

With that he turned, walked briskly to the door and out.
Somewhat weakly, Sara rose also and turned to go upstairs.
She stopped dead as a surge of adrenaline shot up her body
and then back down again, leaving her dizzy.

Ari stood not four paces from her, watching her with a
martial look in his deep, gray eyes. How long had he been
there? How much had he heard? Desperately Sara cast her
mind over the conversation with Moshe.

"So, Sara," he said in a tone of fierce control. "You think
I don't want explanations, that I won't understand. Try me."

Struck by painful dismay, she realized he'd heard everything.

"Now seems a good time, Sara," he said, walking forward,
taking her arm and pushing her, not terribly gently, back into
the chair she'd so recently vacated.

He, too, sat down, pulling a chair around until it blocked
any hope of escape.

Chapter 8

What could she possibly say to him that hadn't already been said? She'd seen—*felt*—the anger, the implacable fury he'd projected at her when he first found out about Danny; she'd heard the unmistakable ring of revulsion in his voice just before he'd walked away from her in the nursery garden that night. *What in God's name have you done, Sara?* She'd seen the chill in his eyes this morning before his first rapprochement with Danny.

And this was all from the present, didn't even touch the wounds of the past, the wounds he hadn't forgotten.

He'd never forgive her, even if he could forget. And if he could forgive... he'd never forget. Because he was a man of black and white, a man of absolutes.

Unless...

Moshe's words settled heavily upon her heart. *What if Moshe was right? What if the capacity for forgiveness lay within herself?* Was there a modicum of hope?

"Talk to me, Sara," Ari said now, leaning forward, his expression guarded, his deep, gray eyes fierce and unyielding. His forearms rested upon his thighs, his hands dangling loose, too near her legs for comfort. One flick of a finger and he would touch her, and if he touched her, she would scream, would cry, would fly apart, as surely as the glass had flown from the windows only days before.

"Sara . . . ?"

"What do you want me to say, Ari? That I'm sorry? That I've made mistakes? We've said it all."

A bitter smile twisted his lips. He looked down at his empty hands for a moment, turning them, looking at them as if they were a stranger's hands.

"You know, in some ways we are lucky, you and I."

"Lucky?" Sara asked blankly.

"Yes. Most people . . . most *lovers* . . . have to grow up together, learning life's lessons, sharing every joy and pain. And so often, that very familiarity makes people grow apart, bores them."

He looked up at her finally.

"But you and I, Sara, we grew up apart, we learned those lessons in different settings, with different people. So that now, here, we are lovers and strangers all at once."

He paused, meeting her eyes with a cold detachment. The very fact that he could sit there, talking so calmly of things that ripped her apart, that had ripped him apart, sent a chill down her spine. Ari couldn't be that changed, that different.

"And since I believe now that strangers is all we're ever likely to be, I think we can safely talk about the past."

"Strangers . . ." she repeated. *All they would ever be.* Did he really believe that? Could he? The words settled coldly into her soul.

"I heard what Moshe said about polarities. He implied that I judge others, while you judge yourself."

Even as he spoke, a flash of anger lighted his face, but he controlled it almost immediately.

He continued. "I've never been one to give too much time to self-analysis, Sara, so maybe he's right. It doesn't matter. All I want to know now is the real reason why you left. Why you didn't tell me about Danny. Why you took so long to let me find out."

"I told you that," she said. "I *told* you in the garden."

"No, you fed me a bunch of crap about being young, too young to know your own mind, too young to handle a love you'd sworn was greater than the wind, stronger than the ocean. Those were your words, Sara. That's what you called your love for me."

His expression was fierce now. Oddly, it made her more comfortable than the cold control he'd shown her earlier. This was the Ari she knew, and while he still made her uneasy— perhaps because he called up an answering anger—it was still a man's passion she recognized.

"I didn't lie," she said between her teeth.

"I'm not talking about lying, Sara! I'm talking about hard facts. You told me one thing, you did another. You took the best part of me, Sara, and then you raised my son, without ever letting me know about him."

"That was *my* decision!" she snapped, shaking inside, feeling a dangerous uncoiling of a long-withheld anger.

"Is that what it was all about, Sara? You wanted to feel you had a *say* about something? You wanted to take some kind of a *stand*? So you ran off and had *my* baby and then raised him, without even *telling* me about it?"

"Of course not," she retorted, but his words flayed her. Hadn't there been some of that?

She tried another tack. "Are you upset because I ran away or because I didn't *tell* you about Danny?"

"Both, damn it!" he yelled at her.

"I told you why I left, I told you that day. I told you in the garden. You *know* why I left!"

"Then you've been kidding yourself, Sara. You didn't leave me because I had so much intensity that I would burn you up, you didn't leave because you were afraid of my condemnation. You left because you were afraid, all right, but it was because you were afraid you were *just like me!*"

The world shifted crazily for a moment. "No," she said faintly. "No..." For the hundredth time in the past few days, Sara felt as if she'd been slapped.

"That's right, Sara. You have that same burning passion for causes, for justice, for loving and living. You can't hide it any more than I can. The only difference is, I don't try to deny it."

Was he right? Dear God, was he right? A thousand different conversations shot through her mind, snatches of Jason's, of Moshe's, of Hannah's words. ... *too quick to judge...think first, act later... think with your heart...* Could he possibly be right? She could only stare at him, too shocked to do more than murmur a denial.

"Passion, Sara. I'm talking the passion for living, the passion for grabbing life and living every second of it. That's what we had together. That's what you left. That's what you couldn't stand."

"How dare you sit in judgment on me, Ari Gaon! No one has ever made me as angry as you have. No one has ever made me totally—" She broke off, aghast at what she'd been about to accuse him of.

"No one has ever made you totally what, Sara?" he asked with a deceptive coolness in his voice. "Totally a woman? Totally lose that rigid control of yours? No one else has ever made you totally aware of the passion in you?"

"Totally forget reality," she said with as much dignity as she could muster.

He stretched out his hand and lightly stroked her bare shoulder with the backs of his fingers. "This kind of reality, Sara?" he asked.

"Don't..." she whispered, feeling her skin break out in goose bumps, her head light.

"Don't what, Sara? Don't make you remember? Don't make you see that passion you have in you? Don't turn the key and unlock it for you?"

"Please..." she murmured. But whether she was asking him to stop or to go on, she couldn't have said.

"I don't know you, Sara," he said softly, raising a hand to caress her throat, the hollow behind her ear. "And you don't know me. We're strangers."

"You...said that's all...we'll ever...be." She couldn't draw in enough breath, and the light touch of his knuckles was driving all the air she had out of her lungs.

"Oh, yes..." he murmured back. "But what strangers."

"I...don't want to be...strangers."

"Why not, Sara? That's what you've made us."

She closed her eyes against the truth in his words. It had been *her* choice to leave all those years ago. And because of that choice they *were* strangers. Different. They would always be different.

Almost sadly he said, "I know that talk cannot eradicate the past, can't make it disappear. And I can't hide the fact that I'm confused, angry even. But talking about it would help me to understand it."

When she still said nothing, he shook her hands slightly.

"I'm not yelling at you now, Sara."

No, he wasn't yelling at her, he was hypnotizing her with his caress, with the feather-light touches that made her mind fly elsewhere and her body too aware of his proximity.

"Won't you talk to me?"

As if his hand against her skin and the scent of him opened some door in her, she found she could talk to him now. This was Ari, not a stranger. She could tell him anything. Especially now that he knew the worst.

Slowly she said, "If you only knew how badly I feel about the other morning, about your having to find out that way."

He smiled without humor. "It wasn't the smoothest of ways I could have found out, was it?"

"No," Sara said in a small voice.

"When I asked you to tell me about Danny's birth, about Jason, about your life…" He paused, drew a deep breath, and continued. "I wanted you to tell me about what was in your *heart,* Sara. What you *felt* about Danny, what you *dreamed* about with Jason. I wanted you to tell me if you had thought about me in all those years, if you had—had *felt* me thinking about you."

His hand gripped hers fiercely. He shook them again. "Tell me, Sara. Please … ?"

"It's hard to say what was in my *heart* at different times," she said finally. "Sometimes whole weeks would go by, when I didn't think of you at all, and then Danny would do something, say something that reminded me of you. And then you'd haunt me for days and days."

To her surprise he answered easily, "It was like that for me, too. Mostly in the spring. I'd see the flowers blooming and—"

"You'd remember the flower chains we'd made."

He nodded, smiling a little. This change of mood daunted her somewhat. It was so uncharacteristic of him to be so gentle, so nostalgic. But it made her feel as if he'd been right to say that strangers was all they would ever be. She didn't know this side of him. But she knew it made her sad that she didn't. It made her even sadder to think that she wouldn't.

Sara smiled wistfully and, trying to match his mood, she said, "One day, maybe five years ago, I remember … it was raining outside, that steady drizzle that seems to come in the early days of autumn. And I was home for some reason or another, I can't remember why, and I was just sitting by the window of our brownstone in Georgetown. Just sitting there, watching the rain running down the windows, and I realized that our time together had been so short that we had never even spent a rainy day together."

"It only rains in the winter in Israel," Ari said softly.

"I know," she answered sadly. "And that day, watching the rain, I remember thinking that it seemed terribly wrong that something that had happened so many years before and had been for so short a time should still have the ability to make me cry, to affect my thoughts."

"But you had a living reminder of that time," Ari commented. It wasn't said with rancor, but it shocked her nonetheless, made the guilt rise in her once again.

"Yes," she said, but she shook her head. "It was more than that. It was as if those days with you that spring and summer... it was as if they were a separate thing. All I had to do was think of you, and I would remember every moment, every day, everything you'd said to me, everything I'd said to you."

"Like they were mental videotapes," he said reflectively.

"Just like that," she answered. "To be played over and over again, sometimes making me smile, other times making me feel sad."

"I know," Ari said. "I know."

And Sara knew that he did. And she wondered if all first loves had that power, that incredible power to totally burn into memory every thought, every word, every touch of a time that had happened eighteen years earlier.

Why did this feel and sound as if they were saying farewell? As if now, now that they had yelled at one another, had lanced the festered wounds of the past, they could talk quietly, sweetly even, letting their last words together be kind ones?

"When we were together the other night," Ari said, bringing up their loving for the first time since that dreadful morning, "that was the first time that the memories subsided. It was as if only by touching you now that I could erase the past."

She had been right, she thought. This was farewell. This was the end of the story she'd kept locked in her heart for eighteen years. She looked at his face, at the sorrow and the regret etched in the fine lines. Yes, he was saying goodbye to her. The thought snuffed out the single flame of hope that had continued to flicker in her.

"It wasn't like that for me," she said slowly.

"No?"

"No." She didn't elaborate. She couldn't have. It had meant too much to her, had touched her too deeply.

"You tried to tell me about Danny that night, didn't you?" he asked.

"Yes."

"But I stopped you."

"Yes, but I should have gone ahead, anyway."

Ari shrugged. "Sara . . . if you hadn't been sent here, if you hadn't had to come to Israel, would you ever have told me?"

"I don't know," she said honestly. She felt as if she were standing around that tiny, snuffed hope, pulling at the wick, searching among the blackened strands for a glow.

"I'm glad I know about him now," he said.

"Me, too," she echoed. For a long while they said nothing. Sara couldn't shake the feeling that there was so much more to be said, to be exposed to the harsh light of the overhead bulbs, but with the bleak thought of goodbye in her mind, she couldn't utter the words that were in her heart.

"Why wouldn't you have told me?" Ari asked, his voice so low she had to lean forward to hear him.

She wanted to scream, *Never mind that now!* Either tell me you want me or tell me to go to hell, but don't sit here raking over the past, until I'm dying from it.

"Sara?"

She sighed. "Because I hadn't told you before he was born, because he was already grown . . . because it didn't seem fair to you to spring a fully grown son on you."

"I don't know why it is, but I feel as if my whole life has changed with knowing about him. Everything is different."

"Better . . . worse?"

"Different," he repeated. "Neither good nor bad. Just unalterably different."

His words provoked a bittersweet memory. "That is how I felt at the moment of his birth. That life had changed, that I had changed forever, and it was a strangely ambivalent feeling—Oh, I had no ambivalence toward Danny, none at all, I loved him absolutely—but life was now changed."

"Yes," he said. "That's it. That's how it feels."

His hand grazed her collarbone, then dipped lower and rose again. This was torture, she thought. Cruel torture.

"You haven't asked how I feel about you, Sara."

Her heart constricted and she caught her breath.

"I don't think I want to hear this," she murmured.

"Why not?"

"Don't, Ari."

He ignored her, tightening his hand around hers even more. But this time Sara returned the pressure.

He closed his eyes swiftly, pulling in his breath with a hiss, then opened his eyes and met her gaze. In the depths of gray she could read hope, uncertainty and that raw vulnerability he'd allowed her to see on the night they'd lost themselves in each other.

"I'm more confused than I have ever been about someone before, Sara. You see, I told myself I never stopped loving you. Not once in all of those years. I loved my wife. She was a strong, fine woman. But I never loved her as I loved you. It was as if that part of loving, that part of me that could love without restraint, the best part of me, was reserved for you and you alone."

It was Sara who closed her eyes this time.

"And now you don't know?" she asked.

"And now I don't know. I'm not sure about anything anymore."

"Because of Danny... ?"

"Because of Danny, because of the past, because you came back and you're the same and yet so different."

Sara thought that whoever came up with that old saying about sticks and stones, and words never hurting, was a total idiot. Nothing hurt worse. She would rather be physically injured any day than live through this pain.

Ari looked down at the hands still clasped in his. Slowly, gently, he stroked the knuckles of her fingers, her slender wrist.

Finally, in a low monotone, he asked, "And if I said forget about what I think or feel about Danny, that the past makes no difference, that only the future matters... ?"

Slowly she shook her head.

"You wouldn't believe me."

He said it with such sadness that her heart, which she had thought damaged beyond repair, twisted to a new level of pain. Numb, she shook her head again.

"You believe I couldn't forgive you," he said.

"I wouldn't believe you, Ari, if you said you did," she said sadly. "No one could. Even if you forgave me, you could never *forget.*"

His thumb stilled, and so did her heart's erratic beating, then he resumed the mesmeric caress. His eyes rose to meet hers once more. "And if I said that I did? That I had?"

"I wouldn't believe you." She could scarcely see him now for the blur of tears.

"Sara," he said, his eyes not wavering. "You're right. I couldn't forget. That's impossible. All I have to do is look at Danny, think of Danny, and the whole past comes crashing in."

A wave of despair swept over her, through her, making her fingers twitch in his hands, making the tears she'd forced to remain quiescent rise to the surface. She heard the slam of the back door, recalling her to her surroundings, to their position, to the world. She blinked rapidly, trying to sit up.

He continued, ignoring whoever might have come or gone, the grip on her hands telling her he was not oblivious to her agony. "But Sara, it's not up to me to *forgive* you. You said it yourself. You did what you had to do. Right or wrong, good or bad, you made decisions and you carried them out. Right or *wrong,* Sara, I made my decisions, too. And I lived by those decisions, as well."

When she said nothing, completely stilled by the nuances of his words, he raised her hands to his lips and pressed a gentle, salutary kiss upon them. *This, then, is goodbye,* she thought.

"Danny said I was wrong to judge you, Sara. He was right. I can't judge you. I didn't follow you, I didn't try to find you. I didn't make it my business, my life, to know what had become of you."

The tears that had threatened to spill were checked and she blinked at him in uncertainty. *What was he saying?*

"Forgive? What the hell does that even mean? There is no *forgiveness* in loving, Sara. Whatever has been done has been done. Whatever happens as a result, happens."

Again he lifted her hands and shook them. "I can't forget, you said it yourself. No one could *forget,* but that doesn't mean that I can let you walk away from here without telling you that I want you. I want you now. I've always wanted you."

She stared at him, her heart thudding in a painful, half-hopeful rhythm. *What was he really saying?* She stilled, her breath catching in her throat. What more? How could she bear any more?

"You thought I wouldn't be able to forgive you, Sara. You think that. Can you...forgive me? Can you forgive me for not listening? For not understanding? For not trying to find you all those years ago? For letting you raise our son without me?"

She closed her eyes. Her back sagged into the cushions behind her, yet she didn't feel the pressure of the material. She felt disembodied. His words reached into the most vulnerable part of her heart and probed deeply. She had lived with the fear, the anger, the pain for so long now that she had almost forgotten their existence, had accepted them as parts of her life. *How had he known?*

"Ah," he said brokenly. "I was right."

Tears squeezed from beneath her tightly closed eyelids, coursing down her cheeks. She made no effort to check them now; they were healing tears, the release of a pain too long withheld, too deeply buried. They were the result of indecision and decisions made eighteen years ago.

"Don't cry, *leva sheli*. Of all things, don't cry," he said brokenly.

Her fingers were released abruptly, and she felt his warm, broad hands caressingly cupping her face, his thumbs brushing the tears away as rapidly as they fell. But his words encouraged a new wave of tears. He'd called her *my heart;* she'd never thought to hear those words again, had never thought to hear them said in just that way.

She opened her eyes and saw him through a blur that melded the glow of the overhead lamp with the silver highlights in his hair. Ari seemed to take up the entire room.

In his words, in his broken voice, she heard everything, *all* she had ever wanted to hear. She raised her own hands to his face, stroking the sun-burnished skin, the soft flesh at his temples, the curve of his working jaw. With the slightest of pressures, she drew him forward, while she herself leaned toward him.

They met, not with the wild passion, the fierce intensity that had always gripped them, but with the most gentle, most tender of kisses, tongues lightly touching, hands overlapping, spanning the distance between them, emotion spanning time.

Slowly, her heart renewing itself with the promise of his touch, she let him know how far she had traveled, how far she understood he had.

Hesitantly, lowering all barriers for her, he allowed her to know how deeply he was moved, how much he cared. Tongue met tongue, lip brushed lip, hands blended and clung together, pressing lightly, firmly against temples, bared throats.

The sound of young laughter made them start. Ari jerked his head around, his expression dazed, as if he had only just now remembered the bright, well-lit room. A young couple, eyes only for each other, made for the stairs and soon disappeared. They were gone, but the reminder was timely. Ari looked back at Sara somewhat ruefully.

Slowly, as if afraid to break the mood that hung over them, he rose, not releasing her hands. He drew her to her feet and without resistance pulled her forward.

"Come," he said.

She could not have refused if heaven had depended upon it. He expected her to go away, had called them strangers, had said "want," not "love," but this was the single ember of hope she'd been looking for. She *had* to go with him, had to know the touch of his hands upon her again. If only in farewell, in goodbye.

Willingly she followed, not up the broad stairs, as she had expected, but through the plywood doorway and across the dew-laden grass to Ari's rooms.

He paused as he depressed the handle on his door, looking across at her solemnly, a question in the now almost black depths of his eyes. She stepped through the doorway in answer and turned to meet him.

He flicked on the lights, blinding her, then off again, adding to her disorientation. Then he drew her into his arms.

Sara melted into the embrace, stunned by the *rightness* of it, awed by the sense of completion she felt there. She couldn't have said what her surroundings were; a sofa clung to one wall, a bookcase to another. All she really knew was that she was once again locked in Ari's arms.

But this time, this rare time, it was not with the immutable passion that had until now always sparked between them. No, this time the passion was blurred by wave upon wave of utter tenderness. It was a tender, gentle goodbye, an affirmation that between them there had been wonderful things, and that while these things could never be again, they could at least have this night.

One of his hands was pressed against the small of her back, not in demand, but in need, while the other threaded through her hair, cupping the base of her neck. His cheek rested against hers, and his heart slammed against her chest, as if trying to enter her. She felt her own heart answering the rapid beat.

She held still, as still as he, savoring, fully taking in the bond that held them. Her mind soared, even as her heart swelled. Right now, at this very moment, he was right, they were the same. They were the *same*.

So slowly that she scarcely felt the shift of his body, the hand at her back rose, trailed along the curve of her waist and traced the swell of her breast where it was pressed against his chest. The other hand eased caressingly down her spine.

His lips covered her own even as she sighed. Their kiss was like none before, a benediction of sorts, a healing, restorative kiss. It was the tender spanning of the years, the fragile bridge to cover all the hurts the past had created. The parting would be the sweeter because of this, and all the harder to bear.

Lightly, questingly, his tongue met hers, and at her tentative reply withdrew, only to come back stronger, more insistently.

His hands were as tender as his kiss. Trembling slightly, they followed the curves of her waist, the lines of her body. When he raised them to the catch of her sundress, she lifted her own, undoing the buttons of his loose shirt one by one. His hands stilled as she trailed kisses in the wake of her fingers' progress. When she found the hard nubs of his tiny nipples, she first brushed them lightly with her lips, then flicked at them with her tongue, finally grazing them with her teeth.

He drew in his breath in a shrill hiss, his hands once again in motion. Swiftly, yet still with that unspeakable tenderness he'd displayed throughout the evening, he dispatched the catch and zipper of her sundress. Uttering a soft moan of satisfaction, he teased the slim straps from her shoulders, and the sundress slid to form a pool at her feet.

So softly that his lips might have belonged to the air around them or to the darkness blanketing them, he lowered his lips, first to her collarbone, then down, meeting the throbbing, arched, tipped point of one breast, then the other, finally caressing the sensitive skin of her stomach. Slowly, achingly slowly, he drew the silky material of the last barrier between them down her legs, his lips following like the burning, evanescent trail of a comet.

His arms wrapped around her legs, his hands were at her bottom, supporting her, holding her upright, even as his tongue explored her. First the buckling knees, then the soft, quivering thighs, and finally, with a groan of want, or perhaps satisfaction, the very core of her.

Her fingers tangled in his hair, she tried raising him, but he, in this unusual, wholly giving mood, did not shift, did not respond to the demand in her hands.

"Ari...!" she gasped, hands dropping to his shoulders, gripping them, pleading with him. His only answer was to let her collapse into his waiting arms, guiding her to his lap and onto the floor, carpeted more thickly by their clothing, made softer by the cushions of his hands.

The pressing concerns of the past few days, of the whole eighteen years, evaporated at his touch. Thoughts of empty tomorrows, bleak futures and of her lonely house in Georgetown all fled. The question of how she might feel the next morning, knowing this was farewell, dissolved into the liquid want he roused in her.

Neither past nor future mattered in the here and now of his lips against hers, his body, lean and hard, brushing against her own.

He rolled over her, an extension of the darkness around them, fully caressing her now, exhorting and pleading, all in the same fluid, stirring motion. He paused above her, his hands splayed beside her head, elbows rigid, lifting his body from her, his very stillness a question.

Her legs parted, lifted, and wrapped around him in tender answer. She arched to meet him, her hands on his shoulders, her breasts seeking the comfort of his chest. So slowly that it seemed to last forever, he entered her, filling her, fulfilling her. No longer content with the distance that separated them, Sara's elbows pushed at Ari's and brought him to her, taking his weight gladly.

He withdrew and Sara gasped, running her hands to his buttocks to restrain him, but he was already sliding in again, slowly, deeply, pausing, only to repeat the action. He groaned in deep satisfaction, in earnest, exquisite agony and at her answering murmur began to move faster, driving ever and ever deeper, making them one person, one thought, one desire.

They rocked, fluid and warm, their bodies enacting the dreams of a thousand nights, uniting them, healing them. Like the opposites they were, Sara thought, their bodies imitated polarities: parry and thrust, restrain and incite, question and answer, seek and find.

His back arched and he lowered his mouth to her breast, taking the hardened nipple, suckling, arousing her to the point of insanity, and all the while he never stopped his deep, rhythmic thrusting, his purposeful questing.

One hand in his hair, the other at his lower back, she pulled him to her, drawing him ever deeper, pressing him to greater speed, urgent and demanding. "Please, Ari," she begged now, her voice hoarse with want, her throat dry with need.

He raised his head only to transfer his moist mouth to her other breast, giving it the same thorough attention he'd given the other. But he drove faster now, deeper, moving against her, inside her, rousing a storm in her body, inciting a riot in his own.

He lifted his head and his full, hard lips met hers, tongues meeting, warring, imitating their loving, withdrawing only when the swift demand in their bodies demanded more breath, greater freedom. And in that moment when thirst seemed quenchless, when the hunger seemed unassuageable, when the need seemed insatiable, Sara felt that burning, spreading detonation of her senses. Her legs and arms locked around him, clinging to him, flying with him, feeling the implosion of total sensation taking her, threatening to separate them with its intensity.

Ari cried out, joining her, exploding, shuddering, holding on to her as if afraid he would be swept away in the after-shock.

As she had before, as she had always felt with Ari, Sara drifted in a new universe, one where none but the two of them lived, which none but the two of them, joined as one, could ever touch. She clung, he drove, and together they spiraled to the perfect culmination of all they had been before and into the dream of what they could have been.

Ari ran his fingers through her hair, his lips pressed against her shoulder, his body covering her, but he displaced his weight as she drew in great gasping breaths.

"Sara, lovely, lovely Sara," he murmured against her temple, his lips caressing her damp cheeks as he spoke.

Though the knowledge held her in its thrall once again—when the cordon was lifted, she would be gone from his life and he from hers—she couldn't resist the urge to stroke his cheeks lovingly, his shoulders, his back, telling him with her hands how much she loved him, had always loved him. Asking his forgiveness, kneading the past from his mind.

She drifted, more content than she had been before, as sated and as profoundly whole as she had only dreamed of being.

Later, much later, Ari frowned at the insistent tapping at his door. Dawn light was filtering into the room, highlighting Sara's hair, imbuing her body with a rosy, dewy glow. He'd been awake for some time, watching her, studying this remarkable woman.

He didn't understand her, didn't understand her need to bury the passion that welled up from her inner depths, didn't understand why she couldn't accept life . . . and *him* . . . for exactly what they were. When he'd mentioned her going away . . . almost as if testing the waters between them, she hadn't argued, hadn't protested. She'd always intended to go. She'd left once before, hadn't she?

They had drifted in and out of sleep, talking sometimes, caressing sometimes. They had made love again, leisurely, sweetly and a third time with wild abandon. They had shared the language of lovers everywhere, recalling the moment when they'd first met, the young reporter, the eager commando. They had soothed the pain of their parting, she with tears wetting his shoulder, he with a voice no longer choked because she was there now, lying in his arms during the telling.

The tap sounded again, more insistently now, changing from tap to knock. Carefully, so as not to arouse her, Ari slid his arm from beneath her neck and rolled away, snatching his pants and pulling them on as he rose.

"What is it?" he whispered, opening the door a bare crack.

Hannah Naveret stood unflinchingly before him, but her hands, he noticed, were clasped tightly around her body, as if physically holding herself in control.

Her eyes dropped to his bare chest, then to his bare feet, then she looked away, a slow and obviously painful blush staining her tanned cheeks.

"I'm sorry, Ari," she mumbled. "I waited as long as I could. But I can't stand it any longer. I'm worried to death."

"What is it?" he asked quickly.

"It's Danny," she said quietly, her voice catching on a note of panic.

"What about him?"

"He's gone," she said.

Chapter 9

"What do you mean, he's *gone?*"

Hannah stepped back a pace at the harsh growl.

Away from the shadow of the doorway, looking out into the gray dawn light, Ari could see that she'd been crying. This made him afraid as nothing else could have; Hannah Naveret had never cried in all the time he'd known her.

"What happened, Hannah? Tell me quickly."

Oblivious of the open door and Sara's recumbent form behind him, he stepped out and bracingly took Hannah's arm. She looked up at him, numbly at first, then with a tremulous smile.

"You'll think I'm an old fool," she said.

"Never," he said quickly, trying not to rush her, but wishing, nonetheless, that she'd hurry up.

She drew a deep, shaky breath that seemed to steady her as much as his grip on her arm.

"Apparently young Shlomo had some plan to go to Na'asum—"

"Across the border?" Ari asked incredulously.

"Yes," Hannah answered. "Because of the skirmish this morning...yesterday morning...he asked Danny to go along."

"They couldn't have been that stupid!" Ari burst out. But he could remember the excitement on Shlomo's face yesterday, and recalled now with dismay the dull flush of pride on Danny's. A pride he'd encouraged.

Hannah didn't respond to his misbegotten assertion, but he continued as if she had.

"If they were to get there—and I don't say *if* lightly—what do they possibly hope to accomplish?"

"Moshe said they were planning to blow up the new P.L.O. headquarters."

"Dear God," Ari said fervently. "This is no kid's prank."

"No, Moshe seemed to think it might be Sternit."

Ari's mind reeled at her words. Danny was mixed up with Sternit? Shlomo was? Yes, he thought, it fitted. He'd seen Shlomo's restlessness, seen the apparent impotent fury whenever the boy heard of some new skirmish, learned about a death of an Israeli. A wave of guilt washed over him. He'd *known* about the boy, yet had done nothing but fob him off with extra duties, more responsibility, praise for his actions of the day before. He'd been so wrapped up in problems of his own that he'd allowed Shlomo's to go unresolved.

And *Danny,* Danny was with him?

Ari said, "You said Danny was gone. They've already left, then?"

"Yes . . . less than two hours ago."

"What!" he roared.

Again Hannah flinched, but she spoke bravely enough.

"They went on foot, up and to the east."

Already Ari's mind was plotting a strategy by which he could stop the young, would-be heroes. They were on foot; he could talk to Harry at the border and secure clearance. They had a hell of a hike across rough terrain; he could get to the very border in less than thirty minutes by jeep. There was a slim chance he could stop them.

He couldn't allow himself to consider the alternative. If he didn't stop them, and they made it into Na'asum, they not only would create an international incident, but would surely be killed. The other side wasn't likely to allow the boys to live, and they would broadcast their outrage to the four winds in as many languages as possible.

Ari suppressed his scream of outrage, outrage at his son's involvement, at the injustice, the fact that these kids had out-maneuvered him as completely as possible.

"How many?" he asked. At Hannah's blank stare, he shook her arm slightly. "How many of them are there?"

He felt a soft hand at his back and started. He should have known Sara would awaken, yet jumped, nonetheless. He hadn't exactly forgotten she was there; it was just that he'd been so terribly focused on Hannah's revelations.

"Four, plus Moshe," Hannah said.

"Moshe!" Ari burst out. He felt temporarily stunned by the news that the old man was out climbing a mountain with an offshoot of Sternit.

"He went after them?" Sara asked from behind him.

"Yes," Hannah said, no shock on her face at hearing Sara's voice, at the implications of her being in Ari's room at this hour. "Moshe said to come wake you if he didn't return in two hours. But I couldn't wait that long."

Ari whirled to Sara. "You heard?" he asked.

"Yes," she said calmly.

He stared at her for a moment, somehow shocked that she could sound so calm, look so unruffled by the disclosure that her son—their son—was somewhere up on a mountainside heading for certain suicide. But a closer look told him she was far from calm. Her lips trembled, much as they'd done beneath his the night before, and her hands were shoved deep into the pockets of the skimpy sundress she'd apparently pulled on by guesswork, because one shoulder strap hung limp over her arm.

Her hair was tousled, her cheeks were flushed and her lips slightly swollen from their loving. The sight of her thus, leaving no doubt how they'd spent the night, jolted him, made him feel oddly vulnerable, spotlighted, as if her presence was a living reminder that he'd failed in his duties as director.

"Can we stop them?" she asked calmly.

Her simple question, the fact that she could pretend to be calm when she must be feeling every bit as panicked as he, gave him the strength to be steady, as well. If she could stand there in the early-dawn light, looking more as if she were ready to go back to bed than react to the news that her only son was in danger, then so could he.

He turned back to Hannah, forcing his features into an air of calm he couldn't feel, trampling the emotions that threatened to burst from him.

"How did Moshe know about this?" he asked.

For the first time Hannah couldn't meet his eyes. "Danny came to us last night. He was very upset by something he thought you two had said."

"Which was?" Sara interjected smoothly.

Hannah met Sara's eyes.

"He seemed to have the idea that he was in the way. That the two of you would be happier without him."

Ari saw the color drain from Sara's face. He felt it drain from his own.

Hannah rushed on. "He apparently overheard you two talking in the lobby of Alef, and jumped to some crazy conclusions."

Sara moaned softly, and for a moment Ari thought the tenuous calm she was maintaining was going to totally collapse. But she held on to it.

"We tried to make him see reason, but it seems that he'd only gone there to tell Sara about Shlomo's plan."

She paused, then looked directly at Sara.

"He thought it might help you with your story."

"But when he heard us...when he *saw* us...?" Sara asked, almost choking.

"He said he didn't think he had much to lose."

"You couldn't stop him?" Ari demanded.

"No. We tried everything. But finally he just pushed Moshe out of the way and ran out of the door."

"Why didn't Moshe come get me?" Ari asked. "We could have stopped them."

Hannah started to cry, slow tears rolling down her soft cheeks. "He said he owed this to you. To Sara."

"Owed it to me—to us?" Ari exclaimed. "Owed it to us to do what? To let our son get killed?"

"To save him for you!" Hannah cried, dropping her head into her hands, tears spilling through her fingers.

Ari checked himself at the sight, but asked, "And after he left? Why didn't *you* come get me?"

"I promised Moshe I wouldn't." Her breath caught on a deep sob, then she said, "I *promised*."

Over her bent head, he met Sara's gaze. Hannah's words, more than her body, stood between them. *I promised.* How many promises they had made...and broken. And now the one promise left was running up a mountainside, immolating himself on the altar of self-sacrifice.

"Did you know he would do something like this?" Ari asked coldly.

"How could I?" Sara asked, her eyes widening with shock at his question.

"You're his mother. You know him better than anyone. He came after you from France."

"I didn't expect him to do that, either," Sara said with some heat.

"You should have," he snapped.

"Oh? And I suppose you would have guessed what he was up to," Sara spat at him.

"If I had known him better, yes!" Ari threw back.

"The hell you would have! You've seen what he was capable of every bit as much as I have! *You're* the one said he snuck in with the soldiers, *you're* the one who stopped me from chewing him out over yesterday's shooting incident, *you're* the one who praised him for those kinds of actions! Don't try to slap me with the past, Ari! It won't work!"

"I'm not *slapping* you with the past!" Ari bellowed. "I'm just saying you should have *known* what the child you've raised for seventeen years was going to do!"

"How would I have known this?" she screamed back.

"If you had *been* there for him, *listened* to him, instead of—" He bit his tongue against the next words.

Sara pounced on them coldly. "Instead of *what . . . ?*"

"Never mind," he mumbled.

"Instead of *what,* Ari? Instead of listening to your *lies* about forgiving the past? Instead of *being* there for *you?*"

When he didn't answer, struck dumb by her tone, by the searing flames in her eyes, she pressed on.

"I asked you last night how you dared sit in judgment of me. I'll tell you what, Ari Gaon, I judge you. And I find you contemptible! There are no rule books on parenting. There are no neat little packages full of tips on how to avoid saying damning things that hurt your children and make them want to run out and join a group of counterterrorists!"

Ari blinked at her for a moment, as shaken by fury as she, but feeling slightly ridiculous. She was right. It didn't make him any less angry, but she was right. There were no rule books. There was nothing he could say to eradicate the past few minutes, and if he were to even have a chance at stopping Danny from sure suicide, he would have to go now.

"Never mind all this," he said. "I've got to go."

He could feel her heat as he passed her, feel her eyes glaring at his back. He flicked on the overhead light and crossed to the narrow closet against the far wall. His movements were jerky as he dragged a shirt from a hanger and yanked it onto his arms. Whether the jerkiness came from anger, frustration or worry, he didn't stop to consider.

He called to Hannah, whom he'd all but forgotten in the yelling match with Sara. "Who else is with them besides Moshe?"

"Avram Feldboy and Ehud Bar-on."

Young hotheads, Ari thought. Too bright for their own good, always into some mischief or another. But he'd never dreamed they would embrace Sternit, would never have considered them self-destructive.

"Hannah! Rouse Yehudi in the garage and tell him to bring a jeep around the front."

"You are going after them?" she asked, her tear-drenched eyes meeting his directly, and for the first time with a glimmer of hope.

"Of course," he said tersely.

He dragged on socks and shoes, his mind on the necessary phone call to Harry at the border, on what things he should take with him. He flicked a glance at Sara, who still stood just outside his doorway, her eyes on the doctor's retreating figure, on the silver footprints in the dew-laden grass.

Her face was pale now, where it had been flushed with anger. Her arms and fingers hung limp at her sides. She looked the picture of defeat. He was surprised, therefore, when she turned and met his gaze steadily, a residue of the fire still there.

"Do you think we'll be able to find them?"

To anyone else she might have sounded calm, even dispassionate. But to Ari, who had held her in his arms, had heard her declarations of love, of guilt, of pain, there was a wealth of anguish in her words.

Ari pushed to his feet, part of him wanting to reach for her and comfort her, the other too driven by the need for action to pause now.

"I'll find them," he answered almost offhandedly.

He stepped back to the closet and with a violent sweep, shoved the rest of his clothing aside. He kept his Uzi there, and extra clips.

"With any luck at all, I will find them before they cross the border."

"And if not?"

He didn't look at her as he checked his weapon. "Then I'll cross too."

"I'm going with you," she said quietly.

He looked up at that. "The hell you are," he said.

"I have to," she said with no inflection in her voice. It was quiet, soft, even-toned, but utterly implacable.

Ari swung the submachine gun over his shoulder. He met her eyes and saw the complete determination that rested there. She was asking to go with him on a desperate rescue mission dressed in a light, crumpled sundress and sandals, he noted with detachment.

Somehow it didn't strike him as ridiculous. It struck him as pathetic, rather heroic, and added to his own sense of desperation. He shook his head slowly. Her hands rose to her hips, and he was reminded of a drawing he'd seen once of Hera reprimanding some lesser god.

"I have to," she repeated.

Her mussed hair, swollen lips and shaded eyes should have made a mockery of her request, but somehow did not. Ari thought he'd never felt so much in sympathy with her before, so in tune with her drive to go find their son. She had never looked so desirable before, might never look as achingly strong again.

He shook his head and turned to shove a small automatic pistol into the belt of his pants.

"Ari, we don't have time to argue about this."

"There is no argument, Sara," Ari said as gently as he could. "I am going alone. You are staying here."

"Ari. He's my *son* . . . and I'm going with you." Her voice quavered.

This time Ari couldn't resist touching her. His hand curled around her shoulder. "He's my son also, Sara. And outside these gates, you are more of a liability than an asset. As you said, we don't have time to argue about this."

She said nothing for a long while, but lowered her eyes to the hand on her shoulder. It was as if he could actually feel the chill from her stare. He let his hand drop to his side, his elbow banging against the gun he was carrying.

"How far away is Na'asum?" Sara asked.

"Thirty kilometers, more or less," he muttered, turning from her, heading toward the door. "As the crow flies."

He would need a blanket, he thought, and possibly water, medical supplies of some kind. All would be found at the infirmary, and it was on the way to the front gates. He could stop there without any more loss of time.

"Ari, I have to go with you. I *have* to," Sara said behind him, the urgency in her voice reaching out and grabbing at his heart. It was less of a plea than a fevered demand. Her words tore at Ari's gut. Not from sorrow for her, far from it. They tore at him because they were so true, true for her, and because of her, true for him.

"Don't you see, Ari? He's out there because of me, because of what I said. Because—"

"I *know*, Sara. My God, don't you think I know how you feel? Don't you think I don't feel it, too? It's as much my fault as yours, more perhaps, because I made him feel as if he came between us. I didn't take the time with him to tell him how I might feel about him. I didn't let him know how much I really cared."

Sara shook her head vehemently, then as if the weight of the fear for Danny was too great a pressure, the vehemence disappeared and her slender shoulders slumped.

"If you understand, then you must know why I have to go with you."

"None of that matters now," Ari said gruffly, again stepping toward the door.

Sara rushed past him, stopping in the doorway, her body a barrier to his exit.

"Sara . . . there's no time to lose."

"I'm going with you," she declared. She raised her hands to the doorjambs.

"You can't," Ari said, attempting to push past her. She avoided his touch, but didn't move.

"I have to," she said again.

"This is not a game, Sara. This is not Washington, he is not missing in a big city. He is crossing a war-torn border. He is trying to get into a village where the P.L.O. is currently head-quartered."

When she merely set her mouth and crossed her arms, still blocking his exit, anger caught up with the fear in him.

"Damn it, Sara! He is in *extreme* danger!"

Any other woman would have shrunk from his words, from the anger spilling out of him, but not Sara.

"Exactly," she said. "I am not going to stay here wringing my hands and worrying about him, worrying about what could be happening out there. I won't get in your way. I'll do what-ever you say, but I *won't* stay behind.'

"Sara—"

"If anything happens, Ari, I *have* to be there. I can't stay here. I can't stay and *wonder* if he's all right. Wonder if *you* are all right. I can't stay here while Danny still believes I don't love him. Don't you understand?"

"Sara . . . please," he said, as gently as the urgency of the moment allowed. "I said I do understand and I do. But I can't let it make any difference."

"I am *going with you.*"

The longer they argued, the less chance he would have of finding Danny before he crossed the border. Ari believed he knew the point Shlomo would make for, but he had no time to stand there arguing. With a ruthlessness born of fear for his only son, Ari grabbed Sara's wrist and yanked her from the doorway.

She fought him as he'd known she would, but he forced her down until she sank to her knees. Once, it seemed ages ago now, he had wanted to drive her to her knees. Now that he had, he could only feel a sick horror in his soul at seeing her face flushed with anger and hurt, her eyes luminescent with unshed tears, her lips parted in pain and desperation.

Oh, Sara . . . he thought, and wanted to kneel beside her and draw her into his arms.

"Don't be afraid, *leva sheli,*" he said softly. "I will find him. I'll bring him back safely."

When she didn't answer, her eyes swimming with unshed tears, her hand covering the one that held her so cruelly, he sighed heavily, releasing her wrist.

Or I won't come back, either, he added to himself. No, if he couldn't stop Danny, couldn't find him, then he would never be able to look into her eyes again or look at his own reflection in a mirror. If anything happened to the boy now, because of him, of *them,* because of what they'd said and done and not said or done in the course of seventeen years . . . there would be no forgiving himself.

Though her hand automatically covered her bruised wrist, she didn't rise, and his last impression of her as he swept out the door, slamming it behind him and breaking into a run, was that he'd left marks upon her wrist and tears in her eyes.

Sara raised a shaking hand to her forehead, shielding her tear-filled eyes from the piercing rays of the sunlight, watching as Ari's loping figure disappeared into the infirmary. She had leaped to her feet at the slam of the door and wrenched it open as she uttered a sobbing imprecation. Now she stood there, rooted to the ground in pain, every beat of her heart a confirmation of her fear for her son, for Ari.

She heard the roar of a jeep as it sliced the morning silence with a shrill whine of tires. It rounded a broad sidewalk and swung onto the pavement leading to the main gates. With another screech of its tires it halted, idling noisily.

She couldn't stay behind. Once, a thousand years ago, that might have been possible. The ever-present cowardice in her would have held her there, as it had done when she was younger, when Ari went out on patrol, when she'd lain awake all night worrying about him, almost sick with relief at the sight of him the next morning. That was the way it would always be, Moshe had told her, when she had tearfully poured out her fears to him one sunny afternoon.

"Ari has no fear," he'd said. "There is nothing that frightens Ari Gaon."

Moshe had been wrong, Sara thought. There was much that frightened Ari Gaon, but he took care that no one ever saw that.

And she'd been too afraid he'd see all her fears.

But she wasn't that girl anymore. She was a woman, and more importantly she was a mother. It was *her* son that was out there somewhere, in danger, stricken to the core because of words *she* had spoken.

Where the idea came from, she had no idea. Nor did she stop to question it. For once in her life she merely reacted, responding on an instinctual level. She whipped back into Ari's room, ruthlessly pushing through his closet, knocking clothing askew, not bothering to pick up anything she dislodged. But within seconds she'd pulled a long-sleeved, army-green shirt from its hanger and a pair of Ari's trousers from another. With these items in hand she turned, her eyes raking his room. She grabbed a ball of socks from his drawer and scooped up a blanket from the narrow, flat sofa. She was almost at the door when she spied a first-aid kit on a shelf nearby, and quickly hauled it down from its dusty home.

She ran out of the room, heedless of leaving the door standing wide, and bolted for the front gates. Her feet scarcely seemed to touch the grass. She ran as if all the demons of her nightmares were at her heels; in many ways they were. Danny was in trouble, hurt because of her words, because of her actions. Once again, Ari would be angry with her, would turn into that cold stranger she'd encountered so many times in the past few days.

Still she ran. She ran for hope, ran for the sake of her life. As she rounded the building, she could hear the dull groan of the jeep's idling engine. A few more steps and she could see the waiting vehicle, could see the two guards at the gate working on the locks, Uzis loose and dangling from their shoulders. Hannah stood beside them talking urgently.

To Sara's intense relief, Ari wasn't there yet. She ran to the jeep and jumped inside before the other three could respond to her presence, almost before they'd spotted her.

"This is for the director," one of the guards said, swinging the gun readily into his hand, aiming it at Sara in his startlement. Hannah put a hand upon his arm, quietly saying something. Whatever she said apparently satisfied him, for with a shrug he lowered the deadly weapon.

Hannah approached the jeep. "He'll be angry," she said.

Sara nodded slowly. Her heart seemed to be trying to burst from her chest, from her frantic run, the very real fear of Ari's reaction and the undiminished fear for her son. She sat there, her mouth dry, her breasts heaving, clutching the borrowed clothing to her chest as if it were armor and the first-aid kit a shield.

Hannah studied her for a moment, her eyes on the bruise on Sara's wrist, then she leaned against the jeep, untying her shoes. She pulled them from her feet and dropped the rubber-soled footwear through the opened window to land with a clatter at Sara's feet.

"We are about the same size, I think," she said. No smile crossed her face, but Sara could read the understanding approbation in the older woman's eyes.

A noise behind them made Hannah turn her head, and Sara's heart accelerated painfully.

"He comes," Hannah said, stepping back.

Sara felt as if her entire being were focused on the upcoming encounter. Her eyes seemed devoid of moisture and burned; her throat was raw from her ragged breathing. Her mouth was closed tight to prevent a scream of fear and rage from escaping her lips. Nothing he could do, nothing short of shooting her would get her from this jeep. Nothing.

Ari hadn't seen her yet. She sat perfectly still, not even flinching when the back of the vehicle was opened and something heavy deposited in the rear, making the jeep shift with the impact.

Ari barked a question at Hannah, something about fuel, then slammed the back shut. Sara swallowed painfully.

"Hannah!" he called, wrenching open the driver's door, "I have already alerted the border to expect us and to keep a watch out for them. I have a radio. You know the coordinates. Radio me if you should hear anything."

"I will," Hannah said. "Be careful! And *bring them back.*"

Sara noted that Hannah's eyes were carefully trained on Ari. She never so much as glanced in Sara's direction.

Ari started to get into the jeep, then turned back to Hannah. "Look after Sara, won't you?"

Without waiting for her answer, Ari slid behind the wheel, shouted to the guards to open the gates, depressed the clutch, and shoving a protesting gearshift into first, shot the jeep forward. He glanced left, then right as he sought to clear the half-opened gates without waiting.

His foot automatically slammed on the brake as he saw Sara sitting beside him. He swore viciously, as both of them lurched forward in the rocking, but otherwise still all-terrain vehicle.

"What in the bloody hell are you doing here?" he demanded. "Get out!"

"No," Sara said as calmly as her feelings would allow. "I'm going with you."

"The hell you are," he snapped, reaching past her for the door release. He popped the handle and flung the door open.

"Get out. *Now!*"

When she didn't move, he swore again, an ugly darkening sweeping over his face. Sara had never seen him so angry, so completely devoid of words, completely stymied. An oddly detached part of her acknowledged that she'd never thought she'd live to see the day when Ari Gaon would be without words or action. Men of passion seldom were.

She forced herself to think of Danny, to remember Ari's painful grip on her arm, to think of Moshe, old and traveling with aching corns on his feet, to remember to show no fear to Ari. And she did this all in an attempt to quell the quaking in her, as she saw him looking at her as if she were some poisonous viper whose bite killed within thirty seconds.

She bit her lips to stop herself pleading with him, telling him that he had no right to keep her from this rescue. He had no right. She was no primrose weakling to be left behind, wringing her empty hands. She was a tough journalist, the mother of an intrepid son and the lover of the kibbutz director. Or had been the night before.

"What is this?" Ari demanded, though Sara knew he understood what it was perfectly well.

"I'm coming with you," she said. Her voice shook slightly, and she neither cared nor regretted that he heard it. His eyes flickered once, taking in the bundle of items she held tightly to her breast, then moved back to her face.

"We've been through all this," he told her through gritted teeth.

"No, you've been through it. I said I was going, and I am."

His arm shot out, and she flinched automatically, her hand raising to block him.

"I wasn't going to hit you," he grunted. "Merely *push* you from this jeep."

"No," she said, scooting her feet beneath the seat to wrap them around the metal supports.

He didn't touch her. "Don't do this, Sara. Please."

"I have to, Ari. I don't have any choice." She met his gaze for a long, steady moment before transferring hers to the front window. She stared straight ahead, ending the conversation, ending the argument.

"Damn you!" Ari said slowly with total meaning. "I won't be blackmailed on this. It's too important!"

"It's important to me as well, Ari," Sara said coldly. "We're wasting time arguing."

She didn't look at him again, but could feel his eyes on her profile, felt the hard, burning fury in him, fury directed at her.

She heard him depress the clutch and shift gears. The jeep moved forward, less forcefully this time, gliding through the now wide-open gates in a sure, smooth exit.

Sara, still keeping her feet beneath the seat, surreptitiously reached out and closed the passenger door.

Silent, the anger in the jeep a third, conversation-stealing presence, they swung along the road leading to the border. With the cordon there was no traffic, making the road seem at one and the same time peaceful, quiet and ominous.

Sara half expected sniper fire to burst from behind a stand of pines or a large boulder. But the only sound to be heard in the still morning air was the grinding of the jeep's gears and the pounding of her own heart.

Ari sat beside her, rigid in his anger, implacable in his fury. Barely allowing herself to relax beside him, Sara nonetheless shifted her arms, lowering the bundle of items she'd gathered to her lap. His eyes flicked to her and back to the road again. There was no softening in that hot gaze.

Sara had the distinct feeling that Ari's whole being was focused on not turning around to take her neck into his hands and shake her until she begged for mercy. She felt grateful for the curving, mountainous road, for if it had been a straightaway, he might have given in to such murderous thoughts.

Dragging her eyes from his rigid profile, Sara tried to concentrate on their ride. Tall, thick pines and steep, sandy embankments bordered their route, and often, where the road had been left untended for some time, large rocks were strewn in a small landslide of rubble at the sides, encroaching upon the asphalt.

A rusted metal truck, once having been painted a reddish purple, lay dizzily on one embankment, a reminder of the skirmishes fought along these border roads. Sara knew that similar, unplanned monuments were scattered throughout Israel, and all bore the unmistakable signs of battle, bullet holes, engines destroyed by explosion. This one served to bring home the danger to her son, the danger to Ari and herself.

Sara felt like that truck, dizzied, abandoned, a living example of the devastating effects of love—mother love, passionate love, deep and true love—devastating, because even if they did by some miracle manage to find Danny and the others, there was now no hope at all of recovering Ari's love. They had made love in gentle farewell the night before.

There would be no gentleness now. She could see it in his face, in the white knuckles of his broad hands. A man of extremes, he could either love or hate. She had spurned the one years ago, run from its intensity, from the intensity buried within herself. She had relearned a taste for that love in their two passionately tender encounters. But after this morning, after the yelling, the accusations and now this direct disobeying of his orders, she could see by the set of his jaw, by the averted gaze, that he had more than likely flipped that trigger-ready switch on his emotions.

After driving for perhaps twenty minutes, they reached a fork in the road. A large, wooden sign declared in Arabic, Hebrew and English that they had reached the end of the highway. It cautioned them against proceeding any farther without official sanction; this was not a crossing point, and all travelers wishing to cross into Syria must do so by air, via the official airline of the Syrian government. It further noted, by means of a large metal diamond imprinted in Hebrew letters, that all travel at present was government restricted.

One of the forks led down the other side of the mountain range, down to the Sea of Galilee to Jerusalem. The other, narrower, led up and over the last mountain and then on to Syria.

Ari spoke, his voice almost friendly, though Sara was undeceived. "You had best put those clothes on now."

He put the jeep into gear and turned onto the fork that led to the border. Slowly, with shaking fingers, eyeing him warily, Sara did as he'd suggested, dragging on the trousers beneath her sundress, having to rise in the seat to fasten the baggy pants. She caught his hard gaze on her bare midriff for a moment. There was no desire in that look, unless it was a desire to murder her.

Her fingers shaking even more, she quickly undid the catch at the back of her sundress and pulled the whole affair over her head, catching his scent and her own, as well. A wash of color swept across her cheeks.

Swiftly, turning from him slightly—though she'd hidden nothing from him the night before—she pulled on his shirt and buttoned it. She shoved the long tails of the shirt into her—his—pants. When the pants were still so large around the middle that they threatened to fall off when she stood, she tore at her sundress until she had a sufficient length of material and then drew it through the belt loops of his pants, tying the ends securely. Finally she took off her sandals and tugged on the pair of socks she'd stolen from his drawer. She pushed her feet into Hannah's heavy shoes. The doctor had been right; they were very nearly the same size.

"You made yourself right at home, didn't you?" Ari observed sarcastically.

Sara didn't bother to answer. Ari raised a hand to his face and rubbed it. He stopped abruptly, a curious expression on his features. He withdrew his hand, glanced down at it as if it belonged to someone else and shot her a dark look. He turned his gaze back to the road without speaking.

He didn't have to speak, Sara thought, remembering his scent on her sundress. Hers, apparently, was on his hands.

She drew a deep, rather shaky breath. Now that she was dressed in shirt and trousers, she felt much better, much more prepared. There was something about long sleeves and heavy shoes that made one feel capable of any action, she thought idly, her first truly idle thought since hearing the knock at the door that morning.

"Sara?" Ari asked, without turning to her.

"Yes?" she answered, forcing a chill note into her voice.

It would be better if he didn't know how truly frightened she was. Even as she thought this, her mind was leaping forward, picturing Danny injured, worse. *Danny!* her heart cried.

"I . . . *nothing*," he grunted.

She didn't have long to wonder what he'd been about to say, for they rounded a curve and came face to face with a large, heavily patrolled roadblock. Ari ground the jeep to a halt, but didn't cut the motor. Immediately they were surrounded by dedicated soldiers, guns at the ready.

One leaned into the window, saying, "Papers, please."

Ari shoved his identification card at the soldier and rapidly explained that he'd called ahead and they were expecting him.

"Of course, sir!" the soldier said, and though he didn't salute, the wave of his M-16 semi-automatic rifle had much the same effect, only more menacingly.

Ari put the jeep into gear once again and passed beneath the wooden painted bar before it had completely risen. Sara heard it graze the top.

"We are at the border now," he said, and without looking at her, edged the vehicle onto a rough dirt track to the left. "We go this way. It runs the length of the Syrian border."

"Will we get there in time?" she asked, the first full phrase she'd uttered since she'd thought he was going to strike her back at the kibbutz.

"We have to," he said.

They bumped along the dusty track for several minutes, Sara clinging to the seat, trying to stay where she was.

"Sara," he said again, and again his voice held a note of friendliness that didn't deceive her. She turned to him, however, watching his face.

He turned to her, as well, but she could read nothing other than a cold, icy fury in the dark gray depths of his eyes. When he spoke again, his voice was colder still.

"If anything happens to Danny because you were in the way, may God forgive you, because I certainly won't."

Chapter 10

Ari didn't feel the next lurch of the jeep, didn't notice that his head came into sharp contact with the metal roof of the vehicle. It was neither more nor less than what his heart and mind were experiencing. He felt the sharp, jagged edge of despair cutting at him, and it wasn't only from the dull look of pain in Sara's eyes; it was also from the self-awareness that if anything happened to Danny, whether or not she was there, he would, as he'd threatened Sara, never be able to forgive *himself*.

And in the back of his mind, that niggling thought he'd had earlier rose to the surface: if anything happened to Danny, there would never be any mending things between Sara and himself. Never. The only possible bridge left between them would be destroyed.

Not that there was much hope of mending things between them, anyway. Her defiance of his orders, her demand that he take her with him were bagatelles compared to the bruise on her wrist and the way she'd flinched when he reached for her. That single drawing away from him, drawing away *in fear,* had demoralized him as nothing she could have said would have done. She'd held her arm up as though to block a blow, and he'd seen then what he'd done to her earlier. The bruise had stood out clearly on her wrist, a dark blue testament to his strength and anger, a bitter indictment of his fury with her, an expression of fear for his son.

Now there was another fear to contend with, the fear for Sara. He might be angry with her, but he didn't want her harmed. Never that.

And *Danny.* His heart wrenched at the thought of his son. His newfound son, half man, still a child. He'd only known of the boy's existence for a few days. *Danny,* he thought again, the cry repeating itself in his heart, in his soul.

Ari told himself sternly that the boy could take care of himself. He'd seen that all too clearly the day before. And yet, perhaps because he'd not had a hand in the training of him, perhaps because he hadn't seen the boy reared, either, and therefore had only a fragmentary idea of how the boy would react when exposed to stress, to fear, to life-threatening *danger,* he felt all the more protective.

Maybe it was because he'd already lost one child; that agony he would take with him to his dying day. The recent discovery of another child was like being given a second chance, like a new breath of life, and in the space of a very few days, a glance, a touch, a handshake, he'd transferred all of those burned-out hopes and dreams to the square-shouldered young man whom Sara brought him. As a result he knew that he couldn't go through that loss again.

The night before, with Sara in his arms, he'd known instinctively she was kissing him with the taste of goodbye on her lips. He'd casually . . . oh, so carefully . . . hinted at her staying, questioned her leaving. She'd made it clear she was leaving. In her touch, in her caress, in her anger.

He wasn't certain he could bear to lose Sara again, either.

He glanced at Sara's stony profile, wanting to tell her some of this, wanting to explain his immediately regretted words. If the three of them came through this intact, perhaps he could tell her then. Perhaps. But perhaps too much had been said and done for forgiveness now.

Why did everything they did or said to each other always seem to spiral around forgiveness? He'd told her there was none of it in love. He had felt the truth in the words then, the rightness. But now he suspected he'd lied, or had at least not understood. Now he understood that forgiveness was what love, real love, was all about. When all else was said and done, it was the only thing that mattered—accepting mistakes, condoning actions, pardoning words better left unsaid, excusing the million little annoying traits and habits. Wasn't that what love really was?

He shot a quick glance at her stark features. Shadowed rings, faintly blue, smudged the hollows beneath her eyes, her mouth was small, drawn tightly closed, as if by a drawstring, to hold in her emotions. The throat his overlarge shirt exposed was taut with tension. Her slender frame, lost in the excess of material covering her, was tight and rigid on the seat beside him.

"You shouldn't have come," he murmured, scarcely able to hear the words himself. But she heard them. Her head turned stiffly, as if she were a puppet beneath an inexpert puppeteer's fingers.

"If you mean I shouldn't have come to Israel, I agree with you. If you mean that I shouldn't have come with you today, you're wrong. Danny is my son. When he's in trouble, I'm there."

The implication was clear: he hadn't been there, hadn't stood by the boy in all his seventeen years.

Ari's jaw tightened in swift anger. "Don't throw the past at me, Sara. You have no right to do so."

She didn't say anything, but he saw her hand cover the bruise on her arm. The gesture, unintended though it might have been, served to burn whatever vestige of a bridge remained between them.

A particularly deep rut grabbed the jeep's tires and they skidded for a terrifying, wheel-spinning second. Ari, turning the steering wheel into the skid, quickly righted the vehicle, but the lesson was timely: he should keep his eyes on the road, his mind on the danger at hand, forget about the bruise hidden beneath her delicate fingers and the anger that had caused it, the anger that still filled him.

Yet he couldn't drive the sight of her tear-filled, pleading eyes from his mind, no more than he could dismiss her present aloof manner.

The pines around them parted for a brief clearing; Ari could see a makeshift checkpoint blocking the far side. Two Israeli soldiers, alerted already by the drone of the jeep, stood at the ready, machine guns pointed in their direction.

Like a mirror image, roughly two football fields away from the first pair, two more soldiers, dressed in the grays and red of the Syrian army, stood with guns also pointed at their vehicle.

Out of the corner of his eye he saw Sara stiffen, her eyes on the Syrian border patrol.

"They won't shoot unless we fire at them," Ari told her.

"Or if we tried to cross?" Sara asked.

"It amounts to the same thing," Ari said. "That would be the only way we *could* cross."

He stuck his arm out the window, waving in a demanding salute, yelling his clearance, his name to the Israeli soldiers. They, perhaps because they had been primed for his arrival, or—less likely—because they had no wish to be run down, swept the rough sawhorses from the narrow track and jumped back out of the way.

"No word . . ." one called as they raced by.

"No word," Sara repeated on a half sob.

"We're not there yet," Ari said. This was the final checkpoint before the road, such as it was, forked for Na'asum. The pines once again closed around them, darkening the terrain, blotting the bright sky. Let them arrive before Danny, before Sternit, before any of them could cross the border. His mind scanned the mountains, almost as if he were with the small group of would-be terrorists.

With the force of habit, after the long years of training, a cool, almost serene detachment settled upon him, infusing his heart with assurance in his ability, investing his limbs with strength and purpose, making his mind feel sharp and clear.

According to the latest reports, the Syrians had posted guards all along the border, particularly on their border with Lebanon, but the least populated spot was along the road to Na'asum. It was thought that no Israeli would be foolish enough to attempt crossing at that point. And that was probably accurate, Ari thought, unless the people attempting to cross were a group of untried teenagers. As if he were with them, he knew the path the group of would-be terrorists had taken, could *feel* the rightness of his choice. They would make for this weak link in the border not realizing that the road would be lined with soldiers.

But if he could get there first . . . maybe he would be able to avert disaster. Maybe *they* would be able to, he thought, glancing at Sara.

They drove for perhaps twenty minutes, each pit in the road that slowed them down calling forth invective from Ari. As he rounded yet another bend, the dirt track opened onto a wider road. He knew this was as far as they could go without being seen and *heard* by the border guards.

He pulled the jeep off the track, cutting the motor and letting it roll silently into a space between the trees. He could only hope that they were far enough away.

Sara said nothing, merely looked a question at him.

"I suppose it would be useless to ask you to stay here," Ari said by way of answer.

"Yes," she responded.

He jumped lightly from the jeep, leaving the door ajar. As he slid around to the back, he felt rather than heard Sara imitate his action. He opened the back door and slung his Uzi over his shoulder. The weight of the gun settled against his ribs like a comforting hand. Sara materialized at his side.

Without a word he handed her the smaller automatic he'd shoved into his pants back at the kibbutz. After a slight hesitation, she took it gingerly and wrapped her fingers around the grip. To his relief she held it properly, if somewhat cautiously. He shoved extra clips into her baggy pockets, then pulled a roll of duct tape from the jeep. He took the first-aid kit Sara still held in her free hand, pushed it to her waist and wrapped the tape around her several times, securing the kit there, tearing the end of the tape with his teeth. In so doing, his head brushed her full breasts and he felt her recoil. He rose and looked at her, feeling strangely shaken.

They might not survive this, he thought with awful clarity. He wasn't going to die without kissing her one last time. He stared at her for a long moment, then slowly pulled her to him. Her eyes, widening as she caught his intention, never left his. When her lips parted, he crushed her to his chest and brought his mouth almost violently down upon hers. She struggled against him, pushing at him, then, as if unable to resist the demanding kiss, clung to him, drawing him even closer.

Whatever the outcome of this morning would be, whatever the future might hold for them, whatever inevitable parting

would take place, he would have this moment, this kiss to remember. And he would have last night.

When he released her, almost roughly, with awful reluctance, she looked dazed, lost. Her lips were still parted and
moist, her eyes soft and unfocused. Her hands still grasped his
shirt, as if by releasing it she might fall.

He, on the other hand, felt cleansed, strong, ready for
whatever might happen next. He let loose the ghost of a
chuckle, a laugh of pure triumph, of acceptance of the vaga-
ries of battle, of life. At that precise moment he felt invincible. Always after kissing Sara, making love with her, he felt as
if he could conquer the world, the universe.

"Let's go get our son," he said, grinning broadly.

"Didn't anyone ever tell you that macho went out with bell-
bottoms?" Sara whispered.

He'd already turned to push his way into the dense forest,
but at her words he swung around. He knew his grin was mis-
timed, but couldn't hide it.

"If more men had a little macho in them, I suspect that
women would be a lot happier," he whispered back.

He turned to the trees again, ignoring her exasperated oath.

Ari said, "You can stay there, if you want. I'm going this
way."

He almost laughed aloud at her indignant snort. But seconds later he felt her close behind him.

"Stay crouched down once we're out of these trees," he ad-
vised softly. For the life of him, he couldn't seem to stop
smiling. It was a strange moment to feel so insouciant. It must
come from Sara, the effect she had on him. He hadn't felt so
young, so capable, so invulnerable since . . . since she left. His
grin slipped somewhat.

"Follow my lead," he said.

They threaded their way through the dense trees to the left
of the jeep, to the left of the clearing . . . to the south of the
border.

"How will we know where they are?" Sara breathed behind him.

He didn't answer. If he told her that he just *felt* it, she would
probably laugh . . . or argue with him again. The truth was that
although he wasn't sure, he knew Shlomo well enough and
Avram and Ehud, too, to figure they would make for this too-
obvious crossing point. Now if only he and Sara weren't too

late. The thought sobered him. He clamped his mind down
against that possibility.

They moved swiftly through the trees, their movement
impeded by thick underbrush and the necessity for crouching
into the protection provided by the growth. He thought of
warning Sara what their chances were of getting through this
without gunfire, but didn't. He considered telling her how
much danger they—all of Israel—would be in should the crazy
boys actually get across the border, but couldn't. Her thoughts
were all for their son, and to Ari it seemed better that way. If
she thought only about Danny, she might just do what he
asked.

They were almost around the clearing, when a sudden shout
from their right, from the other side of the border, sliced
through the air. The word shouted was in Arabic, but Ari
understood it; apparently so did Sara, for she froze instinctively.

Equally instinctively, Ari grabbed her arm and yanked her
flat against the ground. Even as his mind grappled with the
fact that he hadn't *seen* the invisible guard, his body covered
Sara's with his own. He could feel her quivering beneath him,
struggling for breath.

"Who's there?" the voice called in Arabic.

"Shhh," Ari breathed.

"Who's there?" the voice called again. There was a note of
desperation that spoke to the extreme youth of the guard. Ari
heard it with a cold satisfaction. Inexperienced, he thought
with an element of superiority. He could be tricked. He had no
wish to kill the guard; that in itself would cause a problem for
Israel. Reprisals and incursions were one thing, but killing
posted guards represented an infringement of the other nation's rights.

But before he could formulate a plan whereby such trickery
might succeed, another voice called out, this time some distance behind them and to their left. From their side of the
border. It, too, called in Arabic.

"It's me, Ja'mal! Don't shoot!"

For a moment Ari froze. He realized that he and Sara were
trapped between the two voices, then, even as he slowly rolled
off Sara, his gun pointed in the direction of the second voice,
he recognized the name as that of the man Danny and Shlomo

had vanquished the day before. It was Ja'mal who was currently a heavily guarded guest of Kibbutz Golan.

Almost as an afterthought, Ari realized he recognized the voice, too. The impersonator was Shlomo Havinot.

He was almost amused by the simplicity of Shlomo's plan. He might even have applauded it, if the action Shlomo clearly contemplated were not so dangerous, if what they had planned were not so destructive. But this was no heroic mission, no just cause. This was a foolhardy attempt by a group of teenagers and one reluctant old man—if, indeed, Moshe had caught up with them—to enact a reprisal that might result in the deaths of many, or at the least, in their own deaths.

Several options sprang to mind. He could yell out, denouncing the boy as a liar; he could fire a round of ammunition into the air as a warning; he could lie quiescent and then stop the group when they tried to pass; he could rise and draw the fire of the guard himself. All these possibilities swept through his mind in the time it took for one heartbeat to pass, and Ari liked none of them.

Sara, however, took the matter out of his hands.

"Danny!" she called in English. "Don't come any closer, Danny!"

Ari didn't even have time for the curse that sprang to his lips.

The forest around them was suddenly alive; the ground jumped, dirt spurting upward in little puffs of dust, and the leaves over their heads splintered and dropped onto them like a gentle rain. Sara cried out once more, but her half-formed scream was drowned by the earsplitting recoil of the border guard's machine gun. Like thunder and lightning, Ari thought, one could count the distance of a machine-gun recoil from its origination point. This one was far too close. The noise stopped as soon as it had started, though leaves continued to fall.

The guard firing at them had made a serious error, Ari thought coldly. He had no business, no *right* to fire into Israeli territory. Young he might be, foolish he probably was and trouble he certainly was.

"Ja'mal . . . ?" the Syrian youth called out.

There was no answer.

"Ja'mal?"

As the guard called again, Ari ran nearly nerveless fingers over Sara's white face, limp arms. He did this automatically, but his mind was on the group of boys behind them.

"Are you all right?" he breathed.

"Y-yes." She turned terrified, wholly apologetic eyes in his direction. "You?"

He shook his head.

"I'm so sorry..." she whispered back.

"Never mind," he whispered back. This was no time for an involved discussion on the merits of her impulsive action.

"I could have gotten us all killed... Danny, too," she murmured, closing her eyes in a gesture of self-recrimination.

Good, Ari thought. While she was stewing in guilt, she wasn't likely to put up much of a fuss about his next plans.

"I'm going to go see if I can find them," he whispered. "Stay here."

Again the options he could employ flashed before him. Although a little less sanguine about the young border guard, now that he'd fired into Israeli territory, Ari still had no wish to harm him; this was none of his doing, he deserved nothing for merely doing his duty—albeit overzealously. But how to incapacitate him long enough to turn the situation around?

He pushed to his elbows, half expecting more gunfire, but none was forthcoming.

He made certain the smaller gun was still in Sara's grasp. "Stay down," he whispered into her ear. "Use it if you have to, but for God's sake, aim for the border, not toward me."

"Where are you going? What are you going to do?" she whispered back, her free hand frantically clinging to his shirt-front.

His eyes met hers, and it seemed to him that a ricochet of electricity passed between them, yet even as it did so, he removed her hands from his shirt. "Stay here," he said coldly. "You've already done enough."

Her eyes shuttered and closed. He hesitated, wanting to tell her what he really thought, but pulled away. This was not the time.

"Please save him," she murmured, as he edged toward a break in the underbrush. "And Ari?"

He looked back at her, their eyes meeting across the green pocket they'd found. He felt once more that curious connection they'd always shared, that transfer of electrical energy.

"Yes?" he whispered.

"Come back to me," she said softly, her hazel eyes luminous, her parted lips full and trembling.

"I will," he promised, and both his promise and her words served to spark that irrational sense of invincibility again. If he didn't go now, if he stayed to say anything else, lingered for one last look at her beautiful face, he wouldn't be able to go at all. He turned his face away and with no more hesitation, slunk into the thick mass of weeds and vines.

Sara watched him go with a sick, sinking feeling. When he'd told her to stay behind this time, she couldn't have argued. She wasn't even certain she could move. She hadn't told Ari, hadn't wanted him to know, but when she'd called out so rashly, not all the gunfire had missed them. She had felt an acute, burning jab in her thigh, just above her right knee. In the first second of impact, had she not been aware of the gunfire, she might have assumed it was a wasp's sting. But she'd known the moment her skin had been pierced that she'd been struck.

Had she ruined all with her cry? She had been hit; had Danny? Had Moshe? She could hear nothing, not even Ari slowly crawling away from her. She strained her ears, thinking she heard something, a whisper. But the nervous calling of the border guard and the pain in her leg dulled her senses.

She raised herself slightly, peering down at her leg, noting with an almost detached coolness that Ari's pants were stained dark red and that the ground beside her was growing damp with ruddy color.

Almost as if her fingers belonged to someone else, she tugged at the tape holding the first-aid kit to her waist. It gave a single inch with a loud, ripping tear, a noise too harsh in the quiet.

"Ja'mal!" screamed the border guard.

Sara gave up the effort, loosening her makeshift belt instead. This, with a bitten-off cry of sharp pain, she wound around her leg, pulling tightly, despite the waves of nausea rising in her throat.

She dropped back to her shoulders, panting somewhat, filled with guilt for her cry to Danny, wishing she hadn't acted so rashly, hoping, *praying*, that Danny or any of the others hadn't also been shot—or worse—because of her cry. She wished she were with Ari, angry as he was with her, wished she knew what was happening.

It seemed she lay there forever, suspended in time, her mind awash with the danger at hand, her body in pain, her heart so thoroughly shattered that, like Humpty-Dumpty, it could never be put back together again. She knew that the events of the morning, at least her part in them, had completely destroyed any hope she had of a life with Ari. They were too different, and at the same time too much alike. There were too many mistakes between them, too many harsh words. They could never go back now.

"Ja'mal!" the border guard called yet again, this time nervously, his voice cracking.

A few seconds later she heard a shout to her left, a scuffle, and a short burst of gunfire. To her right she heard the frantic cries of the border guard, just before the world once again exploded into noise, and the leaves began to rain down upon her.

"Please..." she whispered, not knowing exactly what she was pleading for. Just *please*...

Reluctant though he had been to leave Sara alone in the underbrush, Ari felt he had no choice but to crawl to where he had heard Shlomo's voice. This was as deadly a course as walking straight into the border guard's gun. The teenagers would be wired as tightly as a poorly done electrical job, and could spark fire at the merest sound.

He kept to his stomach, using his knees and the toes of his boots to push him along. And with each push he whispered, "Moshe...Danny...Moshe...Danny..." It was so soft a whisper that it seemed more an extension of his thoughts than any sound.

He froze as he thought he heard some slight movement to his left and forward some ten meters. "Moshe...? Danny?" he breathed. "It's Ari...."

A heavy boot kicked at him from the underbrush, connecting with his shoulder. If he hadn't been half-prepared for the blow by the sudden shift in the plants, he would have taken the hit on the head, but he had seen the plants shake violently and had half rolled to the side. A low moan escaped him despite his efforts to avoid any noise.

Instinctively his free hand shot upward and grabbed the foot that had kicked him. He twisted it viciously, pulling at the same time. With a shout, Shlomo Havinot rose up, falling out of the brush and over Ari's prone body.

One of the group with Shlomo—Ehud, Avram or possibly even Danny—released a brief round of fire just above their heads. From behind them, just beyond Sara, Ari heard the border guard do the same, though he didn't aim into the air.

Shlomo, flailing against Ari with nervous, adrenaline-inspired strength, swore at Ari, trying to get free.

"It's me, you fool!" Ari snapped, grabbing hold of the boy's hair and pulling his head back so that the youngster would look at him.

Much of the fight went out of him then. His face went slack with the typical young boy's combination of stunned recognition and having been caught doing something he shouldn't have been doing.

"Shlomo?" A voice called softly just to their left.

"Here," Ari called back equally softly, scarcely more than whispering.

Avram pushed his head through the thick growth and would have immediately retreated, but Ari grabbed his shirtfront and held on. The high flush of fear and excitement drained from the boy's broad, swarthy face the instant he saw who was holding Shlomo, who was holding his own shirt.

"Sir," he breathed, the single word sounding more like a plea for pardon than any acknowledgment of Ari's status or presence in the forest.

"Where are the rest?" When the boy didn't answer, Ari shook his shirtfront meaningfully.

"B-back there," the boy said with a slight jerk of his head.

"Are they all right?" Ari asked, loosening his grip on Shlomo to roll closer to Avram.

Avram shook his head, his fear of Ari's reaction all too evident. But at the shake of his head Ari's heart froze, a fear too great to acknowledge seizing him.

"Let's go," he said, pushing at Shlomo to make him move before him, pushing at Avram to turn around. "Stay down."

The three of them crept through the brush, Avram uttering short, high whimpers, out of fear of the director's retribution, Ari thought; Shlomo with a sullen, but equally scared deliberation, and Ari grimly holding back the sick dread that threatened to scream out of him.

He figured they must have crawled about eight meters when the brush thinned out somewhat, and Ari could see the results of the morning's work. Ehud lay in an awkward position, one leg sprawled sideways, blood staining his chest. Beyond him, Danny was half sitting, half lying, holding Moshe's head against him.

Alive, Ari thought. My son is *alive.* A wild, potent exultation swept through him, followed by an almost debilitating wash of relief. Ignoring the two boys at his side, Ari pushed ahead, making straight for his son. His son, who still lived and breathed.

Danny looked up at the sudden, silent approach, his eyes widening when he saw Ari.

Ari couldn't read the expression on his son's face, but if he'd had to choose from the many possibilities, he would have said the strongest message was one of profound relief. And hope. A cautious faith that the nightmare could be ending.

"Are you hit?" Ari demanded, seeing the whey-colored shock settling in upon the boy's features.

As his mother had done only minutes before, the boy shook his head. He looked down at Moshe's cradled head.

"Moshe . . ."

Ari crawled the rest of the way to them, reaching out his hand for Moshe, but unable to resist touching his son's arm, hand, face. The boy shuddered, but didn't draw away.

"He's hit," Danny whispered brokenly. "He grabbed Shlomo. They fought. Ehud tried to stop them. When the gunfire started, they were both hit!"

Ari focused his attention on the older man, running his fingers lightly over Moshe's shoulders, down his arms, over his legs. But there was really no need to do any of that. The wound was in Moshe's chest. Blood was seeping slowly, sluggishly, from between Danny's fingers, from beneath Danny's palm pressing tightly against the wound. Moshe's face was white and his lips were stained blue, but he was still breathing. Shallow, overrapidly, stertorously, but breathing, nonetheless.

With the practice of many battles and with his knowledge of wartime first aid, Ari quickly shrugged his shirt from his shoulders and wadded it into a small bundle. He loosened his belt and yanked it free of the loops. He pulled Danny's hand from Moshe's chest, ripped the sodden shirt aside and pressed his own shirt over the rupture that was now visible.

"Lift him," he told Danny and as his son did so, he stretched the belt around Moshe's back. When it was obvious that the belt wouldn't meet in the front, Danny shifted slightly and tugged his own belt free. This he handed to Ari with an impatient thrust. Ari met his eyes briefly, a strange, urgent sort of connection taking place, then he quickly bent over the belts. He fastened the catch of Danny's belt through the last hole on his own, then threaded the catch of his own belt over the end of Danny's and pulled hard, pressing his shirt tight against Moshe's chest.

"Will he live?" Danny asked anxiously.

Ari looked up and met his son's gaze. "I don't know," he said, and regretted his honesty when his son flinched. He pulled Moshe's shirt closed again, noting with detachment that his fingers were stained red.

Without another word he slid over to where Ehud lay. Like Moshe he had a chest wound, but unlike Moshe his breathing was easier, his lips showing none of the telltale blue about them that indicated either damage to the lungs or possible internal bleeding.

"Give me your—" Ari began, but broke off when Avram pressed his shirt into his hands. Ari glanced at him and was sorry, for the boy looked younger than ever without his shirt. Skinny arms hung loosely from bony shoulders. No hair covered his chest, and his ribs, despite the number of times Ari had seen him go back for seconds in the dining hall, were prominent.

Avram's belt followed, and he swiftly moved to Ehud's shoulders, lifting him slightly, telling Ari he had missed nothing of Moshe's doctoring. This time they needed no extra belt. Ehud, like Avram, was almost painfully thin. Ari shook his head; their thinness didn't come from not getting enough to eat, it came from extreme youth. They were scarcely more than little boys, too young for the army, too ripe for mischief.

Ehud stirred a little, moaning.

"Keep him quiet," Ari whispered, turning away from the two and looking across at Shlomo.

Shlomo's lip was puffy, and a bruise darkened his cheek. Ari knew he'd done that to the boy, and for a moment he wished he'd done more. It was this boy's fault that all of them were here, that two were wounded, and a trigger-happy border guard was still out there, waiting to shoot them down. He would have to save the reprimand for later, because now they had to get Moshe and Ehud to safety. And Sara.

Dear God, he thought, he'd almost forgotten about Sara, lying back there alone in the underbrush, in the direct line of fire.

"We'll have to get them to the kibbutz," Ari whispered.

"How?" Avram asked, a note of pure panic in his voice.

Ari thought for a second, a glimmer of an idea taking root in his mind. "You have explosives with you?"

Neither Avram nor Shlomo answered. It was Danny who finally whispered, "In that bag."

He nodded his head at a large canvas backpack some three feet from where Ehud lay. Ari rolled over to the bag, biting off an expletive as a sharp stone jabbed into his bare belly. He jerked up the flap on the bag and reached inside. Grenades.

He looked up and met Shlomo's sullen gaze with hard fury. "You were going to Na'asum armed with nothing more than a handful of grenades?"

Shlomo's head dropped. So did those of the other boys.

"So. You all have a lot to learn, and if we live through this, I'll see that you do. The hard way."

"Sir?" His son's voice. Why did it wrench him so that his son called him sir? Would he ever call him *Abba,* would he live to call him Father?

"Yes?" he asked, shaken.

"My mother . . . ?"

"Is back there," Ari answered tersely.

"Is she hurt? What is she doing up here? What are you doing here?" Danny asked, his whispered questions wholly perplexed.

Ari met his gaze evenly. He was like Sara, this boy of his loins, always looking for explanations, for deeper significance. There wasn't time for answers now, he thought pragmatically, and there certainly shouldn't be the need.

"How did you get here?" Danny persisted. "How did you get in front of us? You were—" He broke off, the first color rising in his cheeks.

Ari shook his head. "That doesn't matter now," he said. "We have to get out of here."

"But how?" Avram asked again.

"I believe I've got a plan."

Danny looked up at that, a faint hope showing on his fine features, and something more. A wary pride? A confidence of sorts?

Ari looked away, too afraid to hope. He hardened his voice. "I don't want any more shooting unless it is absolutely necessary. And that border guard . . . I want him left alive."

"Why?" Shlomo burst out. "He's an—"

"Keep your voice down, you idiot," Ari snapped. "Do you want to get us all killed? What that border guard is, is an international incident! And so was what you were planning to do!"

Ari swallowed the rest of his tirade, but had to get the point across to the leader of the foolish mission.

"You are in very big trouble, boy." He shared his cold gaze with all three boys. "All of you are. Now you'll do as *I* say!"

He outlined his plan quickly, then took a grenade from the satchel.

"When I say the word, Shlomo and Danny, you pull Moshe through the brush, that direction. Avram, you follow with Ehud. Try not to make any noise. Follow that slight opening in the underbrush until you reach Sara. She'll take you on to the jeep. If I'm not there in twenty minutes, get out of here and alert the Israeli border patrol. Now get out of here."

Ari waited until all three boys had started their slow, awkward progress from the clearing, then he pulled the pin from the top of the grenade, and with his hand firmly holding the handle pressed against the side of the explosive, he counted. When he reached fifteen, he threw the grenade as hard as he could, far to the left of them.

The ground shook and the explosion resounded seconds later. And as if angry, the forest flung leaves and sweet-smelling earth down at them, covering, hiding them.

"Go!" Ari called, snarling at the boys who had paused, ducking at the explosion. He was heedless of his voice now, for the roar of the grenade's detonation and the answering gunfire from the border guard hid any sound he might make.

The boys quickly went back to work, staying down as told, grimacing as they pulled Moshe and Ehud out of the clearing and into the underbrush.

Ari waited until the gunfire stopped, then pulled another grenade from the bag, repeating his actions of a few minutes before. Once again the forest cried bruised leaves and black dirt clods, and once again the border guard fired.

But this time, as Ari had devoutly hoped he would, he fired in the direction of the explosion.

Ari couldn't see the boys anymore; they had been swallowed up by the underbrush, and with his ears deafened by the explosion, he couldn't hear them, either.

The border guard, clearly caught up in mindless panic, continued firing long after the grenade's thunder subsided. When he stopped, Ari dipped his hand back into the bag and pulled out a third grenade.

He thought of the look in Danny's eyes, the hope, the tentative confidence in his father, the extended belt, the linking of their belts. It was a symbol of sorts, Ari thought. A profoundly moving symbol.

He pulled the pin of the grenade, and again holding the handle tightly against the rounded, ribbed side, he counted again, but this time his mind was on the linking of their belts, father's to son's, joined in a union as old as life itself, a never-ending circle.

And he thought of Sara. For the first time since the first moment he'd seen her in his office, he realized that there was hope for them. There was hope because he could look at the past and see it for what it was—the past. There was hope because of that linking with his son; their eyes had met and understanding had passed between them, and as a result he could see a future. Together.

If they got out of this, if she listened when he talked with her, if he could love her once again, holding her slender body to his, telling her everything his pride had never let him say before, there could be a tomorrow and a thousand more after that.

He pulled back his arm and flung the grenade as far to the left as he could.

The ground exploded, just as surely as had the past.

Chapter 11

Alone, frightened, Sara's mind conjured up horrible images of Danny, of Ari. If we get out of this, she vowed, there will be no more lying to myself, no more lying to Ari, no more hiding the truth from Danny. Ari knew about Danny now, so one lie was already exposed.

But the deeper lies, those caused by years of dodging the truth about herself, about how she felt about Ari Gaon, how she *really* felt, those had to be exposed, too. She had always assumed she had run because she wasn't able to handle the intensity of Ari Gaon, but had discovered she'd fled because she feared she didn't have enough herself. And she might have continued to believe that, had not first Moshe, then Ari made her confront that streak of passion she possessed.

Ari had said she was just like him, but that she denied her own intensity. What did that mean? What could that mean to the two—the three—of them?

If she were to admit that of all things she had feared the burning drive for causes, the aching passion that raged within her, where would that leave them? Would Ari admire her any more or less?

An explosion seemed to rock the earth and with its roar, with the scream that rose into her throat, and the rapid reports from the border guard's gun, she felt as if something had exploded inside her, as well.

It wasn't Ari's admiration or condemnation that mattered, but Ari Gaon himself. That was all that should matter. If they all came through this, no matter whether Ari ever spoke to her again, if he ever forgave her the cry that had brought down the gunfire, forgave her for running from him eighteen years ago, forgave her Danny, she had to tell him how she felt about him. She had loved him then, as a young girl will love, and she loved him now, as a woman loves, with a raw and brilliant intensity, a deep and unshakable passion.

After the explosion, Sara heard nothing but the too-rapid beating of her own heart. She closed her eyes, trying to imagine herself on any other cool hillside but this one, lying beneath thick branches of pines, resting on a soft bed of ivy. But her imagination wouldn't create the image for her, for no birds sang, and no insects chirped a spring song. They, like Sara, were also quiet, waiting, hiding somewhere, breath held and chests on fire.

When the second explosion thundered through the forest, Sara almost screamed aloud. She had to press her fist to her mouth to keep from doing so. On the heels of the roar came another nervous report from the border gun, but as before, it wasn't directed toward her.

Where was Ari? Where was Danny?

Painfully she rolled to her stomach, and with a soft moan pushed herself in the direction she'd seen Ari take. She could no more have remained there now, worrying, wondering if Danny was all right . . . wondering if *Ari* was, than she could have risen and run straight for the border guard.

She was deafened by a third explosion and yet more gunfire. She dropped flat to the ground, covering her head and ears. Would this nightmare never end?

As the noise died down, she heard other sounds, a scuffling, a whisper and the unmistakable slither of something heavy being dragged in her direction. She looked up with hope, with fear, and pushed her way toward the sounds.

Within a few seconds she saw someone's back and head, then Danny's—*Danny's*. The two young men were crawling on their sides, pulling someone between them.

"Thank you," Sara mouthed. "Thank you." Tears of relief sprang to her eyes, and she didn't bother wiping them away.

"Danny . . ." she whispered lovingly.

His head whipped around at the sound of her voice, and his shoulders sagged. His face crumpled as the boy in him visibly overtook the man. "M-mom," he said brokenly. "Oh, God, Mom!"

He released his hold on the person he was dragging and slithered to her as rapidly as any snake. It was only when he was reaching for her that she saw who it was he'd been pulling.

"Moshe!" she exclaimed.

"Oh, Mom! It was all my—"

Yet another explosion rocked the forest floor, and in swift desperation Sara jerked Danny's head down, covering it with her own. She could feel his shoulders shaking, and knew the moisture on her cheeks was as much from his tears as from her own.

He is safe, her heart sang, even as her mind questioned, with terrible guilt, *but at what cost?*

"Where's Ari?" she demanded.

"Back there. He's covering us," he said, a note of pride in his tremulous voice. His eyes met hers with diffidence.

"I'm sorry about all this, Mom," he said.

"You should be," she told him, her hand on his face, her eyes looking deep into his, all the love she felt for him pouring out of her.

His lower lip trembled, and Sara's heart was wrenched at seeing the very small boy peeking out.

"I'm s-scared, Mom," he whispered.

"Me, too," she answered, drawing a hint of a smile from him.

"You said he was covering you. The explosions?"

"Yeah . . . we're supposed to go to the jeep."

He pulled away from her, looking over his shoulder at Moshe's still form. Sara could hear the labored breathing from where she was.

"Moshe," he murmured. "Moshe's hit. Ari said to take him and Ehud to the jeep. He said you know the way."

"But Ari's okay . . . you said he was okay?"

Another explosion answered her question, and when the roar died down, Danny confirmed it.

"That's him making all that noise. We gotta get Moshe and Ehud out of here," he whispered urgently. With renewed strength he again took his position at Moshe's shoulder and with a nod at Shlomo, started pulling Moshe's battered body along the forest floor.

Sara scrambled out of the way, then, as the two sets of boys pulled their unconscious burdens past her, she moved as swiftly as she could with her injured leg.

With the chaos that Ari was creating behind them, and despite their injuries, they managed to make fair haste through the heavy growth, until they were finally once again in the deep woods that led to the jeep.

It was a relief to stand semierect, Sara noticed, and with the only stab of humor she'd felt throughout the long morning, realized that the tourniquet she'd made for her leg had been her makeshift belt, so that if she tried to walk erect, her pants would slide down around her ankles. She slung the gun over her shoulder and clung to the front of her pants. Ari's pants. They made their way through the deeply wooded stretch, and though her leg was throbbing, other concerns drove much of the pain from her mind.

She had come to Israel to do a story. That was the ostensible reason. And here it was, in all its infamy. In all its unglorious, realistic sordidness. This, then, was her story, she thought, not the deeds of misguided youth, but those misdeeds of unguided youth, of their parents.

They heard another explosion and the echoing volley of gunfire. They stopped as one, each panting, looking down at the two men they were so unceremoniously dragging between them.

Sara put her hand upon her son's arm and summoned a reassuring smile when he started. She turned his wrist to look at his watch. It was scarcely 9:00 a.m. So much had happened in so little time, she thought. She looked up and met her son's dulled gaze.

"It'll be all right," she said.

He looked at her as though she were a complete stranger, speaking another language. His face was slack after the shock of the morning's actions, the morning's disaster.

"Buck up," she said, using Jason's bracing advice for a much younger Danny.

He didn't smile back, but he did move ahead.

They resumed their unsteady progress through the thick underbrush. Somewhere in that brush, in the trees behind them, Sara thought with each agonizing step, was the man she loved, desperately hurling grenades to allow them passage to safety.

Pausing only to catch her breath, Sara was struck by the magnitude of what he was doing. He'd been right, though it had angered her at the time. If men were a little more macho, many women might be happier. At least, she amended, he made her feel that way. His very strength and confidence lent her some, his courage and indomitable spirit made her feel courageous, as well. Courageous enough to face this nightmarish wood, to have faith in her own convictions, her own beliefs. Courageous enough to tell Ari Gaon once and for all that she loved him.

For the first time she understood the insufferable grin that had crossed his face upon their arrival in the forest, understood his crushing kiss. She felt a wild surge of faith course through her veins, felt hopeful for the first time that morning. Truly hopeful.

But even as she thought this, she recalled that it had been her own incautious cry that had resulted in the gunfire that might have killed—perhaps *had* killed—two men.

Ari would never forgive her that. Never. He'd said so, hadn't he? And she'd seen the hard, cold expression on his face. Even knowing this, knowing he couldn't forgive her, she still would tell him how she felt about him. She had to. It was the single, most honest emotion in her life, and she owed it to him to tell him. She owed it to herself.

Forcing herself to weave through the trees as she had done earlier with Ari, Sara tried any number of distracting thoughts to drive from her mind the pressing worry about Ari's safety. But she met with no success. There was simply no getting away from it.

"Mom?" Danny asked. "You're really pale. Are you okay?"

She nodded slightly, but his eyes were raking her face, sliding downward. With a cry he drew back from her, his eyes focused now, his expression one of profound shock.

"You're hurt!" he cried. "You've been hit!"

"It's nothing," she lied, propelling him forward.

He craned his neck to see her better, but she pushed him onward, forcing him to pay attention to Moshe, to the need for urgency.

Three more explosions sounded, and three more barrages of gunfire strafed the forest while they struggled to drag Ehud and Moshe into the narrow apertures of the jeep. Shlomo had tersely outlined Ari's plan for their getaway, and each time Sara heard the thunderous detonation, she knew a moment's gratitude that Ari was still safe, was still alive.

In between the explosions, Ehud, after being roughly shoved into the back seat, groaned and roused for a brief moment, long enough to complain of a pain in his shoulder, then drifted off again at the touch of Sara's fingers on his brow.

During the aftermath of the second explosion, the joint efforts of Sara, Danny and Shlomo had contrived to place Moshe in the back of the jeep in a semireclining position. During all of the jostling, Moshe didn't stir at all. What with his pasty color, the blue around his mouth and the hitches in his breathing, Sara was afraid they might be too late. But while there is breath, she paraphrased mentally, there is hope.

They used the medical supplies Ari had collected in the infirmary to patch Ehud and Moshe as best they could. They covered each of the wounded with one of the thick woolen blankets, then climbed into the jeep themselves to wait.

Sara again turned her son's wrist to look at his watch. They had been waiting for Ari for fifteen minutes now. And there had been no explosions in the last ten. Nervously, impatiently and now fearfully, she drummed her fingers on the steering wheel.

When he had still not appeared after twenty minutes, and no explosions or gunfire had sounded, she slid from behind the wheel and hopped painfully to the ground, favoring her damaged leg.

"You boys go on—"

"No way, Mom!"

She continued as if Danny hadn't interrupted. "When you reach the last checkpoint, stop and tell them what's happened. Tell them Ari Gaon is still out there. That I'm going in to get him."

"You can't do that!" protested Danny. Shlomo lent his voice to the argument.

"I can and I will," Sara said. "Shlomo, you drive. And if I hear later that any of you stopped anywhere but at the checkpoint and Kibbutz Golan, I will have all of your hides for lunch."

How odd it was, Sara thought, watching the embarrassed flush creep into the three boys' cheeks, that they'd all reacted as if they were the small children she was treating them as. A few hours earlier they had been desperate men on a desperate, misguided mission. Now they were young boys again, caught out and in trouble.

"Tell them I'll find him and—" She broke off, aghast at her own thoughts. She'd been about to say, "If I find him alive...."

She continued bravely, "And when I find him, I'll be dragging him down the hill, away from the gunfire, toward Kibbutz Golan." Before any of them could argue, she asked Avram to pass her the blanket she'd taken from Ari's sofa. Luckily Ari had brought others, so after reassuring herself that Moshe and Ehud were both properly covered, she signaled Shlomo to get in on the driver's side and start the motor.

He did so with overt reluctance. Danny again tried to remonstrate with her, but after giving him a hard, silencing look, she turned her back and started for the trees, forcing herself not to limp in too pronounced a manner. She felt as calm and collected as though she were going to cover some Fortune 500 press conference, and as nervous as though she were about to enter a haunted forest. Which she was, she thought wryly. It was haunted by thoughts of Ari Gaon's death or injured body, of what he would say to her if he turned out to be fine, of the love she had to tell him about.

"Wait," Shlomo called, grinning, holding what looked like a snake outside the jeep's window.

It wasn't a snake, it was his belt. Grateful, she came back for it and threaded it through a few of the loops on Ari's pants, cinching it tightly.

"Hurry now," she said to the three wide-eyed boys. "And don't forget to tell the border patrol where we are or will be. Tell them to come quickly."

The jeep roared into life, and with considerable skill Shlomo turned the vehicle around and slowly started down the rutted dirt road. Danny, hanging out of the passenger window, watched her with agonized eyes. Once again she realized that if anything happened to her—and if something happened to Ari—he wouldn't have anyplace to go. There was a will, of course, and a kindly third cousin of Jason's who had agreed, when Danny was born, to take the baby should anything happen to Jason or herself. She hadn't seen that cousin in a little over thirteen years.

She watched the jeep until it rounded the final curve and disappeared from view. A cold determination sank into her limbs, infusing her with greater energy, making her feel strong and capable. She would not leave Danny alone, and she would make some measure of reparation to Ari—and herself—by finding him. She didn't allow her mind to dwell on *how* she might go about finding him, nor on what condition he might be in *when* she found him.

Once again she entered the deep forest. With her leg, handicapped as it was with a bullet lodged in it, and her arms burdened with a large woolen blanket, she was hardly a speedy rescuer. But the chill in her veins propelled her forward and onward. She was almost lighthearted when she reached more open terrain, and once again took to the thick ground cover.

She heard no sound from the Syrian border guard, but took no chances, staying down, hugging the ground as if it were a dear lover. She called for Ari, but in a faint, scarcely audible whisper.

"Ari..."

Sometime during her slow and careful search, she substituted other words for Ari's name, sometimes in English, sometimes in Hebrew, but all were terms of endearment, all calls from the heart.

"Ari... *love*... darling..."

She passed the stretch of cover where she and Ari had last been together, then a few minutes later passed it again. She pressed deeper to her left into the underbrush, following the bent grass and scuffed dirt trail that the boys had made to drag Moshe and Ehud to safety. She was sure Ari would have followed that trail, as well.

"Ari..."

She reached the clearing where the group had obviously been. The ground cover was disturbed, and traces of blood were still visible. She had missed him, she decided with a sinking heart. Which meant he hadn't heard her, which meant . . .

Which meant she had to backtrack, that was all. She turned and once again crawled along the trail, but now her heart was thudding in terrible, painful beats, and the throbbing in her leg seemed to grow to a fever of agony.

For the third time she saw the clearing where she had waited with Ari, had waited for him, and finally had had the first glimpse of her son. But this time the sight provoked a help-less, hopeless despondency. *Where was he?*

She shifted, and a jagged rock pressed against her wound. A sob of pain, a moan of weariness and defeat escaped her lips.

It echoed in the greenery, low and deep.

Such was her despair that for a few seconds she didn't real-ize the significance of that echoing groan. When it struck her with all the force of a sledgehammer, she whipped around, holding her breath, afraid to move, afraid not to.

"Ari?" she whispered urgently, louder, almost heedless of the danger of gunfire from the border guard. Tears of relief, tears of hope stung her eyes.

"Ari!"

Another low moan answered her.

Until that moment, until she had heard his moan, she hadn't really allowed herself to consider all the ramifications of her fears for his life, her fears for her own, if he should be dead. Had he died, in a very real sense she would die, as well.

Swiftly, her hand frantically pushing aside tendrils of ivy, ignoring the pain in her leg as she scuttled to her right, Sara was upon him, before she even saw his prone body.

For a single, blinding second, despite the fact that she had heard his moans, she thought he must be dead. He was lying on his stomach, his bare back covered with scratches and moist earth. His silver hair was encrusted with dirt, and one hand was curled into the ground, as if, even after having been shot, he had tried to crawl along the path. The other arm lay be-neath him, hidden from her.

Not dead . . . she begged inwardly. Please, not dead . . . Her heart jolted once, harshly, painfully, then righted itself as he moaned again.

"I'm here," she whispered. "Shh, now. I'm here, dar-ling." She touched his back lightly with a shaking hand.

For only a moment did she hesitate, uncertain of what to do. Then some instinct she'd never known she had kicked in, and despite her trembling fingers she spread the blanket beside him. Crawling to the far side, biting her lips against a cry of pain as her leg came into contact with a broken branch, she hitched herself onto her hip, hunching forward, keeping her head well below the protective brush. Grabbing hold of his free arm, she pulled him over and toward her, stifling a cry at the sight of his bare and bloody shoulder, an open wound lined with dirt and still oozing fitfully.

He groaned, a deep growl of pain, as his shoulder brushed against her leg.

Frantic now, yet coldly aware of the need for silence, Sara pressed her fingers to his parted lips to quiet him. When he seemed to sigh, but didn't utter any more loud moans, she withdrew her fingers and groped for the kit taped to her waist. Again she didn't hesitate, but did what she should have done earlier when attempting to treat her own leg. Instead of trying to unwind the tape and making enough noise to attract the most wounded of border guards, she sucked in her breath and wrenched the small plastic box forward and down, freeing it from its nest against her stomach, ignoring the scraping against her sensitive skin.

She eased the catch open and rapidly studied the contents. Using her teeth, she tore open a large roll of gauze. Transferring it to her left hand, she opened another packet of no-stick pads. A moment later, unscrewing a small vial of hydrogen peroxide, she drew a deep breath and again bent over him. Mindful of his probable groan of pain, she lightly covered his mouth with the hand holding the pads and roll of gauze, then with hardly more than a flinch, poured the vial of peroxide over the wound.

He bucked, and would have cried out but for the hand covering his mouth. His eyes flew open, and his hand rose as if to fight her off.

"Shh!" she commanded. She willed him to meet her gaze. At last, as if fearful to do so, he did.

Sara had no idea what he could see in her face, but after a moment of staring at her uncomprehendingly, he blinked then seemed to relax somewhat. The merest hint of a smile flickered in his eyes. Through the cotton she felt his breath, hot and rapid, slowly expelled into her fingers.

"I had to clear the dirt," she whispered. "Be still now."

A slight nod of his head told her that he'd heard her words, understood what she was doing. Slowly, almost reluctantly, she drew her hand from his mouth and with a light, careful swabbing action with one of the thick pads, cleared the clods of dirt the peroxide hadn't washed away. He flinched twice during her ministrations, and she paused, fearful of hurting him further.

"Go on," he growled.

She did as he commanded. The wound still looked dreadful, a jagged hole of purple and red, but at least it was cleaner. She pressed the remaining pads over it, and loosening the roll of gauze, used it as another, larger pad. With the help of her fingers, her teeth and a series of whispered imprecations, she freed the adhesive from its awkward metal spool and covered the gauze with the sticky tape.

She heard his swiftly indrawn breath as she pressed the tape into place, and grimaced herself. Glancing at his face, she couldn't withhold a whimper of empathy. His eyes were tightly closed, and his lips were drawn inward in a sneer of pain.

His shoulder was already hot with fever, and from the flush on his face, so was the rest of his body.

"Sara..." he breathed. "Sara..."

"Shh," she insisted lovingly. She raised her hand to stroke the side of his dirt-streaked face.

"You've got to get out of here," he whispered. "Go now. Go with the others."

She hesitated; she hadn't the heart to tell him they were already gone.

"Where are they? Are they safe?"

"Yes."

"Where?"

She hesitated. "They've gone for help."

"They got away."

"Yes, thanks to you."

"What are you doing here?" He couldn't seem to focus on her face. His eyes dropped to her stained and earth-dampened shirt.

"You are filthy," he said, the ghost of a grin on his lips now.

A slightly hysterical giggle bubbled in her.

"So are you," she murmured.

His good arm rose, and his hand brushed her shirt, fingertips flicking clods of dirt from her, but at the same time, lightly

touching her braless breasts. It was Sara who inhaled sharply
this time. Even here, even now, her body responded to the
lightest touch from him.

"So dangerous," he mumbled.

Sara agreed, but she suspected they were not speaking of the
same thing. She took his hand and laid it against his bare
midriff. His hand turned, however, catching her wrist and
keeping her palm pressed against his hot skin. Beneath her
trembling fingers she could feel the crisp hair that pointed like
an arrow to the waistline of his pants, hair that she knew traveled all the way down.

She licked her suddenly dry lips.

"Not scared now," he whispered.

Oh yes, she was, but no longer frightened of the things that
she'd run from eighteen years ago.

Sara lifted her eyes to his flushed face, a smile on her lips.
He was alive! her heart kept singing. He was alive!

He closed his eyes for a long moment, scaring her, but his
breathing was steady, and beneath the hand he still clasped to
his bare skin, she could feel the beat of his heart.

"What are you doing here?" he repeated, his whisper barely
audible. "It's not safe for you."

"Nor for you," she answered softly.

His eyes remained closed, and he was silent for a few seconds, then as he shifted and bit his lips to hold in a cry of pain,
he opened his eyes again, staring at her as if she'd only just
now arrived beside him.

"You came back," he said.

"Yes."

"Eighteen years is too long," he murmured. "Too much has
changed."

Sara felt a chill sweep up her back.

"Different now," he whispered. "So different."

Sara couldn't have spoken. She knew he was speaking in
pain as the fever raged in him, yet he seemed to be saying
things that came directly from the heart—things that cut her
deeply.

"Galit is dead," he murmured.

She laid her hand upon his good shoulder, her heart aching
for him, for the pain in his words, in his thoughts.

"My little Galit."

"Shh..."

"She won't ever pick flowers again."

Tears sprang to her eyes, tears for Ari and the little girl she had never known.

"She used to pick flowers like you did," he said. "I showed her how to make the flower chains you used to make. She made them by the hour. She was so beautiful. So full of life."

Sara could only stroke his face, letting her hands say what she couldn't; her throat was too tight.

"I never cried when she died," he murmured. "I couldn't."

"Don't, my love," she whispered.

"She used to sit on my lap telling me stories, wearing one of her little crowns of flowers. She had such big dreams. Such big dreams. I loved her. I loved her so very, very much, Sara."

He looked directly into her eyes. "You know, don't you? You understand."

"Yes," she said.

"Then tell me, Sara. Why couldn't I cry when she died? Why couldn't I cry for my little girl?"

"Some things hurt too much to cry for," Sara said, tears freely streaming down her own face. The tears he couldn't shed, she could shed for him.

"I tried, you know. I thought if I could just let it out, that I could let her go. But I couldn't. Why couldn't I cry, Sara? Why?"

"Ari..."

"I couldn't go through it again."

"No," she said, not sure what he meant, only wanting to ease the knot of pain in him.

But she understood at his next words, understood how deeply he felt about his son, their son.

"Danny? He's okay?"

"He's fine," she whispered on a sob.

He didn't speak for several minutes, his eyes closed, his breathing harsh. Sara was relieved. This was too painful. She, who had complained that he was black-and-white, was only given to absolutes, had been shown the most shadowed part of his heart, the deepest sorrow of his soul.

When he opened his eyes at last, he gazed at her as if he didn't know her, his eyes meeting hers, but without recognition.

"Ari," she whispered sharply.

"He's Sara's boy. I never knew him," he mumbled.

Sara cried out softly, "You saved him, darling. You did."

"I couldn't go through it again," he repeated.

Her heart racked by his agony, she said the only thing she could think of. "You won't have to, Ari. You won't have to."

"She'll take him away."

"No," she said, unable to argue with him, but hearing in his words a multitude of things, things that saddened her, that meant, no matter how much she might love him, he still wanted her to leave.

"I want him to stay," he murmured. "When she goes, I want him to stay. Ask her. Tell her for me." The grip on her hand grew slack, and his eyes fluttered shut.

"Ari?" she questioned, and only his steady breathing convinced her that he hadn't slipped away to more than sleep.

Gazing at him, close enough to feel the heat emanating from his body, she nonetheless felt miles away. He wanted Danny to stay with him. Delirious he might be, but he'd expressed what was in his heart, on his mind. He wanted Danny to stay...but he hadn't said a thing about her staying, too. *When she goes,* he'd said.

Nothing he'd said could have cut her any more deeply than those words.

He stirred, and through a blur of tears she saw his eyes flicker open again. He looked straight at her, and this time he knew who she was. "Why did you do it, Sara?" he asked. "Why did you cry out like that?"

Sara's hand stilled in the motion of reaching to him. The guilt she felt over that cry threatened to overwhelm her.

"I was weighing what to do," he breathed. "But you called out, before I could think."

"I'm so sorry," she answered.

His mouth twisted bitterly. "Skip the apology, Sara. No apologies, please. It won't help." He closed his eyes again, as if to blot her from view.

Sara sat perfectly still, her mind replaying the words that had gotten her shot, perhaps gotten Moshe killed—that had almost gotten Danny killed. Her heart replayed Ari's last words.

"Don't look like that."

How long had he been awake this time? She met his gaze hesitantly.

"If we get out of this, will you promise me something?" he asked.

"Maybe," she said.

"Promise me, Sara," he whispered urgently.

"Promise you what?"

He struggled to rise to his good elbow, but collapsed onto the blanket, his lips pulled back fiercely, emitting a sharp hiss. "Just . . . *promise* me," he gasped.

"I promise," she said swiftly. "I promise."

His face twisted. "You . . . promised."

"What? What did I promise?"

"That you'll let Danny stay."

"Ari . . . I c-can't," she answered brokenly.

"You promised," he said. "Don't break . . . this one."

"I—I—"

He grabbed her hand again and held it much tighter than she would have thought he had the strength for. "It's my turn, Sara. It's my turn."

"It's Danny we're talking about, not turns," she said.

His eyes shadowed, then cleared, but Sara could see from his face, from the weakening grip on her hand, that his strength was almost gone. "I couldn't bear to . . ."

She closed her eyes, remembering his words. He couldn't bear to go through it again. Losing a child. But could she? For her Danny wouldn't be dead, but he also wouldn't be with her. Ari had made that much perfectly, terribly clear. He wanted Danny to stay, had forced a promise from her. But how could *she* bear to leave her son behind?

"I wish . . ." his voice faded, his eyes closing before he could state his wish. But she thought she knew. It was a manifold wish. He wished he had been able to stop her cry, stop her from coming with him, wished he could know Danny, be with him. He wished things had been different for them, between them.

But they weren't. He'd said that if she did anything that placed Danny in danger because of her presence, then he'd never forgive her.

"Ari . . . ?" she queried.

"Never forgive . . ." he murmured, as if he'd read her mind. He didn't open his eyes, didn't stir.

"I love you, Ari," she said. "I know you can't forgive me for that cry. I don't think you can forgive me for the past eighteen years, either. But I love you. I love you so damned much, it hurts. It always has. I think it always will.''

'' . . . love . . .'' he murmured.

She stared at his recumbent form for several mindless moments of agony, before she heard the distant drone of several vehicles. Even if they represented rescue, Ari and she could hardly stay where they were. She had been shot here, and so had he. If there was more gunfire, they would very likely be killed.

''Ari!'' she whispered urgently, shaking his uninjured shoulder. ''Wake up!''

He moaned, but still didn't open his eyes.

She heard a series of shouts from some distance away; she couldn't make out the words. As they came closer, she realized the voices were speaking in Arabic, so she didn't understand more than one or two words.

Then, shocking her into action, she heard the raucous rattle of machine-gun fire.

Again that instinct she hadn't suspected she possessed swung into action. She jerked the sides of the blanket together, knotting one end around Ari's knees, the other above his head. She shifted, noting with an almost morbid detachment that while her leg felt stiff now, she was no longer in as much pain.

Gunfire, closer this time, served to spur her on. She jerked him around, then, dragging at the knot above his head, pulled him backward, one inch at a time. She dragged him back along the path to the clearing, down the now almost invisible trail in the underbrush. He moaned once and she paused, but when he made no more noise, she continued. Ari was a deadweight in the blanket, impeding progress, but Sara persevered, half-amazed by her own strength, then a few seconds later, lowering her sweaty forehead to her arm, wondered if she had the strength to go on. She had just reached the clearing when she heard once more the distant roar of vehicles.

She didn't stop to wait for potential rescuers. Moshe had been shot here, so had Ehud. The Syrian guard's spray of bullets could reach this far. She couldn't allow another bullet to reach Ari. Luckily, the slope on the far side of the clearing led down toward the valley, toward Kibbutz Golan. And she edged along the ground, her leg numb now, almost useless, her arms tired from dragging the blanket containing Ari beside her. Her throat ached with thirst, ached from the need to keep her sobbing breath silent.

Suddenly she heard shouts, some in Hebrew, some in Arabic, but oddly, there was no gunfire. Tensed, expecting the loud volley of death to begin again any second, Sara could only keep moving, moving farther away from the carnage she was sure was about to begin again. On and on she dragged him, dragged herself, now a foot, then an inch.

After what seemed like hours, all she could hear was the muffled sounds of many feet pushing through the brush. Still caught up in the aftershock of the morning, Sara didn't cry out, too conscious of the need for silence, too conscious of her precious burden. No matter how much he might not be able to forgive her, she still loved him.

No matter that he'd asked her to give the very best part of herself to him—her son. No matter that he'd extracted a promise from her and had flung a past, broken promise into her face. No matter that he didn't, couldn't love her. *She* loved him. Right or wrong, good or bad. His life, whether he wanted her or not, was everything to her.

After what seemed like days, years, she heard a voice calling Ari's name, calling hers.

"Here!" she called weakly. "Over here!"

Within seconds the hillside seemed covered with men. At first Sara could only stare at them dumbly, feeling her eyes blur with weariness, fill with tired relief. When they cleared, she could see that there were only four of them, four incredibly tough-looking Israeli soldiers. One look at them, at the competent confidence they exuded, assured Sara that their rescue was complete.

One of them asked her something, but she only shook her head, no longer able to speak. After that, except for carefully moving her to one side, they largely ignored her, transferring their attention to Ari.

"He lives?" one asked in Hebrew.

"It is Ari Gaon," another spoke over him.

" . . . dead," said one.

Sara struggled to rise, but someone held her down.

" . . . not dead . . ." she murmured.

"Shh. All is well," said the voice at her side, in heavily accented English.

"He is not dead," she said again, this time in their native tongue, despair in her voice, desperation making her claw at the figure beside her.

"Hush, now," the soldier said, holding down her hands. "You will be okay."

"Ari...!" she called. She felt herself lifted and a canteen pressed to her lips. She shook her head, trying to get away from the liquid, trying to free herself of the man's grip. She had to know. She hadn't patched his shoulder, only to kill him by dragging him down the hillside.

"Drink this. You will feel better," the man said, again pressing the canteen to her lips. Suddenly he tipped it upward, trickling the water into her mouth. She gasped and swallowed, the tepid water soothing her throat, lending her a modicum of strength.

"Ari?" she asked again, her eyes meeting those of her attendant, beseeching him to tell her the only truth she wanted to hear.

He looked over his shoulder, nodding in the direction of two of the soldiers who, holding each end of the blanket she'd tied around him, were carrying Ári away from her. They carried him as if he were nothing more than a sack of grain, or, she thought grimly, horrifyingly, as if he were dead.

"He can't be dead...." she whimpered.

"No, no," her soldier said. "He only sleeps. It is easier so. To carry him out."

The relief was almost sickening, and for a moment Sara drooped weakly against the soldier's bracing arm.

"We will check your leg, no?" said another voice. "You have been shot?"

Weakly, dumbly, Sara nodded. She felt a pressure against her leg, then as the makeshift tourniquet was released, the world spun dizzily for a moment; pain crashed in upon her, wave after nauseating wave.

"You will be better now," one of them said.

Before the pain overtook her completely, she had time to consider the young soldier's words. No, she thought, she wouldn't be better now. Or ever again.

One of them gently pried the torn pants from her wound, but no matter how gently he might have touched her, the pain was too intense to bear now, and she drifted away into a gray world of despair and aching loss.

As if from a great distance she heard voices again, felt the jolting and bumping of a vehicle in motion.

"All is good," someone said.

Chapter 12

The light streaming in from the window on the far wall stabbed at Ari's eyes. He blinked rapidly, disoriented, feeling as if he'd had a very important dream, but couldn't recall it, knowing he had to do so.

A nurse materialized beside him and lightly placed her hand upon his forehead. He was sick then, he thought. He was sick and in the infirmary. He shifted, trying to ask her what was wrong, but a sharp, stabbing pain in his shoulder grabbed him and flung him back against the narrow pillow.

"You are awake," the nurse said softly, stating the obvious, though her words made it seem as though he'd been asleep for many days. Her name, he thought, was Ganit.

"What...?" he croaked, but his parched throat and something in his mouth made it impossible to continue.

She lifted his wrist, fingers pressed to the pulse lightly, surely, and said easily, "You've been in here since yesterday afternoon. Do you remember getting wounded?"

"No," he said, but even as he mouthed the syllable, he did remember. The memory shot through his system like a drug, and he half pushed up from the pillow, oblivious to the pain in his shoulder, the needle in his arm.

Calmly she pressed him back down to the bed, releasing his wrist and keeping her palm flat against his chest. "Now, you can't get up, you know."

"Sara?" Damn this thing in his mouth. He could hardly speak, and it rasped his throat almost unbearably.

"Mrs. Gould is resting quietly."

"Why?" he mumbled. He'd dreamed about her. Vaguely he recalled seeing her face, feeling her touch his cheek. She'd been filthy, he remembered, with mud on her shirt, tear tracks on her cheeks. She had been crying . . . for him, he'd dreamed.

"She was wounded, as well," the nurse said quietly, then as he tried to push up again, and she wrestled to keep him down, she added, "In her leg. The doctor removed the bullet yesterday afternoon, and she doesn't foresee any complications."

Sara had been hurt. Shot. Was doing fine. Ari couldn't seem to connect the thoughts, confusion making him quiescent beneath the nurse's restraining hand.

"Danny?"

"Why don't you let me get the doctor so she can take the tube out of your mouth? Then you can ask as many questions as you want."

He reached out and grabbed the hand that she was lifting from his chest. "Danny?" he repeated.

She smiled. "He's fine. Just fine. Not even a scratch. Now you relax and let me go get the doctor."

He let her go and watched as she crossed the small room and whisked out of the narrow metal door. His mind was filled with a thousand questions, not the least of which was Ehud and Moshe's condition. In that clearing in the woods, Moshe's wound looked fatal. He had linked his and Danny's belt around the older man. That, for some reason, stood out in his mind. He had thought it symbolic; for that one moment, that single heartbeat of time, they had been joined, hands, minds, and yes, even hearts working together.

He shook his head. This wasn't his kind of thinking. It was more like Sara's. When, how had she been wounded? Had he enacted a rescue of the son only to have the mother wounded?

Had it been a dream, then, those few moments of conversation, snatched, it had seemed, from the very depths of his soul? Hadn't she pressed her warm hand to his chest, stroked his face? Would he remember the dirt, the pain and the sweet, soft touch of her hand so vividly if it were only a dream? And in his dream she'd said she loved him.

He wanted to see her now. To ask her about the dream, about the words she'd spoken.

But it was the doctor, Hannah Navaret, not Sara, who entered his room. Within seconds the tube was gone from Ari's throat, and a straw was held to his bruised lips. "Drink this, it'll help," she said. He did as she suggested, pulling gratefully at the cool water, despite the pain in his throat.

"You'll have some discomfort for a few days," she said with an apologetic smile, pulling up a chair and sitting down beside his bed. "Ganit tells me you have a list of questions." She smiled.

"Moshe?" His voice was still hoarse, raspy, he noted.

Hannah's broad, kindly face wrinkled in serious concern. "I'm afraid it's too early to tell."

"His chest?"

"Yes. We got the bullet out, but the damage was already done. It pierced one lung and drove through an artery. And he is old," she said sadly. "He'd lost a lot of blood, after already straining himself too hard. The boys said he was complaining of chest pains before the shooting ever began."

"But he will live?"

She shrugged, and her expression was doubtful.

"And Ehud?"

"Like you, a shoulder wound, though as his was lower, we were worried at first. But the bullet missed every major organ. God watches out for fools and foolhardy young boys. He's awake and quaking in his johnny for fear of your wrath."

"Shlomo?"

"Hasn't left the hospital all night. He's the most frightened young man I've ever seen. He thinks you'll probably send him to plow the Negev."

"I should, at that," Ari said with the ghost of an answering grin.

"One thing in their behalf," Hannah said seriously, "and yours—thanks to the fact that you stopped them—is that the border is now so thick with Israeli soldiers that the cordon has been lifted from Kibbutz Golan. According to reports we've been hearing, limited travel is once again being permitted in the border regions."

The cordon was gone. Anyone could come and go now. Ari wasn't sure how he felt about that piece of news. On the one hand he was relieved for the kibbutz's sake, relieved for the worried family members and friends who hadn't been able to visit loved ones. On the other, the lifting of the cordon meant that Danny could leave, could depart for France to rejoin his host family.

And, perhaps worse, it meant that Sara could leave. Could run from him again.

He stirred restlessly. Of all times for him to be bedridden. He might still be lying here like an old man when Sara left. When she left him again.

"Are you in pain?" Hannah asked.

"Yes." Yes, he was in pain. He was in an agony of pain at the thought of Sara and Danny leaving. He'd just barely had a chance to accept the fact that he had a son, let alone learn what made the boy tick. And Sara... He'd spent almost two decades dreaming of her; he couldn't bear to let her go now. He'd told her that, in the dream that didn't feel like a dream.

"Tell me about Sara," he said finally.

"Like Ganit told you, she had a bullet in her leg. She had tied it off with a strip of cloth, but she still lost a good deal of blood. Besides which, dragging kibbutz directors around the mountainside, while lugging a bullet in your thigh, doesn't do anyone much good." Her eyes were bright with humor, asking him to share the joke, but Ari couldn't smile.

This didn't sound like his dream, yet it could account for the dirt on her shirt, the tears on her face. His mind revolved around the fact that Sara had been wounded *before* he had, which meant she'd been wounded after he left her.

He frowned heavily. "There was no gunfire," he murmured.

"I'm sorry?"

"After I left her, there wasn't any gunfire until I ran into the boys...."

"She was wounded before you left for the boys."

Ari stared at her, a sick revulsion growing in him. He'd left her there alone and *wounded?*

"She sent the young men on for help, then went back in for you," Hannah said, incorrectly interpreting his shocked expression. "From what I could gather when they brought you in, she not only found you, but dressed your shoulder—and did a pretty nice job of it, I might add. Then she apparently tied a blanket around you and dragged you out of danger."

"With a bullet in her leg," Ari mused.

"Yes. It's amazing what a person can do when . . . pressed, isn't it?"

Ari was certain "pressed" wasn't what Hannah had been about to say. But he couldn't allow himself to pursue that line of thought; he didn't dare. He'd called Sara a coward. He'd accused her of constantly running, running out on him eighteen years ago, running from the truth, from life.

Yet this same woman had risked her life for her son. Had risked her life for *his*. Instead of running, instead of proceeding as he'd instructed, she had come back for him, saved his life, while all the time wounded herself.

"I shudder to think what would have happened had those boys actually crossed the border," Hannah said now.

Ari averted his eyes, staring at the blank wall. That the boys hadn't crossed the border was only due to Sara. He heard Ganit reenter the room behind him. She said something to Hannah, but caught up in a welter of self-recrimination, he didn't pay attention.

"Thank Sara," he said bitterly. "It was Sara who called out Danny's name and told him to stay back."

"No one could feel more badly about that than I do," Sara's voice said icily.

Ari whipped his head to one side—in time to see Sara waving at Ganit to pull her out of the doorway.

"Wait!" he called out.

"Don't wait, Ganit!" Sara commanded. "I've apologized to Ari Gaon for the last time."

Ari yelled her name again, but she was gone. He stared at the doorway as if sheer force of will could conjure her back.

"Well," Hannah said finally. "Anyone who says being a kibbutz doctor is a boring job needs to spend five minutes around this place."

"She misunderstood."

"Did she?" Hannah asked dryly.

"Of course she did. You said yourself that whatever stopped them from crossing the border saved not only all of their lives, but possibly an international incident!"

"Well, I didn't quite say all that." Hannah chuckled. Ari wanted to throttle her. How dare she laugh? "Not that I don't agree with you."

"Well, then?"

"That's not exactly how you expressed it back there, is it?" She cocked an eyebrow at him. "Listen to me, Mr. Kibbutz Director, fire me for saying this—and I'll warn you now, I've had several offers down in the sunny south, and you've had no applicants for my position—but sometimes you are the biggest fool I've ever met."

She held up a hand to forestall any protestations. "She misunderstood what you were saying, obviously. But did you ever stop to consider that misunderstandings are the largest cause of divorce?"

"We're not married."

"Just so," she said. "Ari, didn't it ever occur to you that when you are bitter for no perceivable reason, and say something that sounds snide, ninety-nine times out of a hundred, people are going to believe you are being snide?"

"It wasn't directed at her!" Ari burst out. "I'm the one who was too busy *thinking* about what to do. She just went ahead and did it."

"So? Why didn't you just say that?"

"She left before I had a chance."

"You could have shouted it down the hall after her."

"I can't believe she thought . . ."

"You've said so many good things about her, to her, that it wouldn't cross her mind that you didn't mean it that way?"

"She should know that!"

"Why? Have you told her?"

This silenced Ari. Had he ever told Sara what he really felt about her? Had he really? Not just that he wanted her, not just that he'd thought about her always.

Hannah looked amused for a moment, then thoughtful, and finally, Ari reflected, angry.

"I see what it is, Ari. You are having a difficult time realizing that little Sara Rosen is a grown-up woman with real thoughts and real feelings."

She rose to her feet. "I suspect if you look back over the years, way back, my dear, you will find that you may have always done that."

She crossed to the door and grasped the metal handle. "Luckily you have a lot of time to think about it." With that she pulled the door closed behind her.

"Mom?...Mom?"

"Coming..." she murmured, her brain insisting that Danny was awake in his crib, waiting to be picked up, ready to start crying any moment. "Coming..." she said again, fighting the urge to drift back to sleep.

"I'm right here, Mom," his adultlike voice said close to her ear, a note of frustration in his tone.

Her eyes opened slowly, blinking at him, seeing his dear face, his broad forehead wrinkled in worry, his lips pinched together.

"Danny," she sighed.

"Yeah. You okay? You've been sleeping for hours. Ganit tells me you were up this morning, but you've been asleep all afternoon."

"I have?" she asked groggily. She couldn't seem to marshal her thoughts. She turned to roll onto her side, but the sharp pain in her leg prevented her. But it did serve to fully awaken her.

"Oh," she murmured, half in physical pain, half in the pain of memory, the memory of Ari's bitter words. She stiffened.

"The doctor—she's a really cool lady, isn't she, Mom?"

Sara nodded. Hannah had been sitting beside Ari's bed when he'd uttered those damning words. But Hannah hadn't looked at Sara with anything but amused sympathy. Why amused?

"She says you probably won't feel like dancing anytime soon, but that there's nothing to worry about. She wasn't lying or anything, was she?"

Sara smiled wanly. "I hope not," she said.

He grinned, then the smile faded from his lips. He looked away, his mouth working, his shoulders drooping.

"What is it?" she asked, a wave of glassy fear coursing through her. More bad news?

"I'm really sorry, Mom," he mumbled, his voice thick.

"Oh, Danny," she said, sagging back against the bed in relief. "I'm the one who should apologize."

He looked up at that, surprise on his face. "Why?"

"It was because you misinterpreted something *I* said that you went up there in the first place."

Understanding flashed across his face, and with it a tacit acceptance of her unspoken apology. Then his head drooped again. "Yeah. Hannah told me what a jerk I was. That wasn't quite the only reason I took off."

He met her eyes again. "See, I wanted to go, I wanted to prove something. I don't know what exactly."

"I can understand," Sara said.

"And I was really teed off at seeing the two of you so cosy."

Sara stilled. Not that there was any likelihood of them being "cosy" again, but she wanted to know why it had bothered Danny... aside from the most obvious reasons.

"It was kind of like him having his cake and eating it, too."

"I don't follow you," she said weakly, though she suspected she did.

"No responsibility for you all those years, then, bam, right back in his arms."

"In all fairness," she said, "I didn't exactly give him a chance way back then."

"We'll never agree on that, Mom."

"You're a good kid, Danny Gould."

"So I should hope," he fired back, but his face seemed to have lost its color. "You know, though. Even though I think that he was wrong back then, in the past, I mean, I think that... I think maybe I was wrong about him on the whole."

"Maybe so," Sara murmured, not sure what he was getting at, not quite sure she wanted to know. She was still too raw from the conversation in the forest and from the overheard words that morning.

Ari had said there was no forgiveness in loving, yet that seemed to be what he wanted: to see her on her knees, begging once again for pardon, exoneration, for forgiveness for the past, for careless, anxious words, for everything she'd said or done since she was twenty-two years old.

"You both could have been killed because of me," Danny said. "I know I wanted to get back at you for what you said... what I *thought* you meant, but I never wanted anybody to get hurt because of it."

"I know that," she said.

"Yeah, but you did get hurt."

"I'll live," she told him, smiling.

"And *he* got hurt. And Moshe is . . ." His voice broke, and a low sob escaped his lips.

"Not dead?" she asked.

He shook his head violently. "Not yet. The doctor says we won't know for a while."

"Try not to—"

"You don't understand!" he burst out, cutting her off. "He came after me to *stop* me. To stop all of us. We wouldn't listen."

"Danny, that was the risk he took when he went after you like that," Sara said.

"You're not getting it, Mom. We ignored him for a while, you know, like sort of shook him off. We knew he couldn't catch up with us. But he kept huffing and puffing up that damned mountain, right on our tails. Then just when we got close to the border, he started calling out that he needed help, that his heart . . ." Danny again halted his speech on a sob.

"Go on," Sara prompted softly. She knew her son had to get this off his chest.

"Ehud and I went back to see what all the fuss was about. He wasn't far behind us. We could hardly see him, because it was just getting light. He was kind of lying over sideways in this clearing, holding his chest, his face all screwed up—like this." Danny imitated the expression. "We, Ehud and I, tried to get him comfortable, like roll him over or something, but nothing we did seemed to work. He just kept gasping, holding his chest with one hand, my arm with his other."

A flicker of suspicion winged its way through Sara's mind. "Did he say anything during all this?" she asked.

"Just 'don't leave me. Don't leave me here to die.' It was *awful*."

Sara's suspicion grew. She remembered Moshe's favorite saying that age and treachery would overcome youth and ability any day, and was more than three-quarters certain he'd used this ploy as a last-ditch effort to stop the foolhardy mission. But she said none of this to her son.

"Then what happened?"

Danny said bitterly, "Shlomo came back then with Avram. He said we should leave Moshe there and get him on the way back."

"Oh, Danny," Sara said.

"Ehud and I said we couldn't just leave him there. Finally, Ehud offered to stay with him. Shlomo was furious. We were all talking in whispers, even Moshe, but it got pretty intense, if you know what I mean."

"I know," Sara responded, half-amused by the ingenuous comment, even though horrified by what he was telling her.

"Well, by then it was starting to get light. Every time Shlomo said it was time to move out, to get going, Moshe would start moaning again. Finally Shlomo said Moshe was faking it. That he was just trying to stop us."

So she hadn't been the only one to see through the old man's bag of tricks.

"I didn't know if he was faking it or not. By then I was pretty well having second thoughts about the whole thing, anyway. I mean, Moshe didn't want us to go badly enough to come chasing after us all the way up the mountain. He said a bunch of stuff about the repercussions if we did get to Na'asum—"

"The least of which was that you would probably have been killed," Sara interrupted dryly.

"Yeah, that too," Danny commented, with the disbelieving insouciance of youth that anything could strike him down. "Anyway, it didn't seem like such a good idea anymore."

"Then what?"

"Then we heard the sound of a jeep off in the distance. Shlomo told us off royally, then said he was going to check it out. He came back a few minutes later, saying he couldn't see anything. But right after that, whether the guard on the other side had seen something or heard us, or maybe he only thought he heard something, but anyway, he called out."

"Who's there," Sara said dully.

"Yeah. After that all hell broke loose."

"Don't swear, Danny," Sara corrected automatically. "But I know what you mean."

"Well, it was part of the plan to use that Arab character's name, but suddenly Moshe grabbed hold of Shlomo's legs and yanked him to the ground. They started to wrestle, then you called out, and Shlomo pushed Moshe away. Ehud jumped Shlomo, and I guess Moshe kind of pushed up to his knees. But the next second bullets were flying everywhere. At first I didn't even snap to what was happening, I only lay there, staring at the jumping bushes, trying to figure out if something was coming through them. I mean they were really shaking.

"Then Ehud sort of folded up, a funny look on his face, and fell backward. So did Moshe. Whether he'd faked that heart attack earlier or not, he sure wasn't faking the blood all over his shirt."

He didn't say anything for a few minutes, then looked up, all trace of his tears gone. "I just couldn't take it in, you know. It was like it was happening to somebody else. I felt like a little kid. I just wanted to go home."

"I know, honey," she said softly, reaching for his hand. She held it firmly, drawing it to her cheek.

"I knew you were out there somewhere. And *him,* probably. I kept thinking that if you weren't killed, I'd never do anything dumb or mean again. I kept thinking..." His eyes filmed over with new tears. "I kept saying to myself that I should have at least given him a chance. Maybe if I'd given him a chance, you wouldn't have thought I was a barrier to you guys, and I wouldn't have run out like any dipstick and gotten everybody into that mess."

"Oh, Danny, don't..."

But now that he'd cleaved an opening for the torrent of guilt inside him, there was no stopping the flood.

"I crawled over to Moshe. I don't know why I went to him first, maybe because he'd tried so hard to stop me from getting there, maybe because he once told me that he owed you something, I don't know. But I crawled over to him. I pulled his head onto my lap, tried to stop the bleeding with ... with my hand."

"Danny," Sara said, shaking his hand a little. "He's still alive."

Danny seemed to shake himself, then resumed his terrible tale. "Then Shlomo whispered that he'd heard something. He slipped out of the clearing, crawling on his belly. A few seconds later I heard him shout and heard him fighting someone. Then, as Avram was going after him—to help him, I guess—Avram went flying. It was *him.*"

"Ari," Sara offered.

"Yeah, Ari." Danny looked away from her again, plainly still remembering. She saw much of how he must have looked as Ari entered their clearing. His eyes glazed, and his face took on a look of dawning wonder, half hopeful, half embarrassed. He turned to her again.

"I couldn't believe it, you know. I mean, it was the first time I really thought of him as being my real father. He looked so mad. So strong. For a second he was like...like everything I've ever wanted to be. You know?"

Sara nodded her head, willing her own rising tears to dissipate. *Promise me, Sara. I promise.*

"This is going to sound really goofy, but when I saw him, you know, just looking at me in this really searching way, a staggering relief on his face, I had the feeling that everything was going to be okay now, now that he was there."

"I know," she said. "He has that effect on people."

"Yeah, but I mean, like it's not a put-up job or anything. He really is that kind of man."

"Yes," Sara said sadly. Hadn't he always had that effect on her? Hadn't she always loved that in Ari, that he was all male, all strong, all hero? And hadn't she run from it, as well? Run from the part of herself that was all female, all strong, all heroine?

She wasn't running now. She'd said she would apologize no more, and she wouldn't. Not for the past, not for the mistakes she'd made. It wasn't Ari's forgivenesss she wanted, it wasn't his pardon, it was his *love*. She'd told him she loved him. If he'd heard her, if he remembered her words, then she could at least carry away the memory of having finally told him. And whether or not he'd heard her, whether or not he would remember her declaration of love, she would always carry the memory of Ari telling her the deepest, most painful secrets of his soul.

This leaving was different. This time it was *Ari* who didn't want her. It was Ari who wanted Danny to stay, but Sara to leave. This time she was merely putting an end to the debts and guilt of the past and present. But why, when she thought about it like this, did the future seem so empty?

"It's kind of a hard thing to live up to," Danny said slowly.

"What is?" she asked.

"Following in Ari Gaon's footsteps. I thought Dad's—Jason's—were tough enough. But Ari's..." His voice faded, and he shook his head.

"I know," she replied, rather amazed that her son had so capsuled her reasons for running all those years ago. She hesitated only a second before adding, "But not for you."

Her son, *Ari's son,* met her gaze hopefully, more than a hint of diffidence in his gray eyes.

"Mom . . . ? I—I think I'd like to get to know him," Danny said finally in a rush. "If he's still speaking to me, that is."

"He will," Sara said, knowing it was true. At the same time, however, she felt a tightening inside. *Promise me, Sara.*

"Yeah, well, he was pretty decent to me when I saw him a while ago."

Sara's heart skipped a beat. He had hinted at a meeting with Ari earlier. "You saw him?"

"He wanted to talk to all four of us. Avram, Ehud, Shlomo and me. We went in there like we'd been called to the principal's office in grade school."

"And?"

"And he was pretty cool. I mean, he chewed us out and stuff like that, but still, he was great."

Unlike his bitter words to her, Sara thought. He hadn't been inclined to grant amnesty to her. Well, she thought, raising her chin, she'd apologized to Ari Gaon for the last time. Which was just as well, she admitted with some chagrin, since he'd told her he'd never forgive her if she placed Danny in danger through her presence. *Never forgive . . .* he'd muttered in his fever.

"What did he say?" she asked at last, feeling as if she were pulling the words from her lips. Perversely, going against her earlier thoughts, she wanted to ask if he'd said anything about her. But she held the words back.

"That we had more guts than sense," Danny said with a slight grin. "He sounded just like Dad. I mean..." He stopped in confusion, the smile changing to a grimace. No wonder Danny always called Ari *him,* adding emphasis; he was actually only having difficulty in designating him, assigning him a slot in his life.

"If you've heard it from both of them, maybe it's something you ought to think about," Sara said slowly, trying to create a bridge between the two men in Danny's life. She was only sorry she couldn't seem to build one for herself. In Ari's arms, in his embrace, yes, but nowhere else, it seemed.

Danny looked at her very steadily for a long moment, then smiled. It wasn't his usual half-cocky, always ready smile, but still it was Danny's smile—Ari's smile, tinged a bit with Jason's acceptance of life, tempered with some of her own hard-won objectivity.

"That's an understatement, if I ever heard one," Danny said. "I'll definitely think about it."

"Did he say anything else?" Had Ari asked the boy to stay with him? Asked her son to stay?

"Not really. Told me I was lucky I wasn't one of the regular kibbutzniks. He'd have my head for washing."

He seemed to have worked the guilt from his mind, seemed to accept both Ari's verdict and hers at full value. She could now go back and discover what he'd meant by his earlier statement.

"Danny, when you said you wanted to get to know him, what did you mean?"

He looked down nervously, then back up again. "Well, that I'd kind of like to stay here. My deal in France would have been up in a couple of weeks, anyway . . . and I doubt if they'd take me back now, even if I wanted to go. And college doesn't start for another three months. I just sort of thought . . . hoped, you know . . ." He wouldn't meet her eyes.

Sara drew a deep, steadying breath. Her entire world seemed dark, shadowed, colored with the blackest sorrow. She hadn't known this request could hurt so much, could rend so deeply, destroy the last defences of the stronghold of her heart. She'd reached the pinnacle of pain.

Everything in her wanted to scream. She had thought that telling Ari about Danny was the single greatest hardship she would ever have to bear, but now she found a new one. Ari wanting Danny to stay, dragging an unknowing promise from her, was one thing. Danny wanting to stay at the kibbutz, to get to know Ari, that was an altogether different matter.

"Mom? Is it okay? I mean, is it okay with you? You like him. I can tell that. Who knows—?"

"Don't!" she cried, his naive words piercing her even more. "Don't say any more," she said.

He met her anguished gaze with a puzzled look, a gaze that narrowed, then grew introspective. "You don't want me to stay, do you?"

"It's not that," she replied, though what he'd said was true. If she'd been staying, too, she would have wanted it with all her heart.

But Ari didn't want her to stay.

"I didn't mean . . . I mean, I didn't want . . . to hurt you, Mom." Danny got out the words with difficulty. "I just thought . . ."

"I won't be here, Danny," Sara said at last.

He thought about this for several long minutes. "Does that matter?" he asked.

When she closed her eyes against this final wound, he said quickly, "I mean, of course it matters, but I'll be home soon enough. In time for college."

"Danny, I'm a little tired." She wasn't lying; she was weary to the very depths of her soul.

"Oh, yeah. Right. I'll check on you later," he said, pushing to his feet. "See ya."

This was the ultimate debt to pay, the last expiation for the guilt she'd carried for so long. She had laid every card upon the table and had lost everything. Lost them both. Ari and Danny. Was she strong enough to lose them both, to turn her back upon Israel, to say goodbye to Ari Gaon a second time? She would have to be. For her son's sake. For her own. And possibly for Ari's. Once she had thought it best, years ago. Now she knew she had been right. Where she'd been wrong was in coming back at all. If she hadn't come back, her son wouldn't be wanting to stay, and her heart wouldn't be torn into a thousand little pieces, wanting Ari, wanting Danny, wanting a family—and knowing it was only in her own mind.

If she left Danny here, allowed him to stay . . . ? It would be the best, the finest thing she had ever done. She had once married to give her son a father, to give a lonely man a son. Now she could leave to do the same thing, only this time it would be real, blood to blood. But it would be so hard.

"Oh, I almost forgot," Danny said, coming back into the room, digging into his shirt pocket. "He asked me to give you this." He handed her a scrap of notepaper, folded in half, with her name scrawled in Hebrew on the outside.

Slowly, her fingers trembling, her heart vacillating between wild hope and flat dejection, she unfolded the slip of paper.

"We have much to talk about. Come see me when you are able," was all the note said. Sara read it three times, searching for hope, searching for anything that might reveal some concern, some *love* in the two lines.

She found none.

Chapter 13

When night fell and Ari still hadn't heard from Sara, he felt the heavy weight of misdeeds, mistakes and shattered dreams settle in upon him. He had too little pride left to walk down the corridor and rap on her door. He'd sent her the note, a note that had cost him a great deal, the two awkward lines conveying, he hoped, all that he couldn't say without seeing her in person, watching her expressive face, without telling her some of what he was thinking, feeling. He'd waited, far more patiently than he'd waited for anything in his life before. And she had not come. Had not asked after him.

She had not come.

He'd asked Ganit if she was well enough for visitors. But yes, Ganit had said. She'd received many. Had even asked for a typewriter to be brought to her room and had typed most of the evening.

So, he thought, drawing the mantle of what little pride he had left around his weary heart, that was that.

But as the night lengthened and the infirmary grew quiet, Ari knew that *wasn't* that. There was too much left unsettled, there were too many things left unsaid.

Was Hannah right? Had he ignored the real changes in Sara? Or was his confusion more basic, so that he had never really seen Sara, Sara the woman, Sara the strong partner? He'd said they were alike. Why couldn't he seem to accept that himself?

If she had changed, it had been for the better. She had come back to Israel, faced him, if not honestly at first, then totally openly, and finally with a dignified honesty, a woman grown, with a woman's pride and depth. And he had treated her as if she were still the girl who had wounded him years ago. It was she who had changed and grown, he who had responded to her in exactly the same way he had so long ago. And if she was the same as she had been? Then it was he who had been at fault eighteen years ago; it was he who was at fault now.

With what he knew to be rare introspection, he studied their relationship, their eighteen-year-old love affair that had been tumultuous from the first meeting and had risen like the sharp upswing of a roller coaster, only to plummet, out of control, losing contact with the track.

Sara had acknowledged those changes, had displayed them easily, so he could see now, but at the time he hadn't wanted to see them. Hadn't wanted things to be different. And now, with his words, his actions—not to mention their son—standing between them, it was all too late. She had come to his arms willingly, giving all of herself, and he'd taken that gift gladly, yet some very terrified part of him had believed she would come to him, only to leave again, taking his heart with her. And as a result he'd been angry the next day, as furious with himself and his foolish trust as with Sara for her supposed betrayal of that trust. In the first place she'd not told him about Danny, and secondly she'd flagrantly disobeyed his order to stay behind.

Now he'd hurt her again—Sara, who had risked her life for his—Sara, who had given him everything he wanted most in life, her trust and a son.

He threw off the covers. He felt stifled, confined, and wanted to walk, to move, to let physical action subdue his restless, self-condemnatory thoughts.

He paced, thinking. Thinking about how he'd felt eighteen years ago when she'd said she was going back to the United

States, leaving him, that dark day when he'd believed the only perfect dream he'd ever had was gone. He thought about how he'd felt when he saw her again that morning less than a week ago, when the desire for revenge had warred with the urge to take her into his arms and kiss her until the world spun for her as her presence had always made it spin for him. And he thought about how it had felt to have her in his arms once again, drawing on that power she seemed to pour into him, that power to make him feel invincible, masterful, strong in heart and mind.

He thought about it all, every single moment, every touch, every feeling, and stopped pacing. He couldn't face losing her again. He wouldn't allow it to happen. He couldn't taste her lips, know her touch, hear her laughter and understand her tears, only to have her go away a second time. His mind stumbled over the echo of a phrase in his mind, a phrase from his past, now in his present: *I couldn't bear it.*

If he could ignore that stubborn pride of his, could swallow it long enough to go to her, to try to tell her what he felt, what he thought about her, then maybe the misunderstandings that Hannah had accused him of fostering, that he had to admit were real, maybe then he could make them fade away.

He drew a deep breath, half afraid, half determined. If she wouldn't come to him, he would go to her. It might be too late, she might turn a cold shoulder to him, but if he didn't try, he was no better than he had been as a young man, letting her go without trying to make her stay, no better than what Danny had accused him of being, no more than the coward he'd called her.

He couldn't let her go again without telling her what was deep in his heart. He couldn't let her go this time without asking, *begging* her to stay. He'd made that mistake once; he couldn't make it again and still be able to live with himself.

He swung across the room and with a wince of pain, shrugged into the short terry bathrobe at the end of his bed. His shoulder and arm were wrapped tightly, taped to his chest, leaving the right sleeve of the robe empty so that it flapped loosely as he moved. Walking quietly, not caring to be impeded by the night nurse or whoever else might choose to stop him, now that he'd decided on his course of action, he slipped from the room and down the hall to the one Ganit had said was Sara's.

He depressed the handle slowly, careful to conceal any sound, and pushed the door open.

Light from the hallway spilled into the dark room, creeping across the small space like a shadow in reverse, sliding beneath her bed, over it, crossing her, throwing his silhouette onto her lap, as if in the shape of a shadow, at least, he joined her, touched her.

She lay with her face to the door, her eyes open, hands touchingly tucked beneath her cheek, the way a child sleeps, lips slightly parted, long lashes casting shadows upon her cheeks. Her clean, tawny hair, tousled by sleep, was spread in a halo on her pillow, surrounding her face, feathering against her slender throat. She was achingly beautiful.

"Hello," he said, feeling the word magnificently inadequate.

Her eyes widened as she perceived who was disturbing her rest. For a moment he thought he saw joy spring into them, and perhaps something more, but a second later they were shuttered, blocking any sign of emotion.

"Hello," she said, but her voice was guarded, wary.

"I'm sorry to wake you," he said formally.

She neither waved his apology away nor accepted it, only rising a little onto one elbow. The hospital johnny slid from her shoulder, revealing the rounded tops of her breasts. Flushing, she pushed it back into place with shaking hands.

He stepped into the room, pushing the door closed behind him. At the sudden absence of light Ari stopped, momentarily blinded. Then, as moonlight cleared the room of swirling shadows, he stepped forward again, drawn by the glow in her eyes. Drawn to Sara as he'd always been, unable to resist her then or now, he moved toward her.

"I finished my story," she said, before he could speak. The words seemed to fill the air around them, assuming a greater volume than they might have if the room had been brighter, if he'd been able to read her face.

"I see," he said slowly, not certain that he did. With the cordon gone and the story done, and with his words, with the

past, creating a wall between them, there was nothing concrete to keep her here. Was that what she was telling him?

"I talked with Danny today," she said. "After he spoke with
you."

Ari felt as if he were smothering in nuances. Why didn't she
just stab him clear through and get it over with? He wanted to
just grab her and kiss her into complying with his wants, his
needs, his most primitive of wishes, but the realization of the
changes in her, in himself, stopped him.

"He says..." She paused, but only to clear her throat. "He
says he would like to stay."

"To stay," Ari repeated blankly. His heart seemed to actually stop beating for a moment.

"Here. With you."

A thousand conflicting emotions coursed through him.
Danny, his son, the son he'd never thought to have, never
dreamed of before the last week, wanted to remain with him.
Fierce exultation was shot with fear of the future, mingled with
a sense that now there was a future, and was clouded by a note
of sorrow in Sara's quiet voice. They had talked about this in
the dream.

I promise, Ari, she'd said. But what was it that she'd promised him?

"Is that what you want?" he asked.

"Yes," she said simply.

"You want him to stay here after you go?" he questioned,
trying to see if he had it right, to understand what she was
really telling him. *Don't go....*

"Yes," she whispered.

"Why?" he asked.

She flinched, and he felt it in the deepest part of him. He'd
meant, "Why are you leaving?" He was asking *why* she
wouldn't stay herself.

She answered the most superficial of his questions. "Because he wants to get to know you. Because he admires you,
admires what . . . what you are."

Even as his heart seemed to swell at her words, he took note
of what she so carefully omitted. This was what Danny
thought, not what Sara thought. Hannah's warning about
misunderstandings rang in his mind.

But before he could ask what she really meant to say, she continued. "And, I suppose, because I promised."

His heart seemed to buck. Had the dream been real, after all?

"And you?" he asked. "How do you feel about him staying?"

She didn't answer for a long time. Instinctively he stepped forward, his hand outstretched, reaching for her face. He could no longer see her eyes and suspected they were closed. His hand met her dry cheek. She pulled away almost violently.

He dropped his hand.

"I think . . . I believe it would be good for him."

Ari would never know how it had hurt her to say that. To say those words, after he'd asked how she felt about Danny's staying there, but not how she felt about leaving? He'd taken her departure for granted. After you leave . . . he'd said.

"There's no denying I would like him to stay," Ari said now, his hand, the hand that had seemed to burn her skin, once again at his side.

"He was afraid that after what he'd done, you wouldn't want him to. But I told him I thought you would welcome the chance."

Though he was very close to her, his face was in shadow and she couldn't read him. She wondered briefly, detachedly, how a blind person dealt with the terrible gaps in conversation, and realized how much she relied on reading a person's face. He sighed.

"You were right," he said. "Though it surprises me a little that you would permit it." His tone was cold.

"He's your son, Ari," she said brokenly. "He needs two parents."

As he had done when she was treating his shoulder, he pulled in his breath with a sharp hiss. But when he spoke, it was on another subject.

"I didn't get a chance to thank you for what you did for me. My shoulder," he said stiffly.

"I—it . . . was nothing."

"Do you mind if I turn on the light?"

Since her face was now covered with tears, she did mind, very much.

"Don't," she said quickly.

He disregarded her plea, and she heard the metal pull of the bed lamp rasp across the connection. She turned from him abruptly, hiding her face, closing her eyes, biting off a cry of pain as her leg tangled in the sheets, placing pressure on her sore leg.

"Sara...?" he asked softly, then with a harsher note, "Are you crying?"

"It's nothing. It's the drugs or something," she said. Just go away, she pleaded silently. Just leave now, before I beg you to stay, beg you to let me stay.

"It seems all we do to each other is cause pain," he said ruefully.

When she didn't—couldn't—answer, he sighed heavily.

"Sara, I didn't mean to make you cry. If it will hurt you that much, don't leave Danny here. Take him with you."

"It's not that," she said honestly, though that hurt was so great, she couldn't believe that there was anything greater.

"What is it, then?" he asked, his voice hoarse, racked.

His hand lightly gripped her chin, drawing her around, turning her to face him.

"If it's not Danny, the thought of letting him stay here, that's making you cry, what is it, Sara? I need to know."

She shook her head. There was too much to say to answer that question. Her entire heart, her whole life were wrapped up in the response.

"Sara, I've never been too much for long speeches. I've always believed that actions speak louder than words. But I don't know what to do here. I feel like talking is the only hope left. Except for this..."

She stared at him helplessly as he bent over her, his eyes never leaving hers, deep grief etching his features, until his lips met hers. Lightly, so softly that they might have been a dream, his lips brushed her mouth. Tenderly, gently, his mouth velvet, he kissed her, then withdrew. Didn't he know what torture this was?

"Sara...why are you crying? Is it because of what I said this morning? Because you thought I was angry with you over calling out like you did?"

She shook her head, a new hope dawning in her, the fear of that hope keeping her silent.

"Because you thought I wouldn't forgive you for that?" He drew her against his good shoulder, his free arm wrapped around her back.

She pushed him away. She couldn't be in his arms, loving him, and have him hold her out of pity, hold her out of nothing more than human compassion. She wanted all of his love, all of his passion, not this tender forgiveness.

He pulled back, his jaw tightening, his eyes pained.

But he said gently, "There's nothing to forgive, Sara. I sounded bitter this morning because I couldn't stop thinking that you acted so much quicker than I, so much faster. I was still thinking about what to do, when you called out.

"If you hadn't called out like you did, they might have rushed that guard, they might have all been *killed,* instead of only two of them wounded. They might have killed that guard, they might have sparked an international incident."

Some of the weight on Sara's shoulders lessened, but the pain in her heart remained as sharp and as biting as it had been all afternoon, all night. As it had been for eighteen long years.

"Sara...?" His gray eyes darkened with some deep emotion.

"I didn't know," she murmured, wishing it mattered, glad that he would forgive her that cry, but wanting him to ask her for much more than absolution, wanting to give him much more in return.

"Hannah told me that misunderstandings are the chief cause of divorce," he said quietly.

Sara nodded slowly, the fear of that single flame of hope making her too afraid to answer, too afraid to add to those misunderstandings.

Jason used to say the same thing. But Jason had never allowed misunderstandings to last. He'd taught her to never say good-night with a grievance or a question on her mind, a wound in her heart. Had that been Jason's gift to her? Teaching her how to unlock the door of communication, to unlock the chest of understanding?

"She's right," Sara said, taking the key Ari had unwittingly offered her.

She drew a deep breath, determined that tomorrow morning when she woke, she could at least know that she had told him everything, told him the truth about herself, her feelings for him, about the dreams she carried within her.

"Ari...?"

"Yes?"

She jammed the key into the lock and turned it.

"When we were in the forest... Did you hear what I said to you?"

"I thought it was a dream," he said, an odd expression on his face.

Remembering Jason's words, remembering Hannah's, Sara hesitated, then asked, "What? What did you think was a dream? Tell me what you can remember."

"When I was looking for Danny, when I was crawling through that brush, I thought that if anything had happened to him, I wouldn't be able to bear it. I'd already lost one child. I couldn't lose another."

Sara sat perfectly still as some of the words spoken in his pain delirium began to make sense. Half-afraid of what he was trying to tell her now, she remembered other words he'd uttered then.

"Did I tell you about that in the forest? It seems I did."

"Yes," she said.

He continued heavily. "And I told you about Galiti."

"Yes," she said softly.

He paused for a long while. "I can't remember everything I told you, but I know I said things I'd never told another living soul."

"I know...." Sara answered unevenly.

"When you left Israel, I thought that part of me had died, Sara. I believed that absolutely." His eyes bored into hers.

"And then Galiti came along. She was so special, so much a part of the land, of the sky. She hardly seemed to touch the earth when she walked. I found I still had love in me. It was different, of course, but I could love."

She must have made some sound, for he stopped, looked at her searchingly, then continued.

"And then she died. There aren't any words to describe the depth of that pain."

"I know," Sara said brokenly. "Oh, Ari, I know."

"In my dream," he said, "I asked you why I couldn't cry when she died."

"It wasn't a dream, Ari."

"And when I asked you, you said that there are some things that hurt too much to cry."

She'd been so right, she thought wildly; the pain in her now was too great for tears. Too deep for weeping.

"I . . . I can't cry now, Sara," he said. "Because the pain is too great. If you go away again, I . . . I don't think . . ."

The hope that had been a single flame leaped and found other hopes and dreams. They caught fire, rousing a blaze of joy in her, giving her the courage to speak.

"When I . . . thought you didn't want me—"

"Not *want* you!" he burst out, interrupting her, sweeping across the room to her bed.

"I thought you wanted me to leave. I thought you couldn't forgive the past . . . couldn't look at Danny and not always see that I had never told you . . . couldn't look at me and not remember that I'd cheated you of knowing your son for eighteen years."

"Sara . . ." he said, pushing her hand aside more gently than the look on his face portended. "As I told you the other night, you're right, I can't forget. But as for forgiving . . ."

He stopped, reaching toward her, but not touching her. He leaned toward the bed, but not over her. When he spoke, his voice was so low that she had to strain to hear it.

"I said the other night that there is no forgiveness in loving. I was wrong, Sara. I was *wrong*. There is *only* forgiveness in love. That's all it is. And when you love someone as much, even half as much as I love you, then there is *nothing* on earth you can't forgive, there is *nothing* you don't love about that person."

Sara stared at him for several heartbeats. "You love me?" she asked tremulously.

"Of course I love you!" he snapped back. "I've loved you for eighteen years! I never *stopped* loving you!"

"Then . . . why . . . ?"

"Sara," he groaned. "That first morning when you came back, all I wanted to do was grab you into my arms and never let you go again."

"You looked as though you wanted to kill me," Sara said.

"Well, that too," Ari admitted, his grin surfacing for the first time.

As if his smile were the one thing to add faith to the blaze of hope within her, she smiled back.

She said, "Before you came charging in here to tell me all of this . . . I was lying here in the dark thinking about what I was going to say to you tomorrow morning."

He stiffened slightly, his features guarded. "And what was that?" he asked.

"I was going to come to your room to visit you."

"And?"

"And I was going to tell you that I loved you."

He made a move toward her, but she held up her hand again. He stopped, wariness still clouding his face.

"And then I was going to tell you that you couldn't get rid of me that easi—"

She never had a chance to finish what she had been going to tell him on the morrow. He dragged her into his good arm, pressing a ferocious kiss onto her lips. It was as if they had never kissed before, had only dreamed of it for eighteen long years.

She melted into the embrace, her hands coming to his face, her body pressing tightly against his, her hospital gown an open invitation to his heated hand.

"If you ever . . ." he mouthed against the base of her throat, " . . . torture me like that again . . ."

"Torture *you!*" she protested, her voice catching on a gasp as his lips met the sensitive hollow of her collarbone.

A sudden rap at the door brought them back to earth in a bound. The handle was jiggled and pressed down before they could fully separate. As one, they turned to the intruder.

It was Danny, his face flushed, his mouth already open, ready for speech. Then he obviously realized that his mother wasn't alone, that he'd interrupted them.

Whatever he'd been about to say, he lost it, his face flushing an even deeper red, his body automatically backing out of the room.

"Sorry," he said, then again, "Sorry."

"Danny!" Ari barked.

Danny stopped.

"Wait, I . . . *We* . . . have got something to tell you."

Danny's eyes went from Ari to Sara and back again. A wariness stole over his features.

"I've asked your mother to stay here in Israel with me."

When Danny didn't say anything, Sara allowed her voice to fill the silence. "Actually," she said, "he didn't ask me to stay, Danny. I told him I was going to, whether he liked it or not."

Danny stared at her as if not taking in her words, then finally a slow grin crossed his face.

"It takes a stubborn spitfire to know one," he said.

Ari laughed out loud. Sara thought it was the first time she'd heard him laugh in just that way in eighteen years.

"Would you mind?" Sara asked quietly. Beside her Ari stilled.

"Mind?" Danny asked.

"That I want to stay here. With Ari."

A strange look crossed Danny's face, then he grinned, the old Danny grin. "I'm kind of relieved, actually," he said. "Hannah and I had this whole elaborate plan worked out to get you two together, and now I don't have to get typhoid or whatever it was she wanted me to have."

Both Sara and Ari laughed, and under the cover of that laughter Ari took Sara's hand into his own. His hand was warm and broad. With that simple gesture she felt loved and secure.

"Was there something you wanted to tell me, Danny?" she asked.

"What?" her son asked blankly.

"I thought something was up when you came bursting in here," Sara observed. She glanced at the bedside clock. "Especially since it's after midnight."

"Oh!" Danny said, blushing in remembrance, blushing anew at having interrupted them. "It's Moshe! He's going to make it. Hannah said he's going to be all right!"

Sara sagged against Ari's good shoulder for a second. "Thank God," she murmured.

"Yeah! And you know what his first words were? He wanted to know if he'd paid his debt."

"What debt?" Sara asked.

"That's what we asked him—Hannah and me. He said that debt he owed you."

"He didn't owe me anything."

"Well, he said he did. He told me something about owing you one a couple of days ago, but he told me he'd probably never tell me what it was."

Danny met her eyes with a look of triumph. "But I know now. Moshe felt like he'd given you some bad advice a long time ago. That if he'd handled things differently, you would have never left Israel."

Having said this, his expression grew doubtful. "But if you hadn't left," he said, "I guess . . . I guess I wouldn't be the same, would I?"

Sara shook her head, but it was Ari who answered.

"None of us would be, Danny. I'll never wish that Sara had gone, all those years back, but if she hadn't, I wouldn't have had Galit, my daughter . . . your sister. If Sara hadn't gone, you wouldn't have known Jason Gould, you wouldn't be the man you are now."

Danny stared at Ari with some respect. Finally he said slowly, "I wish you two could have met. I think you'd have probably liked each other."

"I think so, too," Ari said. "He did a fine job of raising a certain kid I know."

"Yeah?" Danny asked, his face bright at the praise, his eyes alight with mischief. "Mom? I think you ought to marry this guy right away. He has excellent taste."

"I agree with you there," Ari said, lifting her hands to his lips.

"Oh, that reminds me," Danny said, his grin fairly well covering his face. "Hannah told me that the only thing that

Moshe really needed now was bed rest. Seems like it might be a good thing for you two, also.''

Laughing, Sara pitched her pillow at him. It fell short by several feet. Laughing in response, Danny picked it up and tossed it back. ''Okay, I can take a hint. I'm outta here.''

He whisked out the door, closing it behind him. No sooner had Ari reached for her again, however, than the handle clanked down and the door swung open again.

''Now that everything's hunky-dory, is it okay if a couple of us take a run down to Yam Kinneret? I've never seen it.''

''No!'' Sara said.

''Sure,'' Ari said.

Danny looked from one to the other. ''Which is it?'' he asked.

Sara met Ari's eyes. His brows were raised in a question, lips curved in a relaxed smile. He'd lost years in minutes, she thought irrelevantly. He was her love, her dear, wild love.

''Ask your father,'' she said, not looking away from Ari, almost having to bite back a cry at the sudden pressure on her fingers.

Ari didn't turn his head to look at Danny. He kept his eyes locked with Sara's.

''Yam Kinneret is beautiful at this time of year. I suggest you stay for several days.''

''Oh, I get it,'' Danny said with a laugh, and backed out of the room for the second time. He opened the door again almost immediately.

''Can I borrow a jeep?'' he asked.

''No!'' they said in unison.

''Okay, okay, just asking,'' Danny said.

As Danny pulled the door closed for the third time, Ari rose. He crossed the room and flipped the lock. On his way back to her bed, he pulled the light switch, plunging them into darkness. Sara waited for him with a faint smile on her lips.

Ari . . . she thought, and for the first time in eighteen years she didn't feel the knife blade of sorrow cutting at her heart.

Slowly, almost as if he were afraid he would break her, he drew her against his good shoulder.

''Is there anything else we haven't talked about?'' he asked.

"I told you I loved you. You said you loved me. Danny accepts it, even likes it. There doesn't seem to be much of anything else," she said with a laugh.

"That almost covers everything," he murmured, his lips brushing against her shoulder.

"What else is there?" she asked, pulling him down beside her.

"This . . ." he whispered. "A lifetime of being able to *show* you how much I love you."

*   *   *   *   *

SILHOUETTE·INTIMATE·MOMENTS™

IT'S TIME TO MEET
THE MARSHALLS!

In 1986, bestselling author Kristin James wrote A VERY SPECIAL FAVOR for the Silhouette Intimate Moments line. Hero Adam Marshall quickly became a reader favorite, and ever since then, readers have been asking for the stories of his two brothers, Tag and James. At last your prayers have been answered!

In June, look for Tag's story, SALT OF THE EARTH (IM #385). Then skip a month and look for THE LETTER OF THE LAW (IM #393— August), starring James Marshall. And, as our very special favor to you, we'll be reprinting A VERY SPECIAL FAVOR this September. Look for it in special displays wherever you buy books.

MARSH-1

 *Silhouette Books*®

presents

SONNY'S GIRLS

by Emilie Richards, Celeste Hamilton and Erica Spindler

They had been Sonny's girls, irresistibly drawn to the charismatic high school football hero. Ten years later, none could forget the night that changed their lives forever.

In July—
ALL THOSE YEARS AGO by Emilie Richards (SSE #684)
Meredith Robbins had left town in shame. Could she ever banish the past and reach for love again?

In August—
DON'T LOOK BACK by Celeste Hamilton (SSE #690)
Cyndi Saint was Sonny's steady. Ten years later, she remembered only his hurtful parting words....

In September—
LONGER THAN ... by Erica Spindler (SSE #696)
Bubbly Jennifer Joyce was everybody's friend. But nobody knew the secret longings she felt for bad boy Ryder Hayes....

SSESG-1